WHAT'S DONE IN THE DARK

ANGELA L. WADERKER

DEDICATION

To Ajani and Jalina, for being incredibly patient with me.
"How's that book coming mom?"
It's finally complete. You two inspire me in ways you don't even
know. I love you.

ACKNOWLEDGMENTS

To Trina Davis, thank you for being there in the beginning, and taking
the time to read my early efforts.

To Gail Shackelford, my biggest cheerleader and harshest critic, who
never stopped believing in me. You've been much more than an
editor. Thank you for the phone calls, articles, and honest feedback.

To Monica Cross, thank you for being on standby with bail money, and
continually encouraging me when life gets in the way.

From the bottom of my heart, thank you ladies. Without you, there
would be no book.

1 - World's Best Lasagna

"You're making lasagna aren't you?"

She shifted the phone between her ear and her shoulder as she carefully placed pasta noodles over a layer of ricotta cheese. "You know I am. Why?"

"I really love your lasagna."

Janel closed her eyes and shook her head. "You're not going to make it are you?"

"Probably not, I'm sorry."

"Seriously Dorian? Again?"

"I don't really have a choice Janel."

"This is getting old. Not only is it becoming a habit, but you always wait until the last minute to let me know."

"Baby, I'm sorry. I'll find a way to make it up to you, I promise. How about a day at the spa? The whole day. I know how much you like that."

"How about actually coming home on time for once this month? How about coming home on time for once this *week*."

"Not if you want to keep living in Clover Hills. The house, the cars, DJ's sports equipment and fees. That stuff adds up Janel. If I want a fat bonus this year, I have to finish this project on time and within the budget. I gotta do what I gotta do babe."

"*You* were the one who wanted this house, and you were the one who encouraged DJ to get involved in sports so he could be a mini version of you. And if it's about money, you know I don't have a problem with working. *You* were the one who wanted me to stay home."

"And you agreed."

"Yes at the time, when DJ was little. But he's in high school now. He doesn't need me to put him on the bus or be here when he gets home anymore. He'll be in college soon."

1

"I wanted the house because I wanted you and DJ to have the best.   And it's not about the bonus or you getting a job to help out.   I make more than enough money to take care of this family.   It's about my reputation, my career."

Janel rolled her eyes as she put the pan in the oven. "You've never had to work late so often for this long."

"DJ's home, Tony's coming, and he'll probably bring Sherri so it's not like you'll be eating alone."

"Really?   He's bringing Sherri?   Gee Dorian I can't wait to see her."   Her voice was dripping with sarcasm.

"Be nice Janel, she's not that bad.   Look, I really don't want to argue about this.   I just wanted to call and let you know so you wouldn't be worried about me.   I'll be home as soon as I can.

"Whatever Dorian."

"I love you."

"If you loved me you'd bring your butt home and eat with us.   I have to go so I can finish making dinner."   She hung up the phone and slammed it onto the counter top.

An hour later she was sitting on the couch flipping through a magazine as she waited for her company to arrive.   She dog eared pages that contained recipes that sounded appetizing and scanned through some of the articles whose titles sounded mildly interesting.   The doorbell rang and she tossed the magazine on the coffee table as she got up to answer it.   She checked the peep hole before opening the door.

"Hey Tony, come on in."   He gave her a big hug and a quick kiss on the cheek.   "It's so good to see you, it's been a while.   Where's Sherri?"

"She's not going to make it.   Something came up at work at the last minute and she had to stay late."

"Must be going around, Dorian called and said to start eating without him.   Said he's working late again too.   So I guess it's just you, me, and DJ."

"That's ok, it just means there'll be enough leftovers for me to take some home.   I don't know what you put in your lasagna but it's some of the best I've ever had."   Janel led Tony into the dining room and told him to have a seat. "Where's DJ?"

"In Dorian's entrainment room playing a video game. I'm glad someone's getting some use out of that room as much as it cost to have all of that equipment installed. Have you seen the latest?"

"What's that?"

"The sixty-five inch 3D flat screen television?"

Tony's face lit up like it was Christmas.   "Really?" Janel shook her head in agreement.   "That's one thing about Dorian, he never spares any expense when it comes to his toys.   He always has to have the latest and greatest gadgets."

She set the lasagna and garlic bread on a lazy susan in the middle of the table.   "Yeah but he's so busy most of the time that he's never here to use them, so they always end up becoming really expensive dust collectors."

"You want me to get DJ?   I'm not even going to lie, I've got to see this tv.   It's a guy thing."

"Don't you two get caught up in there or the food will be cold."   Janel said as she went back into the kitchen to bring a cold pitcher of lemonade to the table.   She stuck a long wooden spoon down inside the jar to make sure the sugar was completely dissolved when the doorbell rang. She wiped her hands on a dishtowel and headed for the door.   "Just a minute!"   She called out as she rose up on her toes to look through the peephole.   She was fully expecting to see Sherri.   Instead, she saw the outline of two wide brim hats staring back at her through the fish eye view against the sun in the background.   She opened the door and there were two police officers standing on her doorstep.   "Can I help you?"

"Are you Mrs. Monroe?"

"I am.   How can I help you gentlemen?"   She put her hands on her hips and wondered if their visit had anything to do with her son, Dorian Junior.   He was a good kid, responsible and smart, but she knew some of the kids he associated with at school were known to sometimes get themselves into situations that their parents could easily afford to pay to make go away.   She waited patiently for one of the men to explain why they were darkening her doorway just before she was preparing to sit down and eat.

"Ma'am, we have a situation we need to discuss with you. Would you mind if we came in for a moment?"   The older man did the talking while the younger man remained silent. The younger man was pale, with the exception of his nose and ears which were fiery red, and Janel assumed it was patches of sunburn.   She stood her ground, still confused, and continued to wait for them to explain their presence to her.   She was getting impatient and shifted her weight from one foot to the other.

"I don't mean to be rude but I was just about to sit down for dinner.   So if we can just get to the point of your visit. How can I help you gentlemen?"   Janel could hear Tony and DJ behind her, chatting and laughing about something as they headed for the dining room.

"Who is it Janel?   The food's getting cold."   Tony commented.

"I'll be there in a minute, just start eating without me." She stepped onto the front porch and pulled the door closed behind her.   The older man removed his hat and the younger man, appearing somewhat nervous now, quickly followed suit.   Janel suddenly got a queasy feeling in her stomach and her neck and face started to feel very hot.

"Ma'am, there's been an accident."

Janel's heart began racing and she felt as if she couldn't catch her breath. She looked the older man in the eye, his face solemn, and she suddenly felt very unsteady on her feet. She was overtaken by nausea and literally felt weak in the knees. The younger man wouldn't make eye contact with her and she knew instantly it was her husband. She bent over slightly and tried to take a deep breath and find her voice. "Where is he? Which hospital?"

The older man shook his head and looked down at his boots, averting his eyes. He began to fidget with the tassel on his hat. "Ma'am, I'm afraid...he passed away at the scene. The EMT says he was already gone when they got there. They believe he probably died on impact and didn't suffer. I'm sorry." Janel let out a horrific scream and crumpled to the ground crying, repeating the word no over and over again as the two strangers tried their best to console her.

# # #

Janel let out a deep sigh as she closed the door behind the last person who'd come by the house to pay their respects. It'd been a long day and even though the funeral was standing room only, she felt more alone than ever. The silence in the house was a complete contrast to the steady hum of conversation she'd heard all afternoon long and it bothered her. Although she was glad the crowd was gone, it was too quiet. She decided the best thing to do was to keep busy, so she walked into the kitchen to start cleaning up.

Tony, the only other person remaining in the house, loosened his tie and unbuttoned the top two buttons of his shirt. "I'm going to stay and help you clean up this mess if you don't mind." He removed his cuff links and slipped them in his pocket, then folded his sleeves halfway up his forearms. He picked up the trash can and starting throwing disposable plates, cups, and used napkins into the garbage. Janel tapped a serving spoon on the rim of a bowl, trying to get the excess potato salad off of it, and then sealed the bowl with its matching plastic lid. She covered a foil pan half full of cornbread and put both containers on the counter in the middle of the kitchen. Once she cleared all the food from the other counter tops, she began wiping them down with a dish rag. "I have no idea what I'm going to do with all of this food but I'd feel bad just throwing it out. I wonder who decided food was the best medicine for mourning?" She kicked off her shoes, pulled herself up onto the counter, and began rubbing her feet.

"I'm sure if DJ were here he'd have all of this food gone in about three days." He said as he swept a pile of crumbs into a dustpan and dumped it into the trash.

"He'll be too busy eating my parents out of house and home over the summer."

"You got that right. And your mom certainly won't

mind, you know how much she loves feeding folks.   Here."
He gestured for her to put her foot in his hand and he began
to rub it.

"It's a good place for him to be for now, while I sort
things out.   That feels great, I feel like I've been on feet for
two days straight."

He released her right foot and gestured for the left one.
"That was a really nice home going.   Dorian would have
loved it, it was finally something that was all about him.
You know how big his ego was."   It was at that exact
moment that it hit her, and she realized her husband would
never be coming home again.   Ever.   The thought
overwhelmed her and for the first time that day, she began
to cry.   She was quiet at first, but with each breath she
drew in, the tears fell harder and harder and she felt as if
she might hyperventilate.

"There, how's that?"   He asked, looking up at her as he
released her foot.   "Aw Janel, I didn't mean anything.   I
was just trying to lighten the mood.   What a stupid thing
to say, I'm sorry.   Come here."   She slid towards the
edge of the counter and put her arms around his neck.
She hung on tightly as a wave of emotion washed over her
and she began to sob loudly, uncontrollably.   He patiently
rubbed her back as she cried for several minutes.   When
she began to regain her composure, she released her grip.
"You ok?"   He asked before grabbing a paper towel and
handing it to her.

"This doesn't even seem real to me."   She said as she
blotted her face dry.   "I can't believe he's gone.   I'm
sitting here trying to remember the last time we really sat
down and talked to each other, it's been weeks."   She felt
guilty as she thought about their last conversation and
started crying again.   He embraced her and she began
concentrating on her breathing in an effort to calm down.
After a few deep breaths she finally cleared her throat in an
effort to find her voice.   "You know what his last words to

me were?   He said I love you.   And you know what I said to him?   'I have to go finish making dinner.'   And then I hung up on him.   I was so angry with him for cancelling on me again at the last minute.   And now, it all just seems so stupid."

"Don't do that to yourself Janel.   It's not like you knew that would be the last time you'd talk to him.   He knew you loved him, even if you were angry and didn't say it back."

"Angry or not, I should've said it."

"Coulda, shoulda, woulda.   Unfortunately you can't go back in time."   She slid down off the counter.   "Why don't you go lie down and get some rest, I'll finish cleaning up."

She glanced around the kitchen.   "No, I can't leave this for you.   We'll have it done in no time if we both work at it."

He touched her on the shoulder to get her attention.   "I got it, don't worry about it.   Go get some rest, take some time for yourself."   She knew he wasn't going to back down so she nodded her head and climbed the stairs to her bedroom.   She untied her wrap around dress and let it fall to the floor, then pulled her slip over her head and tossed it aside.   She peeled off her pantyhose and flung them on top of the slip.   She went into the bathroom and washed the makeup from her face, then plucked each bobby pin out of her hair and tossed them on the floor until her crowning glory fell down around her shoulders.   She pulled back the duvet cover and sheets and climbed into bed, still wearing her underwear and bra.   She balled herself up into a fetal position in an attempt to make herself as small as possible, wishing she could just disappear.   She covered her head with the sheets and cried herself to sleep, hoping that when she woke up that the day's events would all have been a terrible nightmare.

2 – Sherri

Tony hadn't heard from Janel in several days, so he decided to stop by her home and check on her. He rang the doorbell and waited for several minutes. He knocked on the door, then decided to let himself in with his spare key. He called out to her and the sound of his voice sliced through the stillness in the house. Finally, he took the stairs two at a time and tapped lightly on her bedroom door, which was slightly ajar. He waited for a response before pushing it open and poking his head inside. "Janel?"

He saw movement under the bed sheets so he sat down on the edge of the bed. "I tried calling first. We've been worried about you, me, DJ, your parents." He knew she was awake and he waited patiently for her to respond.

"The phone wouldn't stop ringing, and I didn't want to talk to anyone, so I unplugged it." Her voice was raspy and hoarse.

"I can understand that." He waited to see if she would emerge from the covers, but there was no movement. "I would really love it if you would look at me so I know you're ok."

"And I would really love to just continue to lay here."

"If I knew laying here would bring Dorian back, I would strip down to my boxers and lay with you for as long as it takes, but we both know that's not going to happen. If there was something, anything I could do, you know I wouldn't hesitate to do it."

"I know." She whispered. Finally, she slipped her hand from under the covers and he grabbed it, squeezed it, and kissed her gently in the middle of her palm.

"I know you're hurting, but I need to talk to you.   We've got some business to take care of.   I brought the will over, and I was hoping we could go through it and get things squared away legally and financially."

She released his hand, then exhaled loudly.   The bundle of sheets grew larger as she sat up and pulled the covers from her head.   Her hair was a tangled mess and the stress on her face made her look older than she really was.   Her eyes were a reflection of the pain he was feeling over the death of his best friend, and he looked away as he felt some emotion stir within himself.   There was no time for sadness, he had to push his grief aside momentarily and rely on his professional experience as a lawyer to help her in her time of need.   He felt an overwhelming sense of responsibility for her and DJ now that his friend was gone. "I'll be downstairs when you're ready."

He'd waited for nearly fifteen minutes and she finally appeared in the kitchen, freshly showered with her hair brushed back into a ponytail.   "What can I get you?"   He asked as she sat down at the breakfast bar.   She held up her hand and shook her head no.   "You need to put something on your stomach.   How about some tea."   He told her rather than asked, and put some water on to boil. "If you need anything, anything at all, I'm just a phone call away.   If you want to talk, or even if you don't and you just want some company, I'm here for you."

"I know."   She replied, her voice still slightly raspy.

His cell phone began to ring and he checked the display. He put it on vibrate and shoved it back into his pocket as he sat down across from her.   "Let's talk about this will." He said, flipping open a leather portfolio.   "Dorian had me draw this up a while back, so it's probably a little outdated." His phone began buzzing again but he ignored it.

"You can get that if you need to."

"It's Sherri, I'll call her back later."

"I'm surprised actually, I'd been nagging Dorian for a few years to have a will drawn up.   I had no idea he'd actually done it."

"He had a living will drawn up too.   He listened to you more than you think he did."   The water began to boil and he shoved the stool back to get it but she touched his arm and told him to stay put.

"I'll get it."   She asked him if he wanted a cup as she prepared her own and he declined.   She settled back on her stool, her hands wrapped around the hot mug as she blew across the liquid to cool it down.

With a push of his thumb he clicked his pen and started making notes.   "I need to know who your creditors are, how much debt you're carrying, and how much cash you have on hand.   You should call your revolving creditors and let them know what's going on, the cable company, electric company, etcetera.   They're going to want a copy of the death certificate so just tell them you'll send one as soon as you can.   I'll see if I can pull some strings at the courthouse to speed up the process."

She carefully set her cup on the counter.   "That's going to be a problem."

"No, I know a few people.   I can call in a favor."

"I don't know who we owe, Dorian paid the bills."

He stopped writing and looked up at her.   "Say again?"

"Dorian handled the finances.   I have no idea how much or who we owe."

"You're kidding right?"   She shook her head no.   "But you're the one with the accounting degree."

"I know.   I tried to reason with him but he insisted. You know how stubborn he was, so I just let it go.   I learned early on to pick my battles.   How do you think we stayed married for seventeen years?"

Tony rubbed his hand over the top of his head and sighed deeply.   "That's ok, we'll figure it out.   Do you know if he had any life insurance policies?"

"Yes.   He took out a really big policy a while back for five hundred thousand dollars.   I remember because he had to go through this really intense physical before they would approve it.   I'll have to look around for the paperwork, I have no idea what he would've done with it."

"I'll add that to your 'to do' list.   Just keep an eye on the mail and set aside any bills or statements that you receive and we'll figure out your creditors and debt that way. Now let's get into this will."

Tony spent the better part of the afternoon with Janel explaining the will and covering different scenarios of what she could expect from a legal perspective.   As he started answering her questions, his phone began vibrating again. He checked the display, then quickly began to pack up. "I'm sorry, I've got to go.   We'll have to pick this up later."

"What's wrong?"

"I forgot about dinner with Sherri.   I'm really sorry but I've gotta run.   I'll call you later."   He gave her a quick peck on the cheek, then answered his phone on his way out the door.   "Hey baby, I'm on my way.   I just finished up with a client."

He startled the valet as he sped up to the curb to drop off his car.   He checked in with the hostess, whom he was familiar with from several previous visits.   She smiled at him and shook her head.   "You know you're in the doghouse right?"

"Seems to be my permanent home these days.   Is she still here?"

"Yep."   The hostess pointed in Sherri's direction. "And she's on fire."

Tony threw his shoulders back and pulled himself up to his full six foot three inch frame.   He straightened his tie as he strolled across the restaurant with confidence.   He bent to give Sherri a kiss and she turned away.   "Sorry I'm late baby, it's been a busy day."

She looked at her watch.   "Got me sitting here looking crazy for twenty minutes now."

"I had to stop by Janel's and take care of a few things." He sat down, signaled for the waiter, and ordered a drink.

"I thought you said you were with a client?"

"She is a client."

"Is she paying you?"

"She's a client Sherri."

"Why can't she get her own lawyer?   Isn't that a conflict of interest or something?"

"Dorian made me the executor of his will, and he paid me very well to fulfill that role."

"Personally, I don't think you should be in the middle of her business.   He should've picked someone else."

He changed the subject in order to avoid an argument. "Did you order yet?"

"Yes."

The waiter delivered Tony's drink and took his food order.   "How was work today?"

"Busy.   They brought this guy down from corporate, Shawn Dixson, to train us on a new software system.   I've been chosen to train all the new people at the new branch they're opening next month."

"Is this a promotion?"

"Sort of.   It's additional responsibility along with more money.   You know the new branch isn't far from your place, and I'll have to travel back and forth to that location pretty often for the first few months."

He knew exactly what she was hinting at but he refused to take the bait.   They'd been dating two years but he knew he wasn't ready for them to move in together.   His job as a trial lawyer was stressful, and he enjoyed coming home to a peaceful, quiet, empty home.   "You'll have to get up a little earlier to deal with traffic then."   He suggested as he took a sip of his drink.

The waiter set Sherri's food in front of her and she began

to eat.   "How was the funeral?"

"It was nice.   Dorian would've approved."

"I just couldn't get the time off.   I've got a pretty aggressive deadline to learn what I can from Shawn." Tony shrugged his shoulders.   "Do they know what happened yet?"

"They suspect he took the curve too fast.   It doesn't matter, it's not going to bring him back."   The conversation was taking a turn towards uncomfortable territory so he changed the subject.   "I talked to my mom yesterday, she's thinking about coming to visit."

"Good, maybe I'll finally get to meet her.   Did she say when?"

"No, she just said 'soon.'   Seems like every time I talk to her now she's talking about retiring and moving to Lafayette.   She says she's tired of Ohio winters and the snow and cold."

"I hope she does move here, I'm looking forward to meeting her."

The waiter delivered a fresh drink and Tony thanked him as he took away his empty glass.   "That's what you say now," he mumbled before taking a long sip of the lukewarm drink.

"What's that supposed to mean?"

"I'm just saying, my mom can be a trip.   She doesn't have much of a filter."   He was thankful to see his plate of food arrive, and quickly shoved a bite of steak into his mouth and began to chew.

Sherri pushed her nearly empty plate aside and picked up her wine glass by the stem.   "So I was thinking maybe we could get away this weekend.   What does your schedule look like?"   She swirled the burgundy liquid around in the glass as she waited for him to respond.

He paused and looked at her.   "Are you serious?"

"Yes."   She smiled at him and took another sip of her wine.

"I can't." He said, placing his silverware on the table.

"Why not?   We haven't been on a weekend getaway in forever."

"Did you really just ask me why not?"   He shook his head in disbelief at her cavalier attitude and complete disregard for what he was going through.

"It's just a weekend.   We'll be back before you know it."

"For crying out loud Sherri, my best friend just died. Can you give me a fucking break?   It's not all about you right now."   Her mouth fell open and suddenly he could hear his mother's voice in his head saying a drunken man's words are a sober man's thoughts.   He began to apologize but the damage had been done.

"You don't have to get nasty with me, I just asked a simple question."   She raised her voice and the people immediately around them began to stare.

He reached for her hand but she snatched it away.   "I'm sorry, I didn't mean to snap at you.   I've got a lot going on right now, I can't just up and leave for the weekend anytime soon.   I'm trying to take care of Janel and DJ.   That's the way Dorian would've wanted it, and I'm going to respect his wishes."

"Janel is a grown ass woman whose husband made a hell of a lot of money.   I'm sure she'll be just fine once the insurance check clears."

"Can you lower your voice please?   It's not that simple. She needs me right now.   They need me right now."

"It's always something with you, you're always trying to save the world.   When do I get to be a priority in your life?"

"Can we not do this right now?   I'm really not in the mood to argue, especially in public."

"I'm not arguing, I'm just trying to tell you how I feel. As if you give a shit."

"You're saying *I* don't give a shit about how *you* feel? When you call me and I don't answer, don't I always call

you back?"   She stared at him.   "Don't I?"   He insisted.
She reluctantly conceded.   "Yes."

"And when I spend time with you, I don't answer my phone, I don't look at my text messages, and I don't respond to emails.   And you know what I do for a living, this phone is my lifeline.   When I make plans with you, I always keep my word, we do nice things, and you always have one hundred and ten percent of my attention.   I bend over backwards for you.   What more do you want from me?"

She leaned forward and lowered her voice, speaking through gritted teeth.   "I want to be validated.   If you cared about me like you say you do, if you loved me, you'd put a ring on it."   She slammed her left elbow on the table and shoved her ring finger in his face.

Tony took the cloth napkin from his lap and wiped his mouth.   He fished his wallet from his jacket pocket, stood up, and threw a hundred dollar bill on the table.   "I've gotta go, I've got some things I need to take care of.   Tell the waiter to keep the change."

"Oh so that's it?   You're just going to get up and walk away?"

He leaned in close to her.   "When you realize the world doesn't revolve around you, give me a call."   He finished his drink and slammed the glass down on the table before he turned and walked away.

3 - From The Hills to the Flatlands

"I come bearing gifts," Tony said as Janel opened her front door and stepped aside to let him into the house.   He gave her a big bear hug and kissed her on the cheek. "How you feeling sweetheart?"

"I'm ok, just trying to stay busy.   How'd things go with Sherri?"   She asked as she shut the door, and he looked at her as if he was confused.   "The last time I saw you, you were late for dinner with Sherri.   How'd that go?"

"Not well."

"Ok, I'll leave that alone.   So what'd you bring me?"

"Food, cause I know you're not eating."   He handed her a bag with a grilled chicken salad in it.   "And this."   He waved a piece of paper in her face.   She grabbed it from him and read it.

"The death certificate?   They told me it would take ninety days, if I was lucky.   How'd you manage to get this?"

"Charm and personality.   And I called in a favor.   I told you I'd take care of it.   I even got you a few certified copies too."

"Thanks.   It feels good to finally have something I can cross off my list.   The bad thing is the list keeps growing."

"What do you mean?"

"I can show you better than I can tell you."   She motioned for him to follow her and she led him into the dining room.   She placed the death certificates in the middle of the table, on top of a thick pile of other documents.

"I see you've been busy.   I assume these are all pieces to the financial puzzle?"

"And you would be right.   Puzzle is definitely the right word for it."

"Talk to me.   What's going on?"

She pointed to the chair across from her.   "Have a seat, you're going to need it.   Before we get into the financial stuff though, something's really been bothering me.   The night that Dorian had his accident, he called me and told me he had to work late.   If that was the case, I don't understand what was he doing on the north side of town?"

"Don't do that."

"Do what?"

"Don't start asking questions that only Dorian can answer."

"I can't help it Tony, it didn't make sense for him to be on that side of town."

"He could've been over there for any number of reasons."

"Like what?"

"Maybe he was getting something to eat."

"Doubtful.   He knew I was making lasagna."

"Maybe he didn't want lasagna."

"*Everyone* wants my lasagna."

"Ok, I'll give you that.   You do make some damn good lasagna.   Listen to me, seriously.   Let it go.   Don't make yourself crazy asking questions about something that you may never get the answer to."

"I can't, it doesn't make sense."

"You have to, because the only person who can answer your question is gone and he's not coming back.   Now, talk to me about this."   He tapped the pile of papers.

"Fine, just shut me down."

"Trust me, it's for the best."   She handed him a document.   "Good, you found the insurance policy."

"I called to see what I needed to do in order to get the money, and they told me the policy lapsed six months ago due to non-payment."

"What?   You're kidding, right?"

"I wish I was.   That's nothing compared to this."   She handed him another document.   "We're four months behind on the mortgage.   And to top it all off, the checking account is overdrawn and the savings account only has a few hundred dollars in it."

"What the hell?   This is crazy Janel.   You had no idea about any of this?"

"None.   We never talked about the bills and no one was calling the house about money so I didn't ask.   I knew he was stressing more than usual about his bonus this year, but I just assumed his project goal was more difficult than usual.   I can only assume he was planning on using that to get us out of the hole.   I've canceled what I could, and paid what I couldn't out of an emergency fund."

"What emergency fund?"

"I have an account that I opened years ago in my maiden name.   A 'just in case' savings account my mom insisted on.   'You never know what he might do.'   You know how she is-was about Dorian.   Over time I added to it whenever I happened to think about it, and it turns out I had a nice balance in there.   It's not enough to get me out of this mess though, and it'll be empty soon."

"I just don't understand.   If he needed money, he knew I had his back.   All he had to do was ask and I would've loaned it to him, no questions asked."

"You know he was too proud for that."

"This is crazy.   I wasn't expecting this at all."

"What am I going to do?"   She looked at him as he ran his hand over the top of his head and stared at the mortgage statement.   "I've got bills piling up that I can't pay, a house that's about to go into foreclosure, a teenage son to support, and no job.   I'm scared."   Her eyes welled up with tears and she dabbed her eyes with her shirt to keep them from rolling down her cheeks.

"I'm not going to lie, this is bad.   But it's not hopeless.   Just give me a minute to think."   She found his words reassuring, and she knew if there was a way out, he'd be the one to find it. "Has anyone from human resources contacted you yet?"

"Yes."

"Did they mention anything about a life insurance policy?"

"No.   He had his pension, which listed DJ as the sole beneficiary, his last paycheck, and some vacation days. The rep told me they'd deposit the money in our account by the end of the month."

"Ok, let's start with the biggest hurdle, the mortgage. Go down to the bank with a death certificate and ask to speak to a loan officer.   Explain the situation and see what they say.   That should buy some time on the foreclosure until I can figure something out."   She nodded in agreement.   "Next, you're going to have to dust off your resume, brush up on your interview skills, and start looking for a job."

"Yeah right.   You make it sound so easy."

"What's the problem?   You've got a bachelor's degree-"

"And no work experience.   I've been a wife and a stay at home mom for seventeen years, who's going to hire me?"

"A company who needs someone who's good at organizing, and has great attention to detail, who happens to have a bachelor's degree in accounting."

"That sounds good in theory."

"Look, you're a smart woman Janel.   Anyone who interviews you will see that within five minutes of speaking to you.   Once you ace the interview-"

"The only way I'm going to get an interview in the first place is by listing some experience on my resume, which I don't have."   She fought to keep her lip from quivering but her eyes betrayed her as two big teardrops rolled down her face.   She got up to get some tissue and he caught her by the arm.

"Hey."   He handed her his handkerchief.

She smiled as she wiped her eyes.   "I didn't know men

still carried real handkerchiefs anymore.   Thanks."

"Look, I know you're feeling completely overwhelmed-"

"This is bad.   I'm in a really bad spot, and I don't see a way out of it."

"It is bad, but I'm here to help.   I'm here for you, and we'll get through this together.   Ok?"   He put his arms around her and squeezed her tight.   "I'm sure there's something we're missing, we just have to keep digging.   Just try not to worry too much ok?"

"What if there isn't anything else?"

"Stop being so negative!   I got this.   You trust me right?   I'm a lawyer, I figure out difficult situations every day.   Now pull yourself together, get down to the bank, and see if you can buy some time on this foreclosure."

# # #

"Hi, I'm here to see a loan officer please?"

The woman glanced up at Janel over the top of her glasses.   "Your name?"

"Janel Monroe."

"What time is your appointment please?"

"I'm sorry but I don't have one.   I was wondering if I could wait until someone is available?   It's important, and pretty urgent."

The woman pressed a long slender finger to the bridge of her glasses, pushing them up on her face.   "Have a seat and I'll see what I can do."

Janel thanked the woman before walking back across the atrium to take a seat in the lobby.   She picked up a copy of Forbes and mindlessly flipped through the pages as she settled in for what she expected to be a long wait.

"Miss Monroe?"   She looked up to find a tall, caramel colored man extending his hand to her.   "I'm Perry Hunter, one of the loan officers on staff.   I understand you need to talk to someone about an urgent matter?"

She stood up and shook his hand.   "Yes, so nice to meet you."

"Come on back to my office so we can talk."   He led her through a small maze of cubicles and into his office where he closed the door.   She took a seat in front of his desk and he settled into the seat next to her, turning his chair in her direction so he could face her.   "So, what can I do for you?"

"Well Mr. Hunter, I'll get right to the point.   I'm four months behind on my mortgage, and it's my understanding that the house is about to go into foreclosure.   I'm here because," she paused.   "Quite frankly I'm in a rather extensive financial bind, and I'm not sure what I should do. I was hoping you could give me some guidance."   She handed him the foreclosure notice and he quickly glanced over it.

"I guess the first thing I need to know is how did you get behind?   Were you laid off?   Did you lose your job?"

"Actually I don't work, I'm a stay at home wife and mother."   She pulled a copy of the death certificate from her purse.   "Unfortunately my husband was the sole breadwinner, and he was killed recently in a car accident."

"I'm so sorry to hear that."

"Thank you.   He also handled our finances, so I'm not sure how we got so far behind."

"Based on your situation, I'm sure I could get you an extension.   We could give you an additional thirty days, maybe a little longer.   How much time will you need? Are you expecting an insurance payout or a legal settlement?"

"I'm working with a lawyer, trying to figure everything out, but right now things aren't looking good."   It was at that very moment that the reality of her situation began to set in for her.   "Honestly Mr. Hunter, I couldn't afford the mortgage payments even if we were caught up, let alone what it's going to take to bring the loan current.   I just need someone to give me some advice, to tell me what my options are, because I have no idea what to do." She held her breath as she waited for him to speak.   He looked at her with gentle hazel eyes and she could tell he was trying to figure out what to say to her.   She was gripping her purse so tightly that her fingers began to ache.

"With this death certificate I can get you a thirty day extension with no problem.   But legally I can't tell you what you should or shouldn't do Mrs. Monroe.   That's a decision you'll have to make for yourself.   Maybe you should talk to your attorney, I'm sure they can offer some good advice."

"I know I'll probably have to sell the house," She struggled to get the words out.   Saying it out loud made the situation real, and she imagined no longer being able to live in the house she'd called home for more than ten years. "What happens if I can't sell it within thirty days?   Does someone just come and throw me and my things into the street like trash?   Help me understand the process so I know what to expect."

Perry's face softened and he looked over his shoulder before leaning in close to her.   "You need a short sale specialist.   The housing market is pretty grim right now, but I know there are a few people in this town that would jump at the opportunity to own a home in Clover Hills. People who can afford it.   You probably won't get an offer that'll cover the entire debt, but you're in the perfect position to submit a hardship case asking the bank to waive the difference.   If they approve it, great, you're debt free as far as the house is concerned.   But if they don't approve it, and there's no guarantee that they will, they'll hold you responsible for the balance."

"Explain to me what the difference is between a short sale and a foreclosure?"

"Think of a short sale as being proactive.   You negotiate the selling price with a buyer, which gives you a better chance at getting the offer you need to pay off your debt.   With a foreclosure, the house goes up for auction, and who knows what it'll sell for.   You might get lucky and it sells for what you owe or maybe even more.   But chances are it'll sell for much less, leaving you on the hook for the balance if the bank doesn't approve the waiver."

"So I need to talk to a realtor?"

"No, not just any realtor.   You need a short sale agent, someone with a lot of experience."

"Can you recommend someone?"

"Legally I can't.   I've already said more than I should. Just ask around, you should be able to find someone fairly easily."

She stood up and extended her hand.   "Thank you for your time, I really appreciate it."

He grasped her hand and squeezed it softly.   "No problem, it's what I'm here for.   Let me walk you out." He escorted her across the lobby and stopped just short of the front doors as he put his hand in his jacket pocket. "Let me give you my card, in case you have any other questions."   She slipped the card inside her purse.   "It's been a pleasure Mrs. Monroe.   It's unfortunate that we had to meet under such negative circumstances.   I hope things get better for you soon."

"Please, call me Janel.   And thanks again Mr. Hunter, you've been a big help."

"If you keep calling me Mr. Hunter, I'm going to start looking over my shoulder for my father."   He had such a beautiful smile that she couldn't help but smile back at him in return.   "If you need anything else, please don't hesitate to call me."

"I'll be sure to do that."

4 – Verna

Tony sat on his living room couch with papers and folders scattered across his coffee table. He was trying to focus on researching a case, but he was tired and kept nodding off. He hadn't been sleeping well because he was worried about Janel, and he couldn't believe the financial mess Dorian managed to leave her in. A mess he had to figure out how to fix. He finally stopped fighting it and stretched out on the couch and let sleep overtake him. He'd barely began to dream when he was awakened by a sharp knock at his front door. He turned over and made himself more comfortable, fully expecting to ignore the interruption, when the knock came again. This time it was more persistent, louder and harder, rudely demanding his attention. Irritated, he got up and looked through the peephole. "Ma?" He quickly opened the door.

"Surprise!"

"What're you doing here?"

"I told you I was thinking about coming to visit, so, here I am. Besides, I hated that I wasn't able to make it to the funeral. You know Dorian was like a son to me."

He couldn't be happier to see her, and gave her a hug and a kiss. "You should've called, I would have picked you up at the airport."

"I figured you'd be working and I didn't want to bother you. Besides, I know where you keep the extra key and I still remember the security code."

"Come on in, let me get your bag. How long you staying?"

"Just the weekend, I'm trying to hang on to my vacation days.   I don't have very many left."

He took her carry-on and set it down in the guest bedroom while she sat down on the couch and took her shoes off.   "You hungry?"

"If I was hungry I'd get in that kitchen and cook myself something to eat.   You know I don't want you making no fuss over me.   I came to spend some time with my son, and see how Janel and DJ are doing.   Come over here and sit down.   Talk to me."   She patted the sofa cushion next to her.   "How are you doing?"

"Just trying to stay busy."

"How are you *really* doing?   Because you look exhausted.   Are you getting any sleep?   And don't lie to me."

"Some."   She raised her eyebrows at him.   "A little." She frowned at him.   "Ok not very much.   I've been working from home, and when I do that, sometimes I get so wrapped up that I don't know when to take a break and walk away."

"Son, you need to take a break and give yourself some time to grieve.   You and Dorian were thick as thieves, and I know you're hurting just as much as Janel and DJ are. Burying yourself in your work is not the answer.   Take some time off and let your partner handle things for a while."

"I've been thinking about it."

"Ain't nothing to think about, just do it.   Today.   Right now."   She picked up his cell phone and handed it to him. "And when you're done I'm going to need you to run me to the grocery store.   I want to cook for you guys tonight so make sure you have Janel and DJ over here by seven so we can eat together."

"DJ isn't here, he's in Michigan with Janel's parents."

"That's too bad, I was really looking forward to seeing him.   I'm sure he's almost grown now.   How long has it been since I've seen DJ and Janel?"

Tony thought about it.   "It's been about two years I think."

"That long?"

"The last time you came to visit, they weren't here.   I think they were visiting family or on vacation or something."

"Well you go on and make that phone call so you can take me to the store.   Then call Janel and tell her you're cooking dinner and you'll pick her up.   Don't tell her I'm here, I want to surprise her."

#

When Janel and Tony walked through his front door, the house smelled of fried chicken and fresh garlic.   "It smells like home in here Tony, I never realized you were such a good cook."

"I don't know about all that.   I do ok."

"From the smell of it you do more than ok."   She turned the corner into the kitchen and stopped short when she saw his mother.   "Miss Gibson?"   Janel went to the woman and gave her a hug and kiss.   "It's so good to see you.   What a really nice surprise."

"I was so sorry to hear about Dorian, I wish I could have made it to the funeral.   How're you holding up sweetheart?"

"I'm doing ok."   The two women took in each other's presence, holding on to each other's forearms, and Janel hugged Verna again.   "It really is good to see you. Smelling all this delicious food brings back good memories."

"Y'all used to eat like they never fed you on campus. Especially the boys.   They were like bottomless pits back then, especially during football season."

"You couldn't get cooking like yours on campus momma. We had to get as much as we could, when we could."

"Nobody could even come close to your peach cobbler Miss Gibson."

"Honey call me Verna.   You making me feel old calling me Miss Gibson.   Y'all ain't in school anymore, you grown. How's DJ doing?"

"I talked to him this morning, he's doing ok.   Still trying to cope with what happened.   We all are.   It kind of feels like Dorian's been gone on a long business trip and he'll be home any day now."

"You know what I think we should do tonight? Celebrate the good times and honor Dorian's memory. What kind of liquor you got over there Tony?"

Verna set the table and Janel fixed the plates.   They sat down together and Tony opened a bottle of dry white wine. Verna raised her glass and Tony made a quick impromptu toast.   "To Dorian, husband, father, brother, son, and friend.   May he rest in peace."

They touched their glasses to one another and took a drink.   Tony was glad to see Janel with a healthy appetite for once; he suspected she wasn't eating much lately.   He hadn't run across many people who could resist his mother's fried chicken.   She'd also made corn on the cob, mashed red potatoes with garlic and chives, fresh string beans with ham hocks, and homemade biscuits.   They spent the evening reminiscing over old times and his mom told Janel a few embarrassing stories from Tony's childhood that she never seemed to get tired of retelling. He got up for seconds and brought a second bottle of wine back to the table.   He offered to refresh the ladies glasses and Janel gladly accepted.

Verna noticed he neglected to refill his own glass.   "Go on and have another glass Tony, you could probably use it."

"I can't mom, I gotta take Janel home."

"Take her home?   She's family, she can stay the night. I'll sleep on the couch and she can have the spare bedroom."

"I can't Verna."

"You can have my bed Janel, I'll sleep on the couch." Tony offered.

"I appreciate it but I can't.   Honestly I'd rather just go home and sleep in my own bed while I still can."

"Ok you've had too much wine.   What does that mean, 'while you still can?' "

"I've got to sell the house Verna, I can't afford to stay there anymore."

"What?"

The doorbell rang and Tony got up.   "I'll get that, probably somebody selling something.   Excuse me ladies." He looked through the peephole to find Sherri on his doorstep.   He opened the door and stepped out onto the porch.   He folded his arms across his chest and waited for her to speak.

"Hey.   I thought about what you said at dinner the other night and I realize maybe I was being a little selfish and insensitive.   I know you and Dorian were really close, and I just wanted to come by and apologize.   I'm sorry."

Tony exhaled loudly as he uttered his own apology.   "I was wrong for snapping at you, you know that's not me. And I was wrong for walking out on you.   I was tired, and frustrated, but that's no excuse.   I'm sorry too."

Sherri looked briefly at the partially closed door, then back at him.   "Ok, this is the part where you invite me in and we have really good make up sex."

"Who is it Anthony?   Your food's getting cold."

"Who is that?"   Sherri asked.

"My mother."

"Your mother's here?   Why didn't you tell me?" Sherri pushed her way past Tony and he followed closely behind her as she made a beeline for the dining room.

"Hi, I'm Sherri."   She shoved her hand in Verna's face.

Verna looked at Tony as she reluctantly shook Sherri's hand.   "Verna."

"It's so nice to finally meet you."   Verna appeared confused so Sherri clarified her relationship.   "I'm Tony's girlfriend."   She let go of Sherri's hand and looked to Tony for an explanation.   "We've been dating for a little over two years now."

Janel downed what was left of the wine in her glass and turned the bottle upside down looking for more.   She cut the uncomfortable silence with a less than enthusiastic greeting.   "Hey Sherri."

She appeared grateful for the interruption.   "Hey Janel. I was so sorry to hear about Dorian.   I wish I could have come to the funeral but unfortunately I couldn't get off from work."   Janel dismissed the woman with a wave of her hand.

The tension in the room was incredibly thick as Verna and Sherri both turned their attention to Tony, looking for an explanation.   He was at a complete loss for words, possibly for the first time in his entire adult life since becoming a lawyer.   As he searched for something to say that would pacify both his mother and Sherri, Janel cleared her throat and stood up on less than steady legs.   "Well, it's been fun fam but I think maybe I ought to be going. It's getting late.   Verna, as always, the food was delicious, and it was really good to see you."   She leaned over and hugged the woman around her shoulders and gave her a kiss on the cheek.

"Stay Janel.   I really want to finish catching up with you."   Verna grabbed Janel's hand and squeezed.

"I can't.   When are you leaving?"

"Sunday evening."

"Give me a call tomorrow and maybe Tony can bring you by the house.   We'll see each other again before you leave."   Janel assured her.   She started towards the door, then stopped.   "I forgot I don't have my car."   She dug around in her purse and mumbled something to herself that Verna apparently picked up on with her supersonic mother hearing.

"You are not taking a cab home.   Just stay here tonight and Tony will run you home first thing in the morning."

"She wants to go home mom.   Come on Janel, I'll take you."   Tony was thankful for the opportunity to leave. "Can you fix Sherri a plate while I'm gone?   It'll only take me a minute."

"No.   She can fix her own damn plate."

"Ma!"

"What?   She grown ain't she?   She say y'all been seeing each other for two years now, I'm sure she knows her way around."   Tony gave Verna a look and she relented.   "Fine."

"I could come with you?   Since you'll only be gone a minute."   Sherri's tone was one of sheer desperation, and it was obvious that she didn't want to be left alone with his mom.   However, the irony of the situation hadn't escaped him as she was the one who pushed past him and insisted on inviting herself in.

Verna pointed her finger at Sherri.   "Naw, you gonna have a seat and eat this plate I'm about to fix Shelly.   He'll be back in a minute."

#

"Thanks for dinner, that was a nice surprise.   I got to see your mom, and she cooked?   It doesn't get any better than that.   I love her, she has such a wonderful spirit." Janel opened her door and disarmed the alarm.

"That's an interesting way to put it, her 'spirit.'   Most people would call it frankness, or candidness.   There are several other colorful adjectives one might use to describe her too; brusque, forthright, outspoken, direct."

"She is who she is.   All you can do is love her."

"Yeah, cause I can't do much else with her."

"You know you love your momma."   Janel set her purse and her keys down on the foyer table and flipped a light on.

"I do.   I know she really enjoyed seeing you too.   She was so disappointed that DJ's not here.   I have to remember to tell him the next time I talk to him."   He closed the door.

"I appreciate you seeing me home safely."

"I wouldn't have it any other way."

They looked at one another for a moment.   "You want to check the house for bad guys?   It would give you a legitimate reason to stall.   Not that I blame you, I'd stall too if I had two queen bees in the same beehive waiting for me when I got home."

"I'm not stalling, I'm just making sure you get in ok."   He smiled at her, then rubbed his hand over the top of his head.

"You really never told Verna about Sherri?"   He shook his head no.   "Never mind.   It's none of my business."

"I'm glad you came over tonight.   It was good to see you smiling."   He took her hand and kissed it, and continued to hang on to it loosely.

"It was good to get out of the house.   It's not so bad during the day, because I can pretend Dorian's at work and everything is normal again.   But at night-"   She paused. "I'm not going to lie, it's hard."

"What can I do to help?"

"Don't worry about me, you've got your own mess to deal with."   He saw her bottom lip quiver slightly.

"Look at me."   He put two fingers under her chin and made her look him in the eye.   "I don't care what's going on at my house, it could be burning down for all I care. Are you ok?"

"I'm fine."

It killed him to see her eyes tear up.   "If you want me to stay, I'll stay.   For as long as you need me to."   He kissed her gently on the mouth.   To his surprise, she kissed him back before gently pushing him away.

She covered her mouth, as if she was trying to keep from telling a secret.   "You better go."   He was concerned about leaving her alone but she insisted.   "Go on, I'm ok."

"You're sure?"

"I promise, go on.   I'll call you tomorrow."   He waited until she disappeared up the stairs and into her bedroom before closing the door and locking it with his key.

5 – Betrayal

Janel was on her hands and knees, pulling weeds from the flower bed in front of her home, when she heard a car heading up the long driveway. She sat back on her heels and brushed the dirt from her gloves as she watched Tony walk towards her with his familiar stride. It exuded confidence, and was reminiscent of Denzel Washington. She tilted her hat back slightly off of her forehead and pulled her sweaty tank top away from her torso, but the day was so humid that the gesture was in vain.

He removed his sunglasses and surveyed her work. "Looks good."

"Thanks. It keeps my mind busy and helps to relieve some of the stress. Plus, I had to cancel the lawn service. I can't really afford to pay them anymore."

"Maybe you can get one of the neighborhood kids to help you." He bent down and put his hand to her cheek and kissed her on the other.

"Kids in Clover Hills don't do manual labor, even when there's money involved. They get allowances from their parents for doing nothing, and they drive expensive cars that most working adults can't afford." She took off her gloves and held out her hand. "Help me up please?"

He pulled her to her feet. "You staying hydrated?"

"Of course." She removed her hat and gestured towards a cooler on the front porch. She opened it and pulled a wash rag from the icy water. She wrung it out and wiped her face and neck with it. "What brings you out my way?"

"Can't I just come by to say hello and check on you?"

"You could, but my intuition tells me there's more to it than that." She shielded her eyes with her hand and looked up at him.   "Tell me you've got some good news, I could really use it."

"I've got some good news, along with some not so good news.   You wanna go inside and talk?"

"Quite frankly I'm beginning to go stir crazy in there.   I know it's hot out but I'd rather sit out here if it's ok with you."   She sat her hat on top of the cooler and stepped up onto the porch of her antebellum style home for what she imagined would probably be one of the very last times. She made herself comfortable in one of the rocking chairs and he pulled his chair closer to hers.   He leaned forward and rested his elbows on his knees, and she could tell he was thinking about what he wanted to say to her.   She took a moment to really look at him, something she'd never done before.   His skin was smooth, the color of dark chocolate, and his full lips were perfectly framed by his goatee.   And even though he was wearing dress slacks, a vest, and a button down shirt with the sleeves rolled halfway up his forearms, she noticed he wasn't sweating. This made her smile, because it was so in tune with his character.   It seemed that no matter what the circumstances, he always managed to remain calm under pressure.

She smiled and waved at a neighbor driving by, but she was ignored, and her smile faded quickly.   "You see that? They ignore me now.   For years I ran their kids back and forth to games and practices.   I sat next to these people in the bleachers and cheered for their children as well as my own.   I   hosted   countless   parties   and sleepovers...neighborhood association meetings.   And suddenly now that Dorian's gone, they act like I don't even exist anymore."

"Give them the benefit of the doubt, maybe they just don't know what to say.   Death can be an uncomfortable subject for most people.   And his death was so sudden, and tragic."

"You know what I've realized through all of this?   I don't have any friends.   Not any real friends anyway." He shook his head in protest.   "No really.   If you think about it, literally everyone that I know, since we moved to Lafayette, I've met through Dorian.   I've been sitting here trying to figure out at what point I managed to lose track of all of *my* friends.   I had friends when I left Michigan, and then we moved, and it seems like over the years I've managed to lose my own identity, apparently along with the ability to make new friends of my own."

He stared at the tips of his expensive leather shoes. "So what are we, if not friends?"

"That's my point Tony, you're my only friend."   She leaned forward in her chair.   "If it weren't for you, helping me through this craziness, I don't know where I'd be right now.   Probably still upstairs in the bed, crying.   I don't have anyone else to lean on, confide in, or talk to.   It's pathetic."

"You talked to and confided in your husband.   And that's what made you such a good wife, because you didn't discuss your problems with other people.   And the Janel I know isn't pathetic, she's a fighter.   You're stronger than you think you are."

"I'm glad one of us has so much confidence in me. Anyway, you said you had some news for me."

"We found a buyer for the house.   We appealed to their sympathy and they've agreed to pay ninety percent of the debt.   In cash, which should be a major catalyst for the bank committee to approve the deal."

"That's good."

"That's good?   That's great!   I thought you'd be a little more enthusiastic.   You do realize that's the *good* news right?"

"I'm just worried about having to pay the balance."

"That's why we're submitting the hardship letter remember?   If your situation doesn't warrant approval, I don't know what will.   Try to stay positive."

"You're right, I'm sorry.   What's the 'not so good' news?"

"In order to convince the buyer to pay ninety percent, we had to be willing to give up something major in return. We promised if the bank approves the deal, you'd agree to be out of the house within two weeks."

"What the hell?   Two weeks?"

"Hear me out Janel, it's not as bad as it sounds.   If we're proactive, we can make this work in your favor."

"How in the hell am I supposed to find a place to live in two weeks Tony?   I don't even have a job yet!"

"Listen.   We don't know how long it's going to take the bank to review the deal.   It could be several weeks or several months.   So in the meantime, you concentrate on finding a job and let me work on figuring out where you and DJ will live."

"Even if I find a job, I'm not going to be able to find a place to rent without a solid work history.   Or references."

"We have time to figure it out.   I promise you, it's not as bad as it sounds."

"Of course it doesn't to you; you have a job and a place to live.   Hell, at this point I may as well move back to Michigan and live with my parents until I can get on my feet."   She rocked her chair faster as she felt her anxiety level rise, and she closed her eyes in an attempt to keep from crying.   She felt his hand on her thigh, and he squeezed until she stopped rocking the chair.

"Listen, I know this has got to be incredibly overwhelming for you, and I'm not even going say I know how you feel, because I don't.   But I can imagine.   I need for you to understand that no matter what happens, I got your back.   Open your eyes and look at me."   She did as she was told.   "How long have we known each other?

I'm not going to let you fall. You're not going to be homeless. I'm going to make sure of that because we're family. And you will find a job. Do you have your resume together yet?"

"Yes. I went through a resume clinic at the library, and a really nice woman helped me take what little I had to work with and make it sound much more interesting than I ever could. She's been coaching me on some interview skills too."

"There you go. A good looking resume leads to interviews, which leads to a foot in the door. That's all you need. I know once you get a job you'll be making good money in no time. You know Sherri mentioned CSC is opening a new branch on the south side. You should give her a call. Maybe she can put in a good word for you."

"Are you serious? What makes you think she would do that for me?"

"Why *wouldn't* she?"

"Because you left her alone with your mother to take me home the other night."

"And?"

"Women are catty Tony. She needed you to defend her against your mother and you chose to leave. With me."

"How else were you supposed to get home? I wasn't about to let you take a cab."

"The point is *you left her*, the reason doesn't matter. Not only did you leave her there by herself, but you left *with me*. Your attention was focused *on me*, not her. In her mind, your attention should never be focused on any other woman whenever she's in your presence. You already know she's jealous, none of this should come as a surprise to you. I bet you haven't heard from her since that night, have you?" She waited for him to answer but he didn't. "That's cause she's still pissed."

She stood up and stretched, and wondered if she had

enough energy to trim the hedges.   He remained seated and took her hand in his, and he pressed his lips around the knuckle of her middle finger.   She got goose bumps as she remembered how those lips felt against hers.

"You should call her."   He said as he leaned his forehead against her leg.

She touched her hand to the top of his head.   "No thanks, I can do bad by myself."   She stepped off the porch, put her hat and gloves back on, picked up the shears, and started trimming the bushes.

"I'll mention it to her, see if you can list her as a reference at least."

She stopped clipping and turned to face him.   "While I appreciate the thought, I really wish you wouldn't."

"Everyone needs a little help sometimes Janel.   It couldn't hurt."

"Are you even listening to me?"

"She's upset with me, not you."

"She's upset with you *because* of me."

"She *stays* upset with me, and she won't take it out on you.   She's not that kind of person."

"Promise me you won't say anything to her."

"I don't understand-"

"You don't have to understand.   Just promise me you won't say anything."   She pointed the shears at him and he threw his hands up in surrender.

"Fine, I won't say anything."

# # #

As Janel showered to rinse away the yard work, she tried to mentally prepare herself to open the box of Dorian's belongings from the accident scene.   She took a knife to the tape, carefully folded back the flaps, and peeked inside. The first thing she saw was his planner.   It was his lifeline, he never went anywhere without it.   She ran her hand over the faded leather and pressed her nose to it, trying desperately to breathe in his scent.   Her eyes welled up with tears and she closed them momentarily.   She unzipped it and flipped through hand written notes and highlighted entries.   Some business cards spilled out of an inside pocket and she carefully tucked them back into place.   Finally, she set it aside, making a mental note to get it to Tony so he could give it a more detailed look.   She was hopeful that he'd be able to find information that might lead them to something they had yet to discover, financial or otherwise.   She picked up a stack of brittle, dirty papers and flipped through them.   They were mostly maintenance records for the car, along with other miscellaneous receipts.   She set them aside to shred later. The only items left were a couple of empty, cracked CD cases and his cell phone.   She picked it up and held the power button down to see if it would power on.   When the display failed to light up, she took it into the kitchen and plugged it into the charger.   She waited a few minutes before trying again and the display lit up.   She waited for it to power up, then opened the picture gallery.   She smiled as she flipped through them, and stopped when she saw one from their anniversary two years ago.   They'd just finished eating dinner and he'd asked the waiter to take their picture.   It was one of the best anniversary celebrations they'd ever had.   She forwarded the picture to her email account, and suddenly the phone began vibrating and chiming, coming alive with notification after notification.   When it finally finished, both the voice mail and text message indicators appeared in the upper corner, next to the signal strength indicator.   She dialed the voice mailbox and listened to the messages.

You have three new voice mail messages.   To listen to your messages, press 1.

Message 1:   "Hey Dorian, it's Brad.   I need you to swap with me and bring in bagels or donuts for the staff meeting tomorrow morning.   I'm not going to be able to make it, I've got an appointment that I forgot about. Take good notes for me, ok?   Thanks buddy, I owe you one.   I'll see around lunchtime."

Message 2:   "Hey baby, I thought you said you'd be able to get away tonight.   Where are you?   I sent you some pictures to give you a sneak peak of what I have in store for you.   I hope you got them.   Can't wait to see you."

Message 3:   "Dorian, this isn't funny, where the hell are you?   Did something come up?   I'm starting to get worried.   Send me a text if you changed your mind or you can't get away."

End of messages.

She immediately recognized the woman's voice from the second and third messages, yet she replayed them three times each just to make sure she wasn't mistaken.   She disconnected from his voice mail and opened up his text messages, selecting the most recent one first.

Can't wait to see you tonight.

She opened the attachment and it was a close up of a woman's cleavage.   The second message contained a picture without any text.   It was a self-portrait of a woman wearing red lingerie.   Her face was obscured by the reflection of the flash in the mirror but Janel knew who she was.   She flipped through text message after text message, getting more and more upset with each message and image she saw.   She finally threw the phone in her purse and headed straight for Dorian's office.

6 - (Almost) Making Amends

Tony took a minute to go over what he wanted to say in his head before he knocked on the door to face the inevitable. Although he hadn't talked to her, he knew Sherri was still quite pissed over his mother's visit. By the time he'd made it back to his place that night, she was gone, his mother was in the bed, and he had no idea what had transpired between the two of them. He called himself giving her some time to cool off, but she wasn't answering his calls and enough was enough. It was important that he see her because he had two missions to complete. Mission one; he was horny, and mission two; he needed her to help Janel get hired on with CSC. He tapped on the door with his knuckles and waited. Just when he was certain she wasn't going to answer, she opened the door as far as the safety chain would allow.

"What?" She spat the word towards him through the narrow opening.

He positioned himself so he could focus on the one eye that he could see. "I came to apologize since you won't take my calls." The single, unblinking, beautiful brown eye stared back at him. "Seriously Sherri?"

"What?"

"Can you open the door so we can talk like adults?" He gestured towards the chain and she slammed the door closed. For a moment he wondered if she would open it again. Finally, he heard her remove the chain and the door opened slightly. She reappeared in the doorway, with the door pulled tightly against her body, blocking the entrance.   Her childish games were tiring, but he stood fast.   He had objectives that he intended to complete.

"You asked me to open the door, I opened the door."

"I'm trying here.   Do you think you can at least meet me halfway?"   When she didn't respond, he gestured towards the door.   "Can I come inside so we can sit down and talk?"   She finally relented and stepped backwards, opening the door completely.   "Thank you."   He said as he stepped past her and into her living room.   She closed the door behind him but continued to stand in the tiny foyer with her arms folded across her chest.   "Can we sit down?   Please?"   He asked, patting the couch cushion beside him.   She rolled her eyes and plopped down on the opposite end of the couch like an angry teenager, crossing her arms and legs, and he knew this wasn't going to be an ordinary apology.   He'd have to go deep, especially if he expected to get some loving, but he had no doubt about his skills.   He knew he'd accomplish mission one by the time the night was over.   Mission two, however, might prove to be a little trickier, but he was up for the challenge.   "First off, let me just say I'm sorry that I left you alone with my mom.   I'm not sure exactly what happened, but I assume it wasn't good or you wouldn't be ignoring my calls."

He'd barely finished his sentence when she let loose on a tirade.   "She didn't even know who I was!   I mean, I didn't expect her to recognize me *physically* since we've never met face to face, but she had *no clue* who I was. Two years we've been dating, TWO YEARS Tony, and you've *never* mentioned me to your mother?   You talk to her AT LEAST once a week at a MINIMUM, and you never said a *word* about me?   I can't begin to tell you how incredibly *stupid* I felt."

He waited to see if she was done before he responded. "In all fairness Sherri, I tried to warn you that my mom can be kind of tough."

"Kind of tough?   That's an understatement.   She is *brutal*, and you left me there *alone* with her!"

"How else was Janel supposed to get home?"

"You should've called her ass a cab!"

"My mom would've never stood for that and neither would I.   I picked her up and brought her over, it was only right that I take her back home."

"She couldn't even get my NAME right!   She kept calling me *Shelly* and *Shonda*."

"That's my mom babe, what can I say?   I admit she can be a little passive aggressive sometimes."   Before he realized it, the corners of his mouth turned up into a slight smile, which propelled her from pissed to completely enraged in 0.6 seconds.

She flung herself forward on the edge of the couch and shoved her finger in his face.   "You think this shit is funny?"

"No, I don't.   Not at all.   Look, babe, if you had just called-"

"What?   I came over your house to apologize to *you*, after *you* blew up and walked out on *me*, and you're trying to blame this on *me* because I didn't call first?"

"Look baby, I'm tired of all this fighting and arguing.   I said I was sorry, what else can I say?   Can't we get past this already?   I'm sorry I didn't tell my mom about you. You may not agree with them, but I had my reasons.   If you called before you came over, I could've explained she was in town, and arranged for you two to meet.   Instead you chose to force yourself into the situation.   Put yourself in her shoes for a minute.   Do you think that she might have felt ambushed and maybe that's why she reacted the way she did?   I'm not saying what I did was right, and I'm not saying whatever my mom said or did was right, but you need to accept some responsibility here too."

"You call this an apology?"

"Damn it Sherri, it's the best I've got. Take it or leave it."

"Leave.   Now."   She stood up and pointed towards the door.

He continued to sit, defiantly so.   He'd made up his mind that either they were going to work things out or call it quits for good.   "Listen.   I told you I didn't know when she was coming.   She literally showed up, suitcase in hand, that morning.   She hadn't even been in my house for twelve hours, let alone a full twenty four when you showed up on my doorstep.   You know how close we are, that she's protective of me because my dad left before I was born.   She just wants the best for me-"

"Are you saying I'm not good enough for you?"

"Stop twisting my words around and just listen to me for a minute.   My mom doesn't think there's a woman on this earth that's good enough for me.   I've only introduced a handful of women that I've dated to my mom because honestly, you're right, she can be brutal.   I wanted you to be prepared when you met her, so you wouldn't have to experience....whatever it is you experienced.   Can you understand that?   I wanted to tell her about you and introduce the two of you in my own time and in my own way."   He took her by the hand and tugged at her arm. "Sit down and listen to me."   She flopped back down on the couch.   "She'll come around, and maybe the next time she comes to visit things will be different."   She was sitting with her arms crossed, her foot bouncing in the air. He knew he only had a little more digging to do to get out of the hole he was in and into hers, thereby accomplishing mission one.   "I'm sorry.   You forgive me?"   He tried to kiss her on the neck and she made an attempt to push him away, but he grabbed her around the waist and pulled her close.   "Come on, baby."   This is the part where we have great make up sex, he thought to himself as he gently bit her nipples through her shirt.   He finally felt her relax and he kissed her.   When she reciprocated, he knew he was in. "You forgive me?"

She faked a pout.   "I guess so."

"I want to show you how sorry I am."   He kissed her again.

"Yeah?"

"Yes.   But first, I have a favor to ask."   He knew he was risking great sex, but he had faith he could talk his way right back to it.

"What's that?"

"You do me this one favor, this one small favor, and I'll do you a huge favor."   He kissed her neck.   "And another favor, and another, until you roll over and start snoring." He pulled her shirt up and started kissing her stomach.

"You know you don't have to *ask* me to do you a favor." She reached for his waistband to unfasten his pants.

"No not that, something else."

"What?"

"The other day you mentioned CSC was opening a new branch on the south side.   I was wondering if you could put in a good word for Janel and help her get hired on?" He winced slightly without even realizing it.

"Are you serious?   What the hell?"   She tried to push him away from her but he held her tight, put his weight on her, and buried his face in her cleavage.

"Come on babe, just one little favor.   She needs a job. I know you're not the hiring manager, but I know you probably know the person who is.   If you could just mention her name, or put her resume at the top of the 'stack.'   Or maybe even let her use you as a reference? Anything that might give her a leg up in the process."

She continued to struggle, trying to break free from his embrace.   "What the hell does she need a job for?   I know Dorian made the better side of six figures easily. How the hell else could they afford to live in Clover Hills? Besides, she's been a stay at home mother and wife for what, twenty years?   What kind of experience could she possibly have?"

He loosened his grip a little as he made the case for Janel. "She's got a bachelor's degree in accounting, and she's done some odd jobs here and there.   Mostly non-profit work, but it's experience.   And you know she's smart.   Two plus two is still four right, how different can things be?"

"You still haven't told me why she needs a job.   Didn't Dorian have any life insurance?   They didn't have any savings or anything?"

He let her go so he could talk to her face to face. "Technically, she's a client, so I can't really discuss her situation."

"I'm your girlfriend Tony, who am I going to tell?"

"It's a matter of ethics, you know that.   When have I ever discussed any of my clients with you?"

"You want to talk about ethics after you just asked me to find a way to get her hired on?"

"I'm not asking you to compromise yourself, I'm just asking if you could help her out if the opportunity should happen to present itself.   And you know me, I would never ask if it wasn't important.   You already know she's smart, she has a degree, all she needs is a foot in the door. I know if she can get an interview, she'll get the job on her own merit."   He rubbed the inside of her thigh, and she rolled her eyes and sighed deeply.   "A foot in the door, the drop of her name, a reference.   That's all I'm asking.   No promises, no guarantees."   He kissed her on the neck again and moved his hand further up her thigh.   "Please?"

"What's in it for me?"

"Whatever you want."

"I want to go shopping.   Shoe shopping."

He knew he wasn't going to get off so easy, but he was willing to agree to almost anything in order to move things along.   "And?"

"I want to go away for the weekend like you promised."

"Is that all?   Cause I can think of a few things I can give you right now."

"Really?"   She grinned at him.

"Yes, really."   He pulled her shirt over her head and she began to unbutton his.   He unhooked her bra and she started unfastening his belt buckle when his cell phone began to ring.

"No, don't answer it."   She said as she quickly loosened his belt and unzipped his pants.

He checked the display and recognized the name, but wasn't sure why they were calling him.   "I'm sorry baby, I gotta get this.   Just one sec, I promise."   He stood up and walked towards the kitchen as he answered the phone. "This is Tony."

"Tony, it's Brad.   I don't know if you remember me but I worked with Dorian?"

"Yes, I know who you are."

"I don't know if you know or not, but I thought I'd give you a call just in case."

"Know what?   What's up?"

"Janel's in jail."

"What?"   He used his peripheral vision to see if Sherri was listening in on his conversation.   She was still lying on her back, staring up at the ceiling.   Probably pissed all over again he imagined.   All of his hard work had just been undone in a matter of seconds.

"Yeah, I kind of figured you didn't know."

He lowered his voice and moved closer to the kitchen, just in case Sherri was trying to listen in.   "What happened?"

"She came to the office and knocked Michelle clean out, literally.   Broke her nose."

"What?   Why?"

"There'd been some talk in the office, before the accident."

"What do you mean?   Talk about what?"

"Dorian and Michelle....and the possibility of an otherwise unprofessional, intimate relationship between the two of them.   Honestly, if there was something going on, I wasn't aware of it."

"Shit.   I'm on my way."   He stuck his phone back in his pocket.   He zipped his pants, buckled his belt, and started working on buttoning up his shirt.

Sherri sat up on the couch.   "On your way where?"

"I'm sorry, babe.   A client of mine is in some trouble and I have to go take care of it."   He leaned down to kiss her but she turned her head away.

"Why can't someone else at the firm take care of it?"

"It's a long time client and their case is....complicated.   I have to take care of it myself, I know the history on this case."

"I'm so tired of this shit Tony.   You need to make me a priority in your life soon or I'm gone."

"It's my job Sherri, you know this comes with the territory.   I have to go.   I'll call you as soon as I can."   He tried to kiss her again but she put her finger in the middle of his forehead and pushed him away.

"Fuck you and your promises.   Stop telling me how much you care and show me or I'm done with this relationship.   I mean it."

"I hear you-"

"Do you?"

"I do, but right now I have to go.   I'll call you later, we'll talk.   I promise."

7 – Jail

"Monroe, you're up." Janel heard the heavy clunk of the locking mechanism and a corrections officer slid the metal door open. She looked up at him as if he were speaking a foreign language. "But I haven't called anybody."

"Look Laila Ali, all I know is your bail has been posted and you're free to go. You wanna look a gift horse in the mouth, be my guest, just hurry up and make up your mind cause I'm about to go on break."

She quickly stood up and stepped outside of the holding cell. After signing for her belongings, the officer led her through a series of locked doors until he finally deposited her into the precinct lobby where Tony was waiting for her.

"You ok?" She nodded her head, avoiding eye contact with him. "Did they x-ray that before they wrapped it up?" He gestured towards her swollen hand.

"It's not broken." She answered, her voice barely above a whisper.

"Let's get out of here."

You could hear a pin drop in the car as they rode along in silence until she realized he was taking her to his place. "I need to go get my car."

"No you don't. We'll get your car later."

"I just want to get my car and go home."

"Oh you're definitely not going home." He pulled the car into his garage, and they sat for a moment in silence. He finally got out and opened the car door for her but she remained seated, staring straight ahead.   "Get out of the car Janel, I'm really not in the mood."

"I want to go home Tony."

"If I took you home right now you'd probably get pissed off all over again and burn the place down.   And you've done enough damage for one night.   I'm not taking you home."

"Then take me to get my car and I'll drive myself."

"You don't get it do you?   I just bailed you out of jail, therefore you've been released into my custody, and I'm telling you you're not going home and I'm not taking you to get your car.   It's damn near three o'clock in the morning, and the only place I'm going is to bed.   If you want to sit out here, be my guest."   He went inside and shut the door.

She continued to sit in the car for a few minutes, wondering how she managed to get herself in such a mess, before she finally went inside.

"Take my bed, you can sleep in those."   He nodded towards a t-shirt and a pair of shorts at the end of the couch as he flipped through channels on the television.   She picked up the clothing and headed for his bathroom where she took a long, hot bath.   Once she got dressed, she poked her head into the living room to see if he was awake. The room was dark but she could sense he was still lying on the couch.

"Are you ready to tell me what happened, or are we going to talk about it later this morning?"   He sat up and she could just make out the outline of his head.   She walked around the couch and sat down next to him.

"He was cheating on me."   She waited for him to react but he didn't.   "I thought we were ok, you know?   Our marriage wasn't perfect, but I really thought we were good. We had our ups and downs just like anyone else, but never anything major.   We always sat down and talked about things, and we always found a way to move on."   She pulled the neck of her t-shirt up and wiped her eyes. "I never imagined he would cheat on me. I feel so stupid."

"He was the stupid one. Who knows what he was thinking."

"Did you know?" She looked at him, her eyes having adjusted to the darkness.

"No."

"If you did, would you have told me?"

He thought about it for a moment. "I don't know. It would've been just as difficult to tell you something like that as I imagine it would've been for you to hear it." He stared down at the floor. "I do know I would've told him to think about what he was risking, losing you and DJ. I would have asked him if it was really worth it."

"It's late, and I don't want to keep you up any longer than I already have." She stood up and touched his shoulder. "Thank you, for everything." She went into his bedroom, shut the door, crawled into his bed, and cried herself to sleep.

# # #

The combination of the throbbing in her hand and the smell of bacon woke Janel up just before noon, and she joined Tony in the kitchen.

"Good morning." He tossed a Walgreens bag towards her. "I figured you'd need this, it's the strongest you can get over the counter. If you need something stronger I'll have to give my doctor a call." She struggled to open the bottle of pain reliever with her good hand, and he took it from her and popped the top with ease. She shook two pills into the palm of her hand. "You'll need at least three. Better put something on your stomach first though."

He fixed two plates and they sat down and ate in silence. When they'd finished and she slid her chair back to get up, he asked her about what happened the night before.

"I went through Dorian's things, from the accident.   His planner was in there, and I set it aside to give to you, and then I found his phone.   There were some text messages, and a lot pictures.   They went back at least six months." She tapped her finger on the table and fought back the anger rising up inside of her.   "I cooked for him, kept a clean house, I had his baby.   I satisfied his *every* sexual need.   I gave up the chance at a career for him."   She bit her lip and fought back tears.   "We had almost twenty years together, and he threw it away speeding to get to a piece of ass.   I could almost understand if she was incredibly beautiful, but she ain't even cute.   It's like the ultimate slap in the face."   She looked at him.   "So what happens now?"

"I try and convince her to drop the charges.   I'll call her in a few days, after some of the swelling goes down."

Janel chuckled.   "She's going to need more than a few days."

"You think this is a joke?   You're being charged with felony assault.   You could get jail time, a year, maybe more, plus probation.   Not to mention the fines."

"Jail time?   I only hit her one time, I didn't beat her with a tire iron."

"You broke her nose and knocked her out!"

"She got what she deserved!   She was fucking my husband behind my back Tony!   I had that bitch in my house!"

"You act like she was in this alone.   It takes two to tango Janel.   He's just as guilty as she is."

"Yeah well he ain't here now is he?"

"No, but beating the hell out of her isn't going to bring him back either!"   She finally broke down and began to cry, and he apologized for raising his voice.   "Look, I don't know why Dorian did what he did.   Maybe it was a mid-life crisis, maybe he just needed to know he still had it, I don't know.   But I do know he took you for granted.

He never really knew what he had in you.   And quite frankly, he could be a real ass sometimes."   He handed her a napkin to wipe her face with.   "It kills me to see you hurting like this.   And I happen to agree with you, she's not cute.   She's got nothing on you.   But that's over and done with.   You've got to move on.   Taking your anger out on her and staying pissed at him is only going to affect your health."   He gave her a minute to gather herself. "Now, while I'm trying to get you out of this mess you've gotten into, I need you to do some things.   First, get back to working out.   It's the best thing to help with your stress level.   I can't afford for you to run around ready to swing on people at a moment's notice.   I know you probably let the gym membership go but I can pick it up for you, or you can swim here, or we can run together, but you've got to do something to stay active.   Sitting around being angry and feeling sorry for yourself isn't an option.   Second, I need you to get out and meet people.   Networking is the best way I know of to get a job.   It's not what you know but who you know.   Hell, talk to some of the people you already know, hit up those so called friends that you haven't heard from since the funeral.   If you run into any of them, put them on the spot and ask them if they know about any job openings.   Better yet, ask them if you can use them as a reference.   Use their pity and flip it in your favor.   You do that and I promise you things will start looking up and you'll get a job."   She nodded and wiped her nose.   "Now I was thinking about something this morning, and I want you to hear me out on this.   I think you should pack up the house and put everything in storage, and you and DJ can move in with me until you can get on your feet."   She started to protest but he held up his hand.   "If you have a better idea, I'm all ears.   It makes sense if you think about it.   Whether or not the short sale is approved, you'll be out of the house which will make it much easier to show to potential buyers."

"Where is DJ going to sleep?"

"In my office.   I'll move my stuff into the garage for now.   He'll have his own room with his own things and his own space.   I'll get you a notarized statement so you can get him registered for school before he comes back home."

"I don't know Tony."

"The only place you could afford right now is something in the wrong part of town, or section eight housing.   I'm not knocking subsidized housing, but that's not an option when I have the means and ability to take care of the both of you."

"I don't want to be a burden."

"Be a burden how?   We're family.   I have plenty of room, I can afford it, and you need a place to live.   Plus, if the situation were reversed, I know Dorian would've done the same thing."

"What about Sherri?"

"What about her?"

"You guys are already having problems.   I don't want to be in the middle of some mess."

"My name is the only name on the deed to this house, and I'm the only person that made any payments on it. Hell, she doesn't even have a *key*.   If she has a problem with me moving you and DJ in here, then maybe she's not the woman for me.   It's the right thing to do.   She shouldn't have a problem with that."

"She will."

"You're my best friend's wife-"

"She'll feel threatened because we could potentially take your attention away from her, and she doesn't like it when she's not the center of your attention."

"I think you're wrong.   Wait a minute, why are we even discussing this?   It doesn't matter what she thinks.   It's temporary, she'll be fine.   If not, she'll just have to get over it."

Janel knew the idea was trouble waiting to happen, but she knew there was no convincing him so she changed the subject. "I need to get my car. I've got some errands to run."

"You can't get your car. It's too much of a risk. Take mine, and pack some things to bring over. I don't want you staying there anymore. Consider this your new address and start making the transition." He gathered up the dishes and she followed him into the kitchen.

"Why is it a risk to get my car?"

"Because I'm sure Michelle has a no contact order against you, so you need to avoid any situation where you might run into her. She could try and use it against you. If you see her, cross the street, head in the opposite direction, do whatever you need to do to avoid her at all costs until I can handle this. I'm serious."

"You really think you can get her to drop the charges?"

He ran a sink full of hot water and started washing the dishes. "Yes, unless she retains a lawyer and they want to play hardball. I'm going to ask her once, nicely, and if she refuses, I'll threaten to make every aspect of her personal life public in order to establish her character. Or lack thereof. If she still refuses, I'll hire a private detective to pull up every piece of dirt he can find on her. Now if her lawyer is smart, he'll try to force us to settle out of court and pay her to go away, but I'll nip that in the bud quickly. The bottom line is if we end up in court, there's no way a judge or jury will rule against a grieving widow, who found out her recently deceased husband was sleeping with his assistant. Ultimately, she'll end up looking like the bad guy and we'll win. But make no mistake about it." He pointed a soapy finger at her. "You were wrong for putting your hands on her."

"I hope you're right. If I end up having to pay her, she'll just have to get in line."

"I know you're not doubting me."   He rinsed his hands and faced her.   "Listen.   There are two things I am absolutely sure of in this world; my skills in the courtroom, and my skills in the bedroom."

"Oh here we go."   She rolled her eyes.   "That's way more information than I need to know."

"Seriously though, I'm not going to say it's going to be easy, but I'm pretty confident I can make this thing go away. It's going to take some time, patience, a little effort, and a lot of planning, but I can make it happen.   Worst case, you may get fined, do a little probation, but that's only if me, the judge, and the jury are all having an off day, and that ain't gonna happen."   He was smiling but she knew he was serious.   And she knew if there was an easy way out of the mess she'd made, he would be the one to figure it out.

8 - Taking Control

Tony's partner Doug began giving him a hard time as soon as he walked through the law firm doors at two o'clock in the afternoon. "You're looking mighty casual today. When I didn't see you here at the crack of dawn, I thought maybe you'd come to your senses and finally took some time off. Obviously I was wrong."

"I can't, I've got too much to do. And I just picked up a new case that I need to take care of."

"There's always a new case. Let one of the new guys handle it, that's why we pay them so well. They're more than competent. We hand-picked them remember?"

Tony motioned for Doug to follow him into his office. He closed the door and Doug immediately walked over to the window and lifted one of the wooden slats of the blinds with his finger. "Did you buy a new car? I didn't know you had it in you, you cheap son of a bitch. That's nice!"

"It's not my car, and I'm not a cheap son of a bitch." Tony said as sat down at his desk. "I spend more money on one custom made suit than most people spend on their entire wardrobe."

"You're cheap, but I'll admit when you spend money, you spend it in all the right ways. Like your BMW, that's a hell of a driving machine."

"I think there's a compliment in there somewhere. Can we get down to business please?"

"Sure thing. What's up?" He said as he sat down.

"The car is Janel's, she's my new case."

"No surprise there, you are the executor of Dorian's will."

"No, she caught a criminal case.   She found out Dorian was cheating on her with his assistant, so she went to his office and broke her nose, knocked her out."

"Shit, that's bad.   We're talking felony assault."

"Exactly."

"Why the hell was he messing with her?   She ain't even cute."

"Can you focus please?   I don't have confirmation yet, but I'm sure the police encouraged her to file a no contact order.   So, I caught a cab to pick up Janel's car to make sure they wouldn't run into each other again."

"She lawyer-ed up?"

"If she hasn't I'm sure it won't be long before she does. I'm trying to get in front of this thing and I want to hire a private detective.   None of the usual guys, I want the one you used when you had that case against that University of Louisiana professor who was sleeping with his male and female students."

"He's expensive."

"I don't care.   His investigation flipped that case for you right?"

"Yes.   But he's really expensive."

"It's Janel, Doug.   She's family.   I need someone who can tell me what color underwear this woman was wearing three weeks ago at exactly four twenty-eight in the afternoon, if I ask."

"He *is* that good."

"He better be if we're paying him top dollar."   There was a knock at the door.   "Come in."

"You got past me before I could give you these."   Pam, their receptionist, handed him some messages.

"Pamela, just the woman I need to talk to."

"I told you not to call me that, especially if you need me to do something for you.   You're pressing your luck Mr. Gibson."   She wagged her finger at him.

"I need you to get a hold of the private investigator that Doug used-"

"He's expensive."

"How do you even know who I'm talking about?"

"I know exactly who you're talking about.   The guy Doug hired to get evidence against 'Professor Molester.' You pay me *very well* to anticipate what you need before you need it."

"Ask him if he's available and if he is, have him call me directly please.   Did you hear what she just said Doug? We pay her very well, which means I'm not cheap."

"Oh you *are* cheap."   Pam said.   "That's why I let you know up front that this guy is expensive so you won't complain when you see the bill."

"I'm not cheap.   Where are you two getting this from?"

"Years of knowing you?"   Doug offered.

"Any day I walk in here, I'm wearing nearly thirty-five hundred dollars' worth of clothing on my back.   That's not cheap."

"Now I'll give you that.   Sometimes I forget I'm a married woman when you walk in here in your tailored suits smelling all good.   I don't know what happened today but I understand even a man as fine as yourself can't look put together all the time.   Anyway, before I forget, Sherri called here for you first thing this morning."

"I had a late night with a client and my phone died.   She was probably worried when she couldn't reach me."

"She sounded more upset than worried to me, but that ain't none of my never mind.   You need anything else?" Tony shook his head no and she closed the door.

"*You* let your phone *die*?   Like totally dead, no charge?" Doug grinned at him.

"I was exhausted by the time I bailed Janel out of jail and took her to my place."

"You took her to your place?   This is getting interesting."

"I wasn't going to take her home so she could sit there and get upset all over again and do something else crazy."

"So you took her home, let your phone die which I'd never believe if I didn't hear it straight from you, and Sherri called here first thing looking for you.   You know you're in deep shit right?"

"I was just taking care of a friend."

"I'm not the one you need to convince man.   Look, if you want me to handle her case I will.   You might be a little too close-"

"I promised her I'd take care of it and I will.   You know I trust you man but I need to take care of this one personally."

"Fine, but at least let me have your other cases so once you're finished with this one you can take some time off. And I'm not saying that as a partner, I'm saying it as your friend.   What happened with Dorian was messed up, and even though I know you'll never admit it, I know it affected you pretty deeply.   You can't keep burying yourself in your work."

"You sound like my mom."

"I love your mom.   She's a smart woman.   She hasn't given you any bad advice that I know of the entire time I've known you.   You should listen to her."

"I'll think about it."

"You do that.   I'll handle things here."

# # #

Tony pulled Janel's car into his driveway, put it in park, and pressed the button to put the top up.   He played around with the touch screen as he waited the mere eighteen seconds for the top to close.   "I gotta hand it to you Dorian, you got this one right."   He turned the car off and tried calling Sherri.   It rang twice and went to voice mail.   Again.   He hung up without leaving a message, locked the car, and went inside.

"That's a hell of a car you got there."   He said as he sat down next to Janel on the couch.

"I have to admit, of all the gifts Dorian bought for me, that's one I have truly enjoyed."

"You ok?"

"Yeah."

He turned off the television.   "I don't believe you. What's up?   Your hand bothering you?"

"Actually the hand is good.   I'm just a little tired I guess. I didn't sleep very well last night."

"Is it the bed?"

"Not at all, the bed is great.   Part of the reason is I'm so used to having Dorian in the bed with me.   It's going to take a while to get used to sleeping alone.   But the biggest reason I couldn't sleep is because I was thinking."

"Uh oh.   About?"

"My situation and how helpless I feel.   When we talked this morning and you mentioned packing up the house, that got me to thinking.   I want to have an estate sale."

"To sell off some of Dorian's things?"

"Not just his things, everything.   Well not exactly everything.   Realistically, there's no way I can afford another house as big as the one I'm in now.   And with DJ leaving for college in a year, it wouldn't make sense to move into something that big anyway.   It's silly to pay storage fees-"

"You know I'll cover those."

"I know and I appreciate it, but it's a waste of money. There's no sense in paying to store stuff I can't fit into a smaller place anyway.   Why not sell some stuff and put the profits towards another place?   If I can come up with a decent down payment, once I get a job and work a little while, maybe I can get into a house instead of throwing money away on rent."

"That makes sense."

"But, I'm going to need a professional to help me, and since you're a professional who knows a lot of professionals, I was hoping you could help me?"

"I might know someone."

"But?   I hear doubt in your voice."

"It sounds good in theory, but can you really go through with it?"

"Absolutely.   There are some things I want to keep that are special to me, and things I'll need like the beds.   But I don't need three sets of China.   I don't need four couches. Only one of them is really comfortable anyway."

"I don't know Janel.   It's one thing to say you don't have an emotional attachment to stuff you've owned for years, and quite another to actually watch someone else pay a lot less than what you paid for it and cart it away.   If you're doing this so you can move out quicker, don't.   You and DJ are welcome to stay here as long as you need to, you know that."

"It's just stuff Tony.   I don't *need* all that *stuff*.   I *need* to downsize."   He ran his hand across the top of his head. "It's obvious you're not ok with this.   Speak your mind, and be honest.   You know I respect your opinion."

"I know financially things might look bleak right now, but I don't want you to do something you might regret. You never know, we might find something in Dorian's planner that we don't know about yet."

"My situation boils down to wants and needs.   I *need* money, and I have a bunch of stuff I don't need.   It makes sense to me."

When he looked in her eyes he knew there was no reasoning with her.   "I'll make some calls and see what I can do."

"I want to sell my car too."

Tony nearly choked on his own spit.   "I'm sorry, say again?"

"I want to put the Jag in the estate sale."

"I must be tripping because I could've sworn it sounded like you said you wanted to sell your car."

"I did."

"The red one with the black top and the custom red duo tone leather seats?   The one Dorian gave you for your birthday two years ago?"

"I can sell the car, use some of the money to buy something more affordable, and put the rest in savings."

"But you love that car.   Hell *I* love that car.   I deliberately took the long way home today just so I could spend extra time driving it."

Janel moaned and covered her face with her hand.   "I know, I love it too.   Don't make this any harder than it already is.   But it's paid for, in excellent condition, and has low mileage which translates into excellent resale value.   I freely admit I will absolutely miss it, but like I said, it's about wants and needs.   I *need* money, I don't *need* an expensive luxury convertible.   You know I can't even afford the routine maintenance on that car, let alone if something were to happen to it.   Realistically I can't *afford* to keep it."

He knew how attached she was to her car, and he had serious doubts about her ability to hand it over to some stranger in exchange for a check, no matter how many zeros were on it.   He could already see how painful the decision was and she still had the car in her possession.

"I know what you're thinking.   I've thought this through, and I can give the car up when the time comes.   I admit it'll be hard, but I'm in survival mode.   I need cash, and I don't have a job, so the only way I can get some is to liquidate."

"The only thing I have to say is sleep on it for a few days and really think things through.   Think about how this might affect DJ."

"I'm not selling any of his stuff."

"I'm just saying, he lives in that house too, and he may be more attached to some of that 'stuff' you want to get rid of than you think.   In the meantime, I'll make some calls, and we can revisit the conversation in a few days and see if you still feel the same way."

"I hear you.   By the way, I brought Dorian's planner over, let me grab it before it slips my mind and it gets lost in the shuffle."   She reappeared from the guest bedroom minutes later and handed it to him.   "I hope you find something useful."

"I want to ask you something," he said as he put the planner on the coffee table.   "And I want you to be honest with me."

"You know I will, you don't even have to say that. What's up?"

"Am I cheap?"   She turned away from him and started laughing.   "I'm serious."

She took a minute to compose herself.   "You're not cheap sweetie, you're frugal.   There's a difference."   She reassured him with a pat to his thigh.   "You're so cute when you're vulnerable, I don't know that I've ever seen you like this.   Why are you asking me this anyway?"

"I was just curious."

"Cut the bull, who called you cheap?   And more importantly, why do you care?   That's so out of character for you."

"It came up in conversation."

"Was it Pam or Doug?"   He smiled without answering her.   "Just because you keep your eye on the bottom line doesn't mean you're cheap.   That BMW is not cheap. The suits you wear definitely aren't cheap."

"That's exactly what I said."

"Personally, I wouldn't care what they have to say because the bottom line is you're debt free.   I don't know too many people who can say that.   Besides, they were probably just trying to get a rise out of you.   I love them both to death but you know how they like to double team you sometimes.   They think it's fun.   Anyway, I'm going to bed."   She gave him a quick kiss on the forehead.   "Good night.   Get some sleep, and think about what I said."

"I will."

9 - New Beginnings

Janel spent her morning visiting businesses she'd frequented in the past, checking to see if any of them were hiring or in need of any type of financial services. She quickly learned that mornings were best spent job hunting and afternoons were better for networking. Although she enjoyed chatting with people she'd been doing business with over the years, she remained unsuccessful in obtaining any job leads. Her only saving grace was the temp agency she'd applied with, who reassured her they would be able to supply her with a pretty steady stream of jobs, some of which she could work from home.

She stopped by the new CSC Federal branch on the south side to see if they were accepting applications but the building was dark and the parking lot was empty. Not to be deterred, she swung by the branch near her Clover Hills home instead and dropped off her resume to the receptionist. Tired and a little disheartened, she decided to treat herself to lunch. She ordered the special, soup and salad, and took the time to make notes about the places she'd applied with, the people she'd spoken to, and when she should follow up again.

"Mrs. Monroe?" She looked up from her notepad to see Perry Hunter, the CSC loan officer she'd sought advice from. "It's good to see you again. How are things? Better I hope."

"Please, call me Janel. I really appreciate the advice you gave me about the short sale. I've got an offer on the house, I'm just waiting to hear if it's been approved or not."

"That's great, I'm glad I could help.   Are you waiting for someone?"

"No, I'm just making some notes."

"You mind if I join you?"

She looked into his luminous green eyes shaded by long thick eye lashes and thought you can sit on my lap if you want to.   "Not at all.   Please, have a seat."   She tucked her notes inside her portfolio and sat it on the seat beside her.

"Any luck with the job hunt?"   He asked as he pulled a chair out and sat down across from her.

"No.   But I've been networking quite a bit so hopefully something will come through soon.   A friend of mine told me it's all about who you know."

"And that's very true.   What kind of work are you looking for?"

"I have a bachelor's in accounting, but I don't have a lot of experience because I was a homemaker for so many years.   I've done some volunteer work, helping out a few non-profit agencies, but it's not like I've done anything earth shattering."

"Experience is experience.   It doesn't count any less because you didn't get paid, so don't let that discourage you from putting everything relevant on your resume.   And trust me, not much has changed since you graduated. Some of the software may have, but basic arithmetic hasn't. Have you applied with CSC yet?   You know we're opening a new branch soon."

"I dropped off my resume just before I came in here. They basically told me they'll keep my resume on file so I won't be holding my breath."

"They pushed back the grand opening because they're implementing a new system, and they don't want to open the new location until all of the existing employees are trained.   I'd try following up in a week or two, they'll probably be interviewing by then."   The waitress brought her soup, salad, and a few bread sticks, and took Perry's order.   Although she was starving, Janel tried to be polite and wait for his food to arrive before she started eating. "Please, eat.   Your soup is going to get cold waiting on me."   She happily dug into her salad after pouring a little dressing on it.   "Tell me where you're from, I can't quite place the accent."

"You think I have an accent?"

"You do.   I'm guessing you're a northerner."

"I am, I'm from Michigan."

"What brought you to Lafayette?   Did you go to school at the University of Louisiana?"

"University of Michigan.   My husband took a job offer here shortly after we graduated.   Are you a Louisiana native?"

"Born and raised in Baton Rouge.   I came to Lafayette to go to school."

"I'd have never guessed.   I have yet to hear you slip into that native Cajun patois that's so prevalent around here.   Not that that's a bad thing."

"I guess I've inadvertently learned to hide it after working in corporate America for so long."

She noticed the absence of a wedding band on his ring finger.   "You married?"

"No ma'am."

"A handsome man like yourself hasn't taken a wife? Why I do declare, what a grave travesty."   She fanned herself with an imaginary fan while putting on a fake southern accent.

"That's not a dig towards my heritage is it?"

"Of course not, I'm just having a little fun.   I'm surprised that you're single."

"I was married to my high school sweetheart for ten years.   We've been divorced for three years now."

"I'm sorry to hear that.   Any children?"

"A son.   He spends weekends with me, and some holidays."

"Ten years is a long time."

"I caught her cheating on me.   In our house, in our bed."

She was taken aback at how candid he was.   "Wow. That's-I don't even know what to say.   That's awful. And bold."

"What happened to your hand?"

She'd graduated from an Ace bandage to a compression glove and the swelling was down quite a bit but not completely.   "Well Perry, since you've shared something really private and intimate with me, I guess I'll share something really private and intimate with you.   I found out my husband was cheating on me with his assistant before he died.   So I went to his office and let her know how I felt about it."

"He left you in a financial bind and cheated on you? Nice.   I can tell you first hand that hitting rock bottom can be a good thing.   There's nowhere to go but up."   He smiled at her and she felt like a school girl with a crush.

"That's sweet of you to say.   I appreciate the encouragement.   How old is your son?"

"He'll be eighteen in November.   He plays football and basketball."

"My son does too!   I'm surprised we haven't run into each other before now.   He's played in every little town from here to Texas and back."

"Clover Hills is in an entirely different division, both the schools and the summer leagues.   Otherwise we probably would've crossed paths before now."

She felt comfortable with Perry and enjoyed the way their conversation flowed with ease.   She was acutely aware that he'd been sitting with her for much longer than an hour, but he didn't seem in the least bit concerned. She didn't want to leave, but she had a few errands to run before the day got away from her.   "It's been nice talking with you Perry but I've got to get going.   I have some things I need to take care of this afternoon, and I'm sure you've got to get back to work."

"I understand, and I probably should be getting back. Good luck with the job search, but somehow I don't think you'll need it.   I don't know if you still have my card or not."   He pulled a business card from his wallet and quickly scribbled something on the back.   "That's my cell number.   I'd love to do this again sometime.   Maybe we could have a celebratory drink when you find a job?   Or maybe have dinner sometime?"

She felt flattered as she flipped the card over to make sure she could read his writing.   "I just might take you up on that offer."   She couldn't remember the last time she realized she was being hit on, but it was a much needed ego boost and a bright spot in her otherwise frustrating day. She slipped the card into her portfolio and he walked her to her car.

# # #

The next day, Janel headed over to her house where she spent most of the day trying to get a jump start on downsizing her belongings.   She decided to start on one end of her walk-in closet and work through everything in it until she'd reached the other side.   The goal was to decide which pile each item should go into: keep, give away, or consignment.   She had to admit it was beginning to feel like Tony may have been right; making decisions about what should stay and what should go was proving to be more difficult than she first imagined.   The idea of earning a few dollars by selling some of the designer clothes and shoes she hadn't worn in a while sounded good in theory, but she seemed to be continually fighting with herself. Her thoughts ran the gamut from 'I haven't worn this in forever' to 'this is so cute, maybe I should hang on to it for a special occasion.'   She finally decided to get tough with herself.   "Look, do you want to eat or do you want to be cute?"   She said aloud as she sat down on her bed. "You've got to liquidate.   It all boils down to wants versus needs, remember?"   Her monologue lecture was interrupted by a knock at the front door, followed the doorbell.

"Come on in!"   She yelled as she headed down the stairs and Tony stepped inside, holding a plastic bag in the air.

"I've some news for you."   He greeted her with a quick hug and peck on the cheek.   "The bank accepted the short sale offer."

"Really?   I guess I'm going to have to kick it up a notch so I can be out in two weeks.   What's in the bag?"

"Supplies for you to use to start tagging stuff.   I found an experienced estate sale specialist.   Not only did I find one, but I talked him into cutting his commission from thirty percent to fifteen after I explained your situation to him.   I'm going to have a portable storage unit delivered to the house.   You need to tag the big things you can't move but want to keep with orange tags, and I'll get some movers in here to move them into the storage unit.   He's going to drop by tomorrow to talk to you about the process, do a quick visual inventory, and take some pictures.   He'll decide what to eBay, what goes to a physical auction, and what stays here for the estate sale.   Are you still up for this?   It's not too late to change your mind."

"Yes.   I can't keep all this stuff."

"There's something else we need to talk about."

"I knew it.   This was all sounding too good to be true. I'm going to sit down for this if you don't mind."   She sat on the stairs and he sat down next to her.

"I submitted the hardship letter to the bank, explaining how you lost your husband in a tragic accident, how he was your sole source of income, and how you don't have a job and you have a child to take care of."

"Don't.   Don't even tell me-they denied it, didn't they?" He shook his head yes.   "You've got to be kidding me. Somehow I knew that was going to happen, I just can't catch a break.   Why was it denied?   Did they say?"

"I don't know.   Unfortunately they don't have to explain why they denied it."

"You're kidding me!   I have to give them my life story and beg them to give me a break but they don't have to explain to me why they denied it?"   She closed her eyes and shook her head.   "What the hell makes them think I have that kind of money?"

"Janel-"

"This has got to be a really, really bad joke."   She stood up and felt as if she were going to hyperventilate.   She steadied herself against the wall and started gasping for air.

"Hey, it's ok."   He grabbed her arm and put a hand on her back.   "Come on now, take a deep breath.   It's not the end of the world."

"Son of a-"

"I'm guessing either they thought we lied about the amount of cash you have, or they assume you're going to come into some money soon because Dorian died in an accident.   Legally they don't have to explain why they denied the waiver, and if you asked they would probably tell you to count yourself lucky they even approved the short sale and didn't put the house up for auction."

"So that's it?   Is there an appeal process?"   He shook his head no.   "Can I make payments?"

"They want it all, and they're giving you sixty days to pay it."

"If I couldn't afford to catch up on the late payments, what the hell makes them think-"   She felt like the air was being sucked out of the room and she began to gasp for air again, trying to catch her breath.

"Sit down." He pulled her to the stairs. "Look at me. Take a deep breath, in through your nose and out through your mouth." She focused on his eyes until she was able to catch her breath.

"I hope this estate guy is good. At this point I'll be lucky to break even."

"If you break even, you'll be out from under the debt of the house. That's a positive thing."

"But I won't have money to put towards another place."

"Stop trying to look down the road and just take things one step at a time. The house is the biggest hurdle. Once we clear that, we'll move on to the next thing."

"I don't like being dependent on someone else. It's great when things are all good, but when the rug gets snatched from under you-I'm-" She balled her fists up and held them in the air. "I'm so tired of feeling helpless. I don't know how much more I can take." Tears spilled over onto her cheeks.

"Look at me. *I'm* the rug now, and I'm not going anywhere. I'll be right here until you can stand on your own two feet, no matter how long it takes."

The longer she looked into his eyes, the faster her anxiety level fell. She found the sound of his voice comforting.

"Let's just focus on right now, and the things you can control. Talk to the estate guy, tag your stuff, and we'll see what happens after the sale. If the money comes up short, we'll come up with a plan to work through it. One step at a time, ok?" He put his hands around her wrists and she relaxed her arms. "You'll get through this, you're stronger than you think you are."

She took one last deep breath and put her arms around his neck and hugged him. "I'm so glad you're here, I don't know what I'd do without you."

10 - Good Morning Sunshine

Tony tossed his bag on the floor near the garage door and pulled a carton of shrimp fried rice from a bag of takeout. He was starving and exhausted, and all he wanted to do was eat and veg out in front of the television for the remainder of the evening. Janel's case had gone from challenging to difficult when he found out Michelle was being represented by one of the best lawyers in town. Although Tony was confident he was a better lawyer, it meant he'd have to work much harder to bring his A game to the table. He'd also given serious thought to taking time off, but he knew he wouldn't feel comfortable doing so until he worked through the rest of his existing caseload. As he was flipping channels, he heard the front door open and close, followed by the sound of keys sliding across the marble kitchen counter top. Janel walked into the living room and plopped down next to him. She looked as exhausted as he felt. "There's Chinese in the kitchen. Your favorite, crab rangoon and Kung Pao Chicken."

"I'm so glad, because I do not feel like cooking. Thanks." She went into the kitchen and returned carrying a wire handled white cardboard container and a pair of chopsticks.

"You ok?"

"I just feel really....frazzled lately."

"How's it going at the house?"

"Good. I got DJ's room packed up today. I can't wait for him to come home, even though I dread having to tell him he doesn't have a home to come back to."

"He has a home, it just doesn't look like the one he left."

"You know what I mean.   The estate sale guy has been awesome.   His experience has made everything so easy for me.   The sale is this weekend, rain or shine, so I'll be out of the house on schedule.   He's pretty confident that I'll make enough money to pay off the loan."

"Selling the Jag should help quite a bit."

"I've already signed the title over to him, and I told him that I don't want to know who the buyer is.   I even asked him to try to find a buyer from out of town so I don't have to see someone else driving it around.   Giving it up is hard enough as it is."

"Any new job prospects?"

"I have two interviews tomorrow."

"You submitted a resume to CSC?"

"I did.   In fact, I was told by a reliable source that they're going to start interviewing for the new location soon."

"I have a feeling you'll get something soon.   Just keep your head up."   She made quick work of the Chinese food and made an attempt to stand up, only to quickly sink back down to the couch.   "Old age sneaking up on you?"

"Please.   You're the same age I am so I don't know who you're calling old."   She winced as she made it to her feet. "The muscles in my lower back are starting to spasm, and quite frankly I'm just sore all over.   I need to take a hot shower, I feel like I'm covered in a layer of dust and sweat."

"Why don't you use my bathroom?   I've got that huge jacuzzi tub in there."

"The shower in my bathroom is fine."

"Why don't you let me run you a hot bath, you can turn the jets on, get a little aromatherapy going.   And while you're soaking I'll make you a drink to help you relax."

She rubbed her lower back.   "That does sound nice."

"Give me a few minutes and I'll take care of it."   He let the water run hot, dropped a capful of lavender bubble bath in the water, and added some epsom salt for good measure.

He laid out a set of his softest towels, lit two candles, and vacated the room so she could settle in.   He went into the kitchen and made her one of his infamous vodka creamsicles in an oversized margarita glass.   He tapped on the bathroom door.   "You decent?"

"I've got bubbles in all the right places."   He opened the door and set the drink on the edge of the tub.   "That's huge!   If I drink all that I'll drown in here."

"Don't guzzle, sip and relax.   You need anything else?"

"I couldn't figure out how to turn the jets on."

"Oh yeah, they're in a weird spot."   He flipped a panel and turned them on for her.

"Perfect."

"Take your time."   He assured her as he shut the door behind him.   He went back into the kitchen and grabbed a beer, then made himself comfortable on the couch as he flipped channels and searched for a movie to watch.   His mind drifted briefly to Sherri, and whether or not it was worth working things out with her.   They were arguing and fighting much more often than usual and he was tired of it.   Plus, she'd never gone this long without taking his calls, so he knew they were at a serious crossroads.   If he decided he wanted back in, he knew she would make him work hard for it.   He had no doubt he'd have to go big and expensive to win her over this time.   The sound of Janel singing over the hum of the tub jets distracted his train of thought, and he smiled at the thought of being able to do something so simple for her that made her happy.   If a hot bath and a stiff drink was all it took to make her smile, then he'd do it for her every night if she wanted.   It was nearly forty-five minutes later before he heard the water start draining and the bathroom door finally opened.   He waited a few minutes for her to step back into the living room, and when she didn't, he called out over his shoulder. "How was it?"

"Like heaven!"   She yelled back.   He expected her to reappear any moment and when she didn't, he got up to investigate.   "Knock knock?   You ok?"

"I loooove your bed.   The mattress is like soft, but firm."   She was laying on her back, spread eagle, in the middle of his bed in a silky red two piece lingerie outfit. She looked as if she might try to make a snow angel on top of his duvet cover.   Even though she was decent, he looked away as if she wasn't.   "You were so right T, my back feels sooooo much better.   That drink really really really really did the trick."

He'd been purposefully heavy handed with the alcohol in her drink, but it was obvious that he'd been too generous. She'd never called him 'T' in all the years he'd known her, which was confirmation for him that she was about five sheets to the wind.   Maybe even six.   "I tell you what, you can have my bed tonight.   You've had a hard day, you deserve it.   Goodnight."   He said as he tried to exit the room.

"Hey!"   She said as she sat up.   "Whoo!   You feel that?   I think the room is spinning."

"Just lay back down and the spinning will stop."

"I'm not gonna take your bed.   Iss your bed.   Maybe you had a hard day."

"I don't think you're leaving that bed unless I carry you, and I don't have any plans to do that."

"You want the bed, I want the bed, issa big bed."   She patted the bed and stared at her hand as she concentrated on what she was trying to say.   "We can share."   The expression on her face suggested she was impressed with herself, as if it was the best idea she'd had in a long time. She grinned at him and he couldn't help but laugh.

"I don't think so.   You stay here, I'll take the guest bedroom.   It's not a problem.   You should probably get some sleep."

She flopped backwards on the bed. "Why are you being so diff'cult?" She turned on her side away from him and he heard her mumble. "I can't sleep when I'm alone."

Her words stirred a pang of guilt within him. Partly because he was the reason she was drunk, and partly because he knew she'd been having trouble adjusting to sleeping alone. In his profession he'd dealt with his share of inebriated individuals, and experience taught him that much like a wind-up toy, eventually they winded down. He decided to lay with her until she fell asleep, or passed out, then he would get up and leave and she'd be none the wiser.

"Fine. Scoot over and make some room." She settled in under the covers, and he laid on his back on top of the covers. She hummed softly as she gently rocked back and forth. He stared up at the ceiling as he waited patiently for her to fall asleep. It wasn't long before her back began to rise and fall in a slow, steady rhythm and he knew she was down for the count. Having gotten comfortable, he continued to lay next to her as he thought back to the first time he saw her at a bar just outside of campus. She was sitting at a pub table, sipping on a drink and laughing with some girlfriends. He was immediately attracted to her but wasn't sure how to approach her. Even though he played football throughout high school and the girls were constantly vying for his attention, he had yet to develop a sense of confidence with the ladies. And Dorian made sure to give him hell about it every chance he could. Despite the fact, he found himself elbowing Dorian in his side and pointing in Janel's direction.

"Yo man, she is fine! You know her?" Dorian asked.

"No, but I'd like to get to know her."

"That's what I'm talking about. Go on over there and see what's up!"

"I don't know man, she ain't no groupie. I don't know what to say to her."

"Man if you gonna hang out with me, you gots to get some game!   Just go talk to her.   Give her a compliment. Tell her she has nice hair or pretty eyes.   Women love that shit."

"Come on man, I can't go over there with a weak ass line like that.   Maybe I should send her a drink?"

"What the-?"   Dorian sucked his teeth.   "Only old dudes do stuff like that.   Let a real man show you how it's done."   And with those fateful words, Dorian made a move on the woman that captured Tony's eye and his heart the very first time he ever laid eyes on her.   And now, nearly twenty years later, Dorian was gone and she was lying in his bed.   He told himself to get up and leave, but he just couldn't bring himself to do it.

# # #

Tony was awakened by the sun streaming through the vertical blinds of his bedroom.   He was still on his back, and Janel was still curled up on her side.   She began to stir and when she awakened, she rolled over to face him. "Morning sunshine."   He teased.

She lifted the sheet away from her body and peeked underneath.   "I'm not naked so this can't be as bad as I think it is."   Her voice was groggy and hoarse.   He grinned at her without responding and she pulled the sheet up over her head.   "That is an evil grin, you must have something on video."

He snatched the sheet away from her.   "I did, but I erased it."   She tried to pull the sheet back up but he held tight.   "I'm kidding."

"What the hell did you put in that drink?   It was good but damn!"

"I may have gotten a little heavy handed with the vodka, but the good news is you shouldn't feel hung over."

"I don't.   That was probably the best night of sleep I've had in a long time.   Be honest though, how badly did I embarrass myself?"

"You didn't."   Her eyes narrowed as she tried to decide if he was still messing with her or not.   "You got in my bed, I said you could have it, you asked me to lay down with you-"   A look of horror crossed her face.   "Not like that. You were under the covers and I stayed on top.   And here we are.   Nothing happened."   He turned onto his side to face her.   "How's your back?"

"I feel really good.   You were right, the tub was the way to go."

"Good."

They stared at one another for a few moments, and all he could think about was how beautiful she was and how lucky Dorian had been.   He brushed a few strands of hair away from her eye and allowed his hand to linger on her cheek.   He leaned in and kissed her, tentatively at first, fully expecting her to reject his overture.   But instead she closed her eyes and kissed him back.   He flipped her onto her back in one fluid motion, and pushed her camisole top up, exposing her torso.   He kissed her softly on her stomach as he reached up and squeezed her breasts.   She pulled his tank top over his head and lightly dug her nails into his back, which turned him on even more.   She pulled the camisole top over her head and he cupped her breasts and sucked her nipples.   He ran his tongue down the center of her stomach and kissed her on her hip bone as he slipped off her silky boy short bottoms.   He shifted his weight to one side and pulled off his boxer shorts, then positioned himself between her thighs where he slowly pushed the tip of his penis inside of her.   She moaned and gripped his hips, pulling them towards her as she spread her legs wider to accommodate him.   Once he was fully inside of her, he dropped his forehead to her shoulder and let out a sigh.   He slowly pulled his hips back and then thrust himself back inside of her in one quick motion.   She cried out and he began rhythmically stroking in and out of her, faster and faster.   He felt her kegel muscles begin to contract and she arched her back.   She bit her lip to stifle a scream as she started to orgasm, and he decided to join her, their bodies reaching a sexual climax together.   Her body went limp and he collapsed on top of her, both of them breathing hard and completely covered in sweat.

"What time is your first interview?"

"Ten."

"You want breakfast?   Bacon and eggs?"

"Absolutely."

He gave her a quick peck on the lips and rolled himself off of her.   He pulled the sheets up and carefully covered her naked body, then slipped on his boxer shorts.   "Don't you go back to sleep."   He warned, shaking a finger at her.

"I won't!"   She insisted, smiling at him.

11 - Is You Is, or Is You Ain't my Baby

Janel showered and dressed for her interview, then joined Tony for breakfast as if their morning tryst never even happened. She was starving and grateful for the opportunity to put a good meal on her stomach before she left the house.

"You look nice."

"Thanks."

"You nervous?"

"A little."

"You'll be fine. Just take a few deep breaths before you go in and try to clear your mind." The doorbell rang and he excused himself from the table. "Be right back."

Suddenly she heard a woman's voice shouting. "What the hell is going on Tony?" She remained seated at the dining room table and finished drinking her juice as she watched Sherri cross the living room and head straight for Tony's bedroom.

"What're you talking about?" He asked as he waited for her to come out of his bedroom. Janel wiped her mouth and took her dishes into the kitchen.

Sherri emerged from the bedroom and shoved her finger in his face. "You know what I'm talking about. Where is she?" She came busting into the kitchen like a Tasmanian devil where she nearly ran right into Janel. "This is what I'm talking about. I came by here last night and I saw her car in the driveway. And what do you know, here she is first thing this morning. I know she spent the night, don't even try to lie about it."

She stared directly at Janel as if she were trying to burn a hole through her soul. The way she was acting was one of the very reasons why Janel disliked her so much. She lacked self-esteem and was full of drama. She debated as to whether or not she should just leave and let Tony handle hurricane Sherri all by himself. The last thing she needed was to be late for her interview because she had to put his neurotic, bipolar girlfriend in check.

"So somebody want to explain what's going on here?" She asked, still staring at Janel.

"Nothing's going on Sherri. If you'd just calm down I can explain." He reasoned with her.

She put her hands on her hips and turned around to face him, cocking her head to one side. "Oh please do. I can't wait to hear this."

Janel, short on patience and wanting to end the drama so she could leave, responded on his behalf. "I had to sell my house. Tony's letting me stay here until I can find another place to live."

"What? What the hell is she talking about? You let her move in here without talking to me about it?" She was practically screaming at him and the last of Janel's patience flew out the window.

"I'm standing right here, so don't talk about me as if I'm not in the room. And I guess you're having comprehension problems because I just explained that the situation is *temporary.*"

Sherri turned towards Janel and snarled at her. "With all the money Dorian left you? Why do you need to stay here?"

"Quite frankly it's none of your business what my husband left me or why I'm staying here. This is between me and him. You should really stay out of grown folks business."

Suddenly Sherri turned into a stereotypical black woman, sucking her teeth and rolling her neck. "Oh I know she ain't talking to me."

Janel wanted to laugh, and wondered if she was going to

kick her shoes off, pull out her earrings, and ask for a jar of Vaseline.   She decided to have a little fun and push her buttons even more.   "Let me get this straight.   You just randomly drove by the house last night, but you didn't knock on the door or call.   That's kind of stalker-ish don't you think?"

"Ok I'ma whoop her ass if you don't get her out of here."

"I'm standing right here.   There's nothing between us but air and opportunity."

Tony positioned himself between the two women but Janel was hardly worried.   "Look Sherri.   Janel and DJ are going to be staying here for a while.   I would've said something to you but you haven't been answering the phone or returning my calls so what could I do."

"I'm out Tony, thanks for breakfast."   Janel picked up her purse and keys from the counter top and walked out, leaving him to deal with the wrath of Sherri.

# # #

After another day of disappointment, Janel returned to Tony's house and the place she felt most comfortable; the kitchen.   She made dinner, but instead of eating, decided to wind down by swimming a few laps in his pool.   She dove in and zoned out as she swam lap after lap.   When she felt as if she couldn't swim another stroke, she took a break and held on to the side of the pool while she caught her breath.   It was then that she realized she wasn't alone, Tony was watching her from one of the loungers.

"You training for a swim meet or something?"

She flicked water at him.   "You told me to get back to working out, so I'm just taking your advice."   She swam to the pool stairs and climbed out, where he met her with a towel which he wrapped around her shoulders.   They sat down next to each other.

"How'd it go today?"

She rolled her eyes. "Not enough experience and no suitable positions available at this time. But, lucky for me, they'll keep my resume on file."

"Have you heard anything from CSC?"

"Nope. And after what happened this morning I probably won't if Sherri has any say about it."

"She was upset but I'm sure she wouldn't do anything like that."

"I'm sorry about all that, I was way out of line. That was between the two of you and I should've just let you handle it instead of stirring the pot."

"No need to apologize. You were in the middle of an awkward situation and you did what you felt like you had to do. I can respect that."

"I'm not trying to get in your business but I heard you say she's not talking to you. What's up with that?"

He removed his suit jacket, laid it across the lounger behind him, loosened his tie, and unbuttoned the top two buttons of his shirt. "That day I left your place, and I was late for dinner with her, we got into an argument at the restaurant and I snapped at her. Then I got up and walked out. Long story short, I went over to her place a few days later to apologize, and she got pissed at me all over again because I had to leave to take care of some business with a client."

"Why would she get upset about that? You're a lawyer, your clients are your bread and butter and she knows that."

"She's upset with me because she thinks I put everything else before her."

"I know for a fact that's not true."

"I know. But, good man that I am, I told my partner and our staff today that I'll be taking some time off as soon as I can wrap up my open cases. And I'm not just doing it for her. I feel like my life is kind of out of balance right now. I could use some down time to figure things out. What happened with Dorian has me thinking that maybe I should look at re-prioritizing some things in my life."

"Good for you, you deserve some time off.   How long has it been since you've taken a vacation?   And I don't mean holidays or a weekend getaway."   He thought for a moment.   "That's my point, you had to think about it way too long.   Speaking of cases, what's the latest news on mine?"

"We're scheduled to go to court in a month but I guarantee she'll have dropped the charges by then.   And she's filed a no contact order against you, so don't be surprised if you see a piece of certified mail soon."

"What do I do when I get it?"

"Sign for it and continue to avoid her."

"You really think you can make this go away?"

"I know I can, it's what I do.   I've hired a private detective to do some digging, and even if he doesn't find anything, which I highly doubt, you'll have sympathy on your side.   When I'm done presenting the facts in this case, the judge will want to order *her* to pay *you* for *your* pain and suffering."   She grinned at him.   "What?"

"I remember when we were in school and you were so quiet and shy.   I'm just trying to figure out when you blossomed into this confident, semi-cocky guy."

"That was a long time ago."

"I'm glad you're so confident, and I don't know how I'm ever going to pay you back."

"I come pretty cheap."   He tapped a finger on his cheek and she leaned in to kiss him, but he turned his head and her lips landed on his.   She closed her eyes and enjoyed the moment, then pulled away, resting her forehead against his.   "I can't tell you enough how thankful I am for everything you've done for me."   She put her hands on his shoulders and stood up.   "I made dinner, help yourself."

She took a shower, put on her favorite t-shirt and pajama bottoms, and started cleaning the kitchen.   "Did you eat?"

He brought his dishes into the kitchen placed them in the

sink. "Yes, and it was delicious. Thank you." She was running hot dish water while she searched for containers to put the leftovers in. "You know I have a dishwasher, right?"

"It's quicker to just wash them by hand." He leaned against the counter and watched her as she put the food away and wiped the counters. When she started washing dishes and he continued to hang around, she wondered if maybe he was trying to find a way to talk about what happened between the two of them that morning. "What's on your mind Gibson?"

"Gibson? I feel like I should be wearing my football jersey."

"Number 75, same as Mean Joe Green."

"You remember that?"

"I do."

He chuckled. "You haven't called me Gibson in years." He hopped up on the counter and leaned his head back against the cabinets.

"I haven't had to ask you what's on your mind in years either. Usually if you have something to say you just say it."

"It's Sherri. All we do is argue and fight lately, and I can never do anything right."

"All relationships have their ups and downs."

"Something else has been bothering me. When Dorian passed, it seemed like it was just another day to her. I understand she couldn't get off work to go to the funeral, but she never even called that day. I buried my best friend, and she never so much as sent a text message to check on me. And that bothers me."

"And it should. She wasn't there for you."

"Don't get me wrong, she's a good person, she's got a good heart. Maybe I should just let it go."

"If you were able to let it go, you would've already. You should ask her about it."

"I would if she were talking to me.   I guess what I'm saying is I'm tired, and I don't understand why things are the way they are between us.   I'm not doing anything differently than I was when we first met.   I need some insight into the female psyche."

"I'm probably not the best person to be talking to about this."

"I disagree.   I trust your opinion and I know you'll be honest."

"It bothers me that someone who claims to care about you so much was not there for you in your time of need. However, in all fairness, you need to ask her about it so she can give you her side of the story.   Personally, I would've done whatever it took to be there for you, if I had to call in sick or whatever.   But that's just me."

"I know you don't like her but-"

"I never said I didn't like her."

"Come on Janel, I'm a lawyer.   I play games with words for a living.   Just be honest with me."

"I don't really know her.   But the little bit of time I've spent with her, she's not someone that I choose to spend time with."

"I call bullshit.   You're not being honest, you're being politically correct.   You and me go way back, just tell me what you think and stop worrying about hurting my feelings."

"Fine."   She turned to face him.   "I don't like the way she talks to you, I don't like the way she treats you, and I think she's looking for a payday.   And it doesn't matter to her if it's a ring and marriage, or a baby and child support, because her biological clock is ticking.   Personally, I think she's trying to do both so she can really hit the jackpot." She turned her attention back to the dishes.

"Tell me how you really feel."

"You asked!   What'd your mom have to say about her?"

"She told me to run the other way."   Janel couldn't help

but laugh.   "I'm not kidding, she hates her."

"I don't think the word hate is even in your mom's vocabulary."

"She said if I love her, she'll tolerate her but she doesn't like her.   And you know my momma, she don't mince words."

"The fact that she actually said something to you about it speaks volumes to me.   Typically we keep our mouths shut about that kind of stuff because the more we say we dislike something, the more our children seem to want it." She pulled the plug in the sink and let the water drain.

"Maybe I should just walk away then, and call it quits."

"Whoa!   You asked my opinion and I gave it to you, but don't go making any rash decisions based on what I think. If you feel like the relationship is worth saving then fight for it.   Regardless of what you decide, I'm here for you. Always have been, always will be.   If you're happy, I'm happy."   She dried her hands on a towel.

"I'll admit she's got some issues-"

"We all have issues, but we learn to deal with them."

"Her mom abandoned her, and she grew up in foster care.   She had it tough, and I think that's why she has some insecurity issues."

"You don't have to justify why you care about her.   I'm not here to judge.   If that's who you want to be with it's really none of my business."   Disappointed they didn't discuss their sexual encounter, she decided to end the conversation.   "I think I'm going to head to bed so I can get any early start in the morning.   Good luck with whatever you decide."

12 - The Elephant in the Room

Tony woke up early feeling tired after a restless night of sleep. He'd tossed and turned continually, disturbed by nightmares about Janel, Sherri, and his mother, arguing and fighting. Sometimes even physically. He opened the blinds and saw Janel sitting next to the pool, working on her laptop. He pulled on a tank top and some shorts and opened the French doors of his bedroom to join her.

"You're up awfully early." Obviously lost in thought, the sound of his voice startled her and he apologized.

"It's ok. It's just so peaceful out here, it's easy to get lost in my own little world. I really love this space."

He sat down next to her. "What are you concentrating so hard on so early in the morning?"

"I was going over some numbers for the estate sale, using some estimates to see how much money I might have left after I pay off the house. Obviously I need a car, and I was looking at how much I'll need for a decent place to live. I was also looking at flights. I was thinking about going up to visit my parents and fly back with DJ. Not that he can't fly back by himself, he's not exactly little anymore."

"You just told me how peaceful this space is, so why are you looking at stuff that's stressing you out? What happened to taking things one day at a time?"

She closed the lid of the laptop and set it aside. "You're right, I'm sorry."

"Don't apologize to me, I'm just saying. Why not chill out in the pool instead, before the sun gets overhead and it gets too hot?"

"Maybe later. You want some breakfast?"

Sensing that he may have hurt her feelings, he attempted to make things right.   "I know it's easy for me to tell you not to stress, but things are going to work out.   You'll get a car, that's not a problem, and you and DJ can stay here as long as you need to.   I mean, I don't think it's such a bad place.   I've definitely stayed in worse places."   He joked, trying to lighten the mood.

"I'd just feel more comfortable moving to my own place as soon as possible."

"That's what I don't understand.   What's the rush? To me, it's like you're putting the cart before the horse."

"With the way Sherri acted, I don't want to put my son in that kind of situation.   The last thing I need is another assault case.   I can't even afford the one we're fighting now."

"I guarantee what happened with Sherri won't happen again.   There are boundaries now and I intend to make sure she understands and respects that.   This is you and DJ's home now too."

"Listen Tony, you know I love you to death, you've been there for me and my family so many times over the years-"

"What's really going on Janel?   I feel like we're dancing around something here.   Talk to me."

"I just think it's best for everyone involved if I move out sooner rather than later."

"Why?"   He pressed.

"I just don't want us to start taking each other for granted."

"You mean you don't want us to keep sleeping together."

"Ok, yes.   That's exactly what I mean."

"You feel guilty?"

"No."

"Do you regret it?"

A beautiful smile spread across her face and he couldn't help but smile too.   "Look, I'm not saying it wasn't nice. It was."

"But?"

"We just lost Dorian, and we're both still hurting.   I think the two of us sleeping together might've been....convenience, a way to find comfort in each other. You know what I mean?"

"I disagree."

"All I'm saying is with Dorian gone and DJ not being here, coupled with the fact that you and Sherri are on the rocks right now, that's a lot of temptation.   It would be easy to make that a habit.   I'm not going to lie, it was nice, but it's a habit that could cause a lot of problems once DJ comes back.   I'm sure he'd be pretty upset if he found out we'd been sleeping together."

"Ok, so when DJ comes back, we stop sleeping together. Problem solved."

She laughed.   "Just like that huh?   You're good, you should look into counseling crack addicts.   'Just stop, problem solved.'"

He racked his brain to find a solution that was mutually agreeable, but allowed him to continue to sleep with her. "Seriously though, I don't want you to focus on moving out right now because you'll only end up hurting yourself.   If you move out before you're ready, you could end up in a situation worse than the one you're in now.   Stay here and concentrate on finding a job and getting some experience under your belt.   The pay will come, and you can move out then.   And in the meantime I'll try to keep my hands to myself."

"The reason this is so important to me is Dorian took care of me for seventeen years, and then he left me hanging. I need to know I can get out there and take care of DJ and myself on my own.   I have to do this."

He knew her mind was set, but he offered one last piece of advice.   "I respect that, just let me offer my last two cents and I'll back off."

"Fair enough, you know I respect your opinion."

"Wait until the estate sale is over before you start making any decisions. At least then you'll know your true bottom line, and you won't be stressing unnecessarily."

"You're right, I agree."

"I'd like to help you, if you'll let me."

"You're already helping me."

"I'd like to get you a car. Something nice, maybe two or three years old."

"I can get a car-"

"Hear me out please. You need to be able to hand over the keys to the Jag pretty quickly once it sells. If you already have a car you don't have to worry about it." He could tell she was open to the idea so he pressed a little harder. "And I don't want you to worry about paying me back, it would be a gift. I can find a way to write it off on my taxes. We can go today, right now, if you want."

"You're not going to work today?"

"I'm the boss, I can come and go as I please. Besides, Doug will probably turn a cartwheel when I tell him I'm not coming in."

She finally relented. "It would be one less thing to worry about. And I need to start getting used to the idea that I have to sell my car, and I can't do that if I'm driving it every day."

"And if you want to visit your parents, I'll foot the bill for that too."

"I can afford to-"

"It's a small price to pay if it's going to contribute to your peace of mind. But if you're going up there to tell them about what happened, my advice is not to do it. Go and enjoy spending time with them, but keep all this to yourself for now."

"I have to tell DJ, what if he says something?"

"Don't tell him until you get back. You get off the plane, we take him to his favorite restaurant for dinner, and you tell him then.   And you tell him not to say anything to your parents."

"What if they try to mail something to the house?"

"It'll get forwarded here and they won't know the difference."

"It wouldn't feel right.   It's deceitful, a lie by omission."

"You know I know your parents fairly well.   And I know telling them right now is the wrong thing to do. Your dad will worry, and he'll try to find a way to come up with some money for you, and your mom will say I told you so and rub it in your face.   You know as well as I do that she never cared for Dorian from the beginning, and you don't need any of that on your plate right now."

"So how do you think I should handle it?"

"I think you should fill them in a little at a time as your situation improves, over the phone.   That way you're in control of when the conversation ends, and you're not dropping this big bombshell on them about how you're homeless and penniless now.   Because you know that's exactly what they'll hear if you tell them right now, no matter what you actually *say*."   He could see the wheels turning in her head.   "I'd like to come with you.   It could be like a mini-vacation, or a precursor to me finally taking some time off."

"I don't want to stay longer than a weekend.   Just long enough to say hello, spend a little time, and bring DJ back home."

"That's fine, it's your call."

"I guess I'll take you up on that offer too then."

"Good.   You let me know when and how much and I'll take care of it."

# # #

Tony returned to the office after a rough but victorious day in court.   It was one more case resolved and one step closer to him taking some time off.

"I heard there was this attorney that was so on point at the courthouse today that some people thought they heard Shaft theme music as he walked down the hallway."

"Really?   I wonder who that could have been?"   Tony asked Pam as he paused at her desk.

"A real handsome man, smooth skinned, mocha colored brother with a goatee.   Wears a suit like nobody's business.   Rumor has it he's with the Gibson and Reed law firm."

"You're not getting another raise Pam."

"I'm merely saying congratulations on your win today. Why must every compliment I give you or Doug mean I want more money?"

"Because I know you and they usually do.   Any messages?"

"I called the private investigator and he's available.   I gave him your cell and he said he'd call you today."

"He may have already, I haven't stopped long enough to check my voicemail yet."

"How many more cases before you take some time off?"

"Three."

"Including Mrs. Monroe?"

"Yes."

"Poor woman.   She deserves to win that one on principal alone.   You eat lunch yet, or do you want me to order you something?"

"I grabbed a sub on the way."   He held up the bag.   "I need to slow down on the takeout, I haven't been getting in the workouts like I should."

"Could've fooled me."

"Flattery will get you nowhere, you're not getting another raise."   He said over his shoulder as he walked to his office.   He ripped the sub bag open and spread it flat on his desk, and just as he was about to bite into his sandwich his cell phone rang.

"This is Tony."

"Mr. Gibson, it's Mike Foster, private investigator.   I hear you've requested my services."

"I've got a client that I'm defending in a felony assault case and I need your help.   The woman's name is Michelle Brooks."   He gave the investigator a moment to write down Michelle's information, then gave him a run-down of what happened between the two women.

"Obviously you want me to work on dismantling her character, find out if she was sleeping with anyone else on staff, if she's done anything like this in previous jobs, etcetera etcetera."

"Exactly."

"You understand I get paid up front right?"

"Actually no, I wasn't aware of that.   I was warned, however, that you don't come cheap.   But you do come highly recommended."

"I charge what I'm worth, and I can assure you I'm worth it."

"You better be if I'm paying you up front.   I'm not exactly in the habit of paying for services before they're rendered."

"Mr. Gibson, I leave no stone unturned.   In fact, I don't leave any rock, sod, pavement, gravel, or sand unturned. I'm thorough, and I deliver results, or else I refund my fee. And in the fifteen years I've been doing this, I've *never* refunded my fee.   I *always* find something, because at the end of the day, we *all* have secrets.   I guarantee results, but I'm not the Rolling Stones.   I don't guarantee satisfaction because you may not be happy with what I uncover."

"You can believe I'll hold you to that, because in my line of work there's always a first time for everything.   It's called a precedent.   I'll have Pam take care of your fee today, and the sooner you can look into this, the better."

"Not a problem.   Give me a few days and I'll let you know what I come up with.   I look forward to proving my worth."

"One more thing Mr. Foster."

"Please, call me Mike.   Mr. Foster is my father."

"I want you to take a good look at her financial records."

"I do that already but you sound like you're hunting for something specific."

"I am.   I want you to tell me if Dorian ever gave her money."

"If there's a paper trail of him giving her money, then he definitely missed the point of having an affair.   Most men in his position give cash, if they give anything at all."

"I don't expect there to be a paper trail, but-"

"I'm five steps ahead of you Mr. Gibson.   I check bank accounts for large cash deposits, and I look for things that don't make sense.   When a woman drives a high dollar car and she lives in a one bedroom apartment in a low rent district, something is wrong with that picture.   If she's wearing a different pair of Manolos every day but she's driving a ten year old beat up Honda Accord and she doesn't work at a shoe store, something is wrong.   I know my fee concerns you but like I said, I've got fifteen years of experience Mr. Gibson.   This ain't my first rodeo, and I guarantee I can dig up some dirt on this young woman.   In these types of cases, unless it's a really young girl, it's usually not the first time the woman's ever had an affair with a married man."

"It sounds like I just may get my money's worth after all Mike.   I'm eager to see what you turn up."

"I'll give you a call as soon as I have something."

He was torn between wanting Mike to find something financially, so he could understand why Dorian left Janel in such a financial bind, and not wanting him to turn up something that would tarnish his friend's memory even more than it already had been.   He knew he wasn't perfect, but it would really disappoint him if Dorian was giving his mistress money or buying her expensive gifts. He didn't seem the type, but stranger things have happened.   If it was a dead end, the next step was to dig through his planner.

13 - To Grandmother's House We Go

Janel was a bundle of nerves on her way to her parent's house in Ann Arbor, Michigan. She agreed that not mentioning her situation was best, but she wasn't sure if she could keep her mouth shut, especially when it came to her father. The good news was she was doing better financially. She'd earned enough money from the estate sale to pay off the house, and selling her Jag left her with a decent sized nest egg for her savings account. And Tony bought her a used Lexus which took care of her transportation needs. All she had to focus on now were finding a job and saving up a down payment for a place to live. She was holding out hope for a call from CSC about an interview, but until then, she'd just have to rely on her temporary work.

They pulled into her parents driveway, and she rang the doorbell before letting herself in.

"Oh my goodness! I thought you weren't coming in till later? And look what the cat done drug in, Anthony Gibson! What a nice surprise!" Anne Marie gave him a hug. "It's so good to see you again, under much better circumstances this time."

"How you doing Miss Anne?"

"I'm good, have a seat."

"Hey momma." Janel gave her a hug and kiss. "Where's daddy and DJ?" She asked as she flopped down in her dad's favorite recliner.

"Playing golf. Said he was only playing nine holes so they should be back soon. Y'all hungry? I'm making ham, collard greens, hot water cornbread, baked macaroni and cheese, and fresh corn on the cob.   And I made peach cobbler for dessert."   She peeked through the living room curtains.   "Here they come now."

Janel couldn't wait to see her son, she'd missed him so much.   When he walked in the door she swore she was looking at a ghost.   DJ looked just like his daddy.   He'd grown a mustache and had to be at least three or four inches taller.   His voice even sounded deeper.   She stood up and tried to contain her emotion.   Seeing him made her realize just how much she missed her husband.

"Mom!"   He hugged her tightly, picking her up off her feet and swinging her from side to side like a rag doll. "Man, I missed you so much."   He kissed her on her cheek and put her down.   "Uncle Tony!   Good to see you too." He offered DJ his right hand and was prepared to hug him with the left but DJ smacked his hand away and gave him a big bear hug.

"You got a little dirt on your upper lip there man." Tony joked.

"You guys don't even know, I'm so ready to go home. Not that I don't want to be here with grandma and grandpa, I'm just saying.   I'm so ready to sleep in my own bed again!"

"You're early Nel, good to see you baby girl."   Roy gave his daughter a hug so tight that she swore he would break a rib.   He kissed her on the cheek and the whiskers from his beard tickled her face.

"How you doing daddy?"

"Anthony, good to see you again."   Roy hugged him and gave him a solid smack on the back.

"Good to see you too pop Roy."

DJ flopped down on the couch between Janel and Tony, and her dad sat in his recliner.   "You look tired mom. Looks like you lost some weight too."   Roy furrowed his brow and gave his grandson a look.   "You look good though, I just haven't seen you in forever."

Anne Marie chimed in. "She does look thin DJ.   Too thin if you ask me.   Looks like you could use a day or two of sleep too.   You really should take better care of yourself Janel."

"Ay Marie."   Roy growled.   "Don't start.   She been through enough as it is."

"I'm just saying-"

"Let it go."   He said, raising his voice.   "Why don't you bring us something to drink?"   Anne Marie narrowed her eyes at him before she went back into the kitchen.   She returned with two glasses of lemonade for Janel and Tony.

"What about me and DJ?   We been out in the sun all day."   Roy asked.

"Get your own damn lemonade.   The food is done if y'all want to sit down and eat."   Tony was the first to stand up.   "Where you going?"

"To make myself a plate, if that's ok Miss Anne.   I'm starving."

"You'll do no such a thing.   Set down, Janel will make you a plate."

"He ain't company, why I gotta make his plate?"

"That man came all this way with you, the least you can do is make him a plate."

"I'll get it Miss Anne, it's no trouble."

"*Set down!*   She'll bring it to you."   Janel rolled her eyes and went into the kitchen as her mom unfolded a tv tray for Tony.

"How long y'all staying?"   Roy asked as Janel sat a plate of food in front of Tony.

"Just the weekend.   I want to give DJ some time to get settled in before school starts."

"Settled into what?"

"In...to a routine, this being his senior year and all.   You know, football practice, getting used to getting up early. You want me to make you a plate daddy?"

"No thank you, we ate at the golf course.   I am a little thirsty though." He said as he cut his eyes towards his wife.

"I don't know why you ate at the golf course when you knew I was cooking before you even left here."

"Woman, don't start with me."

"I'll get you some lemonade daddy.   DJ, you want a glass?"

"Yes please."

Janel was happy for the opportunity to leave the room and get away from the tension and her parent's bickering. She took her time pouring the drinks, and was startled when the kitchen door swung open behind her.

"You ok?"

"Sure.   What you need?"

"Nothing, just checking on you.   But I told them I needed some hot sauce, so I guess I better not go back out there empty handed."   He opened the pantry and grabbed a bottle of Frank's RedHot, and she smiled at the thought of him being worried about her.   "You want me to take those out too?"

"No, I got it."

"Keep in mind it's just one weekend.   We'll be gone before you know it."   He rubbed her back.   "We should take a ride around the campus tomorrow, see if any of our old hang outs are still there.   And maybe we can have lunch at Delhi park?"

"Maybe."   She said as she took the lemonade into the living room.

After a day of hanging out with the family, back to school shopping for DJ, dinner at Knight's Steakhouse, and a trip around campus with Tony to see how much things had changed, Janel was more than ready to hit the sack.   She turned the television down and settled into the pullout couch bed.   Even though she was tired, she just wasn't sleepy yet.   She started flipping through channels, hoping to stumble upon something interesting to watch, when her father appeared in her peripheral vision.   "Hey daddy, is the television too loud?"

"No."   He said as she sat down on the arm of the couch. "I just wanted to talk to you, see how you're doing."

"I'm doing fine."

"I know better than that.   I know you Nel, and I know something's going on.   So why don't you just save us both some time and tell me what it is.   You and Tony plan on hooking up?"

She smiled.   "No."

"I know The Bible says thou shalt not covet thy neighbor's wife, but if the neighbor is deceased, and the wife is a widow, and the man genuinely cares about the woman, I think God might consider making an exception."

"He has a girlfriend daddy."

"If he had a girlfriend, he wouldn't be here with you." He waited patiently for her to say something.   "I can sit here all night.   I ain't even sleepy."

She turned off the tv and sat up, pulling a blanket around her shoulders.   "I had to sell the house, it was about to go into foreclosure.   Dorian's life insurance didn't pay out, it lapsed due to non-payment several months ago."

"If you two were having money problems you know you could've come to me."

"I didn't know.   Dorian paid the bills."

"How much do you need?   I got a little rainy day fund that your momma don't know about."

"Keep your money daddy, I'm ok.   I've been looking for a job, and Tony's letting us stay with him until I can get on my feet and find another place to live."

He rubbed the knuckles of his hands as if they ached with arthritis, and she could tell he was worried. "I know you're grown, and I know this ain't gonna come out right, but if Dorian was making so much money, how come you don't have any of it?"

"I don't know. We're still trying to figure that out. In the meantime, I sold some of the stuff in the house, and my car-"

"Your car? How you 'posed to get around?"

"Tony helped me get another one. He's been such a big help. I don't know what I would've done without him."

"If you say he's looking out for you and DJ, then I got no worries. He's a good man. Always been sweet on you too, but Dorian had your nose so wide open you never even noticed."

"No, you and momma always *hoped* Tony was sweet on me because you didn't *like* Dorian."

"Stevie Wonder could see that man had a crush on you from day one. And I liked Dorian well enough, your momma's the one that had a problem with him."

"And I never understood why. He was a good husband and a great father."

"Seemed to me if he was such a good man, he would've done whatever it took to make sure that insurance policy never lapsed."

"Maybe he did daddy and we just don't know it. It's not like he's here to defend himself."

"You're right, I apologize. What's done is done, nothing we can do about it now. And I can sure rest easy knowing Tony's looking after you. Who knows, maybe you two will end up-"

"Daddy, they were best friends-"

"Don't matter! Dead men can't get angry. Or jealous. And the Lord works in mysterious ways, you never know what could happen."

"Don't tell momma what we talked about, ok?   I don't want her to worry.   I'll tell her when things are a little more stable."

"Don't worry, I won't."

"That's what you say."   She said as she pointed a finger at him.

"I won't!"

"Ok."

"Goodnight sweetheart."

"Goodnight daddy."

#

"Anyone want seconds?   Or thirds?"   Anne Marie asked as she took her plate and placed it in the sink.   She looked specifically at DJ and smiled when she said the word 'thirds.'

"No thanks grandma, I'm good."

"You sure, there's plenty.   Your grandpa and me ain't gonna eat all this food once you're gone."

"Momma, he's not going to starve between here and Lafayette.   We'll be home in a few hours, unless we get caught in traffic headed back to the airport."   She was more concerned that when they arrived in Lafayette he wouldn't have an appetite, and she wouldn't have a reason to take him to dinner and tell him about his new existence.

"He's a growing boy with a high metabolism.   He'll be hungry again in an hour."   Anne Marie insisted.

"Leave her be Ay Marie.   If the boy gets hungry again Tony'll make sure he gets fed."

Janel shot her dad a look, and Anne Marie caught it. "What's he talking about Nel?"

"Nothing momma.   DJ, go pack your stuff.   Take a good look around and make sure you don't forget anything."

Anne Marie waited until the boy cleared the room. "Roy, what you mean *Tony'll* make sure he gets fed?"

Tony looked at Janel and shook his head, but she decided to go ahead and let her mother in on the situation. "Have a seat momma, there's something I want to tell you before we leave." A look of concern came over her face as she sat down next to her husband and grabbed his hand. "Dorian's life insurance never paid out. The policy lapsed, and I had to sell the house and my car to pay off our debt."

"What? That don't make any sense."

"Somehow we missed a payment which voided the policy."

"But he made so much money. You two didn't have any savings?"

"We did, but he handled the finances so I'm not sure what happened to them."

"I'll tell you what happened, he was so busy trying to keep up with the Jones-es that he got in over his head and spent it all. And now you and DJ have to suffer for it."

"That's not true-"

"It is true! He never really cared about you! All he needed you for was to have some eye candy on his arm and to give him a namesake. He was a selfish jackass that only cared about himself and making people think he had it all together."

"Ay Marie-"

"No Roy, don't 'Ay Marie' me!" She said as she smacked his hand away. "How the hell does someone like that make so much money and manage to leave his family without a pot to piss in or a window to throw it out of? I told you she never should've married him."

"Miss Anne, with all due respect, Dorian was a good husband and a good father. And I'm trying to find out what happened to the money. I know he didn't just blow through it, and as his best friend, I feel obligated to try and prove that, and clear his name if I can."

"Tony, you know I love you like a son, but you can't clear his name because he was dirty from the beginning."

Roy slammed his hand on the table.   "Damn it Anne Marie Carter that's enough!   LET IT GO.   It don't matter what you think about Dorian, the man is dead.   Can't none of us go back in time, what's done is done.   We ALL just need to let it go and move on."

"We should probably get going so we don't miss our flight."   Tony offered.

Janel shook her head as she stared at her mother.

"You need anything?"   Roy asked.

"No daddy, I'm fine."   She kissed him on the head.   "I love you."

"Fine how?   You don't have a house or a car."

"I'll be fine momma.   If you would've let me finish you'd know that."   She walked into the living room to get her stuff.

"Miss Anne, Roy.   Good seeing you again.   Let me get those."   Tony offered as he took Janel's bags.

14 - A Change Will Do You Good

Things seemed to be coming together for Tony. He'd cleared his entire caseload, with the exception of Janel's, and once he cleared her case he planned to send an email to his staff letting them know if they had any issues to contact Doug until further notice. He was beginning to look forward to being able to take some time off to relax and not do any work at all, including checking emails. Mike, the investigator he hired to investigate Michelle, touched base with him to let him know he had a few leads, and he reassured him he'd be getting some information to him soon.

It was a bit of an adjustment having Janel and DJ in his home, but one he was really enjoying. He found their presence comforting, a stark contrast to the emptiness he was used to coming home to. And one of the biggest benefits, compliments of Janel, was that he usually came home to a hot, home cooked meal. The only area of his life that wasn't in tune with his proverbial 'Chi' was his relationship with Sherri. He hadn't talked to her since the morning she barged into his house yelling at him after playing inch high private eye. Since he had some time on his hands with only one case pending, he decided to try and make peace with her by surprising her with flowers and taking her out to lunch. And maybe during the meal they could talk about some of their issues. He strode confidently through the door at CSC, flowers in hand, only to be told by the receptionist that he'd just missed her.

"She left about five minutes ago. Would you like me to put those on her desk?"

"If you wouldn't mind.   Any idea where she went?"

"I'm not sure, but I know she goes to that Mexican place on 5th and Hardaway quite a bit."

"Thanks, I'll swing by there and maybe I can catch her."

Within minutes he was at the restaurant, explaining to the hostess that he was looking for an acquaintance.   The place was packed, and he didn't see her face among the crowd.   The hostess finally offered a suggestion.   "We have another section in the back.   You're welcome to take a look."

He thanked her and made his way to the additional seating in the rear of the restaurant.   As soon as he walked into the room he noticed her in the back, in a corner with a man.   Not wanting to make any assumptions, but wanting to make his presence known, he didn't hesitate to approach the table.   "Hey.   I stopped by the office to see if you wanted to have lunch."

"If you had called first, I could've explained to you that I was having lunch with a colleague and it wasn't a good time."

He chose to ignore her flippant comment and focus on her companion instead, who sat stone faced in a poor attempt to appear intimidating.   "'Sup man?"

"Shawn, Tony, Tony, Shawn Dixson."

He ignored the man, who remained silent and continued to stare at him, and turned his attention back to Sherri. "You think we can step outside and talk for a minute?"

"I'm having lunch Tony.   Our food will be out shortly."

He knew she was trying to push his buttons, and although he was upset, he refused to react.   "You know what, I apologize for interrupting.   You two enjoy your lunch."   He left the restaurant beyond pissed, and by the time he reached his car, he heard her call his name.   He stood outside his car as he waited for her to catch up to him.

"What do you want Tony?"

"Nothing.   Go enjoy your lunch with Shawn."   He avoided eye contact with her in an attempt to maintain his composure.

"You asked me to come outside and talk, so let's talk."

"I'm tired Sherri."

"So what are you saying?"

"Are we going to try to work this out or not?"   She brushed her hair out of her face and looked at him without responding.   "I guess I have my answer then."

"What do you want me to say?   We're not going to solve anything right now, standing in the middle of a parking lot."

"You call me when your schedule clears up, but don't wait too long.   Like my momma always says, one monkey don't stop no show."   He got in his car and drove away.

Frustrated and void of any cases to concentrate on, he didn't know what to do with himself so he headed home. He was surprised to find Janel sitting at the dining room table, working on her laptop.

"Hey.   I thought you'd be out hitting the pavement."

"My fragile ego can't handle anymore rejection this week, so I'm concentrating on some temp work.   What're you doing home?"

"The only case I have left is yours, and I'm hoping to put that to bed soon."

"I hope so too."

"What're you working on?"   He asked, looking over her shoulder.

"Payroll for a small business.   The woman who normally handles it is out on maternity leave."

He realized he'd stood behind her a little too long when she looked up at him.   "I don't mind if you watch, just have a seat.   You're hovering."

"Sorry, I was just curious."

"Are you ok?"

"I'm fine.   Why?"

She cocked her head to the side and narrowed her eyes. "You work so much that you don't even know what to do with yourself now that you have some free time, do you?"

"Actually, I was thinking about catching a movie. Wanna come?"

"What's playing?"

"Let me see."   He touched the screen on his phone a few times and read some titles to her.

"Honestly, none of those sound very interesting to me. But if you just want some company, I'll go with you."

"Nah that's ok.   No sense in you suffering through something you're not interested in."   He plopped down on the couch like a sulking teenager, trying to put the incident with Sherri out of his mind.   He browsed through personal email as he realized Janel was right, he didn't know what to do with so much down time on his hands.

"Listen.   Give me a few minutes to find a good stopping point and maybe we can find a pay movie on cable.   We could pop some popcorn and just chill right here.   It'd be cheaper than spending thirty or forty dollars at the theater."

"I can afford to take you to the movies, it's not a problem."

"Sorry, I'm constantly in cost saving mode these days. It's a habit."

"Actually, it's not a bad idea."

"You might want to check and see if we actually have any popcorn.   You have a teenager in your house now.   Food disappears quickly whenever he's around."

"That's ok.   I'll run to the store and pick up a few things while you finish up."

When he returned from the store she was sitting on the couch flipping through the onscreen guide.   "Find anything?"

"Not really."

"Go ahead and start popping the popcorn, I've got an idea." He went into his bedroom and pulled out a few DVDs from the back of his closet; Love Jones, The Color Purple, Coming to America, Boomerang, and What's Love Got To Do With It. He returned to the living room and spread the movies out on the coffee table. She came back with a bowl of popcorn and set it on the table.

"Look at-You've been holding out on me! You know these are some of my favorite movies, right?"

"I know, I remember. They're even better now, remastered for Blu-ray. You pick, ladies choice."

"This is tough, like choosing a favorite child." She finally picked Boomerang, and he put the movie in the player and sat down. After making sure the surround sound was adjusted just right, he made himself comfortable by stretching out on his back and resting his head on her lap. "You comfortable?" She joked.

"Very, thanks."

She stretched her legs out and started feeding him popcorn, and when she was finished, she rested her arm across his chest. Once the movie ended, he tried to convince her to watch another one with him because he didn't want her to get up. He was comfortable and wanted to spend more time with her.

"Although I really enjoyed that, I really don't have time to watch another one. I've got to finish that payroll and then pick up DJ from football practice." She patted his chest. "Come on, get up." She wriggled beneath his weight until he finally sat up. When she stood up, he grabbed her by the wrist. She wriggled free of his grip and held his hand. "When are you going to tell me what's wrong? I know you, something's up."

He put his arms around her waist and pulled her close to him as he pressed his face into her stomach. He inhaled deeply, savoring the scent of her skin. She always smelled so good, like cocoa butter and soap. He felt the tips of her fingers on his head, softly at first, then she embraced it with both hands.   She ran her finger and thumb along his outer ear and gently squeezed and pulled on his earlobes.   A chill ran through his body and he was instantly aroused.   He slid his hands over the back of her thighs and squeezed, pulling her towards him as he slid backwards on the couch.   She moved in sync with him, spreading her legs and straddling his lap, her knees planted on the couch to either side of him.   He grabbed her butt and squeezed hard as she kissed him, thrusting her tongue into his mouth and pressing her breasts against his chest. He eased her shirt up and caressed the small of her back. He slid his fingers along her soft skin, up to the clasp on her bra, and unfastened it with one hand.   She grabbed the front of her shirt and pulled it, along with the bra, over her head in one quick motion, flinging them both aside.   He cupped her breasts and sucked her nipple into his mouth, flicking it with his tongue and biting it gently, then repeating the actions on the other one, giving them both equal time and attention.   He grabbed the waist of her shorts and tugged at them as he brushed his lips across her torso, kissing, licking and sucking her skin.   She unfastened them and stood up, allowing them to fall to the floor.

He raised his hips to remove his shorts while she slowly pushed her panties down over her hips, teasing him before she straddled him again.   She pulled his t-shirt over his head and he raised his hips to meet hers, eager to be inside of her.   She guided the tip of his shaft inside of her, closing her eyes and softly exhaling as she lowered herself onto him.   He kept his hands on her hips and fought the urge to push her down on top of him as his girth filled her.   He felt her relax once he was fully inside, and she settled her weight on her knees, rotating her hips in small circles, then easing herself up and down, teasing him. She arched her back and began bouncing up and down, faster and faster.   He thrust his hips upwards, matching her rhythm.   He fought the urge to come and was thankful when she finally slowed her pace.   She squeezed his shaft each time she raised her hips, flicked her tongue in his ear, and nibbled his earlobe softly before taking it into her warm, wet mouth.   He leaned his head back and closed his eyes.   "That feels so good."

She brushed her soft lips across his cheek and she kissed him again, and he gripped her hips and began pounding into her.   He wanted to feel her nails in his back and hear her call out his name as she came.   She moaned and he asked her if it felt good.   "Yes.   Don't stop."   She whispered.   Their bodies were slick with sweat and when she began to gasp he knew she was close to climaxing. "Come for me baby."   Her muscles began spasming and his pace became frenzied.   "That's right, come with me." He squeezed her waist with both hands, digging his fingers into her skin, and they both cried out as he pushed himself as far inside of her as he could.   She collapsed on top of him as every muscle in his body began to relax, his energy spent.   He leaned his head against her chest and tried to catch his breath.   She leaned her weight to one side to get up but he held her firmly in place with both arms wrapped around her.

"No, not yet.   Stay here for a minute."   He kissed her gently between her breasts and rested his ear against her chest.   He hugged her tight, and she started flexing her kegel muscles again.   "Stop, stop, don't do that."   He finally slipped from inside her and she relaxed on his lap, draping her arms comfortably around his neck.

"I don't know if I'm going to be able unfold my legs. I'm not twenty anymore you know."

"Just stay here with me for a minute."   He ran his hands over her warm thighs, still slick with sweat.   "Please."

"We can't keep doing this."

He kissed her softly on her arm.   "Why not?"

She gently cupped his face with her hands and forced him to look at her.   "What exactly *are* we doing here?"

"We're friends, relieving some stress and finding comfort in each another."

"It's physical and we're friends with benefits."

"It's more than that."

"You have a girlfriend."   She put her hands on his chest.

"I'm not so sure anymore."   He took her hands in his and kissed them, then started sucking on her fingers.

"She'll be back.   You fight all the time."   She said, gently pulling them away.

"It's different this time.   I'm tired."

"Are you?   Or are you just lonely?   Or grieving?" She slowly unfolded her legs and he helped her stand up. "I need to take a shower before I pick up DJ."   She gathered her clothes from the floor and handed him his.

"I'll go get him if you want?   I know you need to finish up that payroll."

"That's ok, I'll get him.   I'm going a little stir crazy, I could use the fresh air."

"We could shower together?"   He suggested, as he pulled his boxers on.

He saw the corner of her mouth start to turn into a smile but she bit her lip to keep it from happening.   "I don't think so.   I'll be late as it is."

He watched her walk towards her bedroom.   "I'm not lonely or grieving.   And it's not a physical thing."   She glanced at him before disappearing into her room.

15 - Things Are Looking Up

Janel pulled into the school parking lot to attend DJ's first Middlebranch football game. Her phone began to ring as she put the car in park. She answered it and balanced it carefully between her ear and her shoulder as she gathered up her purse, locked the doors, and headed towards the stadium. "Hello?"

"Hello. May I speak with Janel Monroe please?"

"This is she. How can I help you?"

"Hi Janel, my name is Anna Turner and I'm with human resources at CSC Federal. We've reviewed your resume and we think you might be a good candidate for a position we're looking to fill. Do you think you'd be interested in coming in for an interview?"

"Yes, I'm very interested."

"We're holding interviews at our newest branch, and if you're hired, that's where you'd be located. Are you familiar with our new location?"

"Yes, I know where it is."

"Would you be able to come in tomorrow at ten?"

"Sure, that sounds great."

"Good, I'll put you down for ten. Just to let you know, our interview process takes approximately two hours. Sometimes they run a little longer, it just depends. I always like to give people a heads up so they can plan accordingly."

"I appreciate that, thank you so much. I'll be there, ten am tomorrow morning." She hung up, let out a whoop, and did a little victory dance in the grass. "Thank you! Finally!" Although it wasn't a guarantee, it was a chance to get her foot in the door and gain some new experience, and possibly land a permanent position.

She took the bleacher steps two by two as she made her way to the top row.   The grin on her face quickly faded as she looked around and realized she didn't recognize anyone.   It was quite the change from football games at DJ's old high school, where she sat with the same clique of Clover Hill parents.   She felt a twinge of guilt as she imagined DJ feeling the same way as he navigated the hallways of his new school.   She hated that he had to switch schools for his senior year, but after talking to him like an adult at great length about their current financial situation he understood.   He still didn't like it, but at least he understood and didn't blame her.

She wondered where Tony was when she heard one of the referees blow his whistle to signal the start of the game. DJ's games were usually a priority to him, and he rarely missed one unless work left him no other choice.   She sent him a quick text message asking if he would make it and waited for him to reply.

The game started out slow, but the action picked up quickly and by half time Middlebranch was up by two points.   By the time the third quarter rolled around, she found herself on her feet cheering for her son just like she did when he played for Clover High, despite the fact she was sitting alone.   In the end, they eliminated their competition 44 to 36, and her son had three carries, two interceptions, and three touchdowns.

She waited patiently in the stands as the rest of the crowd migrated down the bleachers and towards the parking lot.   She'd learned a long time ago that it was easier for her to stay put and have DJ find her than for her to go looking for him at any sporting event.   After nearly ten minutes, she finally spotted him waving his arms at her. As she made her way down the stairs she noticed he was standing with a team mate.

"Hey mom.   Where's Tony?"

"Your guess is as good as mine.   I assumed he'd be here, especially since he's not working.   I sent him a text message but I never got a reply."

"That sucks.   I felt like I was off tonight and I was hoping he could give me some feedback."

"If you felt off it was hard to tell.   You're faster this year, and you're hitting much harder.   I see a big difference between last season and this season.   You're looking really good."

"You think?"

"You know I wouldn't say so if I didn't.   Who's this?" She gestured towards the young man standing next to him.

"This is my friend PJ.   PJ, this is my mom."

"It's nice to meet you PJ."

"Nice to meet you too ma'am."

"Don't call me ma'am, it makes me feel old.   Miss Janel is fine."

"Yes ma'am, I mean Miss Janel."

"So mom, I was wondering if I could go hang out with the guys and celebrate a little bit."

"Who, when, and where?   You already know the drill."

"PJ, now, at Sal's Pizzeria.   The football team gets a discount on game nights, regardless if we win or lose."

"What time do you plan on being home?   You know it's a school night."

"I know, not too late."

"How late?   I need a time."

"Ten?"

He gave her his best pitiful look and she finally caved. "Fine, ten.   You need money?"   He shook his head no. "Who're you riding with?"

"PJ.   I was hoping you'd let me borrow the car?"

"And how am I supposed to get home?"

"I'll drop you off on the way."

She considered his request while both boys stared at her expectantly.   "I guess I'm ok with that, but you know my rule.   I don't know PJ so I need to meet his parents before you leave."

"My mom left already, but my dad is still here."

DJ elbowed him in the side.   "Dude, hurry up and go get him.   I'll meet you in the locker room."

Janel sat down as she watched the boys disappear in opposite directions, rushing through the remains of the crowd.   Almost twenty minutes later the two young men reappeared, freshly showered and wearing a tad too much cologne.   It was just confirmation for her that there was more to their outing than just 'hanging out with the guys.' She was happy that he'd made a friend, and admittedly a little jealous.   At least he had somewhere to be and someone to hang out with.

She checked her phone again to see if Tony responded to her text and he hadn't, which was odd.   He always responded, unless he was in court, and even then if he had a chance he would respond to say he was in court.   She glanced up momentarily and noticed a man walking towards her.   The closer he got, the more she realized she recognized him.   It took a second for her to place his face and when she did, she smiled.

"What a nice surprise.   It's good to see you again Janel. How are you?"

"Perry!   It's good to see you too.   I guess this means our paths are going to cross more often."

"Is that such a bad thing?"

"I feel stupid."

"Why?"

"PJ looks just like you, I don't know why I didn't pick up on that."   He was the spitting image of his daddy, green eyes and all.

"He is my doppelganger, as well as my namesake."   He tried to hug his son but he pulled away in embarrassment. "The boys tell me you're loaning them your car for the evening so they can hang out at the pizzeria."

"I told them they could go if I felt comfortable after meeting PJ's parents."

"How are you going to get home?"

"They're going to drop me off."

"How about we send them on their way and I'll take you home.   Are you ok with that?"

"Umm, sure.   I guess that'll be ok."

"Mom, can we go now?"

"So you're ok with just leaving me here with some strange man?   He could be a crazy serial killer or something."

"You obviously already know each other from somewhere.   Besides, if you come up missing, I know where to tell the police they can find him.   He comes to almost all of the practices.   Can we go now?"

"Fine, smart aleck, go on.   Be careful please, and be home by *ten*.   Not five after ten, or dropping PJ off at *his* house at ten.   Be in the house by ten.   You hear me?"

"Yes ma'am."

"Man, to be that age again..."   Perry said as he watched them head for the parking lot.   "Look at 'em.   They know they want to run to the car but they can't because it wouldn't be 'cool.'   So, you want to get a bite to eat?   I don't like to kill on an empty stomach, and I don't like for my victims to die hungry.   I'm one of those nice serial killers."

"Very funny.   What'd you have in mind?"

"Ever hear of Stella's?"   She shook her head no.   "You're in for a treat, it's a great little spot."

They debated the highlights of the football game as he drove them to a hole in the wall spot that looked as if it might have been a personal residence in a former life.   "This is Stella's, one of my favorite guilty pleasures.   It doesn't look like much but they have some of the best fried catfish in the south."

The waitress hollered out from behind the counter.

"Y'all seat yourselves, I'll be with you in a minute."   They chose a corner booth and she placed two double-sided, laminated menus on the table.

"Thanks but we won't be needing those."

"I already know what you want, you're a regular, but I thought she'd at least like to look at the menu."

"We'll take two catfish dinners, a Coke, and whatever she wants to drink.   And if she's not licking her fingers when she's done eating, I'll leave you a hundred dollar tip."

"Now that's a sucker's bet, I ain't no fool.   I ain't worried no way cause I know you a good tipper honey. Two catfish dinners coming right up.   What you want to drank sweetie?"   Janel ordered a Sprite and the waitress disappeared into the kitchen.

"Guess what?   CSC called me for an interview. Tomorrow morning at ten."

"Good, it sounds like things might be looking up."

"I'm nervous."

"Don't be, you'll be fine."

"You got any tips?"

He motioned for her to come closer and she leaned in close.   "If you really want to ace the interview, this is what you do.   You go in, sit down, relax, be yourself, and then...flash that beautiful smile of yours-that's the one right there, and I'm sure you'll do just fine."

Janel laughed.   "I thought you were really going to tell me something helpful!"

"That right there is some good advice, I don't know what you're talking about."

"I don't think I want to work somewhere that would hire me simply because they think I have a nice smile."

"Seriously though, don't sweat it.   You've got a degree and a little experience, and you'll be working with proprietary software that's new to everyone.   Actually, you're at an advantage because you don't have to unlearn the old system and bad habits."   The waitress placed two huge platters of food in front of them and asked if they needed anything else.   Perry thanked her and she walked away.

"If this tastes as good as it smells, I'm going to gain a few pounds tonight."

"I'm sure it'll be in all the right places."   He winked at her and she felt flush, completely flattered by the compliment.   "Here, try this fried okra, it's delicious." He held his fork to her mouth and she took a bite.   "Save room for the cobbler.   You won't be sorry."

"I'll be lucky to finish this and I'm hungry."   Her plate was piled high with mac and cheese, turnip greens, and a catfish fillet that covered half her plate.   He finished his meal quickly while she struggled to clear half of hers. "I'm sorry, I need a to-go box."

"You want dessert?"

"No thank you.   I'm stuffed."

"You can get it to go and eat it later."

"Why don't we come back sometime, skip the monster platters, and just have dessert?"

He smiled.   "I'll be sure to hold you to that."

"You were right, it was very good.   Thanks for sharing your guilty pleasure with me."

"You're welcome."   He slipped some cash in with the bill and looked at his watch.   "Did you need me to run you anywhere else?   It's still early."

"Actually you could just drop me off at the walking trail in the neighborhood.   I need to walk some of this food off."

"Let's go, I'll walk with you."

They walked a lap around the lighted trail and enjoyed light conversation before he delivered her to the front door of Tony's house. "Nice place."

"You know it's not mine, I'm staying with a friend.   I'm hoping I can start looking for my own place soon though."

"I had fun tonight.   I realize you're not where you want

to be right now, but I was hoping we could see each other again.   Maybe go someplace where we don't leave smelling like we've been deep fried in Crisco.   I'd really like an opportunity to get to know you better."

"I love to dance, and you have my number."

"I do, and honestly I want to use it every day, but I don't want to push.   I know you've got a lot going on."   He gently took her right hand in his and examined it.   "Your hand looks good."   He kissed the back of it and threaded his fingers through hers.

She struggled to think of something clever to say but the words just wouldn't come to her.   "I've still got a little pain and swelling in the joints but it's much better."

"I'll give you a call when I figure out where I'd like to take you."

"I look forward to it."

He reluctantly let go of her hand.   "I guess I should go. I feel like your father's going to come out any minute and tell me it's time for me to go home."

She had butterflies in her stomach and didn't have a clue what to do or say next.   Feeling nervous and awkward, she held up the plastic bag of leftovers.   "Thanks again for dinner."   What a dumb thing to say, she berated herself in her head.

"One of my favorite places.   Can't eat there too often though, my cholesterol would be through the roof.   Not to mention I'd have to spend a lot more time in the gym."

"I better go inside, it would be weird for DJ to pull up and see us standing here talking like teenagers."

"Good point.   You have a good night."

"You too"

"Good luck with the interview, and I'll call you soon."

She watched him walk back to his car before she went inside and closed the door.   She pressed her back against the cool steel and let out a tiny shriek like a school girl with a crush.

16 - A Full House Beats a Flush

Tony got a call from Mike Foster regarding some information about Michelle, and he suggested that they meet for an early dinner at Ruth's Chris Steakhouse.

"If you tell me what I want to hear, this meal's on me. If you give me crappy information, you're on your own."

"Fair enough.   I have no doubt I'll be keeping my wallet closed tonight.   It'll be my pleasure to prove to you I'm well worth my fee Mr. Gibson."

"Put your money where your mouth is and show me what you got."

He placed a legal sized envelope on the table and pushed it towards Tony.   He opened it up and scattered the contents.   There were dozens of pictures, along with a small stack of papers.

"It seems this young lady is quite the kept woman.   And Mr. Monroe wasn't her first or only conquest.   She left her previous job at a small corporation in order to escape a scandal that was brewing between her and the executive vice president.   She's known for trying to sleep her way to the top, and apparently she's sharpened her game over the years.   She's managed to con three older gentlemen, and I'm talking gray haired older gentlemen, into thinking she's a good, monogamous girl.   And in return, they provide the finances to keep her in a comfortable lifestyle.   She's smart about it though, not too flashy, doesn't brag, and she splits her cash across three different bank accounts.   She even has a few successful investments.   The unique thing about Mr. Monroe, from what I can tell, is he seems to be the only one who's ever been to her home.   And if he was giving her money, or anything else for that matter, I couldn't find any evidence of it.   My personal opinion is she thought Mr. Monroe was her best shot at getting a better paying position within the company, and the old guys were simply her financial security until she could get there.   I'm sure the fact that he didn't require a Viagra prescription didn't hurt either."   Tony flipped through the pictures, and there were several that were pretty sexually explicit.   "Quite frankly I don't know why she bothers to work.   If she raised her standards and lowered her age limit a little she could probably quit her day job."

"How'd you get these pictures?   Some of these look like you were so close that you risked being spotted."

"I have high quality, very expensive camera equipment. I don't pocket my entire fee, I do put some of it back into my business.   That's part of the reason why I charge so much. You get what you pay for, wouldn't you agree?"

"I was skeptical but I have to admit you were right. You were worth the money.   There's some really good information here, definitely worth a quality steak dinner and then some.   I'm confident this case won't see the inside of a courtroom once I share this with her lawyer." He flipped through the stack of papers and there were financial records, with the account numbers and social security number blacked out, along with a detailed log containing her every move since the day he'd asked Mike to investigate her.   "How can you be so sure he wasn't giving her money?   You can't exactly track cash."

"She's smart, but she's no genius.   She gets cash from the old men, hangs on to it for a while, then she deposits it into her bank accounts.   She wants her deposits to appear random, but I was able to pick up on a pattern.   The first deposit happens after three weeks, the second one a week later, the third one happens a month from that, and the fourth one happens in two weeks.   Then she repeats the pattern.   I can't prove to you one hundred percent that he never gave her money, but I've been doing this a long time and my instincts are rarely wrong.   The only way I could investigate any further would be to investigate him, and you only paid me to investigate her."

"Now that you've mentioned it,"   Tony removed the envelope from the table and replaced it with Dorian's planner.   "How'd you like to do another job for me?"

"What's this?"

"This is Mr. Monroe's planner.   He earned close to seven figures, and yet when he died he was four months behind on the mortgage, the house was about to be foreclosed on, their checking account was overdrawn, and their savings account was almost empty.   And I want to know why.   I need you to help me figure out what he was doing with his money."

Mike unzipped the planner and flipped through a few of the pages.   "Was he a gambling man?"

"No."

"He have any other vices?   Drugs?   Strip club? Drinking?"

"If he did he did a pretty damn good job of hiding it."

"Can I be frank?"

"Please do.   In fact I'd prefer it."

"Why is this so important to you?   What's in it for you?"

"He was my best friend.   The three of us, him and his wife, we went to college together.   We've known each other a long time, been through a lot together.   I just need to know."

"Did you know he was having financial trouble?"

"No, which is part of the reason why this is bothering me. I know we didn't talk about everything, but something like that, he knew he could have come to me."

"They say pride goeth before a fall.   Why not just ask his wife what happened?

"I have, she doesn't know.   She's the one who asked me to look into it.   You tell me you can take this case, and I'll have the money in your account first thing in the morning."

Mike zipped the planner up and set it aside. "You know Mr. Gibson-"

"Call me Tony."

"I think I like you Tony.   To be a lawyer, you ain't half bad.   No offense."

"None taken."

"I tell you what.   Since you've agreed to foot the bill for this very expensive steak dinner, I'm going to give you my 'friends and family' rate."

"It's not like I'm not doing you any favors, you earned this dinner."

"Never the less, I'm a pretty good judge of character, and I think you're a decent guy.   A scholar and a gentleman, if you will.   I'm going to give you a twenty-five percent discount."

"I appreciate that Mike, it's very generous of you.   How long before you think you'll have something for me?"

"When I have something worthwhile, I'll be in touch. Just like the last time."

The more he got to know Mike over dinner, the more he liked the guy.   He was very intelligent and had quite a bit of insight into people and why they seemed to do the things they did.   After dinner, they shook hands and parted ways, and Tony left the steakhouse with a full belly and feeling as if a huge weight had been lifted from his shoulders.   Armed with the information he'd obtained from Mike, he could wrap a bow around Janel's case.   All he had to do was meet with Michelle's lawyer and show him why it was in his best interest to convince her to drop the case.

Once he got home, he headed straight for his bedroom to change clothes and make a quick call to Michelle's lawyer to set up a meeting.   He slipped on a t-shirt and a pair of shorts and sat on the edge of his bed to make the call.

"Bill, it's Tony Gibson."

"Tony.   You calling to wave the white flag and talk about a settlement?"

"You ought to know by now that I'd never roll over for you.   You're the closest thing to real competition that I have in this town.   You know I'm going to make you work harder than you ever have to get a win over on me.   You think we can have lunch tomorrow and talk about this case?   Just you and me, one on one, without your client."

"I'm in court all day tomorrow."

"How about we meet at Chili's for happy hour?   I'll buy you a drink and we can talk."

"Aw shit!   You're one cheap son of a bitch so if you're offering to buy me a drink you must have something pretty solid up your sleeve.   Why don't you save us both some time and just tell me what's up."

"Come on Bill, what's the fun in that?"   He was genuinely disappointed, he wanted to be able to show him the mountain of character crushing evidence he had against Michelle and actually see the expression on his face when he realized his case had just fallen apart.   "Fine, I'll play nice this time.   Your client has quite a history of sexual indiscretions."

"It's not a crime to be a slut.   If that's all you've got-"

"You have to know I'm coming at you harder than that. Did you know she's got a history of trying to sleep her way to the top in the corporate world?   She's also got a thing for older guys.   She's currently bilking three different senior citizens out of their hard earned cash.   In fact, I'm not even sure why she's working because she could easily be classified as a call girl with the things she's been doing. And those are just the highlights, I could go on."

"And you have proof of all that?"

"If I didn't, I wouldn't have agreed to buy you a drink. I'm a cheap son of a bitch, remember?   I've got pictures and financial records."

"I could still push for pain and suffering.   Ask for some

jail time, and probation."

"You could, but if you do, I'll ride the poor grieving widow train all the way to the bench.   Pair that up with what I've got here in my hands and the sympathy will be so thick in that court room that your client will end up having to pay my client for pain and suffering.   And just so you're aware, my client doesn't have any money to go after.   I'm working this case pro bono.   I have proof of that too if you need it.   Trust me Bill, pursuing this case is a waste of your time.   Worst case scenario, my client gets probation and your client ends up with egg on her face and a ruined reputation.   Even more so than it already is."

There was a moment of silence on the other end of the phone.   "I was so ready to go toe to toe with you on this one.   But it sounds like you really do have an ace in the hole.   At first I thought you were just trying to bluff me, but I can tell you're serious."

"I never bluff my way around a case, not even with the newbies.   I can send you the proof right now with a click of my phone camera.   I do the legwork and get it done, so you can believe what I'm saying to you."

"I was hoping you'd gotten lazy for once in your career. Give me a few days.   I'll talk to my client and get back to you."

"I'll be waiting by the phone."   Tony hung up, laid back on the bed, and closed his eyes.   It was such a relief knowing he'd gotten Janel off the hook, and that he would be able to enjoy some stress-free time off.   He turned onto his side and decided to take a nap before he had to leave for DJ's game.   What he expected to be a thirty minute power nap turned into an overnight event.   When he re-opened his eyes and rolled over to check the clock, it read fifteen minutes after nine.   AM.   And although he felt bad about missing the game, for the first time in a long time he actually felt well rested and refreshed.   He got up, showered, and skipped his morning shave.   It was the first step in an effort to be a bum and do as little as possible during his vacation.   He'd never stepped away from the office without being tied to his work in some way, whether it be taking work home or being tethered through his phone and email account.   He picked up his cell phone and disabled his work email, and noticed text messages from Janel.   He got dressed and wandered into the kitchen where he found her eating a bowl of cereal at his breakfast bar.

"Morning sunshine.   I was just about to come in there and put a mirror under your nose to make sure you were still alive.   I was worried about you.   You feeling ok?"

"I laid down to take a nap and I guess I didn't realize how tired I was.   I hate that I missed DJ's game.   Is he upset with me?"

"Nah.   We were more worried than anything, until we got home and saw you were just sleeping.   You're not getting sick are you?"

He pulled out a stool and sat down next to her.   "No, I'm fine.   I had a few drinks and a heavy dinner last night and I got one of the best nights of sleep in my life."

"You obviously needed some rest then."   She turned the bowl up and drank the milk, then dropped it in the sink. "I've gotta run.   I've got an interview with CSC this morning."

"Good, that's great."

"Wish me luck."   She kissed him on the cheek, then took a minute to run her hand across his stubble.   "I don't know that I've ever seen you with a five o'clock shadow.   I like it, it's kind of sexy."   He walked her out to her car and opened the door for her.   "Are you telling me all I had to do was start growing a beard to get you to call me sexy?"

"I've always thought you were sexy, it just wasn't exactly appropriate to say so in the past."   He leaned into the car, smiling.   "I've really gotta go or I'm going to be late."

He stepped back and let her shut the door.   He tapped

on the window and she rolled it down.   "Let's go out tonight for some drinks and dancing.   To celebrate."

"Celebrate what?   It's just an interview, it's not a guarantee."

"You'll get the job, I'm sure of it."   He leaned on the window sill.

"You got some pull at CSC that I'm not aware of?   Cause I know Sherri doesn't have any love for me."

"You'll get it.   I can feel it in my bones.   Plus, I've got a surprise for you."

"What surprise?"

"Come out with me tonight and find out."

"If I agree to go out with you will you let me leave?"

He stood up and tapped the roof of the car.   "Go, good bye.   And good luck."

"Thanks.   I'll call you and let you know how it goes."

17 - Just When I Needed You

Janel pulled into the parking lot at the new CSC branch, turned her car off, and took a deep breath. "You can do this." She told herself in the rear view mirror. She was greeted warmly at a side entrance by Anna, the HR representative she'd spoken to on the phone.

"It'll be just a moment. They're finishing up another interview so you can relax for a few minutes. There's coffee, tea, and water in the break room just down the hall, you're welcome to help yourself, and I'll come get you when they're ready."

"'They?'"

"Yes ma'am. You'll be interviewing with a panel of three people. We used to have three individual one hour interviews, but we found this process works better for us. It allows all three people to hear your answers, then they get together afterwards and discuss all the candidates to determine who we'll be calling to offer positions."

"How soon do you expect to start calling people with job offers?"

"Probably as early as this afternoon. We've got a pretty tight deadline to get people trained and get this branch open. We've already had to push back the grand opening twice."

"Do you think I have time to step outside for a moment?"

"Sure. I'll come get you when the panel is ready for you."

"Thanks." Janel stepped outside and walked towards the back of the building. She'd never interviewed with a panel and her anxiety level was through the roof. She sent Tony a text message hoping he could offer a few words of encouragement.

Janel: I'm interviewing with a panel of three people! They didn't tell me that on the phone!

Tony: Take a deep breath.   Relax.   You've got this.

Janel: I tried that, it's not working.   I'm really nervous.

Tony: Don't be nervous, you got this.   Go in, be yourself, and YOU'LL BE FINE!

Janel: Gotta run, she's calling me back inside.   Wish me luck.

Tony: You don't need it, the job is yours.   Have a little faith.   :-D

She followed Anna into the conference room where the panel was sitting.   "Everyone, this is Janel Monroe. Janel, this is Tina Falmore, she deals with cash management," Janel shook her hand, "this is Rick Smallstreet, he's one of our internal auditors," Janel said hello and shook his hand.   "And this is Perry Hunter, he's one of our loan officers."   Her eyes registered her surprise but otherwise she was able to keep her cool.   She shook his hand as if it was the first time she'd ever met him. "Very nice to meet you Mr. Hunter."
    "Likewise."   He replied as he smiled at her.
    "You can have a seat there, and just come see me when you're done.   Ok?"   Anna left the room and closed the door behind her and Janel sat down.
    "Are you ready?"   Tina asked.

She borrowed Tony's confidence and replied. "Absolutely."

"Good, let's get started."

When she emerged from the interview two hours and ten minutes later, she felt great. She was confident that the panel was impressed with her responses and that she'd made a positive impression on them. And having Perry on the panel, surprising as it was, couldn't have hurt her chances any either. The first thing she did when she got in the car was call Tony.

"So, how'd it go?"

"If I don't get called for this job, then I must've had some hell-a competition. I'm so in there, I know it. I can feel it."

"When will you know for sure?"

"The woman from HR told me they're going to start calling people this afternoon. They want to get everyone trained as soon as possible so they can open that branch."

"Just make sure you keep your phone handy. You on your way home?"

"Actually I'm starving, I'm headed over near the college to grab some sushi. You want me to bring you something?"

"No thanks, I've already had some leftovers. I'll see you when you get back."

She had to circle the parking lot three times before she was able to snag a spot near the sushi restaurant as they were doing pretty brisk lunchtime business. They were fast and cheap, which is exactly why she'd decided to stop by. She stood in a long but fast moving line and placed her order, then moved to a second, slower moving line to pay. She read the local news on her phone as she waited.

"Janel? Janel Carter, is that you?" She looked over her shoulder and saw a woman eating lunch at a table in the dining room near the window. The woman stood up and moved closer to her and Janel covered her mouth to stifle a scream.

"Rita?   Rita Mae Jones?   Is that really you?"   The two women hugged each other and rocked back and forth. "Oh my gosh, you are a sight for sore eyes.   I can't believe it's really you!   How've you been Rita?"   Janel's eyes actually welled up at the sight of her.   She and Rita were roommates their freshman year, and they'd gotten to be good friends because her boyfriend, Charlie Seidel, was on the football team with Dorian and Tony.   "Are you almost done eating, or do you have time to eat with me?"

"I've got plenty of time, my next class isn't until two."

"Your next class?   Oh my goodness, let me pay for my meal and I'll come sit down so we can catch up."   Janel couldn't pay her tab fast enough before she sat down and joined her old friend.   "I can't believe you're really here. What are the chances?   What are you doing in Lafayette?"

"I just moved here a couple of weeks ago.   I'm recently divorced and I was looking for a fresh start.   The University of Louisiana wasn't my first choice but they offered me the most money so here I am."

"You're a professor?"

"Yes girl, I'm a professor now.   Can you believe it?   I teach economics.   Me and Charlie got married after we graduated and I continued on with school and ended up getting my PhD.   You remember Charlie Seidel right?"

"Girl, how could I forget.   He was a six foot five muscular chocolate bar and fine as hell.   Yes I remember Charlie, very well.   It's no surprise you guys got married, you were always joined at the hip.   I hate to hear things didn't work out for you.   How long were you married?"

"Fifteen years, and we've been divorced now for about six months."

"Any kids?"

"No, and we ended it amicably.   We just decided we're better friends than anything else.   I'll miss him, and the sex-"

"Stop it!"

"Girl I ain't gonna lie, the sex was off the hook!   But we'll keep in touch, and I'm looking forward to starting a new chapter in my life.   Enough about me, tell me about you?   I know you married Dorian after we graduated but then you guys just disappeared.   What are you up to these days?"

"After we got married, Dorian got a job offer we couldn't refuse so we moved here."

"You know I always liked Dorian but he was one cocky, high yellow, pretty boy.   What's he up to these days?"

"Unfortunately he was in a car accident at the beginning of the summer."

"Oh my god, is he ok?"   Janel shook her head no.   "Oh Nel, I had no idea.   I'm so sorry to hear that sweetie. How're you doing?"

"I'm not going to lie, it's been tough, but I'm doing ok."

"Now you guys had kids right?"

"We have a son, Dorian Junior.   We call him DJ.   You should see him Rita, he looks just like Dorian did when we were in school.   Spitting image."

"Then he must be a handsome young man because Dorian was fine.   And whatever happened to his friend? Tall dark skin brother, nice looking.   He was always kind of quiet but he was so good looking, and he had the sexiest smile.   I can see his face but I can't think of his name."

Janel grinned at her.   "Tony."

"Yeah, Anthony Gibson, with his fine, shy, quiet ass.   He and Dorian were tight.   Where's he at now?"

"Here, in Lafayette."

"For real?   Is he married?   I bet he is, to some bitch of a woman who doesn't treat him right.   He probably got a few rotten kids too."

"No, he's not married and he doesn't have any children but he's got a girlfriend." Janel twisted her face up to show her distaste.

"Figures.   I take it you don't care for her."

"We won't even go there.   Anyway, he's a lawyer now and he's doing really well.   He's got his own firm, a fifty percent partnership."

"Nice."

"DJ and I are living with him temporarily."

"Why, what's wrong with your place?"

"I had to sell the house.   It was in Clover Hills.   I was a stay at home wife and mother so without Dorian's income, I couldn't afford to keep it.   I've been looking for a job so I can afford to move out of Tony's place."

"How that's going?"

"Actually I just came from an interview and I think I nailed it.   I should find out by this afternoon."

"That soon?"

"It's a bank, a new branch, and they're trying to open up as soon as possible."

"Well good luck.   Girl, it's so good to see you.   I've really missed our friendship, and I hate that we drifted away from one another over the years."

"You have no idea Rita, I know exactly how you feel." Janel was ecstatic at the thought of having a girlfriend in town that she already had history with.   "Hey, you have plans tonight?   Tony and I were going to go out and have a few drinks.   You want to join us?"

"I'd love to but I have a lot of unpacking to do."

"Girl I promise I will come over tomorrow and help you. Come on out with us tonight and have some fun.   Maybe we'll both meet some new people."

# # #

Janel sent Rita a text message asking where she was sitting just as Tony was turning into the parking lot of The Voodoo Lounge. They walked in together and scanned the crowd, searching for her, while Janel kept an eye on her cell phone in case she replied. The place was pleasantly crowded, which wasn't unusual for a Friday evening since they had a live band and some of the best happy hour specials in town. Janel finally spotted Rita waving her arm near the stage. She tugged at Tony's shirt and they made their way over to the pub table. Rita slipped her slender, petite frame off her stool and gave them both a hug.

"Hey beautiful, how've you been?" Tony asked.

"I am doing great. It's so good to see you. You know, with the exception of that little bit of salt and pepper in your beard, you still look the same. Don't get me wrong though, the salt and pepper is sexy." She winked at him and they all sat down. "You guys look so cute together! If I didn't know any better I would swear you were a couple."

"I'm going to head over to the bar and get a drink. You two want something?" Tony asked.

"A Voodoo Doll, please."

"What the heck is that?" Rita asked.

"It's their signature drink, you'll like it. Get her one too please."

"Voodoo Dolls it is. I'll be right back."

As soon as he walked away from the table Rita moved her stool closer to Janel's. "You slept with him didn't you?"

"What?"

"Don't play stupid with me, I know better. You're sleeping with him aren't you? Hell I don't blame you. He looks even better now than he did then."

"Come on Rita, he was Dorian's best friend.   Plus, I told you he has a girlfriend."   Janel tried to deny it but the grin on her face betrayed her.

"Hey, I'm not judging, you two are grown adults.   And unless there's something I don't know about, Dorian ain't going to be coming back anytime soon, God rest his soul. Lord forgive me for that but I gotta tell it like it is.   And if he's got a girlfriend, I can guarantee he ain't thinking nothing about her tonight cause if he was, he'd be with *her* and not here with *you*."

"What makes you so sure I let him hit it?"

"He walked in here with his hand in the small of your back."

"And?"

Rita sighed loudly as if she was losing patience.   "The small of the back is very intimate.   Platonic male friends don't put their hands there, they touch up here near your bra clasp."   She demonstrated by touching her.   "Men who put their hand in the small of your back have either seen your ass, or they hope to soon.   Trust me on that one, you're welcome."

"That's crazy."

"If I'm so crazy, look me in the eye and tell me you haven't slept with him.   I know it's been a while, but I feel like I still know you just as well as I did back when we were roommates."

"Fine, we've slept together, ok?   Damn!"

"I knew it!"

"Don't you say anything when he comes back either."

Rita smacked her hands together.   "I'm crazy huh? Whatever.   So tell me, how was it?"

Janel couldn't stop grinning.   "It was good.   Real good."

"Damn, I knew it!   Girl, I'm happy for you.   It's nice to see something good come out of such a bad situation."

"Don't get too happy.   We just had a little fun is all. We're not a couple."

"Not yet.   Give it time."

Tony returned to the table balancing six drinks in his large hands, two for each of them.   "This ought to tide us over until the waitress gets a chance to stop by."

"You got that right cause she hasn't come over here yet."

Before they could even catch up with each other, the band began to play making it impossible to carry on a conversation.   The dance floor filled quickly, and Tony grabbed Janel by the hand.   "Come on, let's dance."   She followed enthusiastically.   She loved to dance but it wasn't Dorian's thing so she hadn't been in a long time. The band played two upbeat songs, then made an unusual transition to a slower one.   Several couples left the floor to sit down and she turned to follow suit but Tony grabbed her elbow.   "One more?"   He extended his hand to her. She stared at it momentarily before she finally took it and allowed him to lead her back onto the floor.   She placed her hands on his shoulders, expecting to leave some space between them, but he pulled her close.   He placed his hands around her waist, then slid them around slowly until they were finally resting comfortably in the small of her back.

18 – Busted

Tony and Janel didn't leave The Voodoo Lounge until one, putting them back at the house around one fifteen in the morning.   He gently laid his keys on the kitchen counter and they quietly made their way into the living room.

"That boy ate a whole pizza?"   Tony asked, looking at the mess DJ left on the coffee table.

"You've seen him eat before, that shouldn't come as a surprise."   Janel said as she turned off the tv and leaned over to pick up the empty pizza box.

"Leave it.   Make him clean up after himself in the morning."

"I had the best time tonight.   It felt so good to get out and have some fun.   Thank you so much, for everything. The estate sale guy, letting us stay here, getting the case dropped, believing in me when I'm not sure if I believed in myself.   Keeping me from freaking out before my CSC interview!   Everything."

"I'm glad I was able to be there for you."

"Wasn't it good to see Rita again?"   She slipped her shoes off and held them in her hand.

"It was.   I'm glad you'll have her around, I think she'll be good for you.   Now you can say you have *two* real friends here."

"Yep."   She smiled.

"I guess we should probably say goodnight."

She poked him in the chest as she held his gaze with her eyes. "Yep."   He grabbed her around her waist, pulled her to him, and kissed her.   She dropped her shoes and purse on the floor and kissed him back as she wrapped her arms around his neck. He grabbed her butt, like he was palming two basketballs, and lifted her off her feet. She responded by wrapping her legs around his waist, and he carried her into his bedroom and kicked the door closed with his foot. It slammed loudly and he froze. "Don't worry, he sleeps hard. A freight train could come through here and he wouldn't wake up."

He put her down and locked the door, and she began stripping her clothes off. He quickly followed suit as he watched her crawl onto the bed and wait for him to join her. He couldn't wait to be inside of her again, but this time he was going to take his time getting there. He knelt on the bed, between her legs, and wrapped his hand around her left ankle. He bit her calf softly, then kissed it, and she pointed her toes in the air and giggled. He rested her leg on his right shoulder and stroked it as if he were playing an upright bass made of flesh. He ran his hands over her knee, down her warm, firm thigh, and back up to her calf. Her skin was silky smooth and soft, and smelled faintly of cocoa butter. He grabbed her right ankle and put it on his other shoulder, and she flexed her knees, using her legs to pull her butt up off the bed in an effort to try and pull him closer to her. He resisted, and started biting and licking the inside of her leg, making his way further and further down. He pushed her legs apart and massaged her inner thighs, and she rested her feet on the bed, her legs slightly apart. He settled between them, on his stomach, and kissed her from her hip bone to her belly button.

He put his arms around her thighs and pulled her closer, and she closed her eyes and licked her lips. The smell of her was an aphrodisiac, and he wanted to feel her warmth constrict and release around his member, but first he wanted to make sure she was thoroughly satisfied. He wanted to give her a back arching, toe curling orgasm. He licked his index finger and began rubbing her pearl. She grabbed his hand and moaned softly as he allowed her to control the pressure and speed of his every movement. He finally pushed her hand away and replaced his finger with his mouth.   He flicked his tongue back and forth quickly and her hips began to twist and writhe beneath him.   She grabbed his head, pressed her hips against his mouth, and began to grind against him in a rhythmic circular motion.   He could hear her whisper his name as she arched her back, her breath becoming a series of short gasps.

He stuck his tongue between her folds and moved in and out, slowly at first, then picking up speed.   She dug her nails into his shoulders and relaxed her thighs, opening her hips wider so he could go deeper.   He wrapped his lips around her sensitive spot and began to suck, moving his head back and forth from left to right.   He could hear her begin to pant and her breathing quickened.   She let go of his head and called out to him.   "Oh Tony, don't stop." She pulled a pillow over her head and he heard a muffled 'Oh my god, I'm coming' as her thighs tightened against his face and her hips began to jerk upwards.   She threw the pillow on the floor and relaxed her legs as she tried to push his head away, but he tightened his arms around her thighs and stayed put as she writhed on the bed, her hips still spasming with pleasure.   When he finally felt her entire body go limp, he went in for the kill.

He let go of her legs, climbed on top of her, and slipped his tip inside her wetness.   She inhaled sharply, arching her back again.   He quickly thrust himself inside of her and out again, just once, teasing her.   She folded her arms across her face and bit the inside of her arm to keep from crying out.   He plunged himself deep inside of her, forcefully, and stayed there for a moment.   He closed his eyes and leaned his head backwards, letting out a soft moan, as he enjoyed the spasms of her muscles massaging his member.   She opened her eyes and looked at him as she dug her nails into his butt.   It was painful but it turned him on even more, and he started thrusting himself inside of her as hard and fast as he could.   He could feel her walls spasming and contracting against him and he had to stop and catch his breath in order to maintain his stamina.

He kissed her on her mouth, long and slow, as he tried to take his mind off of the sweet release he was working towards.   Then he propped himself up with his arms so he could watch himself slide in and out of her.   He was covered in her wetness.   Suddenly he pulled out of her entirely, and she dug her nails into his thighs in an attempt to pull him back inside.

"Turn over."   He commanded, and she flipped over onto her stomach and drew herself up onto her hands and knees.   "Bring it to me."   She moved backwards, arching her back and pressing her hips towards him.   He smacked her hard on her butt cheek and she cried out, then he slowly ran his hand over the same spot, and he felt her tighten up, anticipating another strike.   He placed his thumbs on her lower back and gripped her waist tightly. He slid inside of her and began thrusting in and out as he admired her from behind.   He stopped and let go of her waist, and she took over, banging her hips against him, harder and harder, faster and faster.

The sweat dripped generously from his body onto her back and her skin glistened in the moonlight that was streaming through his partially open blinds.   He finally had to pull away from her again to keep from climaxing, taking another moment to catch his breath.   She flipped onto her back and pressed her toes into the middle of his chest.   She was smiling up at him, very obviously enjoying herself.   He was aching, throbbing, and wanted to pound into her until he could finally release himself, but not just yet.   He was going to maintain his stamina as much as he could, even if it killed him.   At least he'd die with a smile on his face.   He eased back inside of her, pulled her legs up, her knees almost to her ears and her ass in the air. The position made her feel even tighter than she already was and he was questioning whether or not it had been a good idea.   He struggled to keep from coming so he stopped pumping and quickly released her legs.   He gently bit down on her shoulder to distract himself.   He knew he wouldn't be able to last much longer, especially with the way she was wiggling her hips beneath him.

She whispered in his ear, "come with me," and tightened her muscles around him.   He propped himself up on his elbows and began pounding her as fast as he could, both of them completely covered in sweat, panting and gasping for air.   She grabbed another pillow and put it over her face and yelled into it as her hips began to spasm again with pleasure.   He put his face into the other side of the pillow and bit down on the foam as he moaned loudly and finally came inside of her.   He collapsed on top of her and she flung the pillow aside.   "Oh my god that was so good," she said as she exhaled loudly.   She completely relaxed and kissed him on his forehead.   All he could manage to do was nod his head in agreement, and shortly thereafter he drifted off to sleep, still nestled between her legs.

#

Tony awoke in the morning on his back, with Janel at his side, lying on her stomach.   Her right arm was resting across his torso and her right leg was resting comfortably over top of his.   The covers were on the floor and they were both still naked.   She was breathing deeply, clearly still asleep.   The clock on his nightstand read five after nine, and he could hear DJ banging around in the kitchen. He shook her gently and whispered her name to wake her. She turned away from him towards the window, curled up into a ball, and started to go back to sleep.   "Janel, DJ's awake." He said, putting some bass into his voice.

She sat up with a sense of urgency. "Shit." She rubbed her eyes, sat on the edge of the bed, and wrapped herself in a sheet. "I thought I'd be out of here by the time he got up. I really don't want to have to explain this."

"Then don't." He attempted to rub her back but she pulled away. "You don't owe him any explanation. We're grown."

"He's going to be upset." She got up and started getting dressed.

"Maybe, maybe not."

"Are you kidding me? You're 'Uncle Tony,' his dad's best friend. He loves you but he *idolized* his dad. He was his hero. Your credibility with him is shot now."

"I'm not just some random guy. I care about you and he knows that."

"That's my point Tony. I'm not supposed to be with anyone but his dad, period. What makes this even worse is you were his friend. That makes me, us, especially off limits. We broke the code. The two people he trusts most in this world broke his trust."

"If it were me, I wouldn't say anything." He slipped on his boxers and a t-shirt. "Maybe he doesn't even realize you're in here?"

"Oh come on!"

"He's a guy, sometimes we don't notice things."

She let out a sigh of disgust. "You're not helping."

"I told you what I thought. If he has a problem, let him come to you, and you talk about it then."

"I don't know what I'm going to do." She said as she stood near the door.

"I know what I'm going to do, I'm going to go out there and make some breakfast."

"I need to go shower."

He put a hand on the doorknob. "You ready?" She shook her head yes and he opened the door. The television was on but the living room was empty.   She headed for her room and Tony joined DJ in the kitchen. He was sitting at the breakfast bar eating cereal, toast, and Pop Tarts.

"Morning."   His greeting was met with deafening silence.   "I'm going to make some omelets, you want one?" It was painfully obvious he was being ignored, so he dropped some eggs in a bowl and started whipping them. "Something wrong?"   He finally asked.

"Nope."   His response was dripping with attitude.

"If there is, you know you can talk to me."

DJ dropped his bowl in the sink, put his food on a paper towel, and left the room.

"Where's DJ?"   Janel asked, fresh from her shower.

He shrugged his shoulders.   "I think he knows, and I'm pretty sure he's pissed about it.   He didn't have two words to say to me."

"I should go talk to him."

"Let him be for now.   Give him a chance to calm down. Because I tell you right now, if he pops off and says something crazy to you, as his godfather, I will step in and handle it.   He's allowed to be angry, but I won't let him disrespect you."

"I don't think it'll get to that point, but if it does, I can handle him."

DJ stepped into the kitchen just long enough to say "I'm leaving" and headed towards the front door.

"Hey, hang on a second.   Where are you going?"   She asked.

"Out."

She cocked her head to the side.   "You need to take some of that attitude out of your voice or you won't be going anywhere.   Out *where*?"

"I don't know, to play basketball I guess."

"You need a ride?"   Tony asked.

"No."   He answered, with even more attitude in his

voice.

"Who the hell-"

"I got this."   Tony said, touching his hand to her arm. "I don't know what's going on with you, but if you have something to say, be the man that you think you are and say it.   And make sure you show some respect when you do."

"You want to talk about respect?   What kind of respect did you show my father by sleeping with my mother? You were supposed to be his friend.   And you," he said looking at Janel.   "How could you betray dad like that? Or were you sleeping with him before daddy died?"

She raised her hand and smacked him across his face. "You may not like me, you may not like what I do, but as long as I'm on this earth you will *respect* me.   Don't you *ever* talk to me like that again."

DJ held his cheek as he stared at her in disbelief.   "I'm out of here."   He said before storming off.

19 - Right Place, Wrong Time

Janel sat in her car and tried to mentally prepare for her first day on the job, and put the events of the weekend behind her. When DJ failed to return home and she began to worry, Tony went out after him. And he found him, in Clover Hills, playing basketball with his old friends. And, he was drunk. It was all she could do to keep from choking the boy when they walked through the door, but Tony assured her he would handle it. And the next day, he did, by working the boy so hard that not only did he get sick, but he vowed never to drink again.

She approached the side entrance and tapped on the glass door and a woman opened it for her. "You here for training?"

"Yes."

"Down the hall on the left."

She took a seat in the training room next to a young blonde woman with piercing blue eyes. She smiled at Janel and introduced herself. "Hi, my name is Jenny."

"Janel. Nice to meet you."

They exchanged small talk as the room quickly filled with thirteen other trainees, and exactly on the hour, the trainer walked through the door and up to the front of the classroom.

"Good morning, my name is Miss Anderson, and I'll be training you this week. You'll also notice a gentleman wandering in and out of the classroom at random. His name is Shawn Dixson, he's from the corporate office, and he'll be evaluating the effectiveness of my training sessions so please don't allow his presence to distract you. I have two simple rules.   The first; if you have a question, ask *me*, not your neighbor.   They don't know any more than you do or they wouldn't be here.   And second; be on time, in the morning and when you return from break.   On time means by that clock on the wall, not what's on your cell phone or your watch.   Anyone anticipate having a problem with those two things?   No?   Let's get started."

Janel died a little inside at the thought of having to spend five days being trained by Sherri Anderson, but she vowed to maintain her professionalism and suffer through it.   By the time lunch rolled around and Sherri cut them loose at five minutes till twelve, Janel was more than ready to be away from her, if only for an hour.   She stood up and grabbed her purse, and resisted the urge to run to her car.

"Are you staying for the catered lunch?"   Jenny asked. Before Janel could answer, she felt a tap on her shoulder.

"Can I speak to you for a second?"   Sherri asked, giving Jenny a look that clearly said get lost.   The girl took the hint and excused herself.   Sherri looked around the classroom to make sure it was empty before she spoke.   "I noticed the young lady sitting next to you had a question earlier."

"She missed a step during one of the procedures and I just showed her where she needed to click in order to catch up."

"Are you going to do her work for her too?"

"Excuse me?"

"If she can't keep up during a training class then maybe she's not qualified to handle the position.   And I can't evaluate her ability to comprehend the training materials if you're helping her."

"She missed a step, it took two seconds to catch her up."

"Like I said this morning, if someone has a question they need to ask me.   Next time, tell her to raise her hand so I can assist."

Janel couldn't do anything but stare at the woman, she

was speechless.   Sherri flashed a fake smile, and she knew she was trying to get a rise out of her, but Janel refused to give her the satisfaction.

She responded with her own fake smile.   "If it happens again, I'll be sure to do that.   Is there anything else?   I'd like to grab lunch and I wouldn't want to break your other rule about being late."   Inside she was seething with anger.

"That's it.   Enjoy your lunch and I'll see you back here at one."

Janel couldn't leave fast enough.   She was so angry that she literally had tunnel vision as she focused on getting out of the building as fast as possible.   She made a quick detour to the bathroom to empty her bladder and locked the stall door behind her.   As she relieved herself, she could hear the distinct sound of someone heaving, but trying to do so as quietly as possible.   She could clearly hear the contents of the woman's stomach hit the water, followed by a flush of the toilet.   Janel finished her business and emerged from the stall.   She rubbed the soap between her hands like she was trying to start a fire, rushing so she could be on her way.   The handicapped stall door swung open and out stepped Sherri, looking peaked, her face shiny with perspiration.   Janel turned the water off, her hands still soapy, and tried to blot them dry.

Sherri looked at her through the reflection of the mirror. "I think I had some bad sausage for breakfast."   Janel focused on her hands, refusing to make eye contact with her.   She could care less what was wrong.   She snatched another strip of paper towel from the machine and used it to open the door, then made a beeline for the exit.   She reached out to push the door open and stopped short when she heard someone call her name.   She closed her eyes and fixed her face to hide her annoyance, and with a fake smile, she turned in the direction of the voice to see Perry smiling at her.   Her fake smile quickly turned into a real one as she was genuinely happy to see him.

"You look like you're in a hurry."

"I'm not used to being cooped up in a classroom all day. I just need to get out and get some fresh air."

"I was just headed out myself.   You mind if I tag along?"

"Absolutely not.   I need to get going though, I have to be back before one."

"If you let me drive, I'll make sure of it.   After you." He held the door open for her and they headed to a sandwich shop nearby.

"How's the training going?"   He asked as he bit into an Italian sub.

"Ok.   I think by the end of the week I'll feel completely stir crazy but it's just five days.   I'll manage."

"I was surprised when I didn't hear from you after the interview.   I apologize if my presence distracted you."

"I admit it was a surprise, but I managed.   I got the job right?"

"I wanted to call you this weekend but I was busy with my son, we're working on a project together.   I'm trying to teach him how to do some stuff around the house.   And I haven't quite figured out where I want to take you yet. I'm not the spontaneous type, I'm more of a planner.   I need to make sure I've got my ducks in a row before I ask you out again."

"Taking me to Stella's was spontaneous."

"The circumstances forced me to be spontaneous.   I had to think quickly to find a way to spend some time with you."

"Did you arrange to be on that panel in order to spend time with me too?"

His eyes twinkled when he smiled at her.   "No, but would it have been wrong if I had?   Unfortunately that was forced spontaneity too, someone called out sick so they asked me to step in at the last minute.   I would've called to give you a heads up but I didn't have time."   He took another bite of his sandwich and wiped his mouth.

"Like I said, it worked out."   She picked up her sandwich and took a bite.   "Will you be working over here now or are you staying at the Clover Hills branch?"

"I'm just over here today to help get the office set up. These new guys are very experienced so there's not much training required.   It's just a matter of getting them up to speed on a few CSC nuances."

She shoved the last bite of her sandwich in her mouth and crumpled up the wrapper.   "I've got to get back, I can't be late."   Or Attila the Hun will make an example of me, she thought.   She kept the comment to herself as she had no idea if Perry knew Sherri and what type of interaction they'd had.   He nested his tray on top of hers and set them both on top of the trashcan, then held the door open for her as they headed back to his car.   When they arrived back at CSC, Janel immediately felt eyes on her. Sherri's uninterrupted gaze followed her across the room until she finally reached the hallway where she could no longer be seen.   She went back to the classroom, took her seat, and checked the clock.   They had five minutes to spare, so she made small talk with Jenny while they waited for Sherri to return.   She made a mental note to pack her lunch the rest of the week so she didn't have to stress about being late coming back from lunch.   She refused to give Sherri another reason to reprimand her.

After having spent eight hours with Sherri, the last thing she wanted to do was go home and deal with her son and his attitude.   But she felt the need to in order to relieve the tension in the house.   She wasn't sure what she was going to say, and she hoped the words would come to her. She knew he was upset and hurt, and she could understand why, and she wanted to give him an opportunity to express how he felt in a more calm and respectful manner.   She stopped by the school and picked him up from football practice.   "Hey son."   She said as he got in the car.

"Hey."

"How was your day?"

"Fine."   He said as he turned his head and stared out the window.   She pulled into the driveway and he jumped out of the car before she could even put it in park.   "Hey." She called after him.   He stopped but didn't turn to look at her.

"We need to talk.   Go put your stuff up and meet me out back please."   She walked past Tony in the living room on her way through the house.

"Hey lady, how was your first day?"

"Long.   We sat in a classroom and trained for eight hours."

"Where you headed?"   He asked as she continued on her way to the pool deck.

"I told DJ we need to talk.   I want to clear the air.   I can't take him walking around here with his mouth poked out."

"Should I join you?"

"No.   I'll handle it."

She sat down and took her shoes off as she waited for DJ to join her, and just as she was about to lose patience, he walked through the patio door and sat down.   He refused to look at her, choosing to stare at his hands instead.   "I know that you've been through a lot these past few months. Losing your dad was hard for all of us.   And I know having to move, starting your senior year at a new school, and having to make all new friends has been difficult.   I get that.   And I'm proud of you because you've managed to handle things very well.   But I can't have you walking around here angry and ignoring us.   This is Tony's house, he took us in, and you need to show him some respect.   So let's talk about why you're upset so we can try and move on and get past it."

"I don't understand how you guys could do that to dad. I mean, I know he's gone, but I still I think it's messed up. And wrong."

"Tony and I have spent a lot of time together, trying to take care of things. And we'd been drinking, not that that's an excuse, I guess what I'm trying to say is we didn't plan it, it just happened. And just to clarify, we weren't sleeping together before your dad passed away. I loved your dad, but eventually I'm going to have to move on. That doesn't mean I'm going to move on with Tony, but I'm going to start dating at some point. I don't want to spend the rest of my life alone." He remained silent. "I know you're hurt, and I'm sorry, but can we find a way to move on from this?" He continued to stare at his hands. "Look at me." She waited until his eyes met hers. "Do you have something else you want to say?

"No. Can I go now?"

She gave up and decided to let him deal with it in his own time and in his own way. "Fine, go." She went to her room and changed into her swimsuit. She opened the sliding glass door, took three steps, and dove into the pool. She swam four laps across the pool, trying to shake the stress of the day, before she realized she was being watched. She swam to the side of the pool and took a moment to catch her breath.

"How'd it go?" Tony asked.

"I explained what happened, but he's still upset. He just needs some time." She pushed off the side of the pool and started floating on her back. Tony stripped down to his underwear and dove into the water next to her. "And what exactly did you say happened?" He asked, wiping his face.

"I told him we'd been drinking, things happened, and that we weren't sleeping together before Dorian died."

"What can I do to help?"

"Just give him some time, he'll come around.   He can't stay mad forever."

"I'm not just talking about DJ, I mean overall.   I can see the stress all over your face."

"Help me get my own place.   If I stay here, we'll just end up in bed again, and I can't have my son upset with me. He's all I have left."

"What am I, chopped liver?"

"You know what I mean."

"I know a woman, a realtor.   I can give her a call."

"You know I'm grateful for what you've done for us, but we need our own space.   It's for the best."

"If that's what you want, I'll do what I can to make it happen.   But what happened between us was more than just physical for me.   And I think it was for you too.   Am I wrong?"

"Don't-."

"Am I wrong?"

"Did you break up with Sherri?"   He didn't answer her. "Look, maybe there's....something here, but...the timing is just-"   She shook her head.

"I'll respect that.   I don't like it, but I'll respect it."

20 - The Good, The Bad, and the Ugly

Tony met Mike Foster for dinner again, but he chose Longhorn instead of Ruth's Chris'. He wasn't sure if the information he had on Dorian would be worth another sixty dollar dinner. He chuckled as he thought about Pam and Doug calling him cheap, and he surveyed the menu as he waited for Mike to join him.

"Tony! I apologize for being late, something came up and I couldn't get away."

"No problem, I just sat down. I wasn't sure what you were drinking so I just ordered water. The waitress should be back shortly if you want something stronger."

"What're you having?"

"Water."

"How about I treat you to something a little stronger?"

"I'm not sure if that means you have good news or bad news, but I'll take you up on the offer. I'll have a rum and coke."

They ordered their food and the waitress brought their drinks quickly. "Your food will be out shortly gentlemen."

"So, what've you got for me?"

"Some good and some bad, but nothing earth shattering. You'll be relieved to know it wasn't drugs or gambling, or anything illegal. He just got greedy. He was doing well with some investments, decided to put all of his eggs in one basket, and lost a lot of money. He wasn't a rookie either, so he probably got an insider tip that didn't quite pan out."

"Is that the good news? Cause if it is, I'm going to need another drink before you give me the bad."

"No, you'll like this." He pulled a folded piece of paper

from his jacket pocket and slid it across the table.

Tony studied the document. "Mike, I owe you an apology. When they told me you were expensive, I thought about using someone else. But this right here, this is worth every penny I've paid to you." The document was a photo copy of a life insurance policy, payable to Janel, in the amount of fifty thousand dollars. "I should be buying you a drink for this."

"Nah, it's been my pleasure. I like it when I can give someone good news for a change."

The more Tony talked to Mike, the more he liked him. He was a good guy with a real passion for his job. And he couldn't wait to tell Janel the good news, he knew she really needed to hear it. They finished their meal and walked to the parking lot together.

"Well Tony, I hope I've made you a believer."

"You have, and if I ever need your services in the future, I won't hesitate to give you a call."

Mike gave him a firm handshake. "Appreciate it man. Have a good night."

As Tony got into his car and buckled his seat belt, his phone rang. "This is Tony." There was a hesitation in the line, so he looked at the caller ID, then put the phone back to his ear. "Hello?"

"Are you busy?"

"What do you need Sherri?"

"I was wondering if you could come by so we can talk."

"I tried that, at the restaurant, remember? You didn't have time for me."

"I'm sorry about what happened at the restaurant. I was angry. I don't like when things are like this between us."

"Neither do I, and it's happening too often. I'm tired."

"That's why I want us to sit down and talk, so we can work things out."

"Look Sherri-"

"Just come by.   If you don't want to do this anymore, I understand, but at least be a man about it and come tell me to my face."

"I don't want to argue with you anymore."

"I don't want to argue either.   I just want to try to work things out.   I miss you."

He tapped his fingers on the steering wheel and, against his better judgment, decided to stop by her place.   "I'll be there in about fifteen minutes."

When he arrived at her house, he stood on her front porch for a few minutes, hoping that things would go differently than they had in the past.   He rang the doorbell and she answered quickly.

"Come on in."   She was wearing a tank top, with no bra, and a pair of cut off jean shorts.   She embraced him warmly around the neck and pressed her body against his as she kissed him.   He shut the door and followed her into the living room, his eyes drawn to her latte colored thighs, shapely hips, and her apple shaped ass.   She sat down and crossed one velvety smooth thigh over top of the other. "I'm glad you decided to come by.   It's good to see you, I've missed you."

He sat on the opposite end of the couch and tried to focus on what she had to say, but he found himself distracted by her body.   He had to admit he missed her physically, and just wanted to take her into her bedroom and have some of the best makeup sex he'd had in a long time.   And while he hoped that might be a possibility for the way the evening might end, he refused to lose sight of the real reason he'd agreed to stop by; to determine if they had a future together.   He needed the conversation to progress quickly, as he was developing a hard on and he wasn't sure how much longer he could hide it.   He readjusted himself, maintained his poker face, and waited for her to continue.

"I just wanted to start off by saying I'm sorry about

Dorian.   I know I wasn't one of his favorite people, but like you said, it's not about me.   I know how close you two were, and I should've made more of an effort to be there for you."

He could hardly believe what he was hearing.   This was not the same woman he'd been dating for the past two years.   She never admitted she was wrong, and getting an apology from her was like trying to get a mule to go someplace it didn't want to go.   Hearing her apologize gave him hope that maybe they could work things out and move forward after all.

"In fact, you were right about everything you said at the restaurant.   And I've been doing a lot of thinking lately, about my behavior.   I was so upset when you let Janel and DJ move in without telling me.   I was upset because I felt disrespected.   But when I sat back and really thought about what you did, it was such a selfless thing to do. Honestly I don't know too many men who would've done that.   And that's the kind of man I want to be with. Someone thoughtful, and caring.   So I just want to say I'm sorry.   For everything.   And I hope we can give this relationship another chance."

He wanted to ask where the hidden cameras were.   Not that he didn't think she was sincere, but working through rough patches with her was never this easy.   In fact, things were going so smoothly that he found himself at a loss for words, which was a rarity for him.

She stared expectantly at him.   "Say something Tony. You know that this isn't easy for me.   You heard me right? I was wrong and you were right.   You win.   I don't know what else you want me to say."

"I heard you.   And it's not about winning, or telling me what you think I want to hear.   It's about...not arguing all the damn time."

"You forgive me?"

"I forgive you."

"Can we move on to the makeup sex now?"

"If that's what you want to do, I'm not going to argue with you." He joked. She jumped in his lap and began kissing him while she unbuttoned his pants. "Why don't we take this into the bedroom?" She agreed, taking him by the hand and eagerly leading the way.

He got up early the next morning, before sunrise, showered quickly, and got dressed. One of the first thoughts to cross his mind was whether or not Janel was worried about him not coming home. And while he'd enjoyed himself with Sherri, he couldn't deny the fact that he spent most of the time fantasizing that he was with Janel again. In fact, he'd come dangerously close to calling out her name, which would have been disastrous. As jealous as Sherri was, it probably would have resulted in her attempting to slice off his manhood.

"Why are you up so early?" She mumbled from under the sheets.

He walked over and gave her a quick kiss. "I've got a few things to take care of today. The early bird gets the worm, right?"

She mumbled something, turned over, and snuggled back under the covers.

Despite thinking about Janel, for the first time in a long time he was hopeful about his future with Sherri. He sat down on the edge of the bed and placed his hand on her back. "Hey, how about we go to New Orleans for a weekend? Catch some live music, eat some good food. You could go shopping on Magazine street." She turned and looked at him. "We'll get a hot tub suite. What do you think?"

"When?"

"Friday. Pack a bag and I'll pick you up from work."

# # #

Tony felt silly sneaking into his own house, but he still made an effort to slip into his home as quietly as he could. It was still too early for DJ or Janel to be up so he was hoping he could go in unnoticed, as if he'd been there the entire night.   He pulled off his shoes and moved quietly through the kitchen into the living room, where Janel was sitting on the couch, yawning and stretching her back. She looked at him and he stopped dead in his tracks, like a teenager caught by his parents trying to sneak in after curfew.

"Good morning."   She whispered.

"Hey."   There was a moment of awkward silence as they looked at one another.   "I'm sorry, I probably should've called."

"Oh, this isn't what it looks like.   I wasn't waiting up, I was watching a movie and fell asleep."   She stood up and rubbed the sleep from her eyes.   "Besides, you don't have to tell me when you're not coming home.   I'm just a temporary house guest and we're both grown."

Her words stung a little.   He thought of her and DJ as much more than temporary house guests.   "You're going to be sleepy in class today.   I know you didn't get a good night's sleep out here.   I should know, I've spent the night on that couch more times than I care to admit."

She winced as she stretched her lower back.   "I'll be fine.   It's nothing a few cups of coffee and ibuprofen can't fix."   She looked at the clock.   "Although I do have a little time to get some sleep before I leave."

"You want some breakfast?"

"No thanks.   Maybe you can make some for DJ as a peace offering.   He'll be up soon."

"He hasn't had more than two words to say to me.   I'm

still very much a traitor in his eyes."

"That makes two of us, he's not saying much to me either.   He's stubborn, just like his daddy.   But he'll come around eventually and you two will be back to being best buds again."

"I hope so."

"I'm going to go lay down, try to get a little sleep."

"Just a heads up, I'm going to New Orleans this weekend."

"Good, I'm glad to hear you're doing something fun with your time off."

"I'm taking Sherri."

"It's none of my business who you're taking.   You don't owe me any explanation."

"I just don't want you to be worried when you don't see me around this weekend."

"If I'm ever worried about you, I'll call you or text you. If nothing else I know you always have your cell phone with you.   Does this mean you two worked things out?"

Tony shrugged his shoulders.   "Working towards it, I guess."

"Great.   If you're happy, I'm happy.   I'll see you later today, ok?"

As Tony stood in the kitchen trying to decide what he wanted for breakfast, DJ appeared from around the corner. "Morning.   You want some breakfast?"

"Don't have time, I'll miss the bus."   He concentrated on tying up his shoes in order to avoid eye contact.

"I can take you to school if you want.   It's not like I have to be at work."

"No thanks."   He said, flippantly, as he searched for something in his backpack.

"Look, I can deal with you being upset with me, but you really need to give your mom a break.   She's got a lot on her plate right now, and you being upset with her isn't making things any easier."

He zipped his backpack and headed for the door.   "I need to go."

"You may not think so because I'm not always here, but I know exactly when your bus comes.   And I know you have at least twenty minutes."

"What do you want?"   He said, with attitude.

"For you to grow up and lose the attitude.   What happened between me and your mom happened, let it go. You have no idea what she's been through, and I'm not going to stand by and watch you treat her like crap.   She deserves better than that."

"My dad was good to her, and she didn't waste any time stabbing him in the back by sleeping with you."

"Unfortunately your dad is gone, and he's not coming back."

"I wouldn't sleep with my best friend's girlfriend.   Even if he broke up with her.   That's the rule, you don't go there."

"It's not like we got together and said 'hey let's sleep together and make DJ really mad at us.'"

"He would've never done that to her.   Or you."

"How can you be so sure?   What makes you think your dad was so perfect?"

"I just know.   He wouldn't have done that."

"Your dad died on his way to sleep with another woman. He was cheating on your mom."

DJ stared at him.   "You're lying."

"Shit."   Tony immediately regretted having opened his mouth, and he could see the boy was devastated.   "I'm sorry, I shouldn't have said that."

"That's not true.   Why would you lie like that?"

"You know I've never lied to you."

"You're lying!   My dad wouldn't cheat on my mom. He loved her."

"He did.   He was a good man, but he wasn't perfect. And your mom isn't either.   The point is it's not fair for you to sit around judging her when she's been busting her butt trying to fix your dad's mistakes and take care of you." As he watched DJ turn and run out the door, he wondered just how much shit he was going to be in when Janel found out what he'd just done

21 - Don't Screw This Up

"What's been going on? I haven't heard from you all week." Rita asked Janel as she took a bite of her chili dog. They were sitting in the bleachers, waiting for DJ's football game to begin. She'd heard that McKinley was one of Middlebranch's biggest rivals and it was evident by the size of the crowd that was quickly filling the bleachers.

"My week started off with a bang. I started training for my new job on Monday. I walk in the classroom, and we're waiting for the instructor, and guess who walks in?"

"Beats me, you know I don't know anyone."

"Sherri." Rita stared at her blankly. "Tony's girlfriend."

"Oh no."

"Oh *yes.* So during class, the young lady sitting next to me asks me a quick question. I lean over and answer her. No big deal right? We break for lunch and Sherri gives me a lecture. She tells me if the girl can't keep up during training then she may not belong there, and that if I keep helping her she won't be able to evaluate her 'comprehension of the training materials.' It took everything in me not to reach out and choke her."

"Please tell me she's not going to be your supervisor?"

"Hell no, thank goodness. But she will be evaluating my work for the next few months, and discussing my progress with my supervisor."

"You need to watch your back."

"Yeah I know. Especially now that they're back together."

"What do you mean they're 'back' together?"

"They weren't talking for a while, but they got back together this week."

"What did you do?"

"What do you mean 'what did I do?'"

"I saw the way he looked at you Friday night, and he wasn't thinking about his girlfriend or anyone else.   You guys had so much fun together.   If he made up with his girlfriend, it means you did something.   Tell me what happened after you left the lounge, and don't leave anything out."

"We went home-"

"And slept together.   Any fool could see that coming. You guys were all over each other on the dance floor."

"Girl, it was good.   I wanted to roll over and suck my thumb when he was done."

"Ok we'll come back to that later because I do want the dirty details.   What else happened?"   She wiped mustard from the corner of her mouth with a napkin.

"We fell asleep, and he woke me up in the morning to let me know DJ was awake."

"Dang, so you got busted?"

"Yep.   It wasn't pretty.   I tried talking to him but he's still upset."

"Of course he is, he probably feels betrayed.   He'll come around though, he can't stay mad forever."

"That's what I said.   Um, we got in the pool, he said I looked stressed, and he asked me how he could help.   I told him the best way to help me was to help us get our own place so that we wouldn't be tempted to sleep together anymore."

"I have a feeling this is where things went south.   And what did he say?"

"He said it wasn't just a physical thing for him, and he asked me if I felt the same way."

"I'm almost afraid to ask, but what did you say?"

"I told him it didn't matter because he's still seeing

Sherri and the timing is all wrong."

"No wonder he went back to his girlfriend!   He bared his soul to you and you crushed him!"

"Come on Rita, what do we look like trying to have a real relationship.   We can't go there."

"Why not?"

"Because.   What would people think?   And it would crush DJ."

"Are you kidding me?   Who cares what anyone else thinks.   And why do DJ's feelings matter so much?"

"He's my son!   You just said yourself how he probably feels like we betrayed him."

"And I also said he'll get over it.   He's not a little kid anymore.   He may not want to think about it but momma's got needs and daddy is gone.   Besides, he'll be off to college before you know it, and he won't care who you're dating."

"I can't chance losing him, he's all I have left."

"And what is Tony, chopped liver?"

"That's exactly what he said."

"You actually *said* that to him?   Now I see why he went running back to Sherri."

"I misspoke!   I didn't mean to hurt his feelings!   I just meant I lost the house and-"

"You rejected him *and* hurt his feelings, so he went back to the devil he knows."

"I just think it would be...weird."

"How?   You've already slept with him!"

"That's physical.   An actual relationship is different."

"You messed up.   He's a good man, he's never been married, he doesn't have kids, and he makes good money. Even better, you've known him for years and he's crazy about you!   And you're sweet on him too.   I don't know why you won't admit it."

"I've got enough on my plate right now just trying to make a new life for myself.   Maybe after I-"

"Ooooh!   I could just shake you right now!"   Rita balled up her fists and shook them at her.   "You need to go to him, apologize, and tell him how you really feel."

"It's too late now.   He's on his way to New Orleans with Sherri as we speak."   Janel's phone vibrated with a text message from Perry.

You at the game?

She responded: Yes.

Perry: Where?

Janel: Under the scoreboard, top row.   Where are you?

Perry: Look down to your left.

She saw him waving his hand and she waved back.
"Who is *that* piece of caramel delight?"
"Perry.   He's DJ's friend's dad, he works at CSC."
"You work with *him*?"
"He's at another branch.   He's the loan officer I dealt with when my house was about to go into foreclosure."
"Foreclosure?   You didn't tell me all that, you just said you had to sell the house."
"When Dorian passed, we were four months behind on the mortgage.   Don't ask why, I don't know, that's a story for another time.   Anyway, we've been out to eat together a few times, and he's made it clear he'd like to get to know me better."
"Good.   Hopefully you won't screw things up with him as badly as you screwed them up with Tony.   When are you guys going out again?"
"I don't know.   He said he'd call me."
"When he does, try not to mess it up.   Think of him as

your Plan B."

The game was intense and ended in a three point win for Middlebranch.   Both boys had a good game, with DJ accomplishing two interceptions and PJ making the play of the night by sacking McKinley's quarter back.   After the game, Janel observed her usual routine of staying put and letting DJ find her.   It was especially important this particular night because the crowd was elbow to elbow thick.   So much so that police presence had been increased for the historic rivalry and they were aggressively encouraging people to move along.   Janel spotted Perry and a woman moving against the crowd and climbing the bleachers towards them.   She was beautiful, model beautiful, with a perfect white smile and unbelievable (or maybe un-be-weave-able) hair.   Her skin was flawless and she wore very little makeup.

"Janel, this is my ex-wife Ayana.   Ayana, this is DJ's mother, Janel."

Just looking at the woman made Janel feel ugly.   Her legs were long and lean and she had large doe eyes and high cheek bones.   She was slender but had curves in all the right places.   If this is what she looked like in shorts and a tank top, she couldn't imagine what she looked like all dressed up with someplace to go.

"It's so nice to finally meet you.   DJ's a great kid, you've done a wonderful job raising him."

"Thank you.   This is my friend Rita, Rita this is Perry and-"

"His ex-wife, Ayana.   Got it.   Nice to meet you." Ayana nodded hello and Perry shook Rita's hand.

"It was nice meeting you ladies but I've got someplace I need to be.   Perry, can you walk me to my car?"

He looked at Janel, as if he were asking permission with his eyes, and Rita looked at Janel to see what her reaction would be.   "Can I call you later?"   He asked Janel.

"Sure."

"Goodnight ladies, have a good evening."   Ayana said as slipped her arm through Perry's, and Janel and Rita watched them walk down the bleacher steps together.

"That wasn't awkward at all."   Rita quipped sarcastically.   "He hangs out with his ex-wife?   Who does that?   He's cute and all but damn."

"Look at the pot calling the kettle black.   You and Chuck are still friends."

"Touché."

"At least they have a legitimate reason.   I think it shows a lot of maturity for them to be able to come together peacefully for the sake of their son."

"She's not being amicable, she wants him back.   In case you weren't paying attention, that was a power play.   She wanted to let you know that he'll do whatever she asks him to, because they have history together."

"She'll never get him back, she hurt him too badly.   He caught her cheating on him, in their house, in their bed."

"That's not going to stop her from trying.   And never say never.   You need to watch her."

DJ appeared at the base of the bleachers with his buddy PJ in tow.   He waved at her, which was surprising, because he was still on minimal speaking terms with her. When her foot touched the last stair, she asked him if he was ready to go.

"I was hoping I could hang out with PJ for a little bit, to celebrate."

"You haven't had more than two words to say to me all week.   Why should I let you hang out anywhere?"

Rita elbowed her.   "They did have a really good game Janel."

"I hope you don't think you're taking my car?"

"I have my mom's car tonight Miss Janel.   My dad took her home."

"Go on.   And you better have your butt home before

eleven." As soon as the boys were out of earshot, Rita spoke up.

"Didn't she say she had someplace to be? And yet she conveniently gave up her car so the boys could go out tonight. I'm sure it had nothing to do with luring her ex-husband to her house for some post game activities. I wouldn't count on getting a call from him tonight."

"That's pure speculation on your part. We don't know what happened. Maybe PJ got the story wrong."

"I speculate she's trying to cock block."

"Let it go Rita, I'm not worried about it."

"Ok. Let's go to The Voodoo Lounge and have a few drinks. You could use one after the week you've had."

The lounge was packed but they were still able to score a two person table along the wall and order drinks from the waitress. While they were waiting, Janel felt her phone vibrating so she checked the display. It was Perry calling. She rejected the call and immediately sent him a text message.

Janel: Can't pick up. At The Voodoo Lounge. The band is playing.

Perry: Sounds fun. Mind if I join you?

Janel: Will you be bringing Ayana along too?

She immediately regretted sending the message. He didn't know her well enough to know she was kidding and it probably came across as petty and jealous. He responded quickly.

Perry: Dropped her off a long time ago. Keep in mind she is my ex. I'm moving forward in my life, not backwards.

Janel: I was just kidding about Ayana.   Didn't mean anything by it.

Perry: There's usually some truth behind every 'just kidding,' but it's ok.   We were supporting our son, nothing more.   I apologize if seeing us together was off-putting. I'd really like to see you.

She showed the text messages to Rita.   "You know, you really suck at this dating thing."
"I haven't dated in almost eighteen years.   I don't know what I'm doing."
"I was married for a long time too but I'm not as bad at this as you are.   Tell him to come down here.   He's obviously trying to get next to you so let him.   Especially since you jacked things up with Tony."   She snatched the phone, entered a reply, and hit send.
"What did you just do?"   Janel checked her phone to see what she'd sent.

Janel: Come on down, I'd really like to see you too.

He responded immediately with 'Great, on my way.' She looked up and smiled at her friend.
"I got your back girl.   I refuse to let you screw this one up."
Perry showed up twenty minutes later, and Rita did something that completely took Janel by surprise.   She stood up and grabbed her purse.
"Have a seat, I'm heading home.   I've got a stack of projects waiting for me that I've got to get graded before Monday."
"You're my ride.   You're just going to leave me here?"
"I'm sure Perry will see you home safely.   He seems like a total gentleman."
"Let me walk you to your car."

"See?   Perfect gentleman.   Thank you for asking but I'll have security walk me to my car, I'll be fine.   Have a seat."   She gave her friend a hug and spoke into her ear. "I want a full report in the morning.   Don't blow this."

The night passed quickly and before Janel knew it, she and Perry were standing on Tony's porch again, at two in the morning.

"I had fun tonight."   He confessed.

"Me too.   I love that place."

"I'd really like to take you some place where we can carry on a conversation.   Can I take you to dinner tomorrow?"   He glanced down at his watch.   "Or later on today.   Technically it's Saturday morning."

"Sure."

"I'll pick you up at seven."

"What should I wear?"

"I'd love to see you in a dress, not black tie formal, but nice.   Halfway between a sun dress and a prom dress. You know?"

She smiled.   "I think so."   She had butterflies in her stomach.

"Sooo, I guess this is goodnight."   He leaned in to kiss her on the cheek, and she could hear Rita's voice in her head telling her not to screw things up.   She turned her head and kissed him on the lips.   He put his hands around her waist and pulled her closer.   His lips were soft, and his cologne made him smell like he was fresh out of the shower.   She was tempted to invite him in, and thankful that her son was inside to serve as a deterrent.   He pulled himself away and exhaled loudly.   "Whoo!   I'll never make it home if we keep doing that.   I'll see you later tonight, ok?"   He made sure she got inside safely before he walked back to his car and pulled away.

22 - Shit or Get Off the Pot

Tony couldn't believe he'd spent an entire weekend with Sherri, in New Orleans, without them having a single disagreement let alone a full blown argument.   He wasn't sure what it was, if she was well rested or was wearing new makeup or what, but she looked really good.   She was a beautiful woman, no doubt, but he found himself even more attracted to her than usual.   And he didn't know if he was just horny as hell or if it was because they'd been apart for so long but the sex was incredible.   It was definitely a step above their normal sexual relations, and they'd had a lot of it.   She couldn't keep her hands off of him.   In fact, they spent more time in the room than they did experiencing the city.   Which was ok with him because it meant he didn't have to spend a lot of money on her shopping sprees.   He calculated the cost of the entire weekend and decided he'd gotten off relatively easy.   He bought her a pair of shoes and a couple of dresses totaling a little less than eight hundred dollars.   And it was worth every penny to be back in her good graces and to be able to relieve the tension between the two of them, both physically and mentally.

They left early Sunday morning and it was a gorgeous day, so they took their time driving back.   They had the sun roof open and the windows down, and Sherri insisted on driving the first leg of the trip.   The fresh air, coupled with the white noise of the wind, lulled Tony right to sleep, but it wasn't long before he found himself waking up again. He opened his eyes to see why they were slowing down, and saw that they were pulling into a rest stop.

"What's up?"

"I gotta pee."

He looked at his watch.   "We haven't even been on the road thirty minutes."

"I had all that orange juice at breakfast."

"Women."   He joked.

"Well I'm sorry I can't just pull over and whip my penis out on the side of the road, or pee in a bottle like a neanderthal."

"Whoa.   Where did that come from?   I was just joking Sherri.   We had a great weekend, let's not spoil it now by getting into a senseless argument."   She got out of the car and slammed the door.   She returned ten minutes later and they got back on the road.   He was unable to get back to sleep, so he pulled out his phone and began checking his work email.   Finally, he decided to finally break the silence.   "I'm thinking about going back to work tomorrow.   The holidays will be here before you know it, and business usually starts picking up around Halloween." She continued to drive in silence, eyes concentrating on the road.   He wondered if she had a case of PMS, or if this was a sign of things to come and she hadn't changed a bit.   The last thing he wanted was for things to go back to the way they were.   He decided to make the conversation about her in an attempt to get her talking again.   "By the way, before I forget, I wanted to thank you for helping Janel.   I know she was really relieved to finally get hired on somewhere."

She remained quiet for a moment before she finally responded.   "Like you said, she's smart and has a degree. It wasn't hard, she was an easy sell.   She did ok with the initial training too."

Training.   How could he forget?   It suddenly dawned on him why Janel had been so stressed all week.   She'd just spent five days training with Sherri for eight hours a day.   Thinking about Janel made him want to call her, but he knew he couldn't without causing more drama with

Sherri.   He decided to send her a text message instead.

Tony: You there?

Janel: Yes.

Tony: Why didn't you tell me you've been training with Sherri all week?

It took a few minutes to receive a response from her.

Janel: Why would I?   I behaved and it was uneventful.   I'm not trying to catch another case.   :-)

Tony: Funny.   On my way home.   I should be there in another hour or so.

Janel: Thanks for the warning.   I'll make sure the house is clean from the party we had while you were gone.

Tony: You're just full of jokes today, aren't you?

Janel: Be careful and I'll see you when you get back.

"Who are you texting?"
"Doug.   I'm letting him know I'll probably be in tomorrow."
"Why don't you just call him?"
"Cause if I do I know I'll never get off the phone with him.   I know you don't want to listen to us talking about boring lawyer stuff for the next forty-five minutes."
She seemed satisfied with his explanation, and he turned his attention back to his email in an attempt to try and catch up with what was going on.   They didn't say more than five words to each other the remainder of the trip, and he was thankful for the peace and quiet.   He dropped her

at her place, carried her bag inside, and gave her a hug and a kiss.   He hurried home but was disappointed when he turned the corner and saw Janel's car missing from the driveway.   He pulled into the garage and couldn't deny the fact that he was really looking forward to seeing her. They'd spent so much time together after Dorian's death, and this was the first time they'd been away from each other for more than a couple of hours.   Admittedly, he'd missed her.   He was surprised when he opened the door and smelled food cooking.   A smile spread across his face and he was happy to be home.   He dropped his overnight bag near the door and headed straight for the kitchen.

"Hey.   I didn't think anyone was here when I didn't see your car in the driveway."

"DJ has it.   He's out somewhere with PJ, probably at the mall.   He had a really good game Friday so I let him go out and celebrate a little bit."

"He talking to you yet?"

"Not past the basics."

"That kid is stubborn."

"Just like his daddy.   At least with Dorian he'd tell you why he was so pissed off and get it out of his system. With DJ, he holds it in for a while."

"Yep, he got his stubborn streak straight from Dorian, because you're not stubborn at all.   Right?"

"Smart ass."

"You should've let him sit in his room and suffer, thinking about all the fun he could've had with his friends. Especially after I had to bring him home drunk from Clover Hills."

"I let him go for me, not him.   I was tired of him walking around here with his face all screwed up and I wanted some quiet time for myself.   I just wanted him out of the house and out of my hair."

"I watched the highlights from the game online.   He's going to have recruiters coming after him soon.   When they do, let me know.   Some of them will say anything to sign a player, and most of them don't have DJ's best interests at heart.   College football is big business, it generates a lot of money."

"I'll be sure to redirect anyone to you.   And I hope they start calling soon, because I certainly can't afford to pay for his education."

"You won't have to.   If he doesn't pick up a sports scholarship, he'll get an academic one for sure."

"How was your weekend?"

"Ok."

"How much did it cost you to get back in her good graces?"

"Surprisingly enough, shopping wasn't very high on her list of priorities so I got off easy.   We had coffee and beignets at Cafe Du Monde, shrimp Po-boys in the Quarter, and listened to some live music at The Howlin' Wolf."

"I've only been to New Orleans once, and it was with Dorian on business so I didn't get to see or do a whole lot."

"We should go sometime.   It's a great town, we'd have fun."

"Yeah right."   She scoffed.   "I'd like to see you run that one by Sherri, the two of us going to New Orleans together."

"How was your weekend?   I hope you didn't spend it cooped up in this house?"   He asked, purposefully changing the subject.

"It was ok."   She turned her back to him and plugged one side of the sink in order to start running dish water.

"I keep telling you I have a dishwasher for that.   And that's a sink full of dishes, so don't tell me it's easier to do them by hand.   You gotta help me start using that thing. I've heard they go bad if you don't.   I never made enough dirty dishes to use it when I was living by myself.   That's why you and DJ should stay around a little longer."

"To help you with your dish washer problem?"   She giggled.   "Sounds serious."

"Don't laugh, it is serious.   Hundreds of dishwashers go bad every year due to neglect and non-use.   I've seen the statistics, it's a real epidemic."   She laughed as he walked up behind her and attempted to pull a dirty dish from the sink.   She stuck her butt out and used it to try and fend him off, but he caught her around her waist and pulled her close to him.   He nuzzled his face in her hair and inhaled deeply.   He loved the way she smelled, and he missed that smell over the weekend.   He brushed his lips against the warm skin of her neck and she dug her nails into his arm and inhaled sharply.   He pressed himself against her so she could feel his rising erection and he whispered in her ear.   "You want me to stop?   Tell me."

He flicked her earlobe into his mouth with his tongue and sucked on it sensuously.   She maintained her grip on his arm but no words fell from her lips.   He slid his hand down between her legs and she pressed it against herself and started to grind against it.   "I take it you missed me too?"   He asked, as he started to grind himself against her butt.   "Turn around."   She did as she was told, and he kissed her as he slipped his hands under her shirt and up her back to unfasten her bra.   He unbuttoned her shorts, then shoved his hands inside her panties and squeezed her butt as hard as he could.   She pushed her shorts and panties down around her hips until they finally fell to the floor.

She snaked her tongue in and out of his mouth and sucked on his lips as she pulled down his shorts and underwear and took hold of his manhood.   He picked her up and put her on the edge of the counter and she eagerly spread her legs.   She wrapped them around his waist as he shoved himself inside of her.   She groaned loudly and he hooked his arms under her knees, giving himself full, unobstructed access to her.   He began pounding himself into her, and the sound of their skin smacking together echoed throughout the kitchen.   "Damn you feel so good. I want to come already." He could feel her muscles beginning to spasm around his member so he decided to let go and allow himself to orgasm. They both moaned out loud as they came together. He felt her legs finally go limp, and he released them as he pulled himself from her. She slipped slowly down off the counter and steadied herself on the floor.

"That was so good."

"This is crazy, we can't keep doing this. DJ could walk in here at any minute. A little help?" She gestured towards her bra as she pulled her shorts back on and buttoned them up.

"If it's so crazy, why didn't you tell me to stop? You can't tell me you didn't want that too." He said as he pulled his underwear and shorts on.

"That's not the point. This is the reason why I need to move out of here as soon as I can." She finished getting dressed.

The front door opened and closed, and they heard the metallic jingle of keys. DJ appeared in the room minutes later. "Hey." He said as he chucked the keys onto the kitchen counter.

Surprised to hear him open his mouth, Tony responded. "Hey."

Janel lunged for the cabinet doors under the sink and grabbed a bottle of cleanser. She began spraying and wiping down the counter tops like a germaphobe, her arm moving in small, quick circles as if she was trying to wipe the color right off of the marble. "I made spaghetti and garlic bread with cheese if you're hungry."

"Hey man, I'm sorry I missed your game but I was out of town for the weekend. I saw the highlights though, and I noticed your name was mentioned. You're looking better this year, you're definitely a lot faster."

He mumbled a quick thanks and headed towards his room.

Janel stopped wiping and put her hand on her forehead. "You need to keep your dick in your pants. What if he walked in here and caught us?"   She whispered.

"You could just say no."

"Obviously not!   I thought you were trying to work things out with Sherri?"

"I am."

"You could've fooled me."

"You're the one that put your butt on me.   You can't just go throwing that thing around all willy nilly.   That thing is lethal."

"Ooohhh!   *We can't do this anymore* Tony.   I'm serious.   If you're going to be with Sherri then be with her.   This counts as cheating too you know."

"And what if I'm not sure about working things out with her?"

"Oh for goodness sake would you shit or get off the pot already?   Either you're going to be with her or not, it shouldn't have anything to do with me or anyone else for that matter."

"It doesn't.   I just don't know if I want to keep seeing her or not.   I'm not going to lie, I care about her, but I have my doubts about things getting better between us.   I don't know if I have the strength to walk away from her just yet." They stood in the middle of the kitchen and stared at one another.   "I've laid my cards on the table Janel, I've shown you my hand.   I don't know what else to say."

"There isn't anything else to say.   I've got dishes to wash."   She turned her back to him and put her hands back in the water.

He started towards his room but stopped in the doorway.   "I had fun this weekend, but you know what they say, there's no place like home."

"I know, that's why I'm trying to find one."

23 - There is No Santa Claus

"The realtor has some houses she'd like to show you this evening. Is that good for you or would another night work better?"

"No, tonight's good. What time?" Janel asked.

"Five o'clock?"

"That'll work. Text me the address and I'll meet you there."

She watched Tony get out of his car as she pulled up to the realtor's office, his tailored suit hanging just right on his frame. "Stop it." She told herself as her mind began to wander to places it shouldn't go. He opened her door for her and they walked into the office together.

"Hi I'm Diane, it's so nice to finally meet you. Tony and I have been talking quite a bit over the last few days and I think I've found some houses that might be right up your alley as far as price. It's definitely a buyer's market right now, I just need to get a feel for what you like. If you don't see anything you like today, it's ok, because at least I'll have a better idea of what you're looking for. Then the next time we meet the houses should be closer to what you're looking for." She licked the tip of her finger and flipped through some papers on her desk. "I've got four houses to show you tonight. Is that ok? Are you ok on time?"

"That's fine."

"Great, let's get started. You're welcome to ride with me or feel free to take your own car, I won't be offended."

"You lead and we'll follow." Tony told her.

It didn't take long for the realtor to show Janel all four homes and she wasn't moved by any of them.   As they stood in the living room of the fourth house chatting, she was visibly disheartened, and Tony asked the realtor to excuse them for a moment so they could talk.

"Obviously you haven't seen anything you like.   Is it really the houses or are you worried about the money?"

"Are you serious?   Did you see that last one?   It may as well have had wood paneling on the walls and a beaded curtain leading into the living room to go with all that nasty 70's shag carpeting.   The last thing I need is a fixer upper. My life is a fixer upper right now."

"She said she could show you some other places once she got a feel for what you're looking for so don't lose hope. It's just four houses, I'm sure there are plenty more.   Just give her some specifics and we'll meet with her again in a couple of days."

"I don't really have any specifics, other than it needs to be zoned for Middlebranch.   I just know that I'll know it when I see it."

"Excuse me?"   Diane poked her head around the corner.   "Sorry, I don't mean to interrupt, but I just thought of a house I'd like to show you if you're interested. It's really nice and it's priced to move."

"What's wrong with it?"   Tony and Janel asked in unison.

She cleared her throat.   "In the interest of full disclosure and in accordance with the law, I have to tell you there was a death in the home."

"Oh hell no.   No thanks, I'll pass."   Janel threw her hand up and shook her head.

"Hear me out now before you say no.   It wasn't a suicide or anything, nothing gruesome.   The home was owned by an elderly couple, and the wife took sick.   She passed away in the living room, in a hospital bed, under hospice care."

"How far away is it?"

"It's close, a five minute ride.   I promise you it's a really beautiful home Mrs. Monroe.   I wouldn't even bring it up if I didn't think it was a good fit.   The couple's children have put a lot of money into it in order to attract buyers in spite of what happened, remodeled it top to bottom. They all have homes and live out of state, and don't want to hassle with renting it.   They just want to get rid of it."

Janel looked to Tony.   "It won't hurt to take a look." He suggested.

"Let me tell you, even if I were superstitious I'd buy this house.   It's one hell of a deal."   Diane encouraged.

"Well I'm not superstitious so let's go take a look." Janel suggested and they followed Diane to the home.   She parked her car along the curb and Tony pulled into the driveway.   Janel smiled as she got out of the car, it really was a nice home.   Diane started trying to tell her about the high points but Janel tuned her out as she stepped up onto the porch and admired the landscaping, which someone obviously put a lot of money and back breaking effort into.   She knew this was the one, without even setting foot inside.   It just felt right to her.

"Obviously there's this great wraparound veranda which I just love.   There are two bedrooms upstairs with a full bath between them.   There's a loft that overlooks the great room, which has a fabulous floor to ceiling fireplace. It has beautiful hardwood floors throughout that are original to the house, and they've recently been refinished. The master bedroom is in the back of the house, on the main floor, and has French doors that open onto the veranda.   It has a fully renovated bath with his and hers sinks, a two person jacuzzi tub, a stand-alone shower, and private toilet.   There's also a combination mud room and laundry room with half bath at the rear of the house that opens onto a porch.   And wait till you see this porch, it's like having your own little private garden retreat.

Personally I think it's the best part of the house.   The backyard is partially fenced in on one side, courtesy of the neighbors, so if you wanted to fully enclose it, it wouldn't cost too much.   This house is zoned for Middlebranch high school, the crime rate is low, and this is an established neighborhood so everyone pretty much knows everyone on this street.   You'll have great neighbors too, so I'm told." Janel held up her hand to signal Diane that she'd heard enough.   "Ok well, take a look around and if you have any questions I'll be out front.   I have a few phone calls to make so feel free to take your time."

Janel made her way up the stairs and wandered into the bedrooms and full bath.   She stood near the railing, looked down on the great room, and grinned at Tony.

"I take it you like this one?   The look on your face pretty much says it all."

"This is the one.   I love it.   It's the perfect size, I love the front porch, and the hardwood floors are gorgeous."

"Let's take a look at the rest of the house before you make up your mind."

She walked down the stairs and rounded the corner. "The kitchen is a little small but I can work with that." She walked through the laundry room and out onto the back porch.   Diane was right, it was beautiful and private. Someone with a green thumb had been working overtime because it was surrounded by lush, well maintained vegetation.

"I love it, this is amazing.   It's nice and private, yet still open and airy.   I'm going to have to budget for someone to come take care of all this greenery.   It's beautiful but I think it might be too much for me to handle with a full time job and all."   She turned and looked at Tony.   "I want this house.   What's the next step?"

"Talk to Diane about the price."

"What if it's not in my price range?   I'd be crushed."

"I'm sure it's in your price range or she wouldn't have

brought it up.   She knows what you can afford."

"Let's go talk to Diane then!"

"Before we do that, there's something I need to tell you. Actually there's two things, and I'm hoping the one will outweigh the other.   Let's go back in the house and sit down."

Janel felt her anxiety level rise sharply as she wondered what he needed to say.   He motioned for her to sit on the stairs while he stood.   "You gave me Dorian's planner and asked me to look into what happened with your finances. I found out Dorian had some investments that were doing exceptionally well.   For some reason, he decided to take a huge risk and put everything into one investment and he lost a lot of money.   Now you and I both know that Dorian wasn't stupid, so I can only guess that he got an insider's tip that he thought was solid and it turned out not to be."

"Ok."   Janel said, waiting for him to continue.

"The other thing I found out was that he had a valid insurance policy.   It's worth fifty thousand dollars."

"Are you serious?"   She stood up and put a hand over her mouth.   He nodded his head yes and she thrust her arms around his neck.   "That means I have a real shot at getting this house right?   I mean even if they ask for a big down payment, I should be able to swing it with this policy and the money I've got in savings."

He gently pulled her away from him and asked her to have a seat again.   "There's something else I need to tell you too."

"What's wrong?   You don't seem happy, and that scares me."

"I slipped, misspoke, and told DJ that Dorian was cheating on you."

Janel sat quietly, trying to comprehend the words that had just come out of his mouth.   "You did what?"

"I was-"

"You had no right to do that.   He didn't need to know."

"I got frustrated, I was trying to get him to understand-"

"You spend hours in the courtroom, dealing with witnesses and judges and other lawyers.   Do you just blurt things out when you get frustrated with them?"

"I was just trying to get him to understand that even though his dad was a good man, he wasn't perfect.   And he shouldn't expect you to be either."

"So you decided to tell him his dad was an adulterer? He didn't need to know that Tony.   He *idolized* his dad. Can you even imagine how much that must have hurt him to hear that?   Why couldn't you just let him go on believing his dad was the hero he thought he was?"

"Because he's not a little boy anymore and he needs to wake up and realize Dorian wasn't some kind of mythic comic book character.   He was a man, with faults and flaws like any other man."

She stood up and jammed her finger in his chest.   "He didn't need to know, and it wasn't your place to tell him."

"You make it sound like I told him there's no such thing as Santa Claus!"

"In a sense you did.   The only difference is you know eventually your child is going to find out Santa Claus isn't real.   Some other kid, or some careless adult is going to tell them, and there's nothing you can do about it.   But this, there was no reason for him to know that his dad cheated on me!   The only people that knew were you, me, Michelle, and a few people on Dorian's job.   And I thought the few people that knew, the people closest to him anyway, actually cared enough about him to never tell him. Apparently I was wrong."   Janel pushed him out of the way and headed for the front door.   "I'll catch a ride back with Diane.   I don't want to be in the same car with you right now."

Janel beat Tony home and headed directly for the pool. She changed her clothes, stood on the deck, and dove in. She could imagine steam coming from her head she was so upset.   When she resurfaced, she heard her son's voice.

"Mom, can I talk to you for a minute?"

"If you've still got attitude with me this isn't the time. I'm really not in the mood."   She said as she wiped water from her face.

"I just wanted to say I'm sorry."

She swam to the side of the pool.   "I appreciate that. And I'm sorry if my behavior hurt you."

"You know, I talked to some people at school, and it made me realize that even though we don't have a house anymore, we still have it pretty good.   And even though it would be weird to see you with Unc-Tony, I don't want you to be alone.   I'd rather see you date him than some jerk. He's a good guy.   And if he makes you happy...."   He shrugged his shoulders.   The level of his maturity left her lost for words.   "Was dad really cheating on you?"

The question caught her off guard, but she decided to be candid with him.   "Yes."

"With who?"

She decided not to be so candid with that information. "I don't know."

"Mom, just be honest with me."

"I don't know, really."

"Then how did you know he was cheating on you?

"I found some text messages on his phone."   She hated lying to him, but the thought of him tracking down Michelle on the job crossed her mind and she didn't want that.

"I would've never thought dad would cheat on you. You guys seemed happy most of the time."

"We were.   Look, I know it's hard when you finally realize that your parents are human.   I think almost everyone goes through it.   Your dad and I both made mistakes, but he really was a good man.   Despite what Tony, grandma, or anyone else may try and tell you.   And I'm sorry that you had to hear about what happened from someone else."   She decided to change the subject.

"Hey, guess what?   I think I found us a house today."

"Really?   Where?   I'm not going to have to change schools again, am I?"

"It's not that far from here, and no, you won't have to change schools again.   I have to see if I can get approved for a loan, then I have to get the house inspected, and if there aren't any problems, I'll make an offer on it.   If they accept the offer, we'll be moving soon."

"Can you take me to see it?"

"I'll have to think about that.   I don't want to get your hopes up."

"Well, if we don't get it, it's not so bad living here.   Did Tony break up with Sherri?"

"They had a rough patch, but they're back together. Why?"

"Because she hasn't been over here.   I'm glad though, I don't like her.   She's fake, and she's rude, and she talks to me like I'm a little kid.   And sometimes she can be kind of mean."

Out of the mouths of babes, she thought.

24 - Making Amends (Again)

Tony picked up a large bouquet of lilies on his way home as a peace offering for Janel, hoping it would help to mend fences between them, but he wondered if it was enough. He knew how wrong he was for sharing the information about Dorian with DJ, and he was truly sorry for doing it. "Where's your mom?" He asked DJ, who was sitting on the couch playing a video game.

"In her room."

"Don't go anywhere, I need to talk to you when I'm done."

"Am I in trouble?" He asked, looking up from the screen.

"No, I am." He raised the vase full of flowers in the air. "Can't you tell?" He tapped on the open guest bedroom door, and she stepped out of her closet and tossed a dress on the bed.

"Come on." She said, without looking at him.

"You got a minute, I came to apologize." She stood staring at him, with her hands folded across her chest. "I'm sorry about telling DJ about his dad. I was wrong, and it wasn't my place. And I'd like to talk to him tonight and apologize to him directly to try and set things right. If that's ok with you. I want to clear up all the tension in the house if I can because I can't take it anymore." He handed her the vase and she placed it on the dresser, but she continued to stand with her back to him.

"I'm really sorry Janel, can you forgive me?" When she failed to say anything, and didn't turn around to face him again, he took a step towards her and caught a glimpse of her face in the mirror. There were tears running down her cheeks.   "You know, men have been conditioned from the beginning of time to believe that flowers fix everything. That's how flower shops stay in business, because we're always screwing up.   So I really hope those are tears of joy."   He went into the bathroom and grabbed some tissue and handed them to her.   "What's wrong?"

She blew her nose and cleared her throat before she finally spoke.   "When Dorian and I would get into an argument, I mean a really big one where one of us would actually leave the house, he would always buy me red roses to try and make things right.   And I always wondered if his apology was sincere, or if he was just being passive aggressive, because lilies have always been my favorites, not roses.   But I never asked, because I figured it would just lead to another argument.   Now I wish I had, because I'll never know."

"You know Dorian-"

"How is it that you, his best friend, know that lilies are my favorite, and my husband didn't after seventeen years of marriage?"

He wanted to hug her but thought better of it.   "I don't know.   I'm a lawyer, I have a good memory.   Besides, men are stupid Janel, we don't always get it right.   But it doesn't mean that he didn't love you any less.   Some of us are just better at the details than others."

"Thank you for the flowers.   They're beautiful."

"Are we good?"

"Yeah.   We're good."   She walked back inside her closet and he could hear her sliding hangers across the rod.

"What are you doing?"

She threw another dress on the bed and went back in. "Trying to find something to wear.   I've got a date this weekend."

"A date?"

"Yeah.   I hear it's this thing that two consenting adults engage in that's supposed to be fun if everything goes well."

"With who?"

She stuck her head out of the closet.   "What's with all the questions Sherlock?"

"Nature of the beast I guess.   I am a lawyer.   Who is this guy?"

"A co-worker."   She threw three more dresses on the bed and held one up against herself in the mirror.

"What's his name?   Maybe I could do a background check for you, to make sure he's not crazy."

"He's not."   She smiled at him as she put the dress down and picked up another one.   She slipped a shoe on one foot to see how they looked together.

"How do you know?   You've been married a long time, and the dating game isn't what it used to be.   It's better to be safe than sorry don't you think?"

"He works at a bank, how dangerous could he be? What's he going to do, bore me to death talking about the stock market?"

"You don't think an accountant can be a serial killer? Maybe he crunches numbers all day and tortures women locked up in his basement at night.   Maybe it's his hobby, and helps him relieve stress."   He made a circle in the air with his hands and pretended to choke someone.

"Who said he was an accountant?   And how did you make the jump from mild mannered bank employee to serial killer?"

"I'm just saying, you never know."

"He's not a stranger.   We've already been out a few times already, and talked on the phone a little."

"When?   He ain't never been to *this* house to pick you up.   Or am I missing something?"

"Back off,   pop Roy junior.   You can put your shotgun away, I'll be fine."

Frustrated that he couldn't get a straight answer from her, he resolved to let it go for the time being.   "Fine. I'm just trying to make sure you're safe.   If you really want to impress him, wear that dress with those shoes.   He'll have a difficult time trying to keep his mind on the conversation, trust me."

She smiled at him.   "Thanks."

"You're welcome."   He left her room with his mouth poked out and sat down on the couch next to DJ.   "Can we talk?   It won't take but a minute."

"Give me just a sec."   Tony waited for him to put his game on pause so he would have his undivided attention.

"I want to apologize for what I said to you the other day about your dad.   It wasn't my place to tell you that, and the way I did it just wasn't cool.   And I want you to know I never meant to hurt you, I was just trying to get you to understand that it hasn't been easy for your mom either since your dad died.   Are we cool?"

"Yeah, we cool."

"Come here man."   Tony grabbed the boy by his head and pulled him close and hugged him.   "I love you like you're my own, you know that right?"

"Yeah I know.   Why don't you pick up a controller so I can kick your butt in this game right quick?"

"Are you forgetting I beat you two out of three last time?"

"That's what I'm saying, give me a chance to redeem myself."

"I can't, I've got someplace I need to be.   Rain check?"

"Sure.   I can embarrass you any time, just let me know."

It felt good to be back in their good graces.   Happy to have managed to successfully remove himself from both of their shit lists, he turned his attention to taking care of his own needs.   He changed out of his suit and headed over to Sherri's place with a pep in his step, in the hopes of engaging in some extra special sexual relations.   She answered the door with a look of grogginess and confusion on her face.   "Hey babe, I wasn't expecting to see you tonight."

"I tried calling but you didn't answer.   I brought food." He held up a bag of take out.   "Shrimp po boys."   She stepped aside and let him in, and he followed her into the dark living room.   "You ok?"

"I guess I fell asleep on the couch."   She said, turning on a few lights and the television.

"You coming down with something?"

"No, just tired.   It's been a long day."   He watched her crumple up a sandwich wrapper and whisk it away into the kitchen.

"You already ate?"   He asked as she returned to the living room and sat down next to him.

"I grabbed a sandwich on the way home, but I could eat again.   I missed lunch today."   She leaned over and gave him a kiss.   "I'm glad you came by, it's good to see you."

He emptied the bag on her coffee table and they watched the news while they ate dinner.   He watched her tear through the entire twelve inches of sandwich, then ask him if he planned to finish his.   "Are you sure you're feeling ok?"

"I told you, I missed lunch today and I had to work late. I had a bunch of back to back meetings, and I've got fifteen new trainees that I need to review and report back to their managers.   I didn't have a chance to get away.   I'm starving."

Once his food settled, they stretched out on the couch together and he got caught up in a prime time show that managed to capture his attention.   By the time it ended though, he was ready to move on to the bedroom and his dessert.   As he kissed her on the back of her neck and pressed himself against her, he realized she was asleep. He shook her gently by the shoulder.   "Sherri?"   She moaned softly but didn't move, still breathing deeply.   He shook her a second time, and tried to extricate himself from between her and the back of the couch.   "Hey.   I'm going to go so you can get some rest, ok?"

She sighed deeply and sat up.   She yawned while she stretched her arms in the air.   "I'm so sorry, I was horrible company tonight."

"It's ok.   Go get some sleep, I'll lock the door on the way out."   She kissed him goodnight and headed towards her bedroom as he turned off the tv and let himself out.

It was eleven o'clock by the time he returned home, slightly more sexually frustrated than when he left.   He planned to spend some time in the bathroom with a little K-Y jelly before going to sleep as he quietly entered the house, but when he hit the living room, the glow of the television illuminated Janel's face.   "Are you waiting up for me again?"

"No, I was watching the news.   I already told you it's none of my business when you come and go in your own house."

"Speaking of houses, I meant to tell you I've got someone going over to inspect it on Friday, and I talked to Diane about asking the seller to come down ten thousand dollars off the selling price."

"You didn't waste any time at all did you?"

"Do I ever?   You said you wanted to move, I'm just trying to make it happen.   Did you follow up on the insurance policy?   I assume you'll put that towards a down payment on the house, right?"

"I called and all I had to do was fax them a copy of the death certificate, put a certified copy in the mail, and they told me I should have a check within thirty days.   And I thought the asking price on the house was fair, especially for all of the work they put into it.   You don't think asking them to come down is going to offend them do you?"

"Diane made the mistake of saying they just want to get rid of it, so I used that information as a negotiation tactic. People in Louisiana are superstitious, especially when it comes to death and the afterlife. They want to know things like were the mirrors covered, and was the body properly draped with their feet pointing towards the door, so the soul could 'cross over into the afterlife.'   The seller can either deal with that hassle, or drop the price for someone who's ready to buy right away with no questions asked.   I'm not worried about offending someone I don't know, and you shouldn't be either.   This is business. The worse that can happen is they say no and you end up paying the original asking price, which I do agree is fair, but I think we can do better."

"You know I don't have any experience with buying a house, past co-signing on the bottom line, so I'm going to trust you on this."

"When are you going to tell me who this guy is you're seeing?"

"I'm not."

"Why not?   Do I know him?"   She stared blankly at him.   "Have you slept with him?"

She smacked him in his arm.   "That's none of your business.   Why are you so worried about it?"

"I just want to know.   I kind of feel like you're my little sister and I need to protect you."

"Listen, seriously.   I know we've spent a lot of time together, but just because we're living together temporarily doesn't give you an all access pass to my life.   I love you dearly, you know I do, but this is a part of my life that needs to remain private.   Promise me you'll respect that."

He rubbed a hand across the top of his head as he ground his teeth together.   It was killing him not knowing who she was dealing with, but he knew if he practiced some patience, in time he would find out anyway.   "Fine. You're right, it's none of my business.   I'm sorry for prying."

"I know you Tony, and I know you know people who can find out.   Look at me and promise me you'll leave it alone and respect my privacy."

"I'll leave it alone."

"Look at me."

"I promise."

"Remember, you promised.   You watching this?   I'm going to bed."

"Nah."   She turned the television off, and when she got ready to stand up he grabbed her arm.   "Stay here with me for a little bit."

"Oh no, I know where this is going. No, I'm going to bed." She snatched her arm away.

"Come on Janel."

"No.   Because if I sit here, we end up in there,"   She pointed to his bedroom.   "And I'm not going to explain to DJ why I'm in your room again when I said it was a one-time thing.   I'm not going to lie, it's tempting, but I was serious when I said I'm not sleeping with you again."

"I just wanted to talk for a little bit."

"I'm not stupid.   I know you came creeping back here because you didn't get what you wanted at Sherri's place. Did you guys get in an argument or something?"

"No."

"Then why are you here instead of there?"   He just shook his head, not wanting to explain.   "I thought you were trying to work things out with her?"

"I am."

"If you were really trying to work things out with her, you'd have gone to bed five minutes ago.   Or, you wouldn't have come back here at all."

"So you *were* waiting up for me?"   He teased.   "It's ok, you can admit it."

"I wasn't!   Goodnight."

25 - Green-Eyed Monsters

Janel leaned forward, trying to read the street names through her windshield as she drove to Perry's house for dinner.   He'd been bragging about what a great cook he was, so she challenged him to put his money where his mouth was.   She made a final left turn and pulled tentatively into his driveway.   The house was a sand colored two story French Creole style home, with a wide front porch and slate blue shutters.   It was located in a quiet, tree lined, well-established neighborhood.   She knocked lightly on the traditional tall, narrow, wooden double doors, then rang the doorbell for good measure. She heard the latch turn and he opened the door, wearing an apron embroidered with the words 'Real men don't use recipes.'

"I see you made it, come on in."   He swung the double doors inward and she stepped inside.

"This is beautiful, not what I was expecting at all."

"What does that mean?   What exactly were you expecting?"

"I've seen you at work in your tailored suits and I imagined you going home to a modern, contemporary home.   Not this beautiful, restored, historic home.   And it's so....eclectic and fun and stylish."

"It's sort of a nod to my family history.   When I was getting a divorce and I moved out, I was lucky enough to happen upon this place.   The guy was working on renovating it, he fell on hard times, and I saw the potential. He gave me a good deal, and I picked up where he left off."

"You did the work yourself?"

"Most of it. I had to hire a plumber and an electrician, but I did all the floors and woodwork, and the painting. And I decorated everything."

"Did you hire an interior decorator to help you?"

"Nope. This is all me."

"I'm impressed."

"Let me show you around." He took her hand and led her towards the kitchen, but stopped before they crossed the threshold. "There's an old Creole superstition that says you shouldn't enter a man's kitchen for the first time without kissing him. It's seven years of bad luck, minimum."

"Too bad I'm not superstitious. And since when does 'Creole tradition' talk about a 'man' being in the kitchen?"

"That was pretty bad huh?"

"If you want a kiss all you have to do is ask."

"May I?" He leaned down and she met him halfway as he kissed her gently on the mouth. He showed her his entire home, including the master bedroom and bath, and the second floor, and they ended up back in the kitchen.

"I love it. It definitely has a Louisiana-New Orleans-type of feel to it."

"Have you been?"

"To New Orleans? Once, years ago. I was with my husband on a business trip so it wasn't exactly a vacation. All it did was pique my curiosity, and I've been wanting to go back ever since." She leaned against the kitchen counter and watched him move gracefully around the kitchen.

"You're in luck because tonight, I'm going to bring a little bit of N'awlins to you. This here is my world famous gumbo. You should actually be wearing a blindfold, but I trust you'll keep the ingredients a secret."

"If it tastes as good as it smells, I think I can be persuaded to keep my mouth shut."

"What you smell is andouille sausage, crab, shrimp, okra, and a few other things that I'm not at liberty to talk about."

"How'd you learn to cook?"

"My grand-mere, or nan nan as we called her.   She believed a man should know how to cook for himself, so he wouldn't starve looking for a wife."   She heard him slip into a slight Cajun, French laced accent, and it gave her goosebumps.   He was a gentleman, cooked, cleaned, or at least paid someone to, and had impeccable taste in clothes.   A Renaissance Man for sure.   Which left her wondering why Ayana would risk losing such a well-rounded man by cheating on him.   She realized she could apply the exact same logic to Dorian, and why he would want to cheat on her.   She was no Ayana in the looks department, but she knew she was a good catch.   Not wanting to ruin her evening, she pushed all thoughts of both of them from her mind, and watched as Perry dipped a spoon in the gumbo.

"Here, taste this."   He held his hand under the spoon to catch any drippings as she sampled his homemade goodness.

"Umm, that is so good."

He kissed her again.   "Yes it is.   Have a seat in the dining room while I make our plates."   He served the gumbo over rice and paired it with a fruity red wine.

"Your nan nan taught you well, this is delicious.   Are you sure you're in the right profession?"

"I have a few specialties, but a chef I am not."

"Did Ayana cook like this?"

"Are you kidding?   She can barely boil an egg.   I think she stood in the 'good looks' line a little too long, and completely missed the 'life skills' department.   Not to speak ill of her, but it is what it is.   I can't tell you how many pink t-shirts and socks I've thrown out over the years from her attempts to do laundry.   She wasn't very domestic, but I knew that going in."

"I guess when you look like her, most men don't care whether you can cook or do laundry."

"Yeah but you'd think she'd pick up some skills over the years.   Unfortunately she never did.   Enough about her, let's not ruin the evening."   She finished her gumbo and savored the rest of her wine which was a perfect complement to the meal.   "You want seconds?"   She shook her head no.   "How about more wine?"

"Sure."   He cleared her plate and brought the wine to the table, along with a second helping of gumbo for himself. "I've been wanting to ask you something."   She said as he topped her glass off.   "Why'd you tell me about catching Ayana in bed with another man?"

He looked down into his plate as he mixed the rice and gumbo together, then made eye contact again with her. "When I first met you, you had to share some very personal information with me in order for me to help you.   I know that was difficult, sharing intimate details of your life with a stranger.   And when we had lunch, the day you dropped off your resume, I thought we really hit it off.   Honestly, I thought if I shared that with you that I could gain your trust and get you to go out with me.   I guess it worked, right?"

"I wasn't sure what to think when you said it, but I'll admit I was impressed by the way you said it so casually. And I agree, we were hitting it off, so it seemed more like two old friends catching up with each other."

"Does that mean there's something here, between us?"

"Maybe.   Let's just take things one day at a time."

"Fair enough.   Sounds promising though."

The doorbell rang, and the front door opened and closed. "Hello?"   A female voice called out, and they heard heels clicking across the kitchen floor.   "There you are." Ayana said as she poked her head into the dining room. "Hello again."   She flashed a fake smile and waved a hand at Janel.

Perry stood and excused himself from the table.   "What are you doing here Ayana?"   He asked as he pulled her into the kitchen by her elbow.

"PJ said he left his football gear over here so I came to pick it up.   You made your gumbo!   That's what smells so good in here.   You mind if I get some to go?   You know how much I always loved your gumbo.   I still think it's the best in all of southern Louisiana, you can't find anything like it anywhere."

"Why didn't you just call?   I would've dropped it off at the school on Monday.   He doesn't have a game this weekend so it's not like he needs it right now."

"I was in the neighborhood so I thought I'd save you the trip and pick it up myself.   What's the problem?"

"The problem is I'm in the middle of dinner.   I have company.   Clearly you could see that from the car in the driveway.   You should've called first.   Or at least knocked and waited for me to answer.   You don't live here.   You can't just come strolling in here whenever you feel like it."

"Ok, I'm sorry." She shrugged her shoulders and starting opening cabinets.

"What are you doing?"   He asked incredulously.

"Looking for something to put some gumbo in so I can take it with me."

He grabbed her elbow again and pulled her out onto the front porch.   "This right here, what you're doing now, it's not cool 'Yana.   And you know it.   I have company, you need to leave.   I'll drop the bag off at school on Monday."

She pointed a slim finger in his face.   "If you're dating her and she's going to be around my son, I have the right to know."

"What?   Her son is good friends with PJ.   She's *already* spent a good deal of time around our son, in case you haven't noticed.   Why am I having to tell you this, how come you don't already know?   Besides, it really doesn't matter.   PJ's almost eighteen, so you don't need to concern yourself with who I choose to date or bring around him."

"Can I get his bag or not?"

"I said I'll drop it off at the school on Monday."

"But I'm already here now-"

"Ayana!   There's a line here, and you've crossed it. Now I admit that maybe that line has been a little blurry in the past, and I take full responsibility for that, but I'm clearing it up, again, right here and right now.   We can hang out together for the sake of our son, but that's as far as it goes.   And I thought I made that clear the night you let PJ borrow your car, and you asked me to take you home from the game.   Call before you come by.   Respect my privacy, as I've respected yours.   You hear me?"   She glared at him.   "Is that clear?"

"Yes!"   She said through clenched teeth and stormed off to her car.   He watched her speed off down the street, tires squealing as they struggled to grip the pavement. He closed the door behind him and rejoined Janel in the kitchen.

"I'm sorry about that.   I don't know what else to say, other than I hope you don't allow that to ruin our evening."

She sipped on her wine, wondering whether or not she should be concerned about what she'd just witnessed. "Does she normally come by without calling and just let herself in?"

"Just so you know, she doesn't have a key.   I left the door unlocked.   But to answer your question, sometimes, not often, she does stop by.   But she always calls first. And she's never just walked in like that."

"Why would she do that now, when she hasn't done it in the past?"   She wasn't stupid, she recognized a jealous woman when she saw one.   "Surely you've dated other women, right?"

"Yeah, I've dated a few."

"And she's never done that before?"   Janel knew the show she'd just witnessed was put on was strictly for her, much like an animal marking its territory.   Unfortunately Rita was right.

"Look, I know how it sounds but I'm being honest with you.   Yes she's a jealous woman, but she's never done that before.   We've been divorced three years now and I've dated other women without a problem."

"Looks like there's a problem now.   Do I need to be concerned?"

"No."

"Are you sleeping with her?"

"I'm not going to lie, I slept with her a few times after the divorce.   But it's been over a year since the last time, probably closer to two."

"I have to be honest Perry, it makes me very uncomfortable the way she just walked in here and completely disregarded your privacy."

"I can understand that.   I apologize, and I promise it won't happen again."

She wondered if she should leave.   He was a nice guy, and she enjoyed his company, but the last thing she needed was ex-wife drama.

"If you want to leave, I understand.   I don't want you to stay where you don't feel comfortable.   But I hope you decide to stay, because I really enjoy your company and I'm not ready for the evening to end."

"I couldn't leave right now if I wanted to.   I've had too much wine to even think about driving home."

"If you want to go, I'll call you a cab or take you home myself.   Seriously.   And, I'll make sure to get your car back to you."   He waited for her final answer.   "And, just so you know, I locked the door on my way back in."   He smiled.

"Then I guess I'll stay for a little while longer."   She smiled back at him.

"Good.   I'll try to make it worth your while."

# # #

She felt weird sneaking in at two in the morning, and she couldn't wait until she was in her own place and didn't have to worry about it.

"How was your date?"

She nearly jumped out of her own skin.   "Damn it Tony, wear a bell or something.   You scared me half to death. Why are you sitting in the dark?"

"I fell asleep."

"Bullshit, you were waiting up for me."

"Getting in kind of late aren't you?"   He grinned at her.

"As far as I know, my daddy is in Michigan.   I don't have a curfew."

"I was watching the news and fell asleep."   He teased, mocking her.   "So how'd it go?"

"You really think I'm going to sit here and tell you about my date?"

"I hope so."

She chuckled.   "Well I'm not."

"I thought we were friends?"

"I'm not doing this with you.   Good night."

"I see you took my advice and wore the dress and shoes."

"Good night!"   She said as she closed her bedroom door.

The next morning she was dreaming about cutting up vegetables with Perry and cooking with him in his kitchen when she awoke to soft knocking on her door.   "Mom?"

"What is it?"

DJ opened the door.   "It's your car.   Come look."

She slipped on her house-shoes as DJ woke Tony up. They stepped outside to find her car vandalized with spray paint, and all four tires were flat.   The word 'slut' was written on one side of the black sedan, in big white letters, and 'bitch' was written on the other.   "What the f-"   She immediately ran inside and grabbed her cell phone.

"Hey Janel, good morning."

"You need to put a leash on your ex-wife Perry.   If you don't handle her, I will."

26 - White Lies and Alibis

Tony gave Janel his car to drive so she wouldn't have to take time off from her job without pay. She hadn't earned any vacation days yet, and he was aware of that, so he took it upon himself to spend the day getting her car cleaned and back into an acceptable, drivable condition. She thanked him as soon as she walked through the door from work.

"It looks good. Thanks for taking care of that for me. I really didn't want to have to miss a day of work and pay when I haven't even been there that long. How much do I owe you?" She asked as she pulled her wallet from her purse and prepared to write a check.

"Don't worry about it, it wasn't that much. The tires were just flat, not cut, so all it took was some air, WD-40, and a good wax job. I went ahead and had them detail the whole thing."

"I know that had to run you at least a hundred bucks, right?"

"Put your wallet away, Janel. The money's not an issue. I just want to know who did it. Do you know?"

"No."

He looked at her in disbelief. "You have no idea who could've done that to your car?"

"I have my suspicions, but it's not like I can prove it."

"Does this have anything to do with the guy you're seeing? If so, just tell me his name and I'll handle it."

"Slow your roll Tony, there's no need for legal or physical threats. He didn't do it."

"But it's got something to do with him, right? An ex-girlfriend? Maybe a current girlfriend?"

"Just tell me how much it cost and I'll pay you back.   I really don't want you holding this over my head."

"I would never do that and you know it.   I'm just concerned about your safety.   This guy isn't married is he?"

"How can you stand there and ask me that after what I went through with Dorian?"

"Maybe he lied to you and you didn't know."

"He's not married and he doesn't have a girlfriend."

"As far as you know.   Look, I want you to park in the garage from now on.   I'll move my office stuff into a storage unit tomorrow so we can both park inside."

"It's not that serious Tony.   I reported it to the police, and they said they'd check into it."

"Unless there's a camera focused on my driveway that I'm not aware of, or they find a witness that just happened to be walking their dog at 3 am in the morning, they're not going to find anything.   I'm a lawyer, remember?   I have some experience with this kind of stuff.   Just tell me what you think is going on so I can help you."

"I got it ok?   It's being handled and you don't have to worry about it.   I promise."

"Look, I'm not trying to get in your business but this is my home.   Your son is here.   I can't keep any of us safe if I don't know what's going on."

She put both hands around his face and pulled it close to hers, and she looked him square in the eyes.   "Sweetie, I love the way that you keep coming to my rescue.   You've been my knight in shining armor through all of this, and I love you for it.   I really do.   But it's time that I start handling things on my own.   So let me handle this, ok? Please.   Just trust me.   And if for some reason I can't handle it myself, you'll be the first to know."   She gave him a quick peck on the lips.

Just like you handled Michelle?   He thought, but would never say aloud.   He looked into her eyes, and against his better judgment, agreed to let it go.   He knew she was dug in and wasn't going to give him any information.   "Fine. But I'm still clearing out the garage so you can put your car in there overnight."

"Fair enough.   I'm really liking the beard by the way. I never thought you'd actually let it grow out."   She rubbed her hands across the hair on his face and he couldn't help but smile at her.

"I always thought a beard looked a little unprofessional in the courtroom, but I've actually gotten quite a few compliments on it.   Judge Elway even told me she liked it, and she's one of the hardest, toughest, by-the-book judges in the county."

"I told you it was sexy.   Maybe she was trying to come on to you?"   She winked at him.   "Maybe if you flirt with her she'll throw a couple of easy wins your way."

"Yeah right.   You remember that scene in Boomerang with Eddie Murphy and Eartha Kitt?"

"Marrrrcuuuuuss."

"Exactly!   The only woman I've found so far that *doesn't* like it is Sherri.   She hates it."

"What?   You need to take her to get her eyes checked. I could see if you let it get all Grizzly Adams-mountain-man long and bushy but it's trimmed up all nice.   Did you tell her it was my idea?"

"No."

"Don't.   She'd hate it on principle alone if she knew that.   She's already giving me enough grief at work as it is, I don't need you to give her a reason to give me even more."

"Come on now, it can't be that bad.   Why would she put in a good word for you, then turn around and give you grief after you get hired on?"   The minute he saw her facial expression change he knew he was in trouble.

"What did you just say?"

He rubbed a hand over the top of his head.   "I may have accidentally mentioned something to her about helping you get hired on, in general conversation."

"Are you kidding me?   I specifically remember telling you not to say anything to her.   That I can do bad by myself.   You promised!"

"I don't remember promising so much-"

"Did she tell you that she had something to do with me getting hired on?   Cause if she did, it's a bold face lie.   I know for a fact how I got my foot in the door, and I got the job on my own merit.   She didn't have anything to do with anything."

"I'm sorry.   I was just trying to help.   I watched you walk out of here every day with your head held high, only to come back here deflated and discouraged.   So I asked her if she could possibly mention your name or put in a good word for you with the hiring manager."

"After I specifically asked you not to?   And you wonder why I won't tell you what I think happened to my car." She shoved her hand out towards him, palm up.   "I need my keys please.   I need to go out and get some fresh air." He fished them out of his pocket and handed them to her. "Thank you.   I'm going to be gone a while so don't wait up."

He was really beginning to question if he could do anything right when it came to women.

# # #

Janel managed to make herself scarce around the house for the next few days, and he couldn't help but wonder where she was spending her time.   He knew the defacing of her car was somehow related to the guy she was seeing, so he doubted she would be hanging out at his place, and putting herself in a position for it to happen again.   There was always the possibility that she was hanging out at Rita's, which made more sense, but he didn't have Rita's number so he couldn't call her to confirm.   He carried a box of documents into the house and sat it down in the middle of his makeshift desk, i.e. the coffee table.   "You got homework?"   He asked DJ as he removed his suit jacket and folded it over his arm.

"No.   You need me to clear out?"   He asked as he paused his video game.

"No, it's cool.   Just turn it down a little, please?"

"Sure.   You want to play me in a game of basketball real quick?   I owe you a beat down, remember?"

"As much as I would enjoy showing you just how weak your game is, I can't.   I've got to prepare for court tomorrow."

"I can clear out of here if you need me to.   It looks like you got a lot going on there."

"No don't worry about.   Keep doing what you're doing, you're fine."   He went into his bedroom, changed his clothes, and made himself comfortable on the couch. "You know where your mother is?"

"She said she had some errands to run.   You guys get in a fight or something?"

"Why would you ask me that?"

"Cause you're asking me where she is instead of calling her yourself."

"Smart ass."   He chuckled at how quick witted he was, and it immediately reminded him of something Dorian would say.   "I wouldn't exactly say we had a fight, but she's not happy with me right now."

The doorbell rang, followed by a quick knock at the door, and Tony got up to see who it was.   "Can I help you?"

"Uh, yeah.   Is Janel around?"

"Who's asking?"

"You must be Tony right?   I'm Perry.   Nice to meet you."   He extended his hand and Tony shook it.

"She's not here right now.   Did you try calling her?"

"Yeah, I don't think she's taking my calls right now.   I thought I'd just try stopping by."

Join the crowd, Tony thought.   At least it confirmed he

wasn't the only one on Janel's shit list.   "Sorry man.   You want to leave a message?"

"Actually I just wanted to reimburse her for whatever it cost to get her car fixed."

"You have something to do with that?"

"No."

"You know who did?"

"Look, I really like Janel, and I just thought since we're dating....I just wanted to take care of it you know, do something nice for her."

"If you didn't have anything to do with it, why isn't she taking your calls?"

"That's a whole other story man.   Look, maybe I made a mistake by coming by here."

"Hey, before you go, I want to ask you something.   You work at CSC right?"

"Yeah.   Why?"

"I've got a client who's new in town.   He's got a financial background, and he's looking for a job.   You guys just opened that new branch and all-"

"Those positions are filled.   Something may open up in ninety days, if some of those folks don't make the cut, but there's nothing right now."

"Understood.   Do you happen to know the name of the hiring manager?"

"Anna Turner did all the hiring for the new branch, but he wouldn't want to call her directly.   His best bet is to submit his resume online, or drop it off at any of the branches.   If something opens up that he's a good fit for, they may give him a call."

"So she would've been the person to hire on Janel, right?"

"What's with all the questions man?"

"Sorry, I'm a lawyer, it's in my nature.   Actually Janel and I were talking, and she led me to believe she had some concerns about whether or not she got the job on her own merit.   She thinks maybe someone gave her a hand up or put in a good word for her."

"Are you talking about me?"

"Well?"

"I admit I did suggest they bring her in for an interview. And it was happenstance that I ended up on the interview board.   But I can assure you she got the job on her own. The other two board members had some minimal concerns about her experience, but she interviewed well and they really liked her.   I didn't have to convince anybody to bring her on.   And I'd be happy to tell her that myself if she has any doubts."

"No that's ok.   It's probably best not to bring it up unless she asks you.   Besides, I think I convinced her that she got the job on her own.   She hasn't brought the subject up again anyway."

"Look, I gotta go.   Can you let her know I stopped by? Maybe convince her to let me pay for the damages?   Or take my calls?"

"I took care of the car, so don't worry about it."

Perry's eyes narrowed and he cocked his head to the side.   "You did?"   He pulled his wallet out of his back pocket.   "What do I owe you?"

"It was nothing.   Chump change really.   Don't worry about it.   That's what friends are for, right?"

Perry continued to stare at him, as if sizing him up, before finally putting his wallet away.   "Let her know I stopped by.   Ok?"

"Sure.   It was good meeting you."

"You too."   He said over his shoulder as he headed back to his car.

Tony pulled his phone from his pocket and called Sherri as he headed back inside.   "Hey babe."

"Hey."

"You asleep already?   You sound like you just woke up."   He looked at his watch.   It wasn't even eight o'clock.

"No, I'm just tired.   I have a lot of new responsibility on my plate and it's wearing on me."

"Maybe you should see a doctor?   Take some vitamin B."

"I'm fine, I just need to stop bringing work home and staying up so late.   What's up?"

"I've been missing you.   I haven't heard from you in a few days and I'm starting to wonder if you still have love for me."

"You know I always have love for you baby.   You don't ever have to worry about that.   Why don't you stop by tonight so I can show you just how much love I have for you."

"Sounds tempting but I can't.   I've got court tomorrow so I've got some studying to do.   You think we can do lunch tomorrow?   I can't give you an exact time though, it all depends on when the judge decides to call a recess."

"Tomorrow's really not good, I've got a day full of meetings.   Can we do it some other day this week?   Or maybe you can just come by for dinner one night?"

"I'll have to get back to you on that.   I guess I'll have to take a rain check for now.   Anyway, I'll let you get back to what you were doing."

"Ok, just let me know.   Bye babe."

"Bye."

He now had two new missions to complete.   The first, to find out if Sherri really had a hand in getting Janel hired on, as she'd told him she did.   The second, to find out whether or not this guy Janel was seeing had anything to do with her car being vandalized.   His intuition told him that something wasn't quite right on both counts, and he intended to get to the bottom of them both.

27 - The Art of Getting Un-Dumped

"Can I talk to you for a second?"   Jenny asked Janel.

"Sure, what's up?"

"I've watched you enter transactions in the new system, but I don't get how you got to be so fast at it.   Do you think you could show me a few things?   Sherri's been on my butt and I don't want to give her a reason to suggest that I don't make the cut at the end of our probation period."

"Sure.   Bring a chair over and I'll show you a few tips and tricks that I've learned."   Jenny sat down and Janel pulled up a document on her screen.   "I'll send you a copy of this, it's a cheat sheet I created for myself.   I just keep adding stuff to it as I learn.   Apparently there are a lot of shortcuts and other things that Sherri didn't show us in training."

"She probably doesn't know them.   And if she did, she wouldn't have shown them to us anyway.   I swear I don't think she wants any of us to be successful."

"And I don't understand that, because if we're all successful it means she did a good job training us right? She would get the glory and that's right up her alley."

"I swear she hates me, and I don't understand why."

"Oh now, don't go thinking your special.   She hates *everyone.*"

"She makes me feel like I can't do anything right. Everything she says to me is negative, and she never tells me about anything I'm doing right.   It's like, 'you should've gone out four decimal places instead of just two' or 'you need to make your zeros more *round.*'   Just random, crazy stuff!" Janel laughed at the girl. "I'm serious! Why would they put someone like her in that position? I don't get it."

"Maybe they don't know she's like that. The only advice I can give you is don't give up. Just try and learn as much as you can to show her that she's wrong, and to prove to her that you do know what you're doing. Don't let her trip you up or intimidate you, she thrives on that. And just keep in mind this is temporary. Once we get through this probationary period, we won't have to deal with her anymore."

Janel worked with Jenny for nearly forty-five minutes, showing her everything she'd learned, and she saw an improvement just within the short period of time. "I don't know what she's been telling you, but it looks like you know what you're doing to me."

"It's because I'm comfortable with you, there's no pressure. They really should let you train any new people who come into this department in the future. I like your style of training much better than hers."

"Don't even say that to anyone else Jenny. I'm serious. If she hears anyone say anything like that, she'll think I want her job and she'll be trying to find a way to get rid of me."

"I won't, I promise. Thanks again for your help. You're a great teacher, and you make this stuff seem so easy."

"No problem. We'll help each other get through this."

"Maybe you should send that document to the other new people too, I think it would help."

"Are you kidding me? I can't do that. If Sherri found out she'd have a fit. She'd find a way to make me suffer, and make an example out of me in front everyone."

"Looks like you've got company." Jenny smiled and nodded her head towards the doorway. Janel looked up to see Perry headed her way.   "He is sooo hot."   Jenny fanned herself with one hand as she grinned at Janel and rolled her chair back to her desk with the other.

"Hey."   Perry said.

"Hey."   Janel said as she shuffled some papers on her desk.

"I apologize for just popping up but I didn't know what else to do since you won't take my calls.   I was hoping maybe we could grab some lunch and talk."

She concentrated on her computer screen as she emailed her tips document to Jenny.   "Look, if you don't want to go to lunch that's fine, but could you at least explain to me why you're so upset with me?   I'd feel silly apologizing when I don't even know what I did wrong."

She opened her desk drawer and grabbed her purse. "Let's go."

He drove her to the sub place where they first had lunch together, and they sat on the patio and ate.   She picked at a salad while he finished his sandwich quickly.   After wiping his mouth, he finally broke the silence.   "Are you going to tell me why you're so pissed at me?"

"I know Ayana vandalized my car.   And if dating you is going to bring this kind of craziness into my life....I just really don't need this right now.   I'm trying to close on this house and I have a new job-"

"So you were just going to shut me out?"

She set her fork down and looked at him.   "The last thing I need in my life right now is more drama. Especially drama I can avoid."

"Wow.   You were trying to dump me without telling me you were dumping me."   She shrugged her shoulders as she was overcome with guilt.   "Look Janel, I've known Ayana a long time.   And I'll be the first to admit that she's a jealous woman, always has been and probably always will be.   But in all the years that I've known her, I've never known her to do anything like this.   Ever."

"You never thought she'd walk into your house unannounced either but she did that too.   Be honest with me, are you still sleeping with her?   Because that's the only thing I can think of that would make a woman do something like that, especially to someone that she doesn't even know."

"I was honest with you the first time you asked.   I stopped sleeping with her almost two years ago.   If you're expecting to catch me in a lie, I haven't told you any lies to be caught in."

"And none of the other women you've dated have had any problems like this?"   He shook his head no.   "This is so frustrating.   I hear what you're saying, but I still believe Ayana did this.   The way she stormed off when you told her to leave, she was really upset.   It's too coincidental. I'm about to move into a new house, and I've got my son to worry about, let alone worrying about my own personal safety.   I don't want to have to keep looking over my shoulder because I'm dating you.   It would be nerve-wracking to say the least."

"Let me ask you this.   If your car hadn't been vandalized, we'd still be cool right?   Cause I feel like we really clicked.   Am I wrong?"

"No you're right.   I enjoy spending time with you, as long as it's not to the detriment of my personal property or safety."

"So what can we do to move past this?   Because you don't have any concrete evidence to prove that it was her, and I don't have any to prove that it wasn't.   What can I do so we can get beyond this?   I've already offered to pay for the damages to your car but Tony told me he took care of it."

"What do you mean you offered to pay for the damages?"

"Since you weren't taking my calls, I stopped by the house to reimburse you for whatever it cost you out of pocket to fix your car, but Tony reassured me he already took care of it.   I offered to pay him instead but he refused."

"He never told me you stopped by.   I had no idea."

"That doesn't surprise me.   He came off as a little overprotective to me."

"His bark is worse than his bite.   He was my husband's best friend, so it goes without saying that he'd be bothered by seeing me with another man.   I'll be out of his place soon enough so don't worry about him."

"Oh I'm not worried, it was just a simple observation is all.   So, is there anything else I can do to try and put your mind at ease?   I'm determined to get un-dumped."

"Un-dumped?"   Janel laughed at him.

"Yes, un-dumped.   I need to get us back to 'officially dating' status."

"What would really make me feel better is for you to ask Ayana point blank if she did it."

"Are you serious?"

"Yes.   She may not admit it to you, but I would think you've known her long enough to know when she's lying, right?"

He took a minute to think about it.   "On something like that, I think I could tell if she wasn't being honest with me." He sat back in his chair and rested his forearms on the table as he folded his hands together.   "You know what?   If that's what it takes, that's just what I'll have to do. However, you have to promise me that you'll accept my opinion and let it go. For good.   If I tell you I don't think she did it, that's the end of it."

"If you tell me that and you sincerely believe it, I'll let it go.   But, what happens if you think she's lying about not doing it?"

"Then I promise to help you get to the bottom of it. Within reason of course, I'm not going to help you do anything illegal."

"I wouldn't ask you to do anything illegal!"   She

playfully smacked him on the arm.

"I want to make sure we're clear."

"We're clear.   I'll accept your opinion for what it is."

"Good."   He pulled his phone from his pocket. "Excuse me for just a minute."   He swiped his finger across the screen of his phone, then put it up to his ear. "Hey Ayana, it's me."   Janel's mouth fell open and he pointed a finger at her, warning her to remain quiet. "Give me a call when you get this, I need to talk to you. Later."

"You work fast don't you?"

"When it comes to something I want, absolutely."

"You know the deal is to ask her face to face right?   So you can look her in the eye and observe her body language."

"Don't worry, I got this.   You just make sure you keep your promise."

As Janel drove home, all she could think about was the fact that Tony didn't tell her that Perry had stopped by. She gave slight consideration to the fact that he may have forgotten, but she knew that was extremely unlikely.   And she wondered if he had been passive aggressive, or even confrontational, because of Perry's comment about him being protective.   She busied her mind by making dinner, then sat down and had dinner with DJ.   She took a dip in the pool, showered, and watched television with her son until he finally decided to go to bed.   She began to wonder if Tony would even come home as she put away the food and cleaned up the kitchen.   Then, just as she flipped the light off, she heard the garage door opener rumble to life.

She went into the living room, flipped to the news, and waited for him to walk in.   She heard the garage door open and close, and saw the kitchen light come on.   She heard him rooting around in the fridge, then in the cabinets, and then she heard a series of beeps followed by the drone of the microwave.   She assumed he was eating at the breakfast bar, or knowing him, standing up, because he was taking way too long to appear in the living room or dining room.   "Oh for the love of Pete, could he be in there any longer?"   She complained under her breath as she slouched down on the couch.   Finally, she saw the kitchen go dark and he turned the corner.

"What are you still doing up?   I figured you'd be asleep by now."   He sat down beside her and let out a heavy sigh.

"Watching the news.   How was your day?"   She knew when he started rubbing the top of his head before answering her that something was bothering him.

"Rough."

"What's wrong?"

"That."   He said, pointing to the television screen. There was a story on about a financial aid counselor accused of embezzling and misappropriating government funds.   "He wants us to represent him.   Doug really wants to take the case, but I have a bad feeling about it."

"Why?"

"I don't know, I can't put my finger on it.   It just doesn't feel right."

"I don't understand, why the struggle?   He normally trusts your judgment right?"

"I don't know, he's been on this kick lately about wanting to take more high profile cases."

"You guys have a really good reputation, and you've already had quite a few high profile cases already.   Like Professor Molester.   That one was just crazy."

"Yeah I don't know.   I think he's worried about us resting on our laurels or something.   Anyway, how was your day?"   He asked as he patted her thigh.

"Busy.   I had lunch with Perry today."   She studied his

face for any type of reaction.

"And?"   He waited for her to continue.

"And, I was wondering why you didn't tell me he stopped by and offered to pay to have my car cleaned up."

He turned slightly away from her before he answered her.   "I don't know, I guess it slipped my mind."

"Really."   She gave him a deadpan look.

"Yes, really."

"I don't know that I believe that."

"I don't know why not, I have no reason to lie to you." He said as he rubbed his eyes.

"He's not intimidated by you, you know.   You can't run him off that easily."

"What are you talking about?"

"He said you came off as more than a little overprotective.   I'm thinking a lot overprotective, because he actually asked me if we'd ever dated before."

He closed his eyes and pinched the bridge of his nose. "Dude is tripping, ain't nobody trying to intimidate him. Solid as he is?   He's probably got a good fifteen pounds on me.   Maybe he mistook my confusion as to why some dude I didn't know was ringing my doorbell and calling me by name as trying to intimidate him but that's far from the truth."

"Somehow I doubt it was as simple as that."

He looked over at her.   "Well who are you going to believe, me or him?"

"It's not about who I believe-"

"Then what *is* it about?"   He snapped at her.   She stared at him for a moment, stunned.   "I'm sorry, I didn't mean to snap at you.   I'm tired and frustrated, it's been a long day.   I'm sorry Janel, you know that's not even me."

She stood up, crossed in front of him, headed to her room.

28 - Verna Knows Best

"You want me to call and order you some dinner before I leave?" Pam asked.

"Nah, I'm leaving in a minute." She gave him a look that said 'yeah right.' "I am." He checked his watch. "What are you still doing here?"

"In case you haven't noticed, business has picked up quite a bit lately. I have to stay late to catch up on those billable hours you guys are racking up."

"Do we need to look at getting you some help? I'm not too cheap to hire someone, even if it's temporary."

"I know you're not, we were only teasing you. You *can* be cheap, but you spend money when it counts, like hiring Mike to help Janel and working on her case pro bono. That was really sweet of you."

"She's family, and you know I take care of family. You're family too, and I want to make sure you're taken care of, so if you need some help let me know."

"I will."

"I don't know if I tell you enough but I appreciate you. I never have to worry about anything around here because you're so organized and you keep things running so smoothly. You even catch *my* mistakes, and that says a lot because I don't make very many of them."

She smiled at him. "What mistakes?"

"See, that right there is what gets you the big raises."

"You need anything else before I head out of here?"

"No. You need me to walk you out?"

"I'm good." She paused in the doorway, a look of concern on her face. "Don't stay too late ok?   You need to go home and get a good night's sleep."

"Is that a nice way of telling me I look a little run down lately?"

"You just seem a little stressed."

"I know you know everything that goes on around here, so I'm asking you to just be straight with me.   If something's on your mind, just say it."

"You're normally pretty laid back, even when we're really busy, but lately you've been a little more direct than usual with some of the associates."

"You mean short."

"Yes.   And you've been kind of ruthless in the courtroom, which isn't even your style."

"So people have been complaining about me?"

"I don't want you to get the wrong idea.   People really enjoy working here, I hear it all the time.   You and Doug have a great reputation in the community, and you get the business.   And I don't think it's about hurt feelings or toes being stepped on, I think people are genuinely concerned about you and your well-being."

"What do you think?   Have I been short with you?"

"No, you haven't been short with me, but you haven't been yourself either.   I know losing Dorian was hard, and sometimes I wonder if you took enough time off.   And, even though it's none of my business, I know from experience that when things get tough in a relationship, sometimes that negativity and drama can seep into your professional life.   Even when you try your best not to let it."

He didn't believe it was either one of those things, but he wasn't going to voice his opinion.   "I really appreciate you being honest with me Pam.   I will definitely do some soul searching, and be more cognizant of my behavior.   You're a good woman Pam, your husband is a lucky man."

"Honey I made him work hard to get me, because I honestly believe, the harder you have to work to get the woman, the more you'll appreciate her when you get her. And he tells me and shows me all the time how much he appreciates me.   Cause if he didn't he knows I'd be trying to have an affair with you, and Sherri would have some real competition on her hands."   She said as she joked with him.   "Have a good night Tony."

"You too, and tell your husband I said hello."

After absorbing what Pam had to say, he decided to call it a night and give his mom a call on his way home.   "Hey mom, how are you doing?"

"The good Lord blessed me to see another day so I'm fine, doing real good.   I know I can't wait to retire and move to Lafayette, it's been snowing here all week long."

"You keep saying that but somehow I don't think you'll ever really get around to doing it.   Moving, not retiring."

"Why not?"

"Because of Joe."

"What's he got to do with anything?"

"Joe got game, he ain't gonna just let you move away from him.   He'll find a way to persuade you to stay, snow or no snow."

"Joe and I are just friends, and there's nothing he can say to keep me here.   If he's going to miss me so much he can come and visit, or pack up and move down there himself.   Ain't nothing holding him here, his kids are all grown and moved away."

"Trust me, as much as I try not to think about it, I know you and Joe are more than just friends.   Besides, you know you would miss him just as much as he'd miss you."

"I'm not saying I wouldn't miss him, I'm just saying he ain't got nothing to do with my decision.   He don't live with me and he ain't paying none of my bills so he doesn't get a say so."

"Fine momma, if you say so.   Let me know when you're serious about moving and I'll start looking for a place for you.   Maybe I'll fly you down here for a few days and we can look at some places together.   Maybe Joe will come with you, he's welcome to stay at my place anytime."

"Speaking of moving, how's Janel doing?   Did she find a place yet?"

"She's good, and she did find a place.   She got a good deal on it too."

"Good for her.   I know she's excited."

"She is.   She's a little frustrated with the process though. You know closing always seems to take forever when you're anxious to move into a new place."

"That's good, I'm happy for her."

"She's dating now too."

"Say what?"

"Yep, she's seeing some guy."

"Who?   Have you met him?"

"Yes.   I talked to him briefly."

"Well, what did you think?   Was he nice?"

"I guess so.   I only talked to him for a few minutes."

"Was he nice looking?"

"He was aiight."

"I'm glad to hear she's trying to move on.   She was with Dorian for so long, I can't even imagine what it must be like for her to start dating.   Anyway, what about you, how are you doing?"

"I'm ok."

"Hmm.   You don't sound ok?   You know I know you better than that."

"I've just got a lot going on right now."

"You always have a lot going on.   What's changed?"

"You know I love my job, but I'm starting to think maybe I need a change."

"What kind of change?   You're not talking about leaving the legal profession, are you?   Maybe you just didn't take enough time off."

"I don't know, maybe we should expand the business and take on some different types of cases.   I haven't given it a whole lot of thought just yet."

"Does this have anything to do with what's her name? Are you still seeing her?"

"Mom."

"What?"

"You know what her name is."

"That don't mean I gotta call her by it."

"Sherri.   Her name is Sherri."

"Are you still seeing her?"   Tony hesitated a second too long and Verna immediately picked up on the fact.   "Do I sense some trouble in paradise?   What's the matter son, cat got your tongue?"

"I'm still seeing her."

"I think the better question is, is *she* still seeing *you*?   Cause you sound a little unsure."

"I'll admit I've been having some doubts lately about our relationship, but don't go doing any cartwheels just yet.   I mean, I care about her, I think I love her, but lately...I don't know.   I guess maybe we're just going through a rough patch."

"What's really bothering you?   You may as well spit it out because you know I'm not going to let you off this phone until you do."

"Things are just different lately.   And I'm not sure if it's her or me.   Maybe it's a combination of us both.   She's got some new responsibilities at her job, and I know that has her stressed out and it's been keeping her really busy. And you know I'm always busy but I've always make time for her."

"Being busy is never an excuse.   People make time for the things and people that are important to them.   What does your gut tell you?"

"That something is wrong, but I can't put a finger on what it is."

"Then you should listen to it.   Listening to your gut is what's made you so successful in your professional life, so don't go ignoring it in your personal life.   God gave us instincts for a reason son.   If you think something is wrong, something is wrong, and you don't necessarily have to wait around to find out what it is.   I say cut your losses now and just move on."

"You don't like her so of course you would say that."

"I'll admit I don't care for her, however, you were the one that told me that you feel like something is wrong.   I'm just offering advice based on the information you've given me.   All I really want is for you to be happy, and if she makes you happy, then I guess I'll have to find a way to tolerate her.   However, I'm listening to what you're saying and you obviously have some reservations about her."

"You know, there is this one thing specifically that's been bothering me.   I asked her if she could help Janel get hired on with CSC, and at first she fussed about it but then she said she would.   And when Janel got hired on, and I mentioned it to her, she told me she helped her.   But I was told a very different story by someone who had first-hand knowledge and who had no reason to lie to me."

"She told you a bold face lie.   Think about it.   Why in the world would she help Janel get a job?"

"Why *wouldn't* she?"

"Did you really just ask me that?   That shouldn't be hard for you to figure out.   I know you're smart.   You passed the Bar exam on your first attempt, and from what I understand that's not an easy thing to do.   Do I really have to break this down for you?"

"I know they don't exactly have a lot of love for each other, but still, Janel's in a bad spot and she has DJ to take care of. I would think Sherri could put their differences aside for a minute and help her get a job so she can get on her feet."

"You cannot possibly be that naive son."

"That's not being naive, it's called having a little faith in my girlfriend that she can put aside some childish pettiness and be a compassionate human being."

"Why in the world would she help Janel get a job when she's managed to pull off what Sherri's been trying to do for two years? Janel is living in your house with you, cooking you dinner, coming and going as she pleases, and Sherri is hating every minute of it."

"You would think that would be her motivation to help her, so Janel can actually afford to move out."

"Women are catty Tony. She may have *told* you she was going to help Janel, but she only said it because she knew that's what you wanted to hear. She didn't mean it any more than the man in the moon."

"Yeah but if she were going to lie, why not just say she didn't know the right people or that she didn't have any pull? What made her think I'd never find out?"

"She took a risk, and she did it to make you *think* she cares. She wants you to believe she cares about the same things you care about, because that's what a good girlfriend and potential wife does. But truth be told, Janel could end up on the streets and I promise you she could not care less."

"I disagree. Sherri may be catty but she's not heartless."

"Who are you trying to convince, me or yourself? That girl is bad news. If she'll lie about the little things, she'll lie about big things too. I'm telling you, cut your losses now and move on. "

"You make it sound so easy."

"I know it's not going to be easy. I know you care about her. I've been where you are and I know it's hard. But with some time and distance, you'll get over her and life will go on. Bury yourself in your work, we both know you're good at that.   Look to Janel for inspiration, she's doing it.   I honestly believe cutting her out of your life is for the best, and I'm not just saying that because I don't care for her.   I know if you have a little faith and kick that girl to the curb that you'll be making room for someone better.   You're a good man, you deserve a good woman. Just think about it."

"All right mom, I hear you.   I will."

"Now I don't mean to rush off the phone but I gotta go, Joe's here.   Call me later ok?   I love you."

"Love you too."

He shook his head as he disconnected the call.   He remained in his car, in the silence of his garage, as his mother's words echoed in his head.   'Cut your losses and move on.'   Having talked about her made him want to see Sherri so he called her.   "I was thinking about stopping by, you in the mood for some company?"

"It's kind of late don't you think?"

He checked his watch, it was five minutes after nine. "Since when is nine o'clock late?"

"Since I've inherited new responsibilities.   You're used to having a ton of work, in fact, you thrive on it.   You have to remember this is all new to me, the additional responsibilities and this new system.   People are coming to me with questions that I don't have the answers to, and I'm having to consult with our corporate contact a lot."

"You're right, I'm sorry.   I didn't mean to bother you.   I just wanted to see you for a little bit.   Give me a call when things calm down, or maybe we can go to lunch this week."

"I can't make any promises.   I don't know what a real lunch is anymore.   I've been eating at my desk."

"I'll let you go then."

"I'll call you when I can."

29 - Tell Him

"I can't believe with all this good food on the menu all you're having is a salad."

"I'm having salad because I can't afford a whole new wardrobe. You do realize this is the third time we've eaten out this week? We're on a first name basis with the hostess and we practically have our own private table." Janel and Perry were eating dinner together at a casual restaurant near the university.

"I can't help it, I like spending time with you. And since you won't come to my house, and you haven't moved yet, I don't have much of a choice. I promise the next time you come to my place I'll cook something healthy for you. And I hope that'll be soon because I talked to Ayana about your car."

"And?" Janel put her fork down, wiped her mouth with the cloth napkin, and gave him her full attention. "What did she say?"

"She was genuinely surprised. Maybe even a little concerned."

"Oh I doubt that."

"No really."

"Has she ever taken any acting lessons?"

"Now she did admit that she purposefully walked into the house unannounced, and that she was jealous when she saw us together. And she admitted that what really set her off is the fact that I made my special gumbo for someone other than her. But she also swore to me that she didn't do it."

"Do you really think she would admit that to you?"

"I never would've thought she would admit to being jealous but she did.   And if you knew her you'd know just how big a deal that is.   The point is, I asked her face to face like you wanted and I believe her."

"Oh come on Perry, who else could it have been?"

"Maybe some kid in the neighborhood, pulling a prank?"

"I doubt it.   If that were the case, why'd they pick my car?"

"You have a son, why do kids do half the things they do? I don't think they even know."

"It had to be her, nothing else makes sense."

"Ok, let's say it was her.   Why did she use spray paint? It's temporary.   Why not key it?   That's more expensive to fix, it means a paint job."

"Spray paint is more visible.   I would think the point would be to piss me off *and* embarrass me.   Keying it may have been too noisy?"

"Look, you asked me for my opinion, I'm giving it to you. I've known Ayana since the seventh grade, and I've never known her to lie to me."

"Are you kidding me?   You caught her in *your* bed with another man!   And you don't think she would *lie* to you? I don't know how you could trust anything that comes out of her mouth after that."

"I hear you, and I don't expect you to understand how I could ever believe her, but I do.   I already forgave her for what she did, we've made our peace, and she knows that I'll never give our relationship a second chance.   She has nothing to gain by lying to me about this."

"She'd lie to you about this in a heartbeat because if she tells you the truth, she knows she'll lose your respect for good.   If that happens, she can't spend time with you after PJ leaves for college.   Because ultimately that's what she's hoping for, to slip back into your heart and your bed, despite anything you say to the contrary."

"The bottom line is I asked, she told me she didn't do it, and I believe her.   And you promised me you'd accept my opinion and let it go."

She let out a sigh and sat back in her seat.   "You're right, I did.   I'm sorry."

"You're going to let it go?"

"I still don't-"

"You're going to let it go right?"   He emphasized each word, then looked at her from under his long eye lashes and waited for her to respond.   "You gave me your word."

She heard what he said, and she knew he was convinced. And even though she wasn't as sold on Ayana's innocence as he was, she relented.   "I made a promise and I'm a woman of my word.   I won't bring it up again."

"Good.   So how about you come over this weekend so we hang out?   I'll cook again and this time I'll make sure I lock the door."

She smiled at his attempt to joke and lighten up the mood.   "I'd like that.   I'm really looking forward to seeing what else you specialize in."   A huge grin slowly spread across his face.   "Get your mind out of the gutter, I was talking about food."

"I knew what you meant."

"Look at you two all cozy over here, giggling like teenagers."   She looked up to see Tony walking towards them.   "Janel,"   He nodded hello.   "And, uh-"   He snapped his fingers as he looked at Perry.   "I'm sorry man, I forgot your name?"

"Perry."

"Seems your memory isn't what it used to be these days. What're you doing here?"   She asked.

"Getting a bite to eat.   I just finished up with a client not too far from here and they highly recommended this place for dinner.   So, I thought I'd drop in, have a beer, and check out the menu."   She studied his face, trying to decide if he was telling the truth or not.   "I would ask your opinion but see you had rabbit food.   What about you man, what'd you have?"

"The porterhouse, medium-well."   Perry responded dryly.

"What'd you think?   I see your plate is clean."

"It was good."

There was an awkward moment of silence, which made it obvious that neither of them were going to ask him to join them, and Janel hoped that he wasn't contemplating asking the question anyway.   "Well, I'm going to head on over to the bar, I'm starving.   Perry, good seeing you again.   Janel, I guess I'll see you later tonight?"

She couldn't decide if he was being braggadocios in pointing out the fact that she would be coming home to him, or if he was trying to insinuate that she may not come home and choose to stay with Perry instead.   Either way, she didn't appreciate his tone.

"Later man."   Perry said in a dismissive tone.

"I'm really sorry about that.   I don't know what he's doing here."

"What do you have to be sorry about?"

"I don't know.   I told you he's like a big brother, way too overprotective."

"Don't be sorry.   You can't control what he does. Besides, I'm a grown man.   I can take care of myself.   He doesn't intimidate me."

"You're right, I'm sorry."

"There you go apologizing again."   She brought her finger and thumb together in front of her mouth and pressed them together, as if she were pressing imaginary lips shut, and smiled at him.   "You about ready to get out of here?"

"Yes."

"I don't want to keep you out too late.   I don't want you to be sleepy on the job tomorrow."   He stood and reached for her hand, and helped her to her feet.   He intertwined his fingers with hers and led her out of the restaurant.   He walked her to her car and gave her a long, sensual kiss. "Those lips get me every time!   Good night."

She watched him walk away, then pulled her phone from her purse.   She needed to talk, and she hoped Rita was available

# # #

"I'm sorry to come over so late but I really need to talk."

"No problem, come on in."

Janel couldn't get her words out fast enough as she explained what happened at the restaurant.

"You think Tony showed up there on purpose?"

"Of course he did!"

"Maybe it was just a coincidence."

"No, it felt very deliberate to me."

"But how did he know you were there?"

"I don't know.   Maybe he followed me."

"And why would he do that?"

"I don't know!   To be nosy, to try and intimidate Perry and make him think twice about dating me?"

"But according to you, he's with Sherri, so that doesn't make sense to me."

"I know it wasn't a coincidence."

"Do you hear yourself?   Are you listening to what you're saying?"

"I'm not crazy Rita.   Perry told me that he came by the house to pay for the damages to my car.   I wasn't there, and Tony never said a word.   And when I asked him about, he told me he forgot."   She made quotes in the air with her fingers.   "And then he snapped at me and asked me why it mattered.   Then tonight, he acts like he can't remember Perry's name."

Rita sighed.   "I'd be less than a friend if I didn't give you a good old fashioned dose of reality.   This thing with

Perry, in my opinion, is purely physical. He's a great looking guy, and if he looked at me the right way with those green eyes, I'd probably throw my panties at him too."

"How can you say it's physical when we haven't slept together?"

"The attraction is the anticipation of sex, the thrill of the hunt. When you talk about Perry, you get a sly, lustful smile on your face. But when you talk about Tony, you light up. You guys have a mental connection as well as a physical one. He's crazy about you, and you're crazy about him too, otherwise you wouldn't be sitting here accusing him of stalking you!   Why can't you just admit it? You two have such a natural chemistry when you're together, and it's so obvious to everyone else around you, strangers included.   Personally, I think Dorian would even approve if you two officially hooked up.   I know Tony was his best friend, but I think he would've wanted you to move on and be happy."

"I could care less about what Dorian would've thought about me and Tony.   In fact, I hope he's spinning in his grave.   Turnabout is fair play."   Rita cocked her head to the side and waited for her to elaborate.   "I found out he was cheating on me.   He was on his way to see his mistress when he crashed."

"I'm sorry Janel, I didn't know."

"It just pisses me off that every good memory I had of him is completely overshadowed by the fact that he was fucking around on me, and I don't know how to get past that."

"Did you know her?"

"Yes, it was his assistant.   I went through his phone.   I was so pissed that I went to his job and punched her in the face and broke her nose.   I knocked her out, in front of everyone."

"You did what?   Girl that's crazy!"   Rita's voice went up an octave as she moved to the edge of her seat.

"It's not like I planned it, I mean, I didn't know what I was going to do.   I just knew that I had to confront her. I didn't plan for it to turn into something physical."

"Did she try to swing on you?"

"No, she never even saw it coming.   I didn't say anything to her, so she didn't know that I knew."

"I'm not going to sit here and say she didn't deserve it, but you can't just go around punching people Janel."

"I wasn't thinking Rita!   Besides, the police were called and I was arrested."

"Did she press charges?"

"Yes, and she got a restraining order against me. Technically it's a no contact order but basically it's the same thing."

"Are you on probation?"

"No.   Tony handled the whole mess, and got me off the hook.   We never even went to court."

"So you settled out of court?"

"No, he got her to drop the charges.   I didn't have to pay her a dime."

"Wait a minute.   You popped this hussy in the face, in front of witnesses, and he handled his business so well that you never even had to set foot inside a courtroom?"   Rita shook her head in disbelief.   "He's a good man Janel, stop playing around and tell him how you feel before it's too late.   You two should be together."

"But he's-"

"And I don't want to hear anything about Sherri.   She's a non-factor, a place holder, a distraction.   He's just passing time with her.   He's just keeping her around for the fringe benefits because he doesn't want to be alone."

She dropped her head and cradled her forehead in her hands.   Maybe it was time to stop worrying about what everyone else would think and face the facts.   She really did have feelings for Tony that went beyond friendship and the physical.   "I wouldn't even know what to say to him."

"Just be honest.   He's not going to reject you.   He feels the same way, he just needs confirmation from you."

"I wouldn't even know how to approach him.   Am I supposed to just walk up to him and say 'hey Tony, I gotta thing for you?   Let's do this.'"

"You're pathetic, you know?"

"I've been married for almost twenty years.   I don't know anything about making a move on a guy."

"You've already slept with him, he's seen you butt ass naked, how hard can it be?   Listen, here's what you do. You wait until you two are alone, just chilling, doing something you normally do together like watching tv or eating breakfast, whatever.   Actually no, I have a better idea.   He's going to help you move right?"

"I don't know.   I haven't said anything to him since he snapped at me."

"He snapped at you because he was jealous.   So let him get back on your good side by helping you move.   Then, at the end of the day, when we're all tired, DJ's in his room, and I leave to go home, you offer him an ice cold beer."

"What if he decides to leave when you do?"

"I doubt that, but on the off chance that he does, find something for him to do.   Put a shelf up, find a specific box, hell I don't know, something.   You bring him a beer, fix something for yourself to help settle your nerves, and you start off by thanking him for everything he's done for you.   And I mean everything, handling the will, letting you stay with him, keeping you out of jail, basically point out the ways he's shown you he cares.   Then just tell him you how much you care about him.   And once you put it out there, however you get it out, he's going to meet you halfway."

"You make it sound easy."

"If you speak from the heart it will be."

"When Sherri finds out, that'll be the end of my career at CSC."

"Who cares?   You can quit that job and find another one.   He took care of you before, he'll take care of you again.   Don't worry about that.   Just swallow your fear and go for it."

30 - Full Disclosure

"I'm pregnant."

"I'm sorry?"

"I said I'm pregnant."

Tony sat up in the bed. "What?"

"Remember New Orleans? We spent more time in the room than anywhere else." She reached out to touch him but he pulled the covers back and sat up on the edge of the bed. "So that's, like, what-"

"Two months."

"Are you sure?"

Sherri sat up. "Yes I'm sure, I've been to the doctor." Tony closed his eyes and rubbed the top of his head. She waited for him to say something else and when he didn't, she became annoyed. "Is that all you have to say?"

"I don't know what to say."

"How about 'that's great' or 'I'm really happy' or hell even an 'I love you' will do. Now there's something I've been waiting to hear for two years now. Better yet you could just say 'let's get married,' how about that? I can think of a thousand and one things you could say." He knew where the conversation was headed, and it was feeling just like old times. He wasn't in the mood, and was still struggling to wrap his head around the news she'd just given him. "Earth to Anthony?" She raised her voice as if he were hard of hearing.

He knew she was trying to push his buttons because no one but his mother called him Anthony, and she only did it when she wanted to get his undivided attention.

Suddenly all he wanted to do was leave.   "What Sherri? I'm sitting right here, there's no need to yell at me."

"Say something!"

"When I have something to say I will."   He got up and pulled his boxers on.   "I just need a minute."

"For what?"

"To process what you just told me."

"What exactly do you need to process?   I'm pregnant. I have a small human being growing inside of me.   This is happening."

"Obviously you've had some time to think about what's happening with your body.   I'd just appreciate it if you gave me a little time to do the same."

"I thought you'd be happy."

"I didn't say I wasn't."

"Then what's the problem?"   He pulled his jeans on and buttoned them up, not bothering to answer her question. He honestly didn't have an answer for her because he wasn't sure how he felt.   She got up and pulled on a pink robe from the back of the bedroom door, and knotted it loosely around her waist.   "It really doesn't matter how you feel because I'm having this baby."

"I'm not telling you not to have it.   Surely you know me well enough by now to know I wouldn't do that."

"I'm not doing this alone either."

"Who said you had to?   Where did that come from?"

"Obviously you're not happy about this."

"I didn't say I wasn't happy-"

"You didn't say you were either."

"Have you given this any thought at all?"

"What the hell is that supposed to mean?   Of course I've given it thought.   I've done nothing but think about it."

"I'm talking about the risks to your health.   We're not in our twenties or thirties anymore.   Will you even be able to carry this baby to term?   Have you considered the health risks for the baby?   Birth defects like Downs syndrome, higher risk of miscarriage.   Have you stopped to think about how old we'll be by the time this child graduates high school?   Is that really fair to do that to a child?   This is a baby Sherri, not a pet.   I'm sorry if I'm not reacting exactly like you want me to.   This is a huge commitment and there are a lot of things to consider here."

"You don't think I haven't thought of all that?"

"That's the point I'm trying to make, you've had some time to think about this.   I've had all of five minutes to process what you've told me and somehow you expect me to have something profound to say.   Just right off the top of my head!"

"You don't have to get pissy with me."

"I've gotta go."   He put his socks on and sat down and tied his shoes up.

"Where are you going?"

"I told you before I'm helping Janel move today."   He pulled his shirt over his head and put his wallet in his pocket.

"At six o'clock in the morning?"

"I need to go home first and shower and get changed."

"Whatever."

"Look Sherri.   I'm not upset, I'm not unhappy, I'm just feeling, I don't know, a little overwhelmed right now."

"And I'm not?"

He picked up his keys and looked at her.   "I'll call you later, we'll talk about it.   I just need some time, ok?"

"Fuck you Tony."   She said before she walked into the bathroom and slammed the door shut behind her.   For Tony it was only confirmation that their relationship had come full circle.   They were right back where he didn't want to be; arguing, fussing, and fighting.

# # #

"Lady and gentleman, I am done.   I have no energy left. Here are your consolation prizes, thanks so much for helping me out today."   He eagerly grabbed the cold beer from Janel's hand as he remained seated on her bedroom floor.   She handed Rita a wine cooler, who was sitting in a chair in front of the French doors.   "It's a mess but at least I have all of my belongings under one roof now.   At least I think I do, I'll have to double check the storage units one last time before I turn the keys in.   Once I find them." She twisted the top on her wine cooler and chucked the metal cap into a box of trash before she plopped down on her bed.

"Let me know if you can't find them, I have an extra set."

"Oh I'll find them.   They charge you a ridiculous fee if you don't turn them back in.   I really want to thank both of you for all your help.   I wouldn't have been nearly as far along if I had to do this by myself.   Making sure the movers put everything in the right place alone would have set me back a whole day."

"You helped me get my place together so it was nothing for me to return the favor."

"I owe this man right here big time.   Without him, getting into my own house would have been a pipe dream. You've been such a big help to me, through everything." She put her hand to her mouth and he watched her try to choke back her emotions.

"Come on girl, keep it together.   If you start crying then I'll start crying and I'm sure Tony doesn't want to be consoling two emotional women after all the hard work he put in today."

"I'm just so thankful to have you in my life.   If it weren't you for none of this would've been possible."

"To Tony."   Rita said, and they raised their bottles in the air.

Tony tipped the bottle back and drank the cold brew straight down, without stopping, and Janel wasn't far behind him.

"Dang, you two thirsty or what?"   Rita had barely taken a sip of her cooler.

"Yes.   You need to catch up.   We've earned these drinks today."   Tony told her.   "In fact, I'm going to grab another one."

"I'll get it."   She said, taking the empty bottle from his hand.   "I'm going to stick mine in the fridge and head home.   My Sealey posturepedic is calling me.   I'm hurting in places I didn't even know could hurt."

"I'll walk you out."   Janel said, taking the cooler from her hand and taking a sip.

"Me too.   Help an old man up please."   He stretched a hand out to Janel and she leaned back as she helped him get to his feet.

"I'll be back tomorrow.   But not too early."   Rita said as Tony opened her car door for her.   "Tell DJ I said bye. He's probably asleep up there by now."

"Probably.   It's been a really long day.   If you make it back tomorrow fine, if you don't, I'll understand."

"You know I wouldn't leave you hanging like that.   I'll see you tomorrow."   She waved before she backed into the street and drove away.

"Come on, I'll get you another cold beer.   You've certainly earned it."   Janel said as they walked back into the house.

"Actually I'd prefer a Jack and Coke if you got it."

"I can do that, if you'll help me find some sheets and towels so I can make my bed and take a shower."

"I think I can handle that."   Tony headed towards the bedroom and sorted through some boxes until he found one labeled 'MB linen closet.'   Janel walked in and handed him a plastic cup and he in turn pointed to the box.

"YES, thank you."

"You're welcome." He sat the cup on top of a stack of boxes, then used a box cutter to make quick work of the multiple layers of tape. "They packed this like it was being shipped overseas or something."

"Sit down and enjoy your drink, I can get that." She gently pushed him out of the way. He sat on the bed and watched her remove a layer of crumpled brown paper from the box. She dug around until she was able to find a set of towels and wash cloths, along with a full set of matching bed sheets. He cleared the bed off as she took the linens into the bathroom, and they worked together to put the sheets on.

"You need anything else while I'm up? I've got one small reserve of energy left before I sit down and enjoy this drink."

"Sit down and rest. If I need anything else, I'll get it myself or it can wait until tomorrow."

Tony sat down and immediately guzzled the drink down. He held onto the cup and stared into the bottom of it as he contemplated telling her the news. "I am really feeling my age today."

"Who you telling?" She said she laid down on her bed. "I'm going to miss seeing you every day. Don't get me wrong, I love this place, but it was nice being at your place too."

"You say that like you moved across the country. We live ten minutes apart."

"I know."

"Honestly, I didn't expect you to move out so soon, but I know how important it was for you to get your own place. I'm glad things are working out."

"I need to tell you-"

"Sherri's pregnant." He blurted out, inadvertently interrupting her. "She told me this morning."

She sat up, her face flush. "Are you serious?"

"Yes."

"Um, wow.   I don't even know what to say."

"Me neither."   He looked at her and waited for her to say something, but she seemed to be at a loss for words. "I'm sorry.   I didn't mean to cut you off.   You were going to say something."

"It's, um, it wasn't important.   How pregnant?"

"Two months."

"I really don't know what to say.   Are you-I mean, is that good news?   Are you happy?"

"You know, she asked me the exact same thing.   I don't know how I feel about it to be honest.   It definitely wasn't planned."

They stared at each other for a moment and the silence was deafening.   "Well, if you decide you're happy, then I'm happy.   And I'm here for you if you need me."   She moved to the edge of the bed and stood up.   "Here, let me get that."   She took the cup from him and he took her hand in his and squeezed.   "It's getting late, you should probably go.   You ok to drive?   If not, I can make up the guest bedroom if you need me to."

At that moment, all he wanted to do was stay with her. He wanted to climb into bed with her and hold her until they both fell asleep.   "What were you going to say?   Tell me."

"Nothing, it's not important."   She said as she pulled her hand from his.   He followed her into the kitchen.   "I hope you're ready, babies are a lot of work."

"You say that like I don't remember when DJ was little."

She smiled as she put the cup into the sink.   "I remember when I went into labor you were the first one to the hospital.   You even beat the doctor."

"I never let Dorian live that down either."

"Don't be a stranger, ok?"

"Never.   You and DJ mean the world to me."

"Things will change."

"They don't have to."

"They will."

"Janel-" He took a step towards her and she backed up against the counter.

"You should go."

"Is that what you want?"

"It's not about what I want, it's about what's best."

"What if I don't want to?" He moved towards her and she pressed her hand to his chest to keep him from getting any closer.

"Staying with me, in my bed, isn't an option. But you're welcome to the guest bedroom. Things are obviously very different now." He took a step back, out of her personal space. "Look Tony, I'm thankful for everything you've done for us. Words aren't enough to express my gratitude. But I'm on my feet now, and I'm on my way to a new life, so don't feel guilty about moving on to live yours."

"You make it sound like I'm going to fall off the face of the earth and we'll never see each other again."

"Before you know it your life will totally revolve around Sherri and the baby, and there won't be room for anyone else."

"There will always be room for you and DJ."

"No, there won't be. She'll make sure of that. She's going to systematically remove every person from your life that means anything to you. And she'll do it in a way that you won't even realize it's happening until she's done. Me, DJ, Doug, even your mother."

"It'll be a cold day in hell before she'll keep me away from my mother. We've been through too much together. She's my foundation, my rock."

"Fine, I'm wrong. I don't want to argue about it. I'm tired, and I know you're tired too. Just go home." He leaned in to kiss her on the forehead, like he always did, but she turned her head away.

"I don't want to leave here with you upset with me."

"I'm not upset, I'm just tired and ready to go to bed. Please, just go."

"I'll be back in the morning.   I'll take everyone out to breakfast before we get back at it."

"Don't worry about it.   I think we can handle it from here.   If I need you, I'll call."

He looked in her eyes to make sure she wasn't angry and she looked away.   "You need something, anything, you call me ok?"   Disappointed and hurt, he let himself out.

31 - Ghosts of Thanksgiving Past

"You ready?"   Perry asked Janel as he gave her a kiss.

"Almost.   You and PJ come on in and have a seat."

"You bring your games?"   DJ asked PJ.

"Yep.   You got the console?"   DJ held up his backpack.

"You think your mom will let you go see a movie tonight? My dad said it's ok with him if it's ok with your mom."

Janel checked her panty hose before slipping on her shoes.   She brushed her hair a few more times and fastened a necklace around her neck.   "I'm ready."

"You look really nice.   Love the shoes."

"Red bottoms.   They're old, but classic."

"Louboutins."

She paused.   "I forgot, you were married to Ayana."

"Exactly.   Besides, they don't sell them in my size."   PJ rolled his eyes at his dad's poor attempt at a joke.   "Heads up."   He threw the keys to his son.   "You guys get in the car, we'll be out in a minute."   She emptied her purse on the kitchen counter and stuck a few essentials into a small clutch.   Perry stood behind her and put his hands around her waist.   "You smell even better than you look."   He kissed her on the back of her neck.

"Ok!   Please don't do that."   She tried to pull away but he held her tight.

"I think I found a sweet spot."   He kissed it again and she spun around and faced him.

"I'm serious Perry.   If you don't back up off my neck we'll never make it to the car."

"I'd be ok with that."   He backed her into the counter and she had a flashback of being with Tony in his kitchen.

"We have to go.   The boys are waiting."

"I'm really trying to respect your wishes and take things slow, but it's so hard when you always look so damn good."

"I tell you what."   She sensually licked her lips and poked her finger in his chest.   "You behave yourself tonight and maybe I'll let you get to third base."

"Really?   Don't play with me woman.   I'll find a triple feature for the boys to go to and they won't be back here until nine o'clock in the morning."

"What're you talking about?"

"They want to go to one of the midnight movies, some new action flick.   If we let them drive themselves, that will buy us at least an hour and a half alone."

"I guess you just might get lucky tonight then.   Let's go, I don't want to be late."

During the ride to Rita's home, Janel tried hard to fix her attitude.   She wasn't thrilled about seeing Sherri, and she certainly wasn't looking forward to the awkwardness that might occur with the four of them being in the same room together.   She was, however, looking forward to seeing Tony.   But she felt as if she wouldn't be able to have a conversation with him without Sherri getting jealous and Perry feeling left out.   She decided to focus on Rita and Chuck instead, and getting to know the other guests she'd invited.

They stood on the porch, arm in arm, and rang the doorbell.   "Hey you guys!   Good to see you."   Rita gave them all a big hug and kisses.   "You two can head on upstairs, first bedroom on the left.   I know you don't want to hang out with the boring adults.   There's a tv up there, and I'll come get you when it's time to eat.   Perry, you need to pull the car into the back yard.   You can't park on the street, they'll tow you.   And don't worry about the grass, it's no big deal."   Both women watched him as he jogged back to the car.   "Girl.   Look at how that sweater hugs his chest and those biceps.   When you gonna let him hit it so we can find out if he's any good in bed?"

Janel smacked her on the arm.   "Stop it.   It's hard enough to hold out as it is."

"So don't.   Give in and live a little."

"I'm considering it.   Tonight."

"Really?   Let me know how that goes."

"You know I will.   Are they here yet?"

"He called and said they might be a little late because she's not feeling well."

"I hope she doesn't show up at all.   I know that's bad but I don't even want to be in the same house with her." They smiled and waved as Perry rode by in the driveway.

"You're not going to worry about them.   You've got a handsome man to keep you busy, and if he's not enough, you can get to know some of the other people here."

"Where's Chuck?   That's who I want to see!"

"He's in there.   Go on, I'll wait for Perry."

She barely set foot inside the house when she heard a baritone voice say "You know you look just like a beautiful young woman I used to know named Janel Carter.   She broke my heart when she ran off and married some hoodlum named Dorian."   She grinned from ear to ear as she took in Chuck's presence.   He gave her a long, tight bear hug as he picked her up off her feet.   He finally put her down but continued to hold onto her hands.

"Charles Siedel.   I don't know what it is about you men, you're all aging so gracefully."

"You know Black don't crack baby."

"With the exception of that little bit of gray in your mustache, you still look the same."

"I've gained a pair of love handles too."

"Could've fooled me.   You're just as fine now as you were back then.   If Rita wasn't my roommate I would've stole you from her for sure."

"She told me about Dorian.   I wish I would've known, I'd have come to the funeral."   He gave her a kiss on the cheek.

"I appreciate that, I know you would have."

"I thought I saw a ghost when I saw that young man walk up those stairs."

"That's his namesake.   Looks just like him doesn't he? I'll introduce you when he comes back down to eat."

"Is the other one yours too?"

"That one's mine."   Perry said from behind her.

Rita introduced them.   "Chuck, this is Perry.   He's the father of that young man that just went upstairs, and Janel's gentleman paramour."

"Paramour?   She got that PhD and got all fancy on us." Janel joked.

"We're too old to be talking about 'boyfriends' and 'girlfriends.'   Paramour sounds more mature."

"Hey man, nice to meet you."   Chuck clasped Perry's hand and they leaned in towards each other and lightly bumped chests.

"There are drinks and hors d'oeuvres in the kitchen but go easy because I'll be pulling the turkey out of the oven within the next fifteen minutes or so."

"Come on, let's get something to drink and mingle." Janel pulled Perry by the hand into the kitchen.

"Wow, that's a big dude."

"And he wouldn't hurt a fly, unless it was wearing shoulder pads and a helmet.   He's such a sweetheart, he'd give you the shirt off your back if you needed it."

"And she's so petite.   It's kind of funny to see them together."   She heard the doorbell ring as she and Perry were introducing themselves to some of Rita's colleagues who were hanging out in the kitchen eating snacks.   Janel poured them both a drink and they shared a plate as they hovered near the butcher block, eating and making small talk.

"Happy Thanksgiving everybody."   Tony said as he came into the kitchen.   He made a beeline for Janel and kissed her briefly on the cheek.   It was something he'd done a thousand times, but on this particular evening it made her feel terribly uncomfortable.   Perry reacted by putting his hand around her waist, which made her feel even more uncomfortable.   She grabbed his hand and held it for a moment, then let it go.

"Happy Thanksgiving to you."

"Hey man, what's up."   Tony acknowledged Perry as he grabbed a small plate and piled it high with snacks.   "I am starving."

"Rita said we'll be eating soon so you may not want to finish that plate.   Where's Sherri?"

"She decided not to come at the last minute.   She's not feeling well."   He poured himself a drink and picked up the plate.   "I'm going to go say hi to Chuck.   I haven't seen that guy in I don't know how long."

Upon hearing that dinner would be ready soon, the kitchen cleared quickly leaving her and Perry alone.   "Are you ok?"

"Yeah, why?"

"I'm not allowed to touch you?"

"I'm sorry, it just doesn't feel right.   I don't want you to think I'm ashamed of you or anything, it's not that."

"Don't tease me with third base and then expect me to keep my hands to myself the entire evening.   I'm just a man.   Help me to understand."   He was smiling but she could see that his plea was sincere.

"This is the first time I've done something like this since my husband passed.   And with Chuck, Rita, and Tony here, it just feels like Dorian should be here too.   Now I'm not saying I wish he was here, or that I wish you were him, it just feels weird to be affectionate with another man around them.   Especially when all they've ever known is me and Dorian."   She grasped his hands with hers.   "I don't want you to think I feel like this any other time we go out because I don't.   It's just this situation, this environment, with these particular people.   It's my first Thanksgiving without him and it happens to be with people from my past.   I hope you can understand that."

"I do.   Do you want to leave?"

"No, not at all.   We'll stay, have dinner, and I'll see how I feel then.   Just bear with me, ok?"   She squeezed his hands and he kissed her on the top of her head.

"Sure.   Whatever you need, I'm here."

"Thank you baby."

All of Rita's guests finally gathered around the dining room table, and once they began to eat and the alcohol began flowing more freely, people loosened up and really began to enjoy themselves.   And despite all the joking, smiling, and laughing, Janel still felt somewhat off.   She excused herself and went to the kitchen, followed closely by Perry.

"Are you sure you're ok?   You're just not yourself tonight."   Upon hearing his concern, she got emotional and tears welled up in her eyes.   "Aw baby, don't cry." He hugged her close.   "Maybe you're not ready for all this yet.   Why don't you let me take you home?"   She shook her head no and he handed her a napkin to wipe her face.

"I'm fine, it's just the ghosts of holidays past."

"Maybe it's too soon."

"I'm fine."

"Then maybe I should pull back a little and give you some space, just until you get through the holidays."

She pushed him away and looked up at him.   "I don't want you to do that."

"If you guys need a room I have a guest bedroom upstairs."   Perry instinctively stood in front of her to hide the fact that she'd been crying but Rita noticed right away. "Nel, what's wrong?"

"I'm fine."

"I wondered if it was too soon.   It's your first Thanksgiving without-"

"Did someone move the party in here and not tell the rest of us?"   The smile faded from Tony's face as soon as he saw Janel's.   "What's wrong?   What happened?"

"It's fine Tony, she's ok."   Rita said, quickly trying to diffuse the situation.

"What'd you do to her man?"

"Me?   How the hell do you just come in here and assume I did something to her?"

Tony took a step towards Perry and Rita stood squarely in front of him.   She put her hands on his stomach to keep him from moving any closer.   "Tony, stop.   Please."

"Why don't you go home and worry about taking care of your own woman.   I got this."

"Don't worry about my woman, she's fine.   Right now she's my concern."   Tony pointed at Janel.

"She's fine Tony.   She just had a moment.   It's ok."

Janel ran warm water over a paper towel and wiped her face.   "I don't want you guys making a big deal out of this. I'm fine, really."

Rita lowered her voice.   "Just let him handle it. You've done a great job taking care of her through all of this, maybe it's time you let someone else do it."

Tony looked at Janel.   "Are you sure you're ok?"

"Look man, I already told you.   I got this.   Go check on your woman."

Tony took another step towards Perry and Rita put her hands in his chest and strained against his weight. "Actually Tony, that's not a bad idea.   Why don't you give Sherri a call and see how she's feeling."   He continued to stare at Perry, feet firmly planted.   "Call her, see if she's feeling better."   Rita tried pushing him out of the kitchen but he stubbornly stood his ground.   "It's Thanksgiving Gibson, we don't need all this tension and hostility."   She felt his muscles relax as he pulled his phone from his pocket.   "You can use my room, out the door, to the right. Give yourself some privacy."   He cut his eyes at Perry one last time and left the room, with Rita on his heels.

"What the hell just happened in there?   He looks pissed."   Chuck asked.

"Janel was missing Dorian and got emotional.   Perry was consoling her, Tony assumed Perry did something to make her cry.   You men and your damn testosterone."

"Tony's got it bad for her doesn't he?"

"She's got it bad for him too!   But just when she got up the nerve to tell him, Sherri turned up pregnant."

"Perry seems like a pretty nice guy."

"He is.   And he likes her a lot."

"But?"

"He's not Tony."   They watched Tony emerge from Rita's bedroom.

"I think I'm going to go."

"Is Sherri ok?"   Rita asked.

"Yeah.   She laid down and took a nap, said she's feeling better now.   She's at the store buying ice cream."

"You headed over to see her?"   Chuck asked.

"No.   I think I'm just going to head home."

"I don't want you to go home and sit around by yourself." Rita said, concerned.

"She doesn't sound like she's in the mood for company, and I don't want to ruin your party.   Don't worry about me.   I've got plenty of work to keep me company.   I'll be fine."   He hugged Rita and gave her a kiss on the cheek, then clasped hands with Chuck and wrapped his arm around his back.   "Hey man, when are you heading home?"

"Monday morning."

"I know you're here to see Rita, but I'd really like to buy you a beer before you leave.   I just want to sit down and catch up with you, so make sure you call me."   They exchanged numbers and Chuck promised to give him a call.

32 - To Rekindled Relationships

"Big Chuck, it's good to see you again." Tony stood and gave his friend a hug as he signaled for the waitress.

"Rum and coke please, hold the ice." She acknowledged Chuck's order with a nod of her head and walked away.

"It's been years man, I can't believe it. You're a sight for sore eyes that's for sure."

"It's good to see you too. What's the best thing you've ever had here?" He asked as he looked over the menu.

"Put it this way, I have yet to have something bad. Where's Rita?"

"She's somewhere in here shopping with my credit card. Janel's here too, they met up in the food court." The waitress returned with his drink and he ordered a salmon fillet entree.

"You let her loose in here on your dime?"

"It's cool man, I trust her. I'd do anything for her."

"I really hate that we lost touch over the years. Where did you end up going after school, and what are you doing now? Rita said something about you living in Virginia?"

"We stayed in Michigan for a few years, then we moved to Baltimore for a while, and now I'm in Virginia. I'm a project management consultant and I love it. There's never a shortage of work, my schedule is flexible, I'm not tied to a desk all day, and I make good money."

"Ok, I gotta ask cause I'm confused. What's up with you and Rita? I thought you two were divorced, but here you are visiting for Thanksgiving. What's up with that?"

"I don't know man." He smiled as he scratched his

forehead.   "I didn't want the divorce, I just did it because I love her and I knew that's what she wanted."

"Are you trying to get her back?"

"Hell yeah I'm trying to win her back.   There's no doubt in my mind that she's the only one for me.   There ain't no other woman that can even come close.   I'm not going to sit here and bullshit you, it wasn't all roses, we had our problems, but I think maybe we just needed some time away from each other or something.   I tell you what, when I got here and she picked me up from the airport, she took me straight to her place and put it on me.   The sex was always good, but being away from each other for a while and then hitting it.   Whoo wheee!   It was better than make up sex, I'm telling you."

Tony nodded and smiled.   He missed make up sex. He missed any sex for that matter.   Since getting pregnant, Sherri was tired all the time, and she experienced more than the occasional bout of morning sickness. Unfortunately sex for him came in the form of self-love in the bathroom with a tube of K-Y Jelly.   And he would usually reminisce about the sex he'd had with Janel on the couch or on the kitchen counter.   Now that Sherri was pregnant, he knew there was no way he'd be able to sleep with Janel again.   In fact, he'd only seen her two or three times since she'd moved out, and each of those encounters was brief.

"I'm not going anywhere, I'm just trying to give her space until she decides she wants me back too."

"I hope it works out for you, you guys make a great couple."

"Thanks, I appreciate that.   I tell you what, when Rita told me about what happened to Dorian, I was tripping.   I didn't even know what to say.   That dude seemed so invincible when we were in school, seems like he was always doing something crazy.   To go out like that, slamming into a tree, that's messed up."   Tony closed his eyes, not wanting to think about it.   "Aw man, I'm sorry. I shouldn't have said that, that was really stupid.   I know y'all were pretty tight.   Did he ever mellow out or what?"

"Dorian didn't know the meaning of the word mellow. I mean, he could spell it, you know he was smart as hell, but mellow just wasn't in his vocabulary.   I will say he matured a little, especially after DJ was born, but other than that he was pretty much the same cat.   And I miss him man.   A lot."

"When I saw his son, I thought I was seeing a ghost. Spitting image."

"Yeah, he's a good kid.   I think he takes after his mom a little more than his dad though.   At least as far as his personality.   He's got a pretty good head on his shoulders, and he's smart too."

"Speaking of Janel, what's up with you two?"

"What do you mean?"

"I thought I sensed a little bit of a vibe between you at the party."

"Aw that, yeah, I'm a little embarrassed about that.   I just don't care for that guy she's seeing is all."

"Come on man.   It may have been a while since we've seen each other but you ain't changed all that much. What's up with you two?"

"Ain't nothing going on with me and Janel."

"Then why you grinning?"

"Cause it's a funny question, that's why I'm grinning."

"I'm so happy to amuse you but I'm being serious man."

"Who had the salmon fillet?"   The waitress asked as she balanced a serving tray on her shoulder.   Chuck raised his hand and she whisked the plate down on the table in front of him.   "And this must be yours."   She said as she placed Tony's plate in front of him.   "You two need anything else?"   They shook their heads no in unison. "Enjoy."   She said as she tucked the tray under her arm and walked away.

"Back to Janel.   Don't think you're getting off the hook that easy."   Chuck cut into his fish and gave the piece a few sniffs before putting it into his mouth.

Tony sighed as he sat back in his chair.   "This has Rita written all over it.   What did she have to say about me and Janel?"

"Never mind what she told me, I'm asking you.   I want to hear it directly from the horse's mouth."

He finished off his beer and signaled the waitress to bring him another as he pushed his food around on his plate, trying to decide what he wanted to bite into first. "There's nothing to tell.   When Dorian passed, I was there for her.   I helped her with the funeral, the will, the house, and some legal stuff.   I think we helped each other get through it actually.   Some things happened between the two of us along the way, but that's all said and done now. She's on her own two feet and doing really good."

"You know that's not going to fly with me right?   I need details man.   What 'things' happened between you two?"

He realized his friend was serious so he decided to level with him.   "All right look, I ain't gonna lie to you.   We'd been spending a lot of time together, things got really rocky with my girl, and Janel and I had sex a few times."   He stuffed a few pieces of broccoli in his mouth and began to chew.

"And."

"And I think we both may have caught feelings.   We realized it was a little more than a physical thing.   I approached her about, you know, getting together for real, like dating, but she shot me down.   Next thing you know Sherri's pregnant."   He thanked the waitress for the fresh beer.

"You love her?"

"Janel?"

Chuck smiled.   "I meant Sherri."

Tony ran a hand over his beard.   "I care about her."

"That's not what I asked you."

"I don't know, I guess I love her."

"You guess? You *guess*? Man please. If you asked me if I love Rita, you couldn't even get the words out of your mouth before I'd look you right in the eye and tell you yes, I absolutely love that woman. With all of my heart, more than life itself, with every cell in my body. And you over there hemming and hawing? Talking about *you guess*? Matter of fact, where is she right now?"

Tony shrugged his shoulders. "I don't know. At home I guess."

"You-you guess? Man if my woman was pregnant I'd be up under her twenty-four seven, catering to her every need. She'd get sick of seeing me."

"I come around when she wants me to, and when she's not in the mood to be bothered I make myself scarce. All those damn hormones, one minute she's laughing, the next she's crying, or she's yelling at me for something I didn't even have anything to do with it. It's crazy man. Shit, truth be told, it was kind of like that *before* she got pregnant. The bottom line is, I care about her and I'm taking care of my responsibility."

Chuck bellowed with laughter, causing other people in the restaurant turn and look. "You say that like you're taking your car in for a tune up or something. Let me ask you this. You plan on getting a DNA test done?"

It was Tony's turn to laugh. "Why would I do that?"

"Because you're a lawyer, and you want to make sure you don't get caught up in no mess."

"She ain't been with nobody else."

"How do you know? You stepped out on her with Janel, who's to say she didn't do the same thing to you, and ended up with a little more than she bargained for?"

Tony thought about seeing Sherri and Shawn having lunch at the Mexican restaurant and the smile faded from his face. "Naw, she wouldn't do that."

"How do you know?"

"She tried to make me jealous once but..."

Chuck raised his eyebrows in doubt.   "You never know man.   Women are smart.   They'll flip it on you like that and you'll never even know."

"I'm not even entertaining that.   The baby's mine, and I'm going to take care of my responsibility.   My dad left my mom before I was even born.   He could be sitting in this restaurant right now and I wouldn't know it.   I've never even seen a picture of him.   And Sherri, she grew up in foster care.   She has no clue who either of her parents are.   I don't want that for any blood of mine.   I need to be there."

"It's not even in you to do something like that.   My point is, it sounds to me like you're settling.   And I don't mean 'settling down,' I mean settling for less than you want or deserve.   If the baby is yours-"

"Don't go there man, the baby is mine."

"Mama's baby, daddy's maybe.   All I'm saying is I just got here four days ago.   I haven't seen you and Janel in years.   But what I saw Thursday night was two people who have a lot of feelings for each other who seem to be settling for being with someone else."

"What you saw was a woman mourning her husband, and a friend who was frustrated that he couldn't be there for her like he has been in the past.   I just need to let go, that's Perry's job now.   Besides, I told you I tried to tell her how I felt and I got shot down."

"What if you knew, without a shadow of a doubt, that she felt the same way?"

"It doesn't matter now.   Sherri's pregnant, and Janel's with Perry now.   It wouldn't have worked anyway, the timing was all wrong.   Besides, I don't have time to worry about shoulda, coulda, woulda, or what ifs for that matter. The reality is we're both moving on now, in different directions."

"It's too bad-"

"Just stop it man.   I know you mean well-"

Chuck held his massive palms in the air in surrender. "It's cool, I'm done."   The two men finished their meal in silence.

Finally, Tony wiped his mouth with the cloth napkin and placed it on the table.   "How come you and Rita don't have kids?"

"Retrograde ejaculation.   I had a groin injury when I was young.   When I come, most of the semen goes into my bladder."

"What the hell?"

"Yeah, it's crazy.   We could've done in vitro, but she didn't want to.   She said if it was meant to be it would happen."

"How did you find that out?"

"I asked my doctor.   I always knew something was off, I'd seen pornos and I knew I couldn't come like those guys."

"Nobody can, it's a porno man!"

"You know what I mean.   He ran some tests and that's how we found out.   I wish I had known that back when we were in school.   All the ass-"

"You still would've been with Rita and you still would've been wearing a condom.   Come on man, let's go walk some of this meal off."   They paid the bill and left a tip for the waitress and wandered out into the mall.

"What's up with Perry?   I know you already ran a background check on him."

"I'm not going to lie, I did.   I just wanted to make sure she was safe.   He's divorced, makes decent money, never been arrested.   You already know he has a son.   His ex-wife is banging.   I'm talking runway beautiful, like a model."

"Couldn't have been all that if they're divorced."

"Yeah I'm wondering what happened there.   No-fault, and he's the one that filed, not her."

"He seems like a pretty nice guy.   And he's obviously very into Janel."

Tony sucked his teeth.   "He aight."

"*Aight*?   Did you see the way the women were looking at him at the party?   He got them green eyes and that whole Creole thing going on.   Women love that shit.   I'm secure enough in my manhood to admit that if I was a woman, I'd let him hit it.   I hear beige brothers are making a comeback."

Tony stopped walking and looked at him.   "Man, what the fuck is wrong with you?"

Chuck started laughing.   "I'm just messing with you man.   It's been a while so I gotta make up for lost time."

"Bastard."   Tony chuckled.   "You're touched, you know that right?"

"Don't be jealous.   Just cause you got brown eyes don't make you any less sexy.   If I were a woman I'd let you hit it too."

"Stop it man.   Just stop.   Now I've got a visual of you in a dress, and you'd make one ugly woman."   They started walking again.   "This is good man.   You make sure you stay in touch."

"We got each other's number.   You know you can call me anytime."

"Maybe we can look up some of the guys and have a mini reunion or something."

"I promise you, as long as Rita is in Lafayette, I'm going to be in town so often you're going to think I've moved here.   I'm going to get her back, come hell or high water. You watch what I say."

33 - Operation Set Up

"So, how you been feeling?" Rita asked Janel as she flipped through hangers on a clearance rack, quickly inspecting each and every article of clothing.

"You mean since my mini meltdown?"

"It wasn't a meltdown, it's a normal part of the grieving process."

"I'm better. I didn't expect to get so emotional, I was just momentarily overwhelmed. It brought back memories for me. I was the one who always threw the holiday parties." She picked up a dress and held it against herself. Rita scrunched up her nose and shook her head. "I played the hostess, I made the drinks, I had the cute holiday dishes and glasses." She put the dress back on the rack and moved on to another one.

"I trust Perry took good care of you?" Rita held up a skirt. "For you, not me." Janel shook her head and she put it back.

"He did. He's a sweetie."

"You think maybe you're moving too fast? Getting back into a relationship? Not that I'm being judgmental, I'm just asking the question."

"I'm always going to miss Dorian, there's no question about that. Hell I can't help but think about him every time I see my son. But I'm ready to give a relationship a go, and Perry's very respectful of the fact that I want to take things slow."

"What about DJ? How's he doing?"

"He has his moments, and I don't think he knows I know that, but he's doing ok. And he seems to approve of me and Perry.   They hang out a lot, especially since he's friends with his son, and they get along really well."

"That's good."   She moved on to different rack.   "Did you let him hit it this weekend?"   Janel smiled and turned her back to her friend as she stifled a laugh.   She whirled back around with a shirt held up to her torso.   "Now that I like."

"Did you let Chuck hit it this weekend?" Janel fired back.

"Of course, several times.   But we're not talking about me, we're talking about you."

"I can't have this conversation with you on an empty stomach.   I'm calling a time out so we can hit the food court."   The ladies exited the store, picked up some sandwiches and a drink, and hunted for a clean table. They barely sat down good and Rita was grilling her again.

"Did you finally let the man hit it or what?   The suspense is killing me and I can't seem to read you on this one."

"Yes."

"And?"

"It was....ok."

"What the hell does that mean, 'ok?'   That can't be good."

"Don't get me wrong, he's well equipped, there was some foreplay, and he was very gentle and attentive.   He waited for me to get mine, and he got his, and then it was over."

"So he was a minute man?"

"No, no problems in the stamina department.   He seemed to really enjoy himself I guess.   It wasn't bad, it just wasn't good.   There was no....excitement, no creativity."

"So he was boring?"

"Yeah, I guess that's what I'm trying to say."

"He didn't have a 'move?'   All guys have a move, right?"

"If he does he kept it to himself."

"He didn't go downtown?"

Janel shook her head no.   "He kept it right here."   She made a sweeping motion starting below her boobs up to her head.

"Girl.   Now that makes me wonder.   You did say Ayana cheated on him.   Maybe it was because he didn't spice it up enough in the bedroom."

"And I need spice."

"But, if that's the case, it's an easy fix.   You'll just have to tell him, or show him, what you like in bed.   You said he's working with some nice equipment right?"

"Yes ma'am.   Great body, stamina, length and width. And I did get mine."

"I say he's train-able.   Give him another chance. Maybe he didn't want to pull out his bag of tricks too early. If you let him hit again and things start going back down the same boring road, take charge.   You know some men really get off on that.   Flip him onto his back and ride him like a cow girl.   And if you really want to put it on him, reverse cowgirl him.   When he sees your butt bouncing up and down in all its glory, he'll catch on real quick.   Now *that* ought to spark his creativity."

"I hope so.   I don't think I can stay with a man that I'm not sexually compatible with.   I know that probably sounds bad but I gotta be honest.   I had good sex for seventeen years, I'm not about to settle for mediocre or bad sex now.   Call me shallow if you want but I need it.   It's a requirement."

"I don't think there's anything wrong with that, we all have different needs.   Give him another chance.   He's cute, he's a nice guy, and he's really into you.   And if you have to work with him a little bit, so be it.   I think he's worth it."

"So what's up with you and Chuck?"   Rita turned her head and feigned hearing loss.   "Uh huh, now it's my turn to grill you.   You're not getting off that easy."

"Fine, bring it on."

"Why did you spend the money to divorce him when you two clearly act like you're still married?"   Rita took a minute to think about her response.   "If you have to think about it, do you really think you made the right decision?"

"I felt like we were growing apart.   And I wanted to end it before things went bad."

"Did you try counseling?"

"You know Black folks don't go to counseling."

"You sound like Dorian.   He and I were going through a rough patch and I finally talked him into going.   We learned a lot, and having someone who was non-biased serve as a mediator really helped.   It was a lot of work but once we started using the skills we learned things did get better."

"The first time I brought up counseling he flat out refused to go.   He said he didn't want some stranger all in our business.   Then when I brought it up a second time and insisted on it, he only agreed to it because he knew I wouldn't back down.   But then I changed my mind because I knew he agreed to go because I wanted him to. He just wasn't open to the idea.   How'd you finally convince Dorian to go?"

"I closed my legs and suddenly he was real open to the idea."

Rita let out a laugh.   "Are you serious?"

"Yes.   Sometimes as women we forget the power we hold between our left thigh and our right.   Give it a try the next time you want Chuck to do something that's *really* important to you.   It works, just don't use it too often, and only as a last resort."

"I don't think I could hold out for long.   I have a weakness for Big Willy and the twins."

"So what happens now?   Do you start dating other people?   Are you just trying to see if the grass is greener? I'm curious because whatever problems you had, clearly you two are still into each other.   Maybe you should have tried a legal separation instead?"

"Maybe, hind sight being twenty twenty."

"You still love him, I know you do.   And he's just as head over heels in love with you now as he was when we were in school."

"I'll always love him.   There's no doubt in my mind about that."

"So where do you go from here?"

"I don't know.   I guess I take some time to figure out what I really want.   Do I move on with my life and we remain friends, or do I go back to what I know?"

"You and Chuck, and the phrase 'just friends' don't even belong in the same sentence.   And he's just going to keep flying down here to see you until you give in and come back to him.   Have you even dated anyone since the divorce?"

"No.   The thought of dating scares the hell out of me. Why do you think I live vicariously through you?"

"You're a hot mess."

"Seriously though, I think stepping away, and being in different states, will help us both develop some clarity. And I believe that we'll figure out what's best for us."

"What happens if he finds clarity with someone else while you're trying to figure it out?"

"If he's truly happy, then I'll be happy for him.   Then I'd just have to move on and do my own thing."

"You want me to ask Perry if he's got any single friends?"

"Does he have a brother?"

"No.   He has a sister?"

"Funny.   I may be divorced but I'm still rooting for the men's team.   I appreciate the support but this is something I've got to deal with on my own."

"You know I'm here for you if you need me."

"I'm glad we've run into each other again after all these years.   I need a friend right now."

"Me too.   It was divine intervention."

# # #

"Good morning."   Jenny said as Janel got settled at her desk.

"Good morning."

She walked over, leaned in close, and whispered: "The wicked witch of the west is here.   I saw her fly in on her broom right after I got here."

"I know, I'm her first victim.   I've got an eight o'clock scheduled with her for my final ninety day review.   I've got about fifteen minutes to enjoy a cup of coffee before I head into the gallows."

"Mine is at ten.   Aren't you glad we're almost done dealing with her?"

"YES!"

"Good luck."

Janel took a moment to close her eyes and meditate. She really needed to focus on her attitude, and her body language in particular.   She'd been lucky that she didn't have to deal with Sherri in her personal life.   In fact, she hadn't seen her outside of the job since the incident at Tony's house.   And she got extremely lucky when she cancelled for Rita's holiday dinner.   She couldn't wait to be through with her on a professional level too, and she looked forward to not having to see her again unless it was at the quarterly city-wide company meeting.   She took a deep breath and exhaled slowly.   "After this, I will be free. No more Sherri."   She whispered to herself.   She took ten minutes to enjoy her coffee, and then headed to the conference room that served as Sherri's makeshift office for the day, with five minutes to spare.

"Come on in, I'll be right back."   She walked across the hall and returned with a bottle of water in hand.   Janel couldn't help but look for the tell-tale signs of pregnancy, and think childish, petty thoughts like she hoped she'd gain a hundred pounds and look like a beached whale.   She guessed she was about three months, according to what Tony told her the day he helped her move.   Her skin looked good, which was typical, but her boobs didn't look any bigger.   She wasn't showing yet, and Janel didn't expect her to be unless there were multiple babies.

"Let's get started."   She said with a matter of fact tone as she opened the bottle of water and took a long drink.   "I don't have anything different to tell you this review that you haven't already heard.   You're fast, and accurate, and doing markedly better than your colleagues.   Your margin for error is remarkable."

Janel had to concentrate in order to maintain a poker face.   She thought she just heard Sherri give her a compliment.   Hell was bound to freeze over any minute. "Thank you."

"I have an opportunity for you.   A project."   She slid a folder across the table.   "I've already discussed this with your supervisor, and I think if you're successful in completing this, it will go a long way towards securing you a full time position and a sizable raise after your probationary period is over."   Janel reluctantly pulled the folder towards her and opened it up.   "That's a list of all the problem accounts that haven't been transferred into the new system yet because of various issues.   I want you to work on reconciling these accounts as quickly as possible so that we can get them moved over into the new system before the new fiscal year starts in January."

Janel flipped through three pages.   She estimated approximately fifty accounts per page ranging anywhere from three to five years old.   "What's wrong with them?"

"That's what you need to figure out.   It could be anything from missing paperwork, typos, accounting mistakes, or they may have just slipped through the cracks due to staff shortages."

Janel knew she was being set up for failure and wanted to throw the folder in Sherri's face.   "You want me to reconcile approximately one-hundred and fifty accounts in a little less than a month?"

"If possible.   The goal is to clean them up before year end so if there are any accounting errors they won't carry over into next year."

"What happens if I don't?"

"You won't be penalized.   Ideally, if you can't complete the project by year end, the end of January would work. I've already given you access to the old system, and I'll email you with instructions on how to access it.   Feel free to get started as soon as possible, like I said, I've already cleared it with your supervisor."

Her inner voice was pitching a fit.   You mean I gotta be tied to this bitch another two months?   Who did I piss off to deserve this?   "What if I can't fix all of them?"

"It won't be held against you.   Just make a note and we can discuss them.   If there are more than a handful, we can schedule a meeting to figure it out.   Believe me, any help you can provide will reflect positively.   If you have any questions or need any help, contact me and we'll figure it out."   Janel bristled at the thought of having to ask her for help on anything.   That feeling, along with the fact that she felt like she was being set up, fueled her desire to complete the project and prove Sherri wrong.   Besides, it sounded like she didn't have much of a choice, she was being 'volun-told' to do it.   Janel looked up from the folder and her eyes met with one of the most fake and insincere smiles she'd ever encountered.   "That's all I have for you, unless you have any other questions or have something you'd like to discuss?"

Janel closed the folder and tapped it on the table.   "I guess I'll go get started."

"Great.   Good luck."

Janel walked out of the room without even acknowledging her sarcastic dig. She could hear the words 'dead woman walking' echoing in her head as she walked back to her desk.

34 - Merry Christmas Baby

Tony pulled into his driveway behind the wheel of DJ's Christmas present. As soon as he opened the front door, his nose was assaulted with a smell that was probably going to be dinner. Since getting pregnant, Sherri took it upon herself to cook dinner for him several nights a week. Despite her best efforts, cooking just wasn't her forte. But he wasn't going to be the one to tell her that. "Hey babe. How're you feeling?"

"Good."

"What's cooking?"

"Meatloaf. I know how much you love it, so I thought I'd try something new and put my own spin on it."

What he loved was Janel's meatloaf specifically, everyone did, but he wasn't about to tell her that because it would only lead to an argument.

"Where you been? I was expecting to see you about an hour ago."

"Christmas shopping."

"What'd you get me?"

"I bought a car for DJ."

"Excuse me?"

"He's going away to college next year and he's going to need a car. I drove it home, it's out in the driveway. I was thinking I would take it to him tomorrow because I don't know what they've got planned for Christmas day."

"You bought DJ a car without talking to me about it first?"

"I'm sorry?"

"I can't believe you'd make a purchase that big without

talking to me about it.   Those are the kinds of decisions we need to be making together now."

"You're joking right?"

"Do I look like I'm joking?"

"Listen Sherri, I'm going to say this as tactfully as I know how.   We're having a baby together, I get that.   But unless or until we get married, how I choose to spend my money is my business.   And even if we do get married, what I do for DJ will never be up for discussion."

"DJ is almost grown.   Don't you think it's time you stopped playing foster daddy?   Besides, you have your own child to worry about now."

He took a deep breath and lowered his voice.   "I want to make this very clear, and I'm only going to say it once. As long as you and the baby have everything you need, what I do for DJ is irrelevant, and non-negotiable.   As long as I have breath in my body and DJ has a need, he will never go without.   And I can assure you, no matter what happens between you and I, I'll do the same or better for our child.   This is the last conversation we'll ever have about what I do for DJ.   Do you understand?"

"Oh I understand.   And trust me when I say if you don't do for this baby equally or better than what you do for DJ, we will be having a conversation about it.   You can bet on that.   Fix your own damn dinner, I'm going home."   She threw an oven mit at him and stormed out of the house, slamming the door behind her as usual.

"Whatever."   Tony mumbled as he called Janel.   "Hey. I have some presents I want to drop off to you.   Is it ok if I stop by tomorrow?"

"Come early, Perry's taking me to a show in the evening."

"On Christmas Eve?"

"It's a special performance, a play.   It's one of those not-open-to-the-public 'friends and family' things."

"I want to give you a heads up, I bought DJ a car."

"A what?"

"Don't be mad at me.   It's not new or anything, and I had it checked out to make sure it's safe and mechanically sound.   I know I should've talked to you about it first, but I figured you'd be on board with it since it'll save some wear and tear on your car and he'll be a little more self-sufficient."   He waited for her to say something.   "If you're totally against it, I'll take it back.   It's not like he knows about it yet.   I don't want you to be upset with me."

"What about insurance?   And gas?   Maintenance?"

"As long as he keeps his grades up and stays out of trouble, I'll take care of it.   And his grades have never been an issue, you know that."

"Does Sherri know?   The last thing I need is for my son to become a source of drama between you two."

"She knows, and it's not a problem."

"Then I guess it's fine by me.   It's not like I can afford to buy him one.   I really appreciate that Tony, it's very generous of you."

"Good, I'll see you sometime tomorrow then."

# # #

Tony spent Christmas Eve sleeping in, then caught a movie before heading to Janel's.   He pulled the car into the driveway and rang the doorbell, her gift tucked under his arm.

"Uncle Tony!"

"Merry Christmas."

"Merry Christmas to you too.   Did you get another car?"

"Nope.   That's your Christmas present."

"Seriously?"

He handed him the keys and he snatched them from his hand and ran to the car.   "No way.   This is mine?"   He opened the door, sat in the front seat, turned the car on, and immediately started messing with the stereo.   Tony walked over to the car and Janel came outside to join him.

"Can I take it for a drive?"

"Did you even say thank you?"   Janel asked.   She was in a bathrobe, house shoes, and panty hose.

He got out of the car and gave Tony a hug and told him thanks.   "This is the best Christmas present ever.   Can I go now mom?"

"One more thing."   Tony said as he handed DJ a gift card.   "Gas money.   If you get in any trouble or give your mom a hard time, this car will sit in the driveway until you can be more responsible.   You hear me?"

"Yes sir."   He was going to explode waiting for his mom's ok to leave.

"Go on.   Be careful."   He jumped in the car and sped down the street.   "He doesn't even have his license with him."

"He'll be fine."   Tony kissed her on the cheek and gave her a warm hug.   "Nice robe."

"Very funny."

"This is for you."   He said as he handed her the package from under his arm after they'd gone back into the house.

"I have something for you too."   She motioned for him to follow her to her bedroom.   She sat his present on the bed and pulled a small gift from her dresser drawer. "Before you open this, I wasn't sure what to get you.   You don't really need anything, you have plenty of ties, your suits are custom made, and I couldn't even afford to buy the shoe laces in the shoes you wear.   Just keep in mind it's not about the gift, it's the meaning behind it."

He opened the box and found a silver key chain with the words 'World's Greatest Dad' engraved on the front.   He flipped it over and the back read 'To my knight, thanks. - JM.'

"I had second thoughts about the message because of Sherri but then I thought to hell with it.   As for the world's greatest dad, you've been such a great stand in for DJ, and you're about to be a daddy so..."

"I love it, it's nice. Thank you.   Your turn.   And don't do that thing my mom does, where she slowly pulls the paper off like she's going to save it and reuse it.   Just rip it open, but be careful."

She picked up the package, found a seam, and ripped it open in one smooth motion.   It was a framed, color pencil drawing of her, Dorian, and Tony, from when they were in college.   The original photo was tucked into the corner of the frame, which contained not only the three of them, but Rita, Chuck, and several other people as well.   "Where did you find this picture?   And who did this for you?   It's beautiful."

"I called in a favor from a client.   I wanted Rita and Chuck in the picture too, but I didn't give him enough time. It was a last minute idea so I'm just happy he was able to get the three of us done."

"I remember this night.   This was an off campus party and there was so much alcohol.   Dorian made me so mad, he got really drunk.   I was worried about him getting back to the dorm before curfew, because he was already on thin ice with the coach.   But you helped me get him back to campus in time."

"I remember."

"The next day, instead of thanking me, he accused me of sleeping with you.   But he apologized once his hangover wore off."

"He never said a word to me.   At least you got a thank you."

"This is really nice, thanks."   She set the picture on the bed and gave him a hug.   When he tried to let go, she continued to hang on.

"You ok?   Look at me."   She finally pulled away and a single tear was rolling down her cheek.   He kissed it and wiped the trail with his thumb.   "I didn't mean to upset you, the pic-"

She kissed him softly, then slid her tongue into his

mouth.   He lifted her off her feet and she wrapped her legs around his waist as she hung on tightly to his neck. He put his hands under her thighs and squeezed the skin between the top of her hosiery and her garter belt.   He backed her against the wall and began grinding his pelvis against her.   She pushed her hands against his chest until he released her legs, and she dropped the robe on the floor and quickly removed her underwear.   Seeing her in her bra, garter belt, and stockings turned him on even more. He unzipped his pants and let them fall to the floor as he picked her up again and put her back against the wall.   He held her up while she stuck one hand between her legs and guided him inside of her.   She wrapped her arms around his neck and held on as he hooked his elbows under her knees and rammed himself inside of her over and over again.   She bit his shoulder, hard, which hurt so good it made him want to come.   He heard the doorbell ring but he continued rhythmically pounding her.

"I have to get that, it's Perry."   She whispered breathlessly.   He kissed her to keep her from saying anything else.   The doorbell rang again and she tightened up her lower body and loosened her grip around his neck, making it difficult to hold her up.   "I can't just leave him out there."

"Shit!"   He reluctantly released her legs and slid from inside her.   He pulled his pants on and fastened them, purposefully leaving his shirt untucked.   "I'll get it." Why can't he be on CP time?   He thought to himself as he answered the door.

"Tony.   What are you doing here?"

"Dropping off Christmas presents."

"Where's your car?"

"At the house.   I drove DJ's present over.   In fact, he's probably on his way to pick up your son right now."

"You bought him a car?"   Tony nodded as he waited for Perry to come into the house.   "That's one hell of a

Christmas present."

"It's just a little used sedan, nothing special."

"How you getting home?"

"A cab I guess.   You coming in or what man?"   Tony was annoyed by the questions and frustrated at not being able to achieve sexual release.

"My bad."   Perry said as he stepped inside.

"Janel's getting ready.   I think she had a snag in her pantyhose or something.   You know how women are, she'll probably put on a whole different outfit now."

Perry sat down on the couch.   "It's all right, she's worth the wait."

"Yes, she is."   Tony sat down on the edge of the recliner.   "You ever been married?"

"Ten years, divorced for three.   Why?"

"What happened?   If you don't mind me asking."

"She cheated on me, so I left her."   Tony nodded his head.   "Weren't you calling a cab?   I'm sure you don't want to leave your woman alone on Christmas Eve."

"Yes, almost forgot."   Tony pulled out his phone.   "I got an app for that, one of my young clients turned me on to it.   Technology today is amazing."

"How long you and Sherri been together?"

"About two years now."

"You guys ever take a break during that time?"

"We've had a few bumps in the road.   Why?"

"Just wondering.   Seems like I remember seeing Sherri hanging out with some young guy from our corporate office over the summer.   Steve or-"

"Shawn."

"That's it!   Shawn."

"I've met him.   He trained her on the new computer system."

"Apparently she was a pretty good host, showed him around town while he was here.   Outside of business hours."

"That's something most business colleagues would do. It's not unusual."

"I guess.   None of my business really."

"Not really."

"Actually, there's something else you might want to know though.   He was in town over the Thanksgiving weekend.   And I happen to know for a fact that he wasn't here on business."

"What's your point?"

"You sure she didn't go out for more than just ice cream that night?"

Janel emerged from her bedroom and stood in front of Perry.   She spun around slowly to show him her dress. "Was I worth the wait?"   Both men immediately stood in her presence.

"Always."   Perry said as he put his hands around her waist gave her a lingering kiss on the mouth.

Tony was seething over Perry's insinuation about Sherri, but when he thought about the fact that he was having sex with Janel just minutes before Perry arrived, an evil grin spread across his face.

"You could put on a potato sack and you'd still look sexy to me baby."

"Tony, you need a ride?"   She asked as she put her keys in her purse.

"He'll be all right.   He called a cab.   He's got an app for that."   Perry winked at him and Tony wanted to punch him right in the middle of his smug face.   "Besides, we've got to get going.   We're already late as it is."

"I don't want to just leave him here, that would be rude. We've got time to wait with him right?   It can't be too much longer."

"You kids go on, have a good time.   I'll use my key to lock up on my way out."   Tony winked at Perry.

"If it'll get you home to your *woman* and the *baby* any quicker, I'd be more than happy to drop you off.   After all,

it is Christmas Eve, and she probably shouldn't be alone."
A horn began blaring from the street in front of the house.
"Sounds like your ride is here.   Let's go Janel."   Perry
held his arm out for her, and held the door open for Tony.
He glared at Perry as he moved past him through the
doorway to the waiting cab.

35 - Somebody Already Broke My Heart

After the play and a bite to eat, Perry took Janel home and walked her inside. He took both her hands into his. "I really appreciate you spending the evening with me. I know you've got that deadline hanging over your head."

"I'm honored that you asked me to join you." She kissed him.

"Did you enjoy yourself?"

"I had a great time, it was a good show."

"I guess I'll bid you goodnight then." He kissed her.

"Why don't you stay for a while?" She grabbed his tie and pulled him closer for another, longer kiss.

"If you insist."

"I do." She said as she gently backed him up against the door and reached around him to lock it.

"What about DJ?"

"I'm not concerned about DJ right now. He's asleep. You could drive an eighteen wheeler through here and he won't wake up." She pulled him into her bedroom and he closed the door. What followed was a race to see who could pull their clothes off the quickest. Perry won, although he cheated by leaving his socks on, and he plopped down in the middle of the bed with a huge grin on his face. She patted the edge of the mattress with her hand. "Come here."

"What do you mean?" Perry asked, confused.

"Here, on the edge of the bed." He pulled himself to the edge of the bed, still lying down. "No silly, sit up and put your legs over the side of the bed." He did as he was told. "I'm glad you're so happy to see me." She said as she straddled his lap, her knees to each side of him. She kissed him as she rubbed her breasts against him, and he cupped her butt in his hands and squeezed. She put her hands between her legs and guided the tip of his shaft inside of her, and lowered herself slowly. "You like that?" She whispered in his ear once he was fully inside of her.

He stuttered slightly. "Ye- yes I do."

She pushed him backwards onto the bed and began bouncing on top of him. He squeezed her breasts while he shut his eyes and moaned with pleasure. "That feels so good." She bounced faster and after a minute he sat back up again.

"What's wrong?"

"I can't take it, I'm going to come."

"Then come." She said as she began bouncing again. He put his arms around her and squeezed, then started thrusting his hips upwards. The closer she got to climaxing, the further she dug her nails into his shoulders.

Perry finally said "I can't take it anymore. I want to come."

"Come on baby, I'll come with you." He leaned his head back and let out a loud groan, and Janel could feel him spasming inside of her. She continued to hang on to him, even after he relaxed, and he held her close. And then, out of the blue, she began to cry. She held on even tighter so he couldn't look her in the face.

"Sweetheart, what's wrong?" He pulled a sheet from the bed and wrapped it around her, then twisted at the waist so he could sit her on the bed. She wiped her face with the sheet and he stared at her with compassion and concern.

"Was I that bad?" He asked, trying to lighten the mood.

"No. It was nice."

"I don't know that I've ever made a woman cry during sex before.   From what I hear it's supposed to be a good thing."

"I'm sorry.   Between Thanksgiving dinner and this, you must think I'm a basket case."

"I know you well enough not to think that."   He pulled his underwear on and brought her tissue from her bathroom.

"Thank you."   She blew her nose.

"You want to talk about it?"

"I'm not sure what 'it' is."

"You've been through a lot this year.   Maybe you haven't taken enough time for yourself, to mourn and heal.   Maybe a relationship is just too much for you to handle right now.   And I'm not going to lie, even though I care a lot about you, I want an honest shot at a serious relationship with you.   I don't want to be the bounce back guy."

"You're not a rebound guy."

"I'm starting to feel like it, whether you mean to make me feel that way or not.   Look, I'm not saying I'm not here for you, because you know I am.   But I don't think you're ready to move on yet.   And I'm ok with that.   If you need some time and space, I'm willing to give it to you."

"Maybe you're right."

"I wish I wasn't, but I think I am.   I love spending time with you.   And DJ, he's a great kid.   Or young man, I guess I should say.   And it's not like we won't see each other, our sons are friends, and I love hanging out with them.   We'll see each other at work occasionally, and I hope we can do lunch every now and again."   Janel started tearing up again.   "No, don't do that.   We're moving in the wrong direction."

"I feel bad, like I misled you."

"No, you just didn't realize you've still got some things you need to work out."

She wiped her face and blew her nose again. "I'm sorry."

"Don't apologize. It's just not our time, and that's ok. You just let me know when you're ready and we can start over again." He reached up and touched her face. "You still want me to stay?"

"I'd like you to stay, but I feel like it's asking a lot."

"Then I'll stay, but you're going to have to put some clothes on."

She took the sheet into the bathroom with her and reemerged in pajama bottoms and a tank top. "Better?"

"Yes."

"Can we spoon?" She asked as she snuggled up next to him.

"You mean can you put your cold feet on me and press your booty up against my junk? I'm a man Janel, not a machine." She started to laugh. "I'm serious." He smiled.

"Fine." She said as she flopped over to face him.

"I want you to understand how hard this is for me. You're such a beautiful woman, inside and out, and all I want to do is spend time with you."

The smile faded from her face and she suddenly felt bad about asking him to stay. "I'm sorry, I thought I was ready."

"I'll accept some responsibility too. I knew what you'd been through. But I pushed anyway, I was persistent."

"That's what I like about you."

"Yeah but you were vulnerable. It was too much too soon. I feel like I took advantage."

"I needed persistence. It was a boost to my self-esteem after I found out Dorian was cheating on me."

"Speaking of cheating, I know I asked you before if you had a relationship with Tony-"

"You did, so why are we going there again?"

"He's just so...fiercely protective of you. He takes passive aggressive to a whole other level."

"You're dating his best friend's widow, that automatically makes you persona non grata."

"It's more than that.   He acts like he's jealous, like an old lover."

"I'd say more like a brother."

"Yeah, I can see him showing up in the parking lot at my job, telling me to leave you alone or 'bad things' will happen to me."

"At three o'clock right?"   She put her fist up to his right eye, then his left, while she made a clicking sound with her tongue.

"Yeah, kind of like that."

"Don't take it personal. We've been through a lot together, and he misses my husband.   You're a good man, he knows that."

"Honestly, I think he's in love with you."

"I doubt that."

"I don't."

"I'll bite.   Why do you think that?"

"I'm a man, and I've seen the way he looks at you.   It's the same way I used to look at Ayana, when things were good between us."

"He's not in love with me, he's an old friend.   A very good, sometimes over protective *friend*."

"Who happens to be in love with you."

"Who happens to have a *pregnant girlfriend* and isn't thinking about me in that way."

"All that means is the condom broke and he intends to take care of his responsibility.   It doesn't mean he'll stay with her."

"He's with Sherri, he's not in love with me, and I don't want to talk about it anymore."

"Maybe I'm in love with you."

"Doubtful."

"Why not?"

"You don't know me well enough to be in love with me."

"I disagree."

"We clicked, we've had some good times together, and we have great conversation. That doesn't mean you're in love with me, it only means it's the first time you've clicked with someone since you got divorced."

"I should leave, seriously. I can't do this. I don't want to stop seeing you."

Janel sat up and pulled the covers around her shoulders. "Maybe we should just cut ties for a while."

"I don't want to do that."

"I can't give you what you need right now. This is tough, because I enjoy spending time with you, but I don't want to be around you if it's going to be hard for you. If you want to leave, I understand. Don't feel obligated to stay because you think leaving will hurt my feelings."

He stared at her for a moment before getting out of the bed. She watched him get dressed, taking his time as if he needed to look picture perfect. He saved his tie for last, and she got out of bed and helped him put it on. She adjusted the knot just right. "So handsome." He put his hands around her waist and she rested both hands in the middle of his chest.

"I am in love with you, you know. And Tony is too. But if I can get past Ayana cheating on me, I guess I'll find a way to deal with this too."

"Perry-"

"It's ok, really. And it's ok for you to admit you love him too. Let's face it, it's the elephant in the room that we've all been dancing around for months now." She stared at him without confirming or denying his accusation, and he kissed her on the forehead. "Don't look so sad, we'll see each other again. At least I figured it out before I got in too deep." He let go of her waist and smoothed his hand down the front of his suit coat. "Get back in the bed, I'll let myself out.   Good night."   She watched as he disappeared into the darkness of the living room.

# # #

"Can I get another one please?"

"You know, it's really none of my business but whatever you're looking for, you're not going to find it at the bottom of a martini glass."

"Are you cutting me off?"   Janel asked.

"One more, but only because I'm a sucker for a pretty woman.   But after that, it's strictly water.   As fast as you're drinking those, that alcohol is going to hit you hard when you stand up."   He mixed the drink, going light on the liquor, and set it in front of her.   "Last one, enjoy."

"Thanks."   She nursed the drink and fought the urge to cry as she thought about how she managed to break Perry's heart.   She was also incredibly regretful that she didn't tell Tony how she really felt, despite the fact that Sherri was pregnant.

"If he broke your heart he'll regret it."

"What if I broke his?"

"Then shame on you."

"It was unintentional."

"Still hurts the same.   Did you apologize?"

"Yes."

"He'll appreciate that.   A long, long, long time from now."

"You're not helping."   She emptied the glass and he replaced it with two highballs full of water.   "Drink up.   I'd feel bad if you left here and something happened to you."

A young man tapped her on the shoulder and pointed to the seat next to her.   "Excuse me shortie, are you tired?   Cause you been running through my mind all day!   Is anyone sitting here?"

The bartender spoke up on her behalf. "Yes. Plenty of other open seats bruh." The man ignored the bartender and pulled the stool out anyway. "You deaf? Or do I need to call security?" The man held his hands up in surrender and walked away.

"You my knight in shining armor now? I used to have one of those you know, but I managed to screw that up too."

"I'm not doing anything I wouldn't want another man to do for my sister, my girlfriend, or my wife."

"Thanks."

"You're welcome. If you need me to call you a cab, I can do that too. Most people don't realize I'm a man of many talents." She cracked a smile. "Is that a smile me see chile?" He asked with a fake Jamaican accent. She chuckled as she rolled her eyes. "I was starting to think you didn't have any teeth but you have a beautiful smile. You should do it more often. Look, I gotta head to the other end of the bar if I want to earn some tips, but I'll be back to check on you. Maybe we can even talk about why your cell phone has been blowing up on vibrate in your purse for the last hour." She watched him walk away and decided he was cute, so she vowed to enjoy the eye candy while she worked on sobering up.

"Hey girl, I've been calling you, why aren't you answering your phone? I thought we were going to do happy hour together?"

She gave Rita a hug and patted the stool next to her. "I started early, feel free to catch up. Where's Chuck?"

"Parking the car. Sweetie, how long have you been sitting here?"

"Let's see, I went to work and turned in my project to that bitch ass Sherri, and then I asked my manager for some personal time. I'm starting my New Year's eve celebration early."

"How much have you had to drink?"

"I already cut her off, but let's just say she's going to be feeling real good real soon."

"How much is the tab?"

"I'll pay my own tab, thank you very much." Janel reached for it but Rita pushed her hand away.   She paid the bill and added a tip.   "He's cute isn't he?"

"Time to go home love.   Where are your keys?"   Rita picked up her purse and shook it.

"I can't drive."

"I know, Chuck is going to drive your car home."

"Hey Chuckie?   Still here huh?"

"I'm here until the third, can't get rid of me that easy sweetheart."

"Nel, do you have to go to work tomorrow?"

"Nope."

"Good because you're going to have one hell of a hangover tomorrow.   Chuck, can you get her please?"

36 - Wedding Bells

"Are we taking this case or not?" Doug asked as he paced the floor of Tony's office.

"Absolutely not."

"Are you serious? This case is huge. If we win, and I know we will, it would be a distinguished feather in our cap."

"We've already got an exceptional reputation. Any feathers we put in our cap at this point are moot. My gut says if we take it, we'll regret it."

"We need feathers Tony. Society has a very short term memory."

"I'm telling you we don't want this case."

"Explain your gut to me. Please."

"Sit down before you wear a hole in the carpet. I think this girl is lying."

"I don't think so. You've met this guy, he's a jock, he's cocky, and he reeks of a sense of entitlement."

"That doesn't make him a rapist."

"You're killing me! Your gut is wrong!"

"Can I explain, without interruption?" Doug flipped his hand in the air, signaling him to continue. "Here's what I think happened. These two have been dating since freshman year right? Same classes, joined at the hip twenty-four seven. This kid's a basketball god, and this girl knows it. She just knows she'll become his wifey. No doubt in her mind when he signed with the NBA, she was going to be right by his side with a big ol' ring on her finger. But maybe he decided he wasn't ok with that plan. Maybe he decided he hadn't sown enough wild oats, or maybe he thought he was missing out on something, so he decides to break it off with her to see what else is out there. So what does she do?   She gets upset.   But, she's smart. She knows he has a weakness for the booty, specifically her booty, which he's been hitting since freshman year.   So she calls him, he comes over, she comes on to him, he gets nostalgic and they sleep together.   He leaves, she cries foul, gets a rape kit done, and suddenly this kid's college career and NBA dreams are destroyed.   I think this is a case of a woman scorned.   If I'm wrong, I'm so sorry for her, but my gut says I'm right, and I rarely regret listening to my instincts."

"But this kid is such a jerk.   I'd love nothing more than to take him down a few pegs."

"Being a cocky jerk asshole isn't a crime Doug.   I shouldn't even have to say that to you, it's not like you just passed the Bar.   Take the emotion out of it and use your head.   Put that education that you paid so much for to good use."   Doug shook his head out of frustration. "Look, if you really want this, if you really want a win, then fine, take it.   You're good, you can do it.   All I'm saying is I think the girl is lying and you'd be doing a young, cocky but talented asshole an injustice.   If you can sleep with that on your conscious, have at it."

Doug tapped his finger on his desk.   "Fine, I'll turn down the case."

"Thank you. I got something else I want to run past you. I'm thinking about teaching."

"What the hell?   You bailing on me now?"

"No.   You know how much I love being in a courtroom, I'm not saying that.   I just feel like I need a change.   I want to try something different, and maybe free up some time to make room for other things in my life."

"Is this about Sherri and the baby?"

"No.   Maybe.   I'm only talking about doing this part time.   I think I'd enjoy a different kind of challenge, and it could benefit the firm too. We'll have first-hand access to the law students, and we could hand pick the best and brightest for our internships."

"We already have some of the best and brightest associates, most of whom were previously interns. And if you actually let them, they could handle more of your case load and that would give you the extra time you need to spend with Sherri and the baby, or to take a vacation, or do whatever you need to do."

"I love the job, and I love being in the courtroom. I thrive on it. But I just want to try something different for a change. I feel like I have more to offer, and I think teaching will give me an opportunity to do that."

"So you want to teach in order to give back, so to speak."

"Yeah, I guess that's what I'm trying to say."

"You want to grade papers and deal with snot nosed know-it-all kids trying to bullshit their way through school. That's really what you want to do?"

"You know that's only a small percentage of what I'd be dealing with. They're not all snotty nosed know-it-all kids. I'm sure some a lot of them have a passion for learning, and I want the opportunity to nurture that passion."

"Who better to teach them right?"

"Are you saying I wouldn't be a good teacher? Cause I'm a hell of a lawyer."

"Yes you are, no doubt about that. Honestly, I think you would be good at it. I've seen you with the associates. But that's what scares me. I don't want to lose you to a full time teaching gig."

"You won't. Besides, I haven't submitted a resume yet, I wanted to talk to you about it first so it wouldn't come as a surprise."

"If that's what you want to do, I support you one hundred percent. Just promise me if you get into this and decide down the road that you want to teach full time, don't leave me hanging.   Give me a little heads up before you decide to leave the firm."

"You know I wouldn't do that to you.   I'd offer to let you buy me out, or I'd bring in someone equally competent to replace me, but I'd never leave you hanging."

"I don't think you'll ever leave, you love it too much."

"I do, but this is something I feel like I need to look into." Tony stood up and pulled on his suit jacket.   "I've gotta go, I've got a doctor's appointment, but I'll be back."

"You son of a bitch.   Is that why you want to teach? Are you having some health issues?"

Tony opened his office door and patted Doug on the back as he crossed the threshold.   "It's just a checkup."

Doug stopped and looked him in the eye.   "You'd tell me if it were something serious, right?"

"Stop worrying, I'm fine.   I'll be back in a little bit."

# # #

Tony was surprised to see Sherri's car in the garage as he pulled into the stall next to it.   He grabbed his bag and file box from the back seat and managed to balance them and get the door open at the same time.   She was sitting in the living room watching television.   "Hey baby."

"Hey."   He dropped the box and bag on the coffee table.

"I came by to give you your Christmas present.   I made dinner too."

"I appreciate it but I'm not particularly hungry."   He sat down on the couch next to her.

"It's never good when you bring a file box home."

"I'll be up late.   I've got a couple depositions tomorrow."

"I wanted to talk, if you have a minute.   Here."   She handed him a small box wrapped in candy cane wrapping paper.   "It's really hard to shop for you but hopefully you'll like it."   He unwrapped the gift and flipped open the black jewelry box to reveal a sterling silver monogrammed tie tack with matching cuff links. "These are nice, thanks."

She looked at him and raised her eyebrows and shrugged her shoulders. "You have something for me?" He went to the kitchen and pulled her present from inside of a plastic food container.

"I hid it in the kitchen because I knew you'd be less likely to find it there." She unwrapped it to find a small purple velvet jewelry box. Her eyes lit up and she quickly pulled it open. He could see confusion in her face so he offered an explanation. "It's a Mexican Bola."

"A what?"

"It's a harmony ball. You wear it around your neck, and it hangs down to your stomach. And every time you move, it makes a chime sound that the baby can hear. Then after the baby is born, and it hears the chime, it's supposed to help soothe them because they're already used to hearing it." She pulled it out of the box and rolled it back and forth in her hand. "The saleswoman said it's really popular with pregnant woman right now. I took her word for it."

"It's definitely unique."

"I have a gift receipt-"

"No, I like it. It's very pretty. Thank you."

"You're welcome."

"I wanted to talk to you about the other day."

"I already told you what I do for DJ is not up for discussion. If the situation were reversed I know Dorian would've done the same thing for my son."

"I understand that and I'll respect it. I trust your judgment. What I really want to talk about is us. First off, I would like for you come to the doctor with me. That way you'll know what's happening with the pregnancy, and if you have any questions you can ask the doctor directly."

"You know I'm not going to be able to make every appointment, my schedule just won't allow for it."

"I understand that.   All I'm asking is that you make the effort.   I think that's a reasonable request.   This is your baby too."

"Give me the schedule and I'll see what I can do.   Are you going to have an amniocentesis?"

She smiled.   "Someone's been doing their homework.   Yes, it's scheduled for next month.   I have to be at least-"

"Sixteen but not more than twenty weeks.   Let me know when that is, I'll do my best to try and clear my calendar so I can be there.   The rest I'll have to play by ear."

"Fair enough.   You want me to give the dates to Pam or-"

"Just email them to me. I'll add them to my schedule."

"I also want to talk about us."

"What about us?"

"I just want to know what your plans are."

"I'm not following you."

"Now that I'm pregnant, are we going to move in together?   Are we going to get married?   I'm asking because honestly, I don't want my baby to be born out of wedlock.   The two of us have had our own challenges with our parents, and I'd really like it if our child didn't come into this world as a bastard."

"A bastard?"

"Bastard, illegitimate, same difference.   I'd really like it if this baby were born to parents who have committed to one another through marriage."

"Are you serious?"

"I'm absolutely serious.   Why wouldn't I be?"

"Because that sounds like really old fashioned, dated mentality.   You're every bit the 'modern day woman' in every other aspect of your life, so hearing you talk about a concept that seems so antiquated is just foreign to me."

"Are you mocking me?"

"Absolutely not, I'm just surprised to hear you say

something like that."

"Have you given any thought to us moving in together or getting married?"

"Actually no, I haven't."

"Well you need to."

"Why?"

"Because this baby will be here soon."

"It's not like this baby is going to leave the womb going 'all is lost, my parents aren't married and I'm a bastard.'"

"You think that's funny?"

"No I don't think it's funny.   A bit melodramatic maybe, but not funny."

"This baby needs a home."

"And he'll have one."

"His own room."

"He'll have that too.   You've got room at your place."

"My place?   What about your place?"

"They have bassinets, portable cribs.   I need my office and my spare bedroom."

"You turned your entire life upside down and bent over backwards to move Janel and DJ in here, and you won't even bat an eye about creating a nursery for your own child?   Oh, I'm sorry, I'm not supposed to mention or talk about your 'other' family.   Please forgive me."

"I'm just trying to understand why I need to change my entire life within a matter of months to accommodate a tiny human being who won't even be able to walk or talk yet? Why is it that we suddenly have to sell our homes, which will be difficult in this market unless we agree to take a huge loss, and consolidate into one home, and get married before this new life emerges into the world?   Please Sherri, enlighten me, explain to me why the rush?"

"Why are you being so difficult about this?"

"I'm not being difficult.   You know me, and you know I don't rush into anything without thinking things through. Especially when it doesn't make sense to me.   My parents weren't married and my dad wasn't around, and I turned out ok.   You don't even know who your parents are, and you turned out ok too.   What matters is that this baby is wanted and loved by its mother and its father.   The rest of what you're so concerned about is completely superficial."

"I-NEED-TO-BE-VALIDATED!"   She yelled, and tears began to stream down her face.   "I don't want to have this baby as Sherri Anderson.   I want to be Mrs. Sherri Gibson, with a big rock on my finger, and a nice home that we share TOGETHER.   As a married couple."

"And I'm just not ready to take that step yet."

"Why not?   It's been over two years Tony, how much longer do you need?"

"It has nothing to do with time.   It's not like relationships have an expiration date that suddenly turns into a marriage."

"Do you love me?"

"What kind of question is that?"

"A valid one.   Do you love me?   And I don't mean like when you love a friend and you care about what happens to them.   Do you love me?

"Of course I do."

"You can't even say it."

"Look, the bottom line is I'm not going to be guilted or forced into marrying you."

"You're a real son of a bitch, you know that?"

"I'M a son of a bitch?   Because I won't marry you simply because you're pregnant?   When I get married, if I get married, it'll be to the right woman for the right reasons.   And if that makes me a son of a bitch, so be it."

"You know what," she said as she stood up and prepared to leave.   "I don't give a shit what you do.   All I know is I'm not doing this alone.   You better be ready to take care of your responsibility."

"You won't ever have to worry about that."   He said just before she slammed the door.

37 - Project Castigation COMPLETE

Janel couldn't believe January was almost over. Time seemed to be passing much faster than she wanted it to. DJ finally settled on the University of Missouri, where he'd been offered a full scholarship, and she tried to mentally prepare herself for the day he would pack his Christmas gift with almost everything he owned and drive ten hours away to start his new life. And with the new CSC budget approved and in place, the pace at work felt a bit frantic. But she was glad for it because it made the days go by faster. Plus, the more she worked the less time she had to sit around and think about her personal life. She felt as if she'd made her peace with Dorian by forgiving him, which allowed her to finally move past the mess he'd left behind. It also allowed her to truly grieve the man she'd been married to for all those years. She decided that she refused to let the last few months of his life cloud the overwhelming number of good memories she had of them being together.

She also decided that she would meet with her manager and bring up a discussion about her being hired on full time, before her probationary period was over. Feeling pretty confident about her chances, she arranged a meeting with her. She truly believed the work she put into the audit project alone should be enough to warrant serious consideration. She printed out her talking point paper so she wouldn't forget anything and headed into her manager's office.

"Hi Janel, good to see you. Please, have a seat."

"Thanks for seeing me Elaine. I appreciate you taking the time." She closed the door behind her and made herself comfortable.

"Absolutely, I always enjoy chatting with you whether it's work related or personal.   What can I do for you today?"

"I was wondering if it's possible that I could be considered for full time employment prior to the end of my probationary period?"

"Actually, it is possible, and in fact, it's something that I was going to discuss with you later next month once I'd gathered a little more information.   It sounds like you beat me to the punch, but that's ok.   I'm open to discussing it now.   I just want you to understand that legally I can't promise you anything or offer you anything firm because I don't have official authorization from human resources just yet.   This is strictly an informal discussion. But I'm willing to share with you my thoughts regarding the hiring package I'm considering."   She turned towards her monitor and with a few clicks of her mouse, brought up a document.   She turned her monitor around so they could both see it at the same time.   "So here's the offer I want to take to HR.   Full time employment, of course, at forty thousand a year to start.   That includes full benefits of course, medical, dental, vision, and a 401(k) with a four percent company match.   Again, this is only if HR approves it.   They may come back with something totally different.   Typically they'll go with the manager's recommendation, but I have seen them make changes before too."

"While I'm flattered, the work I did on that auditing project alone is equal to the responsibilities of a senior accounting clerk at a minimum.   And, I was able to keep up with my normal day to day responsibilities while I worked on that project.   I was thinking more like forty five.   And if you take into consideration how fast I picked up the new system, forty eight would be even better. That's just below mid-range for a senior accounting clerk in this area."

"I'm sorry, what auditing project?"

"The auditing project that Sherri Anderson gave me, with the problem accounts that needed to be fixed before they could be converted to the new system.   She said she talked to you about it."

"She didn't say anything to me about it.   Now I do know that she was recently promoted because of some big project she completed over the holidays."

"What?!"

"Yes, she was recently promoted.   She got a big pay raise too I'm sure.   It was in the company newsletter, you didn't see it?   Let me check and see if you're on that distribution list, sometimes they forget about the new people."

"That-heifer!   I knew she had something up her sleeve. She took credit for my work.   That was my project.   I did all the work on that."

"That's a pretty serious accusation Janel."

"It's not just an accusation, it's the truth.   And I can prove it.   I completed that project all by myself.   She didn't do any work on it at all.   I didn't even consult with her.   I didn't need to.   I figured everything out on my own."

"Do you want to go directly to HR yourself, or do you want me to take the lead on this?"

"If you can set up a meeting I would appreciate it.   I want you there.   Especially if you're the one who's going to offer me a permanent position, I want you to be involved so you know first-hand exactly what happened.   This is my reputation on the line."

"And you're sure you have proof?   Irrefutable evidence?   I won't be able to help you if you don't, it'll just be your word against hers."

"Oh I have proof.   I knew she was going to try and pull something like this, I just didn't know what.   So I made sure I documented and covered my butt on everything."

"I'll call HR right now and get the ball rolling."

When Janel left Elaine's office and got back to her desk she was fire hot.   She was glad that Sherri didn't work in the same building because if she did, Janel would be in jail again for having assaulted a pregnant woman.   She took her phone from her purse and walked outside.   She immediately dialed Rita's number.

"Talk fast.   I'm headed to class and I only have about five minutes."

"THAT BITCH BURNED ME!"   Janel shouted into the phone.

"What?   What are you talking about?"

"Operation Setup, the project Sherri gave me?   She used my work to get a promotion Rita.   She never said a word about it to my manager, she didn't have a clue!   If I catch her ass on the street I'm going to give her the beat down of her life."

"We both knew she was going to try something dirty so this shouldn't be a surprise."

"A promotion Rita."

"I heard you, that's pretty bold.   She's got a huge set of balls.   Boulder sized.   Listen, I gotta go but do this for me.   Take a deep breath, keep it together, and go back to your desk and maintain your professionalism.   Meet me at the Voodoo Lounge after work and we'll talk ok?   Go STRAIGHT THERE Janel, no detours.   And this time don't start drinking without me.   I don't want to have to bail you out of jail tonight, ok?   You hear me?"

"I hear you."

"I know you're upset but I need you to keep it together. You have to handle this thing the right way.   Legally, not physically.   I know you want to choke her out, I do too, but there's another way.   I'm sorry, I really have to go. I'll see you after work."   She heard the phone click and

Rita was gone.

Janel paced up and down the sidewalk at the side of the building.   Her heart was racing so fast she could hear her own heartbeat in her ears.   "I refuse to have a stroke over this bitch."   She stood still, closed her eyes, and took a deep breath.   "In through the nose, out through the mouth."   She coached herself until she felt her heart rate slow, and once she was fairly calm, she headed back inside. "I'm going to bury her ass.   She wants to play games, we'll play.   She doesn't realize I have all the winning cards."

# # #

Janel went straight to the Voodoo Lounge after work, as instructed, and ordered two Hurricanes as she waited for Rita to arrive.

"I'm here, I'm here."   She gave Janel a hug.   "Girl!   I couldn't wait to get here so I could hear what happened. Is this one mine?"

"Yes."   Janel pushed the drink towards her.

"Tell me what happened today!"

"I went into my manager's office to talk about getting hired on, she mentions an offer, off the record, I counter the offer, using the project I worked on as leverage, and she looks at me like a deer in the headlights.   Then she proceeds to explain to me that Sherri got a promotion and most likely a fat raise, based on some auditing project she worked on.   It was in the company newsletter.   But get this.   Out of all the fifteen new people that were hired on at the same time as me, three of us were missing from the newsletter distribution list.   One of those three people was Jenny.   You think that's a coincidence?"

"That the one person you work most closely with, who knew you were working on that project, was mysteriously left off the list too?   Absolutely not.   So what are you going to do?"

"I asked my manager to arrange a meeting with HR, and I went back to my desk and I put together a presentation to prove my case.   I know there are logs in that system to track who touches a record and when."

"Yeah but she's buds with the system administrator, the guy who trained her, and I'm sure he has the ability to scrub those logs if she asks him to."

"True, but that's not the only evidence I'm relying on. There were certain things I did in that system to help me stay organized that would only make sense to me.   I used fields that no one else is using, because the documentation says they're not required.   And we were told completing those fields would most likely hinder our ability to move through the records as quickly.   You can't alter information in a record if you don't know it's there."

Rita grinned at her.   "You were thinking, that's good. We both knew she would try to screw you.   Let me ask you this though, what happens if for whatever reason, those records are stripped clean, and the only thing they can show is the fact that Sherri touched them all and no one else.   What happens then?"

"I have all of my hand written notes with names of the people I talked to, along with dates and times.   And, I can provide details on each and every one of those records that aren't in the system anywhere.   When I told her I was finished, I essentially gave her the original copy of the records that she handed me, with a few minimal markings on it.   I never gave her a copy of all the notes I made.   I never even brought them in to work, they're still at home."

"I wish I could be a fly on the wall in that meeting.   Is she going to be there?"

"I imagine so.   If someone were accusing me of claiming their work as my own, I would hope I could be in the room to hear the evidence."

"You just have to keep yourself from going over the table at her."

"I don't even need to, I'm going to make sure she's so embarrassed and her reputation is so ruined that she's going to want to leave the company to save face.   But she won't, because she's pregnant and she needs this job."

"That brings up a good question.   Are you going to tell Tony?"

Janel sighed and dropped her head to the middle of her chest.   "I don't know, I need to think about that."

"What?   What's to think about?   He needs to know what a low down, conniving, scheming heifer he's involved with.   If the situation were reversed you know he'd say something to you."

"That's a sticky situation Rita, think about it.   She's pregnant.   For all we know he's made big plans with her. She's probably moved in with him and they might be talking marriage."

"Which is why you need to tell him.   The only responsibility he has is to that child, if it's even his.   Hell this ought to be enough to motivate him to get a DNA test to make sure.   Wait a minute, when's the last time you talked to him?"

"Christmas, when he dropped off DJ's car."

"Are you serious?"

"Other than a few text messages and a quick phone call or two, yes."

"Has Perry got your nose so wide open that you don't have time for your friends anymore?"

"Perry and I aren't seeing each other anymore."

"What happened?"

"He helped me realize that I needed to take some time for me, to heal, after everything I'd been through last year."

"And what else?   There's something you're not telling me."

"He told me he was in love with me."

"Yet you're not seeing each other.   What else?   Stop holding out on me."

Janel didn't want to tell her because she knew what she would say, but she knew she wasn't going to let it go either. "He said I was in love with Tony and Tony was in love with me too, despite the situation he's in.   He called it the elephant in the room."

Rita smacked the table with her hand so hard the drinks bounced up and clattered against the table.   "I told you! Everyone else can see that you two should be together. Look at what's happening!   The stars and the moon are aligning so you two can finally be together.   Once Tony finds out about Sherri, he's going to dump her so fast it'll make her head spin."

"I'm not listening to you.   The last time I listened to you I got my feelings hurt."

"No, if you had listened to me and told him how you felt when I told you to, instead of dragging your feet, the two of you would be together right now and Sherri would be a distant, non-pregnant memory.   Well she might still be pregnant but Tony would be able to say without a shadow of a doubt that the baby wasn't his."

"Are you here to support me or beat me over the head with my mistakes?"

"I'm here to point out to you that this is divine intervention, and to encourage you to talk to Tony.   Not just because he needs to know what kind of person he's dealing with, but for you.   Go to him and tell him everything, and allow yourself to be completely and totally vulnerable.   And if for some reason things don't go your way, at least you'll know you gave it your all and you can move on with your life."

38 - Spurious Child

"Mike!   Good to see you again."

"Good to see you too Tony.   Dinner's on me tonight."

"I hope you don't expect me to object because I'm not."

"I know you're probably anxious to know what I found out so I'll get right to it.   What do you want to talk about first, the guys or the girl?"

"The guys."

"I have addresses and phone numbers for five of the six." He pulled out a sheet of paper and some pictures.   "This guy right here-"

"Carter.   Steve Carter."

"Unfortunately he's passed.   Had a heart attack at thirty-seven, and left behind a wife and two kids."

"Wow.   At thirty-seven?"

"He gained a lot of weight over the years, his cholesterol was bad, and he sat at a desk all day."

"And didn't get any exercise."

"Exactly.   It's a lethal combination."

"You double checked the addresses and phone numbers? They're all good?"

"I'm offended that you'd even ask me that.   This isn't my first day on the job."

"Sorry, it's the lawyer in me.   It's a habit.   How much do I owe you?"

"Nothing."

"Come on man, I gotta pay you something for you time."

"No charge, don't worry about it."

"Why not?"

"I enjoy doing this right here."   He tapped the picture

of Steve.   "Finding your old football buddies so you can plan a reunion, that's positive, and I love positive jobs."

"Does that mean my other job is negative?"

Mike placed an envelope on the table and slid it towards him.   "I'm not going to lie, it's not good."

"I tried to mentally prepare myself for the worst, so I hope you didn't withhold anything."

"I didn't.   I respect you too much to do that. Everything I was able to find out is in that envelope. Scout's honor."

Tony pushed it aside.   "You know what?   Let's eat. I'll look at this later.   I'd just like to enjoy dinner with a friend right now if you don't mind."

"Sure, I think that's a good idea."

# # #

"Hey babe, what are you doing here?"

"You got the results from the amniocentesis today right? I thought I'd stop by so we could talk about it."

"Come on in."   Sherri stepped aside and let him in. "You eat yet?"

"I had dinner with a friend."

"I'm going to sit down and finish mine if you don't mind." He pulled her chair out for her before sitting down across the kitchen table from her.   "How was your day?"   She asked as she scooped a spoonful of pasta into her mouth.

"Interesting."

"Oh yeah?   How so?"

"Aw you don't want to hear about my day.   Just a lot of boring lawyer stuff.   How you been feeling?   You look tired."

"I am a little tired, but otherwise I feel pretty good."

"What did the doctor say?"

"He said everything looks good.   There are no signs of Down syndrome or any other type of genetic disorder, the amniotic fluid looks good, and there aren't any signs of infection.   Our baby boy has a clean bill of health so far."

"A boy?"

"Yeah."   She smiled at him and he lowered his eyes and bowed his head.   "You ok babe?   You seem a little off."

He raised his head and looked her in the eye.   "Do you remember after the funeral, when we had dinner and I got upset and walked out on you?"

"How could I forget?   I was embarrassed, I felt like the entire restaurant was staring at me."

"You know how we weren't really talking to each other, until we made up and went to New Orleans?"

"I do.   Why?"

"I'm going to ask you something, and I need you to be honest with me.   Did you sleep with somebody else during that time?   If you did, I'd understand, and I give you my word that I won't get upset."

"You don't have anything to be upset about because I didn't."

"If you were drunk, or it was out of spite, I'd understand. I just really need you to tell me the truth."

"I *am* telling you the truth."

He stared at the tabletop for a moment, carefully considering his choice of words, before looking her in the eye again.   "Is it possible the baby isn't mine?"

"Of course it's yours, who the hell else's would it be?"

"I had a conversation with a friend about some fertility issues he was having because of a football injury.   Long story short, I was able to relate to some of the things he was saying, so I made an appointment with my doctor to get some things checked out."

"And what did he say?"

"He told me my chances of getting a woman pregnant were pretty slim."

"Well I guess we beat the odds then.   I'd think you'd be happy about that."

He was disappointed, but not surprised, that she would continue to perpetuate a lie when she knew that he obviously knew differently.   He'd hoped against hope that she would come clean, and prove to him she wasn't the person that his mother told him she was.   He knew it was over, but to have it end like this was disheartening to him. He struggled to keep his anger in check.   "I'm shooting blanks Sherri.   I'd have a better chance of winning the lottery than getting you pregnant."

"Maybe you should go buy a ticket."   Her face was void of expression, her attitude non-chalant.

"I talked to the doctor that performed the amniocentesis, and there's enough of the sample left to have a DNA test done.   I'll pay for it, but you'd have to give your consent to have it done since the baby is still in utero."

She leaned forward, her face screwed up with anger, and he felt like he was looking at a stranger.   "A DNA test? Are you kidding me?"

"All you have to do is sign some paperwork.   Once you do that, I pay the fee, and the results will be back between three and four weeks."

"I'm not doing it.   I won't agree to it."

He closed his eyes and rubbed his forehead.   He was tiring of her charade.   At this point all he wanted her to do was agree to have the test done so he could leave.   "Why not?"

"Because I'm telling you this is *your* baby, and as long as we've known each other you should trust me."

"You want to talk about trust?   Really?"   He pulled a small stack of photos from his pocket and spread them across the kitchen table one at a time, like he was dealing a hand of cards.   "Here's what I think about your trust.   It seems to me, from these pictures here, that you and Shawn spent a lot of time together outside of the job too.   You look like old friends in this one, all snuggled up next to each other.   I think this one here is my favorite.   You guys look like such a happy couple in it, the way you're shoving your tongue down his throat."

"Where the hell did you get these?"   She shoved the pictures away.   "You had someone following me?"

He couldn't believe the indignant look on her face, and he was starting to wonder if he ever really knew her at all. "Actually no, I didn't.   These pictures were printed from security camera footage.   You wouldn't believe how many cameras are focused on you at any given time when you're in public.   You know the old saying, Big Brother is always watching.   I just happen to know people who have access to things."

"Fine, you want the truth, I'll give it to you.   I did sleep with him.   But it only happened on-"

"Just stop."

"We were spending so much time-"

"Stop it!"   He slammed his hand on the table and some of the pictures fell to the floor.   "I already gave you the opportunity to tell me the truth, don't give me that fucking song and dance now!   You would seriously fix your mouth to tell me that it only happened once?   Do you think I'm stupid?"   He closed his eyes and pinched the bridge of his nose.   "I don't know what the hell I was thinking.   I actually thought that if you told me the truth, that maybe I could find a way to *eventually* forgive you, that maybe somewhere down the line I could be there for you if you needed me.   Maybe babysit for you sometime if you ever needed a break or something.   But you're a trip, a real piece of work.   I don't want to have shit else to do with you."

"We used a condom.   That's how I know the baby is yours."

"Then consent to the damn DNA test so we can settle this once and for all."

"I don't need a DNA test to tell me the baby's yours, I know it is."

"Did you fall and bump your head?   You expect me to just believe you over irrefutable evidence from a doctor? If that baby is mine it's a miracle, and I'll go out and buy a hundred damn lottery tickets because I'm due to hit big. You better hear me when I say we can do the DNA test now, or we can do it later, but best believe there will be a DNA test.   I don't want you to have any reason to ever darken my doorstep again."

"Come on Tony, this is crazy.   I'm sorry-"

"Oh it's some crazy up in here all right."   He put his elbows on the table and folded his hands in front of his mouth, resting his knuckle against his chin.   "You know what I'd really like to know?   Did you know the baby was his, or were you just going to take your chances and hope it didn't come out with a light complexion and dimples?   Or, did you know and just decided you'd get a bigger pay day if you stayed with me?   You know what, forget it.   I don't know why I bothered to ask.   You haven't told the truth up until this point, and I certainly don't expect you to start now."   He stood up.   "You can keep those, I certainly don't have any use for them.   Put them in an album and show the baby when he's older."

"If you walk out that door, I promise you this is going to get ugly.   I'll come after you for child support."

He leaned down and got right in her face.   "Are you actually trying to threaten me?   I'm the best lawyer in the city, hands down.   Best believe that.   If you can prove this baby is mine, there'll be no need to come after me for child support because I handle my business.   Always have, always will."   He stood up and pulled his shoulders back. "I suggest you call the doctor and sign those papers now, while I'm offering to pay for it, instead of waiting and having me chew you up and spit you out in court.   And if you do it now, at least you'll have something official to go after Shawn with if he refuses to pay child support." When he got to the door, he paused before opening it.   He turned around to face her.   "By the way, how was that ice cream you went out for Thanksgiving night?"

"Fuck you Tony."

"Not anymore."   He said as he shut the door behind him.

# # #

Tony sat at his desk with his head bowed, in the dark, reluctant to pack up and go home to an empty house.   He picked up the sonogram of the baby and stared at it for a moment before ripping it up and throwing it away.   His cell phone rang, and he ignored it, not even bothering to check the display.   When it rang a second time moments later, he knew it could only be one person.   He also knew if he didn't answer it, he wouldn't put it past her to call the local authorities and have them send out a search party for him to make sure he was ok.

"Hey mom."

"I haven't heard from you in a few days, everything ok?"

"I'm fine, it's just been a little busier than usual.   How are you?"

"I know something's wrong, I can hear it in your voice. Don't try to lie to me."

He debated whether or not to tell her what was going on, but he knew, like a dog with a bone, that she wouldn't let it go until he did.

"I broke up with Sherri."   He heard her fumble with the phone, followed by a faint 'thank you Jesus' in the background.   "Don't mind me, I'll hold while you do a few cartwheels."

"I don't mean to rejoice in your sadness son.   Despite what you may think, I really am sorry to hear that.   I know you cared about her, and I know how hard it can be to get over a break up."

"She's pregnant."   The phone went silent.   "It's not

mine though.   I found out my chances of procreating are pretty slim.   Remember that football game in high school where the guy hit me so hard I flipped head over heels, literally?"

"Yes.   He was a really big kid and it was a cheap shot. I wanted to run down there and smack him upside his head."

"Turns out that injury most likely caused the problem. You know, it's not the fact that she slept with someone else. It's not even the fact that I gave her a chance to tell me the truth and she still lied to me.   I was actually kind of looking forward to becoming a dad."

"You already *are* a dad.   You've been just like a dad to DJ, even when his dad was still here.   Who was the first person to the hospital when Janel went into labor?"   She paused, waiting for him to respond, but he simply smiled. "How many times have you picked him up from school, and worked with him on his football or basketball skills?   And who did he stay with when the two of them took kid-free vacations?   Now that his dad is gone, he needs you more than ever.   He loves you like a dad, and you love him just like he's your own flesh and blood.   It doesn't matter what his birth certificate says."

"I know how much you really wanted grand babies."

"Oh please, don't worry about me.   I'm too old to be babysitting some grand babies anyway."

"I know you don't really mean that, but I appreciate you saying it anyway."

"Everything happens for a reason, and unfortunately we aren't always privy to why.   DJ's got a strong father figure in you for the rest of his life.   Take comfort in that and try not to dwell on the negative."

"I love you mom."

"I love you too son."

39 - CSC Showdown

Janel stopped through the Starbucks drive through and ordered the biggest, caffeine-laden beverage available. She hadn't slept well the night before, and she was anxious about meeting with HR to discuss her accusations regarding Sherri. She knew without a doubt that she had her ducks in a row, she just wondered what Sherri's made up side of the story would be, and how they intended to handle it. She also wondered how long it would take to resolve. Time seemed to stand still as she waited for the nine o'clock meeting to begin. At five minutes till, her manager came up to her desk.

"I just want to tell you before we walk in here that I believe you, and I want to wish you luck. Are you ready?"

"Absolutely."

"After you."

Janel led the way to the conference room and they both took a seat among the other individuals.

"First off I want to thank everyone for being here. And since we're dealing with a sensitive, possibly emotional issue, I want to remind everyone that we're all professionals. Also, I ask that you show each another common courtesy and respect. We all want to be able to resolve this matter in a peaceful way, and I have confidence that we'll be able to accomplish that today. Here are the details as I understand them. If anything that I'm about to say is incorrect, please make a note and we'll address it. You will all have an opportunity to speak uninterrupted." Anna looked down at her notes before continuing. "It's my understanding that Sherri recently received a promotion based on a project that she claims to have completed on her own.   And during a recent performance review meeting with Elaine, Janel claimed to have completed an auditing project on her own that Sherri assigned to her as a special assignment.   Elaine wasn't aware of the special assignment, although Janel claims that Sherri told her she'd spoken to Elaine about it.   So here in lies our dilemma, we have two individuals claiming to have completed the same project, without any help from the other.   I want to point out that as soon as this matter was brought to my attention, we removed their access from the old and new systems, and they were given other temporary responsibilities.   Before I open this up for discussion, I'd like to add that I completed a preliminary investigation into this incident, and I'd like to share what I've found.   The new system has an extensive auditing feature, however, that feature wasn't enabled when the system went live. So unfortunately the only audit information available is the user name of the last person to save the record, along with the time and date that the save was completed. According to my investigation, all of the records in question were last saved by Sherri.   I've since contacted our corporate system representative, Shawn Disxon, to have the auditing function enabled immediately because it's a violation of our Sarbanes Oxley policy to not be able to see extensive information regarding any changes made to our financial records.   Unfortunately that doesn't help us today.   Now correct me if I'm wrong, but I think we all have a pretty good understanding of Sherri's side of the story."   Heads nodded and no one spoke up.   "If there aren't any objections, I'd like to give Janel the opportunity to explain her side of the story."

"I'll keep this short and stick to the facts.   I completed that project, on my own, without any help from Sherri."

"That's a lie."   Sherri blurted out.

"Let her speak, please.   You'll have an opportunity to

respond."   Anna spoke up.

"When I met with Sherri for my last review to discuss my performance in relation to the new system, she told me I was doing such a good job that she wanted to provide me with an opportunity.   She gave me this print out,"   Janel slid copies across the table to everyone.   "And explained these were 'problem accounts' that needed to be cleaned up before they could be moved into the new system.   She also told me that she discussed this project with my manager and that if I had any questions or ran into any problems that I needed to contact her directly.   I made a copy of the print out so I would have a clean copy, and a copy to make notes on.   I used my copy to record dates, the names of people I spoke to, the problem with the accounts, and what I did to fix them.   In detail.   As you can see, this is the original, but I made copies so you could see my notes."   She passed out copies of the working document.   "All of those notes are in my hand writing, and I didn't share any of these notes with Sherri.   She didn't help me on this project because I never went to her for help.   I figured everything out on my own because I had reason to believe I couldn't trust her, which obviously turned out to be very true."

"Sherri, do you have any notes regarding the actions you took to reconcile the accounts?"   Anna asked.

"They're all in the system, on each account.   Under the Activities tab."

"I knew she would say that, because that's the same answer I gave her when she asked me for my notes. Unfortunately, it's only partially true.   I made very simple, very concise notes in the Activities section.   All of the detailed information is written on my copy of that spreadsheet, of which I just gave you all a copy of.   In fact, you can ask me about any one of those accounts and I can give you every detail of what occurred and what I did to resolve it."

"What about this guy, Richard Piedmont.   Page three, about a fourth of the way down the page."   Anna asked.

Without even looking down at her copy, Janel rattled off the information.   "Richard's paperwork was completed incorrectly in reference to a personal loan he received.   If memory serves me, he bought a jet ski.   What I found out during my research was not only had Richard paid his loan in full, he'd in fact overpaid because of a discrepancy in his paperwork.   He's due a refund of two hundred eighty-six dollars and seventy-three cents."

"Seventy-four cents actually."   Elaine spoke up.   "Not to put too fine a point on it."   She smiled at Janel.

"Sherri, can you provide any additional details regarding any of these accounts?"   Anna asked.

"Unfortunately I can't.   Like I said before, I put all of my notes in the system."

"I'm curious Anna, when you looked at the audit information, did all of the 'last saved' dates occur on the same day?"   Janel asked.

"I'm not sure, I'd have to double check.   Why?"

"If I were going to claim someone else's work as my own, I would want to go in and perform a save on every record so that my name appeared as the last person to have touched the record.   And if Sherri was the one working the accounts as she claims, do you really think she was able to fix them all on the same day?   Would there not be a steady progression of last saved dates, based upon her progression through the accounts on the list?   Is she just that good at reconciling accounts?"

"I went back through them all to double check the work before I told my manager I completed the project."

"You double checked *the* work or *my* work?"

"I completed that entire project all by myself.   Why don't you just admit it so we can get this over with?"   Sherri glared at her, her jaw muscles twitching with anger.

"I have one last item to present in order to prove that I

was the only person who worked on this project. Unfortunately, I'm only willing to share the details of the information with Anna.   There's something that I've done to mark all the accounts I've worked on in the new system, not just the ones from this project.   It's a system I developed to help me stay organized.   The reason I'll only share the information with Anna is because I have reason to believe that if I shared this information in front of Sherri, she might contact Shawn Disxon to alter the information since he has administrator access to the system.   And if she called him, he might be able to alter the information before Anna can go in and verify that what I'm saying is true."

"My reputation, as well as my career, is on the line because of these silly accusations.   I have a right to know what fictitious 'proof' she's referring to."

"While I'm sure Shawn is a professional and wouldn't try and alter any records-"

"If he did, there's a way to check.   The administrator account has an extensive audit trail that's built in and cannot be altered.   It's a feature that was added by the programmers to prevent Enron-type activity."

"Really?   How do you know that Janel?"   Elaine asked.

"I've done my homework, and I know that system inside and out."

"Once I talk with Janel and I'm able to investigate her claim, I'll be sure to share that information with you because you do have a right to know.   Does anyone have any other questions?"   Anna looked around the room.

"How long before this situation can be resolved?" Sherri's manager asked as she looked through Janel's notes.

"I'm going to speak to Janel privately, take another look in the system based on that information, and hopefully complete my investigation this afternoon.   Then I'll meet with you and Elaine to discuss my findings and suggested resolution, and then you will meet with Sherri to relay the information to her, and Elaine will meet with Janel.   Any other questions?"   The two managers shook their heads no.   "Sherri, do you have anything else you'd like to add?"

"Just that she's lying and the truth will come out soon enough."

"It sure will because what's done in the dark will eventually come to light."   Janel said.

"You all are free to go."   They left the room and Anna closed the door behind them.   "Ok Janel, what is it that you want to share with me?"

"On the Contact tab, in the address field, there's only one address line by default.   When I was trying to learn more about the system on my own, I found out that you can enable a second address line manually on each account. You know, the second line where most companies list the suite number, floor, or information like 'to the attention of mister so and so?'"

"Yes, I understand."

"On every account I worked on, not just the ones for the audit project, but all the accounts I've touched since I started, I enabled the second address line and I put my initials and the date that I last touched the account on that line.   We were never taught how to do that in training, and I never told anyone else I was doing it.   In relation to this audit project specifically, that date will match my hand written notes where I wrote down the date I finished reconciling the account."

Anna smiled at her.   "That's pretty smart.   I'll go back in this afternoon and take a look, and I'll discuss my findings with your manager in the morning."

# # #

Janel took a deep breath to calm her nerves before she rang Tony's doorbell.   It felt like forever before he opened the door.

"Hey."   The surprise in his voice was evident.

"Are you busy?   I apologize for not calling first but-"

"It's ok, come on in."

"We haven't talked in a while.   How've you been?" She asked as they sat on the couch together.

"Yeah I apologize about that.   I've been busy-"

"You're always busy."

"I'm teaching now, I managed to get on at the university. I needed a change."

"Really?   Congratulations."

"Looks like you just got off of work.   How are things at CSC?"

"Actually that's why I'm here.   I have something I need to tell you."

"What happened?"   His brow was furrowed with concern.

"I was working on a project in December, to reconcile some accounts, something Sherri gave me to do."   He closed his eyes and shook his head.   "Long story short, she claimed the project as her own.   She even got a promotion out of it."

"Are you serious?   Please tell me you went straight to HR, right?"

"I did, and I was able to prove it.

"Good.   What did they do about it?"

"They offered me a job, starting at forty-eight, with benefits."

"Good for you.   Congratulations."

"Anyway, I wanted to tell you what really happened in case she tries to tell you something different.   I just needed to let you know what kind of person she really is."

"I already know.   I'm not seeing her anymore."

"I would say I'm sorry to hear that but I'm not.   I'm sorry if she hurt you."

"So what did they do to her?"

"I'm not supposed to know but my manager told me

anyway.   They busted her back down and put her in a probationary program.   And she's no longer responsible for system training.   I am."

"That's great, I'm really happy for you."

"You know now that her money is messed up she's going to try and take you for everything you've got to 'support the baby.'"   Janel made quotation marks in the air with her fingers.

"The baby's not mine.   I'm waiting on the test to confirm it, but I already know."

"Really?"

"Yeah."

"I can't say that I'm upset to hear that either.   You would've been tied to her forever."

"How are you and Perry doing?"

She shook her head.   "He broke up with me."

"Really?   That guy would've drank your bath water if you asked him to."

"It's not like he wanted to.   He said my heart was someplace else."

"He didn't think you were past Dorian yet."

She stared down at her shoe, trying to find the courage to be honest with him.   "He told me it was obvious to him that...I have feelings for you."   She didn't have the nerve to say in love.   "And he could tell you have feelings for me too because you look at me the same way that he used to look at his ex-wife."

"I'd say he's right.   What do you think?"

She looked him in the eye.   "He is."

"So what are we going to do about it?"

"Take it slow, see where things go?"

He took her hand in his and gently squeezed it.   "Hi, my name is Tony, it's so nice to meet you.   Would you like to go out with me sometime?"

She smiled at him.   "Janel.   And I'd love to go out with you sometime.   How about you give me a call?"

40 – Epilogue

"Need a ride?" Tony asked as he pulled up to Janel's job. She was waiting for him in the parking lot. He got out of the car and kissed her before opening the door for her. "Happy birthday."

"Why thank you Professor Gibson."

"You can't call me that." He shut her door and got in the car.

"Why not? I kind of like the sound of it."

"Because only my students call me Professor Gibson, and I have a strict policy against sleeping with my students."

"I guess I'll have to return my birthday outfit then. I was going to dress up as a school girl trying to sleep her way to an A."

"Wait now, let's not be too hasty. I think I can make an exception."

"Where we headed?"

"I made reservations at Le Scarpe Rosse."

"How about we skip dinner, go to your place, and I have you for dinner instead." She put her hand in his lap and rubbed the inside of his thigh.

He grabbed her hand. "Woman, you can't be doing that while I'm driving. As nice as that sounds, I have something really special planned for you tonight."

"Fine, as long as the evening culminates in me and you having salacious birthday sex."

"Oh it will, trust me. I didn't buy two cans of whipped cream, a jar of honey, and a one pound bag of restaurant style nachos for no reason."

Janel started laughing. "Nachos?"

"Yeah, I'm going for something different tonight."

"You're so silly."

Tony left the car with the valet and they entered the restaurant, where the hostess verified their reservation and seated them in an intimate booth away from the hustle and bustle. "I'll be right back. I need to use the ladies room."

"You want me to get you something to drink?"

"Please."

"Long island iced tea?"

"Actually I think I want a glass of wine.   Pick something for me, you know what I like."   He waited for her to walk away before having a seat.

She made her way across the back of the restaurant to the other side where the restrooms were located.   She locked herself inside a stall and emptied her bladder, then readjusted her dress as the toilet flushed automatically. When she rounded the corner to wash her hands, she nearly ran right into Sherri, literally.   "Excuse me."   She said, careful to keep her tone void of attitude.   She glanced down at the woman's belly long enough to see that her stomach was protruding just enough that it was obvious now that she was pregnant.   But not so much so that she was in the miserable stages.   Janel quickly composed herself and used the sink furthest away from her.

"Well look what the cat drug in.   Fancy seeing you here."   Janel ignored her as she turned the water on and waited for it to get hot.   She lathered her hands and focused her eyes on the drain in the sink.   "You can't speak?"

She continued to ignore her as she methodically rinsed the soap from her hands.

"You took my job and my man, the least you can do is acknowledge the fact that I'm talking to you."

The comment caused Janel to pause, but she realized she was simply trying to push her buttons, so she turned the water off and grabbed a few paper towels.   She wanted to completely turn her back to her but she didn't trust her, so she stood where she could see her in her peripheral vision as she blotted her hands dry.

"Are you happy?"

Janel tossed the towels in the trash can, then checked her lipstick in the mirror.

"Really?   You're just going to act like you don't hear me?"

"What do you want Sherri?"   She asked as she turned to face the woman.

"I want to know if you're happy with *my job* and *my man*?   It's what you've wanted all along right?   How does it feel to be me?"

Janel raised an eyebrow at the woman and chuckled. "You *lost* your man because of your own actions, and I *earned* your job because I'm *better* at it.   Some people would call that karma, or reaping what you sow."

"I'm curious, were you ever able to figure out who trashed your car?"   She waved her hand in the air.   "I know it was childish but I have to admit it felt really good to mess up that nice car that *my man* bought for you."   She smiled at her.

Janel's face felt hot as her blood pressure rose, and she instinctively balled her hand into a fist.   She took a deep breath, determined not to let the woman get to her.   "You know, the funny thing about it is he ran right out and took care of it for me.   Plus, he gave me his car to drive while he handled it.   All while he was still *your* man.   Thanks to you, my car looks better than ever now.   But let's not dwell on the past, shall we?   Tony is no longer your man and he's definitely no longer your concern."

"What's with the fist?   I know you well enough to know you wouldn't hit a pregnant woman."   She ran her hand over her stomach.   "You ain't that crazy."

Janel's hand launched from her side with the speed and precision of a snake striking its prey, smacking the woman directly across her face.   "You're right.   I'm much too classy to hit a pregnant woman.   But I'm not above smacking a pregnant bitch." Sherri held a hand to her face, her mouth open, and Janel leaned in close and whispered to her. "You better sleep with one eye open once you have that baby because *my man* is a damn good lawyer, so if I should happen to do something outside of my character, I have all the confidence in the world that he'll be able to get the charges dismissed. And even if he can't, it just may be worth a couple of days in jail to show you I'm not one to be played with." She stepped away from the woman, straightened her dress, and checked her hair in the mirror as Sherri continued to hold her cheek and stare at her. "Best believe I'm very happy. Enjoy your evening." Janel opened the bathroom door, then paused to look at her one last time. "By the way, tell Shawn I said hello and congratulations." She walked through the door and rejoined Tony at the table.

After a satisfying meal, and a birthday cupcake, Tony retrieved the car from the valet and they left the restaurant.

"Where are we headed now?"

"I'm taking you to your birthday present."

"I'm looking at my birthday present."

"No, I have something really special for you."

Fifteen minutes later he pulled into the same storage facility where Janel had stored her belongings prior to moving out. He pulled up in front of a storage unit and turned the car off but left the lights on. "You got me a storage unit for my birthday?" He opened her door and helped her out of the car, then took her hands into his as he faced her. He took a deep breath and exhaled loudly. He shook his head, unable to find the right words.

"What's wrong? You're scaring me."

He let go of her hands, pulled the key from his pocket, and opened the lock. "Open it."

She bent over to grasp the handle and open the metal door, but he moved her out of the way and opened it for her. She gasped and cupped a hand over her mouth. It was her Jaguar.

"I tossed and turned last night, trying to figure out what to say to you.   Hoping you wouldn't be upset with me.   I knew how much this car meant to you, and how difficult it was for you to sell it.   I couldn't just stand by and let some stranger take it from you.   I love you too much for that.   Happy birthday baby."   She started to cry.   "I sure hope those are tears of joy."

"I can't believe you did that for me."

He gently embraced her face.   "I love you Janel, I always have."   He kissed her lips, then pulled a handkerchief from his pocket and handed it to her.

"I love you too."   She told him as she blotted her face and tried not to ruin her makeup.   "How did you manage to keep this a secret all this time?"

"You made it easy when you decided to sign over the title to the estate sale manager.   You said you didn't want to know who bought the car, so I didn't even have to tell him to keep it a secret."

"Thank you so much.   This really means a lot to me.   I know it's just a car, but it has a lot of sentimental value to me."

"I know.   It was the only thing that Dorian bought you that ever really meant anything to you.   How long have I known you now?   I can remember the very first time I saw you, at that club just off campus, where everyone always went after the football games.   Your hair was short, like Halle Berry in Strictly Business, and you were wearing your little Cross Colours outfit with the bright orange Doc Martin boots."

Janel started laughing.   "Oh my gosh, you remember that?   I loved that outfit but I know I must've looked a hot mess."

"No, you looked good.   That was the style back in the day, and you were always on point when it came to style.   Still are.   When I saw you, you literally took my breath away.   I thought you were the most beautiful woman I'd ever seen.   It was like in the movies you know, where everything else in the room went blurry and the only thing in focus was you."

"Oh please." She waved a hand at him.

"No, I'm serious. I wanted to say something to you, but I didn't know what to say. So I pointed you out to Dorian, and I asked him what I should do. And damn it if he didn't walk right up to you and introduce himself, and the rest is history. I let fear keep me from acting that night, and I vowed to never allow fear to keep me from acting again. What I'm trying to say is I've loved you from the first time I saw you. I've loved you for the last twenty years, as much more than just a friend. I want us back under the same roof. I want to come home to you every day, and I want to go to bed with you every night and wake up to you every morning. I know you may not be ready right now but when you are, I want to marry you, and I'll wait however long it takes for you to be ready to take that step with me. You just let me know, ok?" She shook her head, dried her eyes again, and they embraced each other. "You don't know how good it feels to finally be able to tell you about this car and get it off my chest!" He dug down in his pocket and handed her the key fob to the Jaguar. "Race you to my place?"

# # #

"Would you two come on, we're going to be late!" Rita fussed at Chuck and Tony as she slid inside the limo next to Janel.

"It's not like they can start without us." Tony said as he got in and sat with his back against the driver's window. "Get over here!" He patted the seat next to him and Janel happily obliged.

"Vegas baby! So much trouble, so little time. This town doesn't know what it's in for this weekend." Chuck bellowed as he slid in next to Rita and the driver shut the door.

"We need to decide right now who's going to be in charge of the bail money." Tony said.

"Me!" Rita volunteered.

"No." Chuck shot her down. "There are too many places for you to shop."

"I'll hold it, I ain't trying to go to jail again. Been there, done that." Janel said.

The limo pulled to a stop in front of the small wedding chapel, and the two couples got out of the car.

"Welcome, my name is Gus and I'm the director here. This is my wife Shelley, she's the wedding planner. Ladies, if you'll follow her she'll take you to the bridal suite where you can change, freshen up, what have you. Gentlemen, if you'll follow me I'll get you taken care of."

Rita pulled a short, off the shoulder periwinkle blue dress from her garment bag, stepped into it, and motioned for Janel to zip it up. "How's my hair?"

"You look great. Are you nervous?"

"You act like I haven't done this before. This time it really is till death do us part. You and Tony should join us, maybe they'll give us a two for one special."

"This is your day, not mine."

"Suit yourself."

Shelley ushered the ladies outside to a gazebo where Tony and Chuck were waiting. Tony kissed Janel and took her by the hand, and they stood off to the side while Rita and Chuck were officially married for the second time by Gus in an extremely simple ceremony. Once it was complete and Gus told Chuck to kiss his bride, Chuck planted an enthusiastic kiss on Rita's lips before picking her up off her feet and spinning her around. "I love you baby. I love this woman!" He shouted to the treetops.

"I love you too baby."

"So what's next?" He asked, placing her back on the floor.

"I was thinking we could eat, cause I'm starving, then check into our room and get to consummating this marriage."

"I like the sound of that Mrs. Seidel."

"Then let's go Mr. Seidel."   He took her by the hand and they headed for the limo.

Tony looked at the joy on Chuck's face, and turned to Janel.   He grabbed her hands and squeezed.   "Marry me."

"What?"

He embraced her and kissed her passionately.   "Let's do this baby, let's get married."

"Come on Tony."

"I'm serious.   Let's do this, right now."

"Now?"

"Right now."

"What about your mom, and my parents?   And DJ?"

"We can have another ceremony just for them."

"We don't have a license."

"We can get you one within fifteen minutes."   Gus encouraged.

"Really?"   Janel asked, surprised.

"You are in Vegas!"   He confirmed.

"We don't have rings."

"We have a set you can borrow, for a fee."   Shelley encouraged.

"I'll buy you a ring when we get back.   Or hell, we're in Vegas, we can buy nice rings here.   What are we waiting for, I love you, you love me, let's do this."

"Ok, let's do it!"

About the Author

Angela L. Waderker is from Canton, Ohio, and currently lives just outside of Nashville, Tennessee with her two children, and an uppity cat named Jasmine. She is working on her second novel.

Contact information:

http://facebook.com/ALWaderker

ALWaderker@comcast.net

www.ingramcontent.com/pod-product-compliance
Lightning Source LLC
Chambersburg PA
CBHW070536260626
47161CB00002B/403